I0713422

Praise for Stuart R. West's
Ghosts of Gannaway!

"…the story has some truly scary scenes, it is the slow boil suspense that gets under the skin. I'll be reading more of Stuart R. West!"
–Tom Deady, Bram Stoker Award-winning author of *Haven*

"With *Ghosts of Gannaway*, author Stuart R. West pulls back the skin of 20th Century Americana and extracts a magnificent working-class nightmare. It's the kind of tense, creepy thriller that keeps you frantically turning pages. West's talent and mastery of the craft is undeniably enviable."
–Peter N. Dudar, author of *The Goat Parade*

"Filled with tension, excellent characterization, suspense, ghostly presences, and enough twists and turns to keep you glued to the last page."
–Catherine Cavendish, author of *Cold Revenge* and *The Devil's Serenade*

"Captivating…a ghost story full of surprises."
–Joan C. Curtis, author of *A Painting to Die For*

Also by Stuart R. West

Dread & Breakfast

Twisted Tales from Tornado Alley: A Collection of Short Fiction (coming in the Fall of 2018)

GHOSTS OF GANNAWAY

GHOSTS OF GANNAWAY

Stuart R. West

A
Grinning Skull Press
Publication

PO Box 67, Bridgewater, MA 02324

Ghosts of Gannaway
Copyright © 2015 Stuart R. West

Originally published by Books We Love (BWL), September 19, 2015.
Reprinted by Grinning Skull Press, 2018, with permission from the author.

All rights reserved. No part of this book may be used or reproduced in any manner whatsoever without written permission except in the case of brief quotations embodied in critical articles or reviews.

This book is a work of fiction. All characters depicted in this book are fictitious, and any resemblance to real persons—living or dead—is purely coincidental.

The Skull logo with stylized lettering was created for Grinning Skull Press by Dan Moran, http://dan-moran-art.com/.
Cover designed by Jeffrey Kosh, http://jeffreykosh.wix.com/jeffreykoshgraphics.

Published by Grinning Skull Press, P.O. Box 67, Bridgewater, MA 02324

ISBN: 1-947227-14-9 (paperback)
ISBN-13: 978-1-947227-14-9 (paperback)
ISBN: 978-1-947227-13-2 (ebook)

DEDICATION

As always, I'd like to dedicate this book to my lovely wife, Cydney, and my beautiful daughter, Sarah. They're my rock(s). Couldn't do it without them.

Contents

ACKNOWLEDGMENTS.. i
A Note from the Author iii
Chapter One 1
Chapter Two 10
Chapter Three..18
Chapter Four 27
Chapter Five 37
Chapter Six..48
Chapter Seven 58
Chapter Eight 70
Chapter Nine 83
Chapter Ten..97
Chapter Eleven 112
Chapter Twelve 127
Chapter Thirteen...140
Chapter Fourteen...158
Chapter Fifteen..172
Chapter Sixteen 186
Chapter Seventeen 199
Chapter Eighteen 215
Chapter Nineteen 227
Chapter Twenty 243
Chapter Twenty-One 257
Chapter Twenty-Two 275
Chapter Twenty-Three...294
ABOUT THE AUTHOR 303

ACKNOWLEDGMENTS

A big shout-out to the wonderfully weird and twisted state of Kansas. Endlessly fascinating and creepy place to live, lots of fodder for creepy storytelling. Probably why I still live there.

A Note from the Author

This is the tale of Picher, Oklahoma. Oh, sure, I moved the events just over the border to my fictional town of Gannaway, Kansas. And the characters in the book aren't real. But some of them do represent archetypes of the long-passed citizens of Picher, Oklahoma.

Very few people reside in Picher now. They can't. Because of the zinc and lead mining boom of the '30s, the town is now a death trap. In more ways than one. The water's tainted. The air is polluted with poisonous particles lifted off the chat piles. The very few structures still standing have been torn apart by tornadoes. The residents were forced to move. Or die. Of course, there're still a few stubborn folks who reside there. None too friendly either, I might add. You're gonna see a few Confederate flags flying high in the dilapidated living quarters, good reason enough not to linger.

Picher was once one of the most prosperous towns in the Midwest. How do I know? I researched it. It is the most exhausting book I've written yet, and I won't be attempting that amount of research again. Not only does the book take place in 1935, but there's a dueling timeline in 1969 with all sorts of characters, plot lines, and ghosts crossing paths. *Whew!* During the final edit, I nearly had a panic attack when I caught a character in 1969 saying, "That sucks!" Um, no, just wasn't done.

So, I stupidly set the tale in two timelines I knew next to nothing about. I researched clothing, slang, lifestyles, food, autos, the effects of the depression. Then I had to find out about mining. Would you like to know about mining? Neither did I until I realized the book called for it. Now that info's stuck in my head.

I also discovered a lot about hippies and soul hand-shakes and the various movements going on during the "Free-Love" era, then I'd travel even further back and dig deep into unions and the violent labor strikes of the '30s. I learned about the plight of the Native Americans in the Midwest going back years and years and years and...

Just too much. But I hope the research paid off. I tried to make my tale thrilling, chilling, exciting, action-packed, scary, even a little romantic. And a lot of it happened.

Please learn from the past.

Chapter One

1929...

Something looked off about Karl, no doubt about it. Tommy Donnelly saw it in Karl's eyes the minute they got in line. Not the usual red-eyed glassiness that accompanies miners' fondness for moonshine, either. Karl's gaze flicked back and forth, unfocused and yellow, like a desert lizard's eyes.

Tommy didn't know Karl well. Just by reputation and his daddy's mining tales. An old-time roof-trimmer, Karl's responsibilities included clearing loose rocks, making the mines safe for the other men. Apparently, he'd been in the mines since before the turn of the century. But on this gray Kansas morning, Karl stayed to himself, mumbling. He stared into the dirt like he was prospecting for gold. Hardly in keeping with what Tommy'd heard about this legendary miner.

Truth to tell, though, as it was Tommy's first day in the mines, Karl's odd behavior just set him more on edge.

Big Ed took it all in stride, of course, as he did everything. He chuckled deep within his formidable belly. "Kid, first-day jitters? Stay by my side and you'll be fine."

"Thanks, Ed. Guess I'm just gettin' my feet underneath me."

"That so?"

"That's so." Tommy forced a weak smile. It didn't make him feel much better, but the fact Big Ed had taken him under his wing gave him a small cushion of comfort. Tommy's daddy would've wanted it that way. It bothered him no end that Big Ed didn't think Karl's behavior seemed peculiar. But maybe that's the way Karl always acted.

The line of denim-clad, ruddy-faced men snaked across the grounds. The closer Tommy came to the pull derrick, the more his stomach flip-flopped. Watching the men disappear into the earth in a large bucket increased his anxiety.

Big Ed picked at his teeth with a dirty fingernail. *"Pfft, pfft, pfft!"* Big Ed launched his excavated oral debris onto the ground.

"Tommy, you're gonna start as a dummy. I talked to the ground boss, told him I want you. You'll carry my drill bits. You do good, show you're a man who ain't afraid to work, you'll move up to mucker in no time."

Karl lifted an eyebrow, appraising Tommy as if seeing him for the first time. "They're down there. Told me what I gotta do." He stared at Tommy, waiting for a response.

Big Ed ignored him. Tommy followed Ed's lead.

"All greenhorns gotta start somewhere, kid." Ed raised his voice to be heard over Karl's muttering.

"They come to me, no matter the time, day or night, they talk to me, tell me what I gotta do..."

They were next. Tommy hoped Karl would go down in the bucket in a different grouping. No such luck. Luck wasn't on his side today. Never a good thing for miners.

Jim Reaper, a particularly taciturn man who lived up to his name, was hoister man today. The empty bucket clanged down in the shaft as Jim cranked the hoist handle. Every time the bucket banged into the shaft's wooden walls, Tommy's heart jumped right along with it.

Big Ed let out a long sigh and climbed the platform. The

boards creaked beneath his weight with every step. He grabbed the cable and swung a leg up and over the bucket's rim. "Come on, kid." He jerked his chin toward Tommy.

Tommy stepped up onto the platform. Karl followed behind him. *Closely.* So close Tommy felt Karl's breath on the back of his neck. Ed reached out a helping hand, and Tommy hopped in. Karl gripped the bucket's rim and gave it a spin.

"Come on, Karl," said Ed. "Quit horsin' around. Time to get into the mines."

Karl's lips pulled back, showcasing his yellow-toothed smile. He looked around at his surroundings, lost, a man a-wakened from a dream. It rattled Tommy, but at least Karl had stopped babbling.

Didn't take long, though, for Karl to shrug off sanity and resume his ongoing private conversation. He turned, asked a question of someone not there, laughed at an un-heard response. Finally, he hopped into the bucket, his long legs neatly clearing the rim.

The bucket rocked back and forth over the shaft's collar. The bail holding the cable hook above them groaned. The gaping opening sat at about 12 feet wide by 12 feet across. The darkness reminded Tommy of the hole in the ground they put his daddy in when he passed. Miners work underground, die underground, get put back there again when all's said and done.

"All right," said Jim. It was more a declaration than a question, but Big Ed nodded anyway. Tommy grabbed the cable, a tenuous lifeline at best.

Karl stared at Tommy, his eyes dull. Rather, he looked right through him. "They won't let me rest, gotta do what they say..."

"God damn, Karl!" said Ed. "You liquored up or the devil on fire inside your belly?"

Karl didn't answer. He just gave a lopsided, lazy man's grin.

The square of skylight shrank as they lowered into the ground. A few torches lit up the shaft wall's cribbing of strategically placed 2" x 6' timbers.

The light played across Karl's face, shadows obscuring his eyes. Ed hummed a mostly melody-free ditty, something Tommy didn't recognize. When Karl fell silent again, Tommy couldn't help but steal glances at him. His stillness unsettled Tommy more than the constant mumbling.

Karl's arms shot up. He lurched toward Tommy. The bucket rocked, bashed into the walls. Tommy stumbled, his back against the bucket's rim.

"Karl!" Ed roared. "Jesus Christ!"

Karl shot Ed a puzzled look, then reached a trembling hand toward Tommy. He stroked Tommy's shoulder like petting a mining mule. "It ain't time yet," Karl said. "Not yet, they tol' me..."

"Sorry, kid," said Ed. He glared at Karl. "He ain't usually like this."

Echoes rose above and sank below as the bucket landed on a wooden platform four hundred feet below ground. Water bubbled and churned below the wood planks. Tommy couldn't distinguish the sump-pump from the pulse pounding in his ears.

Tommy hopped out of the bucket first. He didn't want to spend any more time with Karl than he had to. Ed must've had the same thought. He hefted himself out with surprising speed for a man his size. Karl dawdled behind as Tommy and Ed walked down the drift.

Ed clapped a hand on Tommy's back. "Time to light 'em up." He struck a long wooden match and held it to the lamp on Tommy's helmet. "Gotta be careful with fire down here, kid." The welcome light illuminated the dark drift. The match hissed out in a puddle at Ed's feet. "You're lucky, boy. Wasn't too long ago we made do with cloth helmets. Didn't protect us worth nothin'. Damn Gannaway was one of the last mine owners in the tri-state area to give us hard helmets."

Their boots squelched through the water. Using the steel rails as guides, they walked toward the light. After three hundred feet or so, the drift opened into a large stope, already mined and hollowed out for the most part. Artificial orange lantern light painted the cavern's walls. Carefully chiseled pillars of unmined rock braced the cavern roof for support. Nothing looked particularly steady. Boisterous voices greeted them.

"Big Ed! Who's the dummy with you?"

"Is he outta his momma's diapers yet?"

"Ground Boss," said Ed, to a sweaty, short, round man, "this is Tommy, my new dummy. Matthew's boy."

The man's eyes brightened. "Matthew was a good man and a better miner. If you're half the miner he was, son, you'll do just fine down here. Call me Ground Boss. Or sir."

"Yes, sir."

Against the wall, a man stood on a tall ladder, twenty-five feet above the cavern floor. Two miners pulled attached guide ropes taut. The ladder man stabbed a ten-foot-long spear into the rock above him. "Look out below!" he yelled. *Clump.* Loose rocks rained down from the ceiling.

"They tell me what to do..." Karl brushed past them, drowning out the Ground Boss's instructions. Karl walked toward the men steering the roof trimmer on the ladder, purpose in his stride.

A mule brayed once, then again.

Water around Tommy's feet bubbled. Invisible raindrops pelleted down, circular ripples spreading outward. The ground trembled. A hush fell over the miners. Big Ed looked puzzled. Worse, he looked *worried.*

The ground shook again. A roar ripped through the cavern walls. Not a horn exactly. Something deeper, more resonant. An inhuman moan, far away and all around them at the same time. A one-note, unending blast from the bowels of the earth.

Tommy felt the vibrations in his legs first. Then it traveled up into his chest, rattling his ribcage.

"Cave in!"

Panic. Water splashed, churned by fleeing feet. Miners dashed by Tommy, running toward the bucket.

Big Ed held his own, solemnly shook his head. "Nope. This ain't no cave-in. Nothin' like one I never heard."

Screams erupted by the ladder.

"What in *God's* name?"

A pickaxe dangled in Karl's hand, a skull-faced grin on his face. A man lay crumpled at his feet. The other rope-holder lunged at Karl. Karl sidestepped and the man went head first into the wall. With the grace of a dancer, Karl swung around and brought the pickaxe down onto the man's head.

A man on the ladder scrambled down. Karl kicked at the bottom rungs. The man flailed his arms about as if trying to sprout wings. The ladder slowly teetered, then crashed onto an outcropping of rock. The miner's eyes popped clean out of his head. His teeth shattered, spreading small white gems out on the rocks.

"God *damn!*" said Big Ed.

Karl propped a boot onto the dead man and yanked out the pickaxe. He licked the tip. Lovingly, almost. He opened his mouth, his smile crimson. Karl snatched the spear from off the ground. Then he raced straight for Tommy.

Tommy froze, standing still as miners rushed past him. The bellowing sound churned his innards, filled his bladder.

Without breaking stride, Karl ran the spear through another man's stomach. The tip poked out the man's back. He gave it a twist and withdrew the weapon as smoothly as a knife slicing through butter. Intestines slithered to the ground, smooth as a snake over a rock.

A bear of a miner tossed his arms around Karl's neck. Karl thrust the pickaxe into the man's neck repeatedly, missing his own face by inches. He studied the pickaxe, then dropped it.

"Good God in heaven!" the Ground Boss moaned.

"Come on! We gotta get outta here!" Ed yanked Tommy's arm. *"Tommy!"*

Karl dug through his newest victim's burlap bag and pulled out a handful of cylindrical-shaped objects.

Dynamite.

The hellish moaning loosened rock from the ceiling. Small pebbles at first, then a thunderstorm of larger debris. Groundwater danced, shimmied, and rippled.

Karl struck a match, held it to the wick of a dynamite stick. *Fssst.* He dropped the dead match, grabbed for another.

Something struck Tommy's cheek, pulling him out of his horrified stupor. Big Ed had his hand pulled back, preparing for another slap.

"Oh...lord," said Tommy, tears stinging his eyes.

"Let's *go,* goddammit!" Ed clamped down on Tommy's arm, nearly pulling him off his feet.

Karl chased after them, cradling the dynamite to his chest while he swung his spear.

They stormed down the drift. Tommy stumbled, his shoulder catching against the wall. The Ground Boss struggled to keep up, his panting loud in the drift. Tommy risked a glimpse back. Karl stood at the drift's entryway. Singing in an eerie, high-pitched tone.

A gospel song.

"If you could see inside insteaddd, you'd see a brand new mannn..."

The bucket had vanished. There was no way out.

From somewhere far away, a mule whinnied, mocking them.

Hysterical shouts echoed down the shaft. The bucket crashed in front of them. The bottom flipped out like an open can of beans. Its broken cable swished back and forth above it like a horse's tail swatting flies.

"Jesus God!"

"...'cause the old man is deaddd..."

Karl walked slowly down the drift, three sticks of dynamite tucked under his arm. He scrabbled at a matchbox. He struck a match against the rock wall. It snapped in half.

"Go!" Tommy pointed at the swinging cable. "Our only chance! God, it's our only chance! *Go! Now!"*

The Ground Boss grabbed hold of the cable, his knees

and ankles entwining around the line. He scurried up inch by inch.

"You would see a brand new man..."

"Ed! Go!"

Ed shook his head. "You go, boy. Your daddy'd never forgive me if I left you down here."

"But I'll be *faster!*"

"More the reason for you to go, kid! *Dammit* all to hell, now *get!*"

As soon as the Ground Boss cleared the top, Tommy jumped onto the cable. Hand over hand, he scrambled up quickly. Faces peered down the hole. The skidoo bell warning clanged.

And over it all, Tommy heard Karl's death dirge.

"... 'Cause the old man is deaddd!"

Tommy looked down. Ed steadied the cable with one hand, his other held out, warding off Karl.

Karl's singing dried up. The loud thrumming noise diminished. Silence. Except for the scritch-scratching of a match head.

Halfway up the shaft, Tommy spotted a niche carved out of the rock. A hole for the workers who laid down the cribbing along the shaft walls.

Tommy knew Ed couldn't make it to the top. Not before Karl lit his dynamite. Tommy swung toward the niche. His arm and leg took hold, and he crawled in.

Tommy heard Ed talking quietly to Karl.

"Ed! Come on! *Move* it!"

Ed squinted toward Karl before hopping onto the cable. With a grunt, he inched his way up. His weight tugged at the cable Tommy held, burning his hands.

Karl shoved the ruined bucket off the platform. He crawled on top and sat down. By all appearances, he didn't have a care in the world. He chuckled and scratched a match.

Ed struggled hard. For every five feet he climbed, he had to pause to catch his breath.

"Just get to me, Ed!" Tommy leaned out of the niche,

extending his hand toward Ed, straining so hard his muscles shook. Willing Ed to keep going.

Ed climbed and clawed, gasping for air.

A tiny spark of light flashed at the bottom of the shaft. Karl stared into the match's flame. Then he wedged a stick of dynamite into his mouth. The fuse caught, sparkled, brightened, then continued on its trail to destruction.

"Oh sweet Lord, Ed, hurry! Hurry!"

Ed surged forward, using every bit of energy he had.

Karl lit the other two sticks of dynamite. Then he lay down like Jesus on the cross, arms outstretched, the lit dynamite in his hands.

Tommy's fingers swept the tip of Ed's outreached hand. *Missed.* Ed jumped up an inch and grasped Tommy's hand. Tommy pulled, throwing himself back. His backside scraped along the rock toward the shaft, Ed's weight dragging him out. He anchored his feet against the niche's edges, slowing himself. But not enough.

"Ed! Climb! You gotta climb more! I can't pull you in!"

Ed clawed a foothold into the niche and rolled in on top of Tommy.

The first explosion ripped through the shaft, followed by two more. Wood-reinforced walls shook. Rock crumbled. Fire roared up the shaft, bathing them in blistering heat. A cloud of black smoke roiled up and out into the open air above. Tommy and Ed clung to one another like early morning lovers.

The flood of falling rocks dwindled, became a rare pebble. The dead quiet after the chaos should have been comforting. Instead, it seemed an additional threat, devouring Tommy with false hope.

The smoke cleared, and Ed and Tommy separated. Tommy had soiled his pants. Ed wouldn't hold it against him, though. Or say anything about it. Ever. He'd done the same thing.

Chapter Two

1969...

The music stuttered, stopped, sped up. Then it faded out.

"Damn it." Dennis pulled the van onto the shoulder of US69. He reached down and tugged at the eight-track cartridge. Wrinkled tape trailed from the player like ribbon on a gift.

The one concession Dennis had asked Meyers for was an eight-track player installed in the research van. He knew Kansas radio would be hellish. Especially out in the boonies. Nothing but country music and preachers ranting about saving souls from damnation.

It didn't matter much, not really. Just moving on and doing something different renewed him with a vigor he hadn't experienced in a very long time. Getting away from Los Angeles, at least if for a while.

Meyers had seemed reluctant to send Dennis to Gannaway, Kansas. He'd never given a reason. But he saw it in Meyer's distrusting look. A look filled with pity and doubt. Obviously, Meyers didn't feel Dennis was emotionally up to the task.

But Dennis needed the job. Anything to take his mind off what had happened six months ago.

A flash of movement caught Dennis's eye. An American Indian man stood just off the highway, knee-deep in dried bushes and weeds. He looked as startled as Dennis, but recovered with ease and tipped his fedora. Dennis nodded a greeting. The man dropped a potato bag and spread his hands in a "what the hell" manner. Then he pointed across the two-lane highway.

A modest home sat on the other side of the highway, nothing memorable. But the yard burst with a carnival of color. A white-painted garden jockey statue guarded the graveled driveway. Psychedelically colored birdbaths decorated the yard, a pop-art fever dream. Metallic pipes and rods clung to one another, pitched somewhere between sculptures and warnings. A giant peace sign covered the garage door. Above it hung a basketball hoop, wind chimes replacing the net.

The man pointed inside the van, and his lips moved. Appearing frustrated, he cranked his hand around like an organ grinder. Dennis scooted across the bench seat and rolled down the window.

The Indian leaned over the sill and Dennis extended his hand. The man surprised Dennis by foregoing the traditional handshake and offering his thumb instead of his hand. Their thumbs entwined in a soul handshake.

"Peace, brother." He gestured toward the ruined cartridge Dennis held onto. "Can I have that?"

"Sure. You know it's no good anymore, right?"

"Can see that."

Dennis shrugged and handed over the tape. The man cradled the draping tape as tenderly as a gardener would an uprooted plant. He eyed the tape's label. "Good band."

"Yeah, real rock and roll."

The man's smile burned warm and brilliant, his teeth dazzlingly white against his sun-drenched skin. "Come back some time and see what I do with it."

"I might just do that. Peace."

Dennis looked back in his rearview mirror as he ambled on down the highway. The Indian flashed the two-fingered peace sign. Dennis stuck his hand out the window and returned the gesture.

He thought he might enjoy the people of Kansas.

Judging by the desolate surroundings, Dennis knew he didn't have much farther to go. The trees lining the highway were barren. Permanently bowed, the dead ushers pointed the way to Gannaway. Tornado devastation had splintered and weathered the roadside signs, but they were still legible. Competing chicken restaurants battled for the traveler's taste buds and cash. Chicken Rosie's, Chicken Greta's, and the underachiever of the bunch, Lazy Harry's OK Chicken. The board demanding passersby to *Cherish God's Gift* seemed miraculously untouched, probably not too much comfort to Gannaway's past residents now.

Hawks nested on sagging power lines, heads craning, watching Dennis's progress. The only sign of life he'd seen for a while.

Dennis nearly missed the faded "Welcome To Gannaway—A Perfect Piece Of Heaven" sign. He parked the van in a lot filled with abandoned tires and hopped out. He took in a deep breath as he walked by the remains of a building, now nothing more than a crumbling stone foundation. A sour tang of metal filled his mouth, so overwhelming he could taste it.

Next to the destroyed building rested a small, fence-enclosed graveyard. A defunct electric tower loomed high above the gravestones, a guardian of the dead.

Across the highway, he spotted the Gannaway Mining Museum, or at least its remains. The wraparound porch slanted like a storm-tossed boat deck, rising and falling by nature's whim. Several of the wood pillars holding the roof over the porch had toppled. The few survivors looked ready to join them.

Dennis's walking tour brought him to the main strip, four stores in a row. What used to be stores, anyway. A bathrobe hung behind a *Closed* sign on the Gannaway General Store's door, the owner's final word on the topic, no doubt. Boxes and a flattened shelving unit spread a-cross the floor. Earl's Machine Shop crumbled to pieces next door, the front window, door, and back wall all blasted out. Graffiti decorated the walls, forgotten artwork for a dead town. The next two establishments were in even worse shape. Impossible to tell what they once were. One block over, the Old Minetown Pharmacy appeared open against all odds, a soda sign lit up in the front window.

Across the two-lane road stood a water tower, bally-hooing the high school's football team: "Gannaway—Home of the Lions Since 1918." Below it, a statue of a lion sat, one paw perched up. Rusted and discolored, it stood proud-ly amid the devastation like the king of the jungle it once was.

Towering over it all were the chat piles. Man-made ant-hills hollowed out from below the surface, the earth's un-wanted refuse stacked skyhigh. They dotted the horizon. For over forty square miles they covered the landscape, some of them perhaps 300 feet in height.

Alongside them, the remains of mining equipment rust-ed away, relics from a different era.

Before he left Gannaway's city limits, Dennis saw the only other open business in town. Durwood Funeral Home. *Telling.*

How could one of the once most thriving mining towns in the country come to this? Once it was proclaimed "A Perfect Piece of Heaven." Now Gannaway felt more like hell on earth.

A knock on the door jolted Dennis awake from his nightmare, the same nightmare that had plagued him for six months. He owed his unexpected visitor his gratitude.

He slipped on his glasses, flipped on the lamp, and checked his watch. Nine-thirty. Early for him to have fallen asleep, too late for a visitor.

"Who is it?"

"County Commissioner."

Dennis opened the door. An overweight man in a sheriff's uniform grimaced at him, toeing at the gravel. The holstered gun at his side weighed down his pants. He constantly hitched them up by the belt loops.

"Um, hi." Dennis rubbed the sleep from his eyes and stuck out his hand. "Sorry, you caught me sleeping."

"You sleep in your clothes?"

"Don't usually. Just wiped out." Dennis stepped back and waved him in. "I'm Dennis Lipstein. What can I do for you?"

The Sheriff waddled in, studying the small motel room's interior. He pulled out the desk chair and fell into it with an exhausted sigh. "I'm Eddie Stokes. County Commissioner and Kwashau, Kansas sheriff. I reckon you can also consider me sheriff of Gannaway, too."

"That's a lotta titles for one man." Dennis sat on the bed.

"I'm a lotta man." Stokes laughed at his own joke, although Dennis thought he just stated the obvious. "Lipstein, huh? You a Jew-boy?"

Dennis blinked, unsure if he'd heard the man right. "Excuse me?"

"Son, I don't stutter. I asked if you was a Jew-boy?" The chair creaked beneath Stokes as he leaned forward.

"Yes, I am. Not currently practicing. Are you an ignorant bigot?" The instant the words tumbled out of his mouth, he wished he hadn't said them. But Dennis didn't tolerate bigotry easily. Not after growing up with it most of his life.

"Did I hear you right, son?" Stokes patted his chest, then his holster.

"Like you, Sheriff, I don't stutter."

Stokes gave a one-note chuckle. "I reckon not. You got a smart mouth on you, son."

"Sheriff, I'm sorry. I apologize. I shouldn't have said that. You just caught me off-guard. I wasn't expecting—"

"Well, now, you've done gone and gotten on my bad side, Mr. Lipstein."

"Dr. Lipstein."

"Come again?"

"I'm an environmental scientist. Dr. Lipstein."

"Well, hell, now, Mr. Lipstein, if this is your'n way of getting back on my good side, you're sure not very good at it."

Obviously, Sheriff Stokes carried around more than a few chips on his shoulder. But Dennis didn't want to begin his stint in Gannaway with the local law harassing him. "Okay, let's start over." Dennis crossed the room, hand outstretched. "Peace?"

"You a hippie, too, Mr. Lipstein?" Stokes leaned back, relishing his intimidation.

"No, I'm not a hippie."

"Smoke a li'l grass, maybe?" Holding two fingers to his lips, Stokes made a sucking sound.

"No, I *don't* smoke marijuana."

"With that long hair and that scraggly beard—"

"What can I do for you, Sheriff?"

Stokes's face turned redder than a twelve-hour sunburn. "Well, believe it or not, it's what I'm supposed to do for you."

"I don't follow."

"Mr. Gannaway told me you was coming. Some high muckety-muck from the United States Corps of Engineers."

"That's right. Wouldn't consider myself a high muckety-muck, though."

"From the looks of things, I wouldn't either." Stokes passed a huge hand through the air. "But Mr. Gannaway told me to give you assistance. *Supervised* assistance. Now, I gotta tell ya', folks around these parts don't cotton much to strangers nosin' about their business. Just what is it you're hopin' to achieve, son?"

"We, ah, don't really know yet. That's what I hope my research will—"

"And you're a scientist? Back in my school days, I learned science is based on hard facts."

Dennis toyed with the idea of asking him what his education entailed, then common sense prevailed. "Finding the facts is my research."

"And what facts are you lookin' for?"

They could go around and around all night. Dennis cut to the chase. "Gannaway used to be one of the richest mining towns in the tri-state area, if not the wealthiest. The zinc and lead mining industry boomed, particularly in the '20s and '30s."

Stokes seemed disinterested, nodded nonetheless.

"It's a fact the mines under Gannaway have been depleted. Or nearly so. Mr. Gannaway shut down his last mine in 1968 due to lack of minerals. And now the overseas countries have grabbed a large portion of the market."

"Damn commies." Stokes scowled. "Still doesn't tell me what you're doing here."

"There've been reports the water's contaminated in Gannaway. Acid mine water from the minerals. Air contaminants are also a concern. There's—"

Stokes jumped to his feet, faster than Dennis thought possible. He yanked his pants up again. "Son, you *still* ain't told me what you're doing here."

"I'm testing the water and the air. Preliminary investigations. Find out—"

"What's the bottom line?" Stokes wandered off toward Dennis's open suitcase on the floor. He leaned over, one foot off the floor, and peered inside.

"We're going to determine what to do with Gannaway. Make recommendations. Maybe turn it into a wetland."

"You know there's still folks livin' in Gannaway. You gonna take their homes from them because of some scientific nonsense?"

"We'll do what we need to do." Dennis crossed the room

and closed his suitcase. "We're trying to save these people's lives. Seems to me there's been plenty of lives lost already in Gannaway."

Stokes prodded a finger into Dennis's chest. "And I'm tellin' you, son, you'd best watch what you look into. It ain't your concern. You may not like what you find." He poked Dennis again before he dropped his rounded shoulders. His face sweetened with a baby's smile. "But I'm here to help you." He tucked a piece of paper into Dennis's shirt pocket. "My number. Mr. Gannaway says I should help you. But don't you go off on your own, now, hear me?"

"I hear you."

"Think I can find my way out." Stokes left the door open behind him. Dennis slammed the door and pulled back the curtain. Stokes sat in his Sheriff's car, speaking into a walkie-talkie. He replaced the walkie-talkie with a flashlight and swept the beam across Dennis's window. Dennis jumped back.

He had to reconsider his earlier assessment. Maybe Kansas was going to be a huge bummer.

Chapter Three

1935...

As he did every day before starting work in the mines, Tommy pitched a penny down the shaft. "Now we can go on down." Not that Tommy had a superstitious bone in his body, but a lot of the miners did. And if the tradition of tossing away a penny gave his men some peace of mind—and made the mine a safer place to work—it seemed like money well spent.

Call it what you will, Tommy couldn't deny his run of good luck since the events of 1929's tragedy. "The Gold Pot Mine Massacre" is what the newsmen called it. Reporters had flocked from all over the tri-state area trying to wrangle Tommy for an interview. They touted him as a hero. He wouldn't have any of it. He didn't want to minimize the loss of lives or the sadness of the tragedy. Referring to it as anything other than a tragedy seemed wrong, too. It certainly didn't make him feel like a hero. He considered himself blessed to have survived.

Didn't stop the windfall of luck that fell on Tommy, though. Even if it'd been born of tragedy. The Ground Boss who'd survived the ordeal keeled over in the mines shortly thereafter. Just put his hands on his hips and fell flat on his face without warning. At the time, Tommy'd already been promoted to a drill man position. The next promotion happened at lightning speed. At the age of 22, Tommy became the youngest Ground Boss in the history of the Gannaway Lead And Smelting Company. Given his tenderfoot status, the other miners respected him well enough, although a few of the old-timers regarded him with a wary eye. Still, they tolerated him.

Tommy hated riding the back of the Grim Reaper to a top mining position. But the Grim Reaper never asked for Tommy's opinion on the matter. Tommy thought something had to be watching out for him. He had a high-paying income. Well, at least as good as could be expected during the hard Depression. Absolutely, he couldn't regret the beautiful family he came home to.

"Fire in the hole!"

Tommy corralled his men by the bucket, the safest place to be when the explosion went off down in the stope. Safety first, always. Even if it seemed Mr. Gannaway fought him tooth and nail on every point.

While the smoke cleared, Big Ed passed the time by messing with a greenhorn.

"So, you see here, you strap this around your waist and pull the strings tight."

"But...that looks like a dad-gum ladies undergarment, Ed!" Definitely a girdle, all right, but pranks on greenhorns were another longstanding tradition. Let the men have their fun.

"Son, this ain't no woman's underwear. It's to help you with back problems." The other miners grunted, barely keeping their laughter in check.

"Well, all right, then. Reckon I'll take your word on it." The greenhorn took the girdle, eyeing it with suspicion. After he strapped it on, Big Ed clapped him on the back, loud enough to explode an echo down the drift.

Another greenhorn, been there a couple of weeks, attracted Tommy's attention. But for a very different reason.

He'd started out enthusiastically, fervent enough to be at a Call-to-Jesus Revival. The first to volunteer, he carried drill bits, filled buckets, and fed the mules. His energy seemed boundless. Then a week in, he changed, started wandering off, his mind clearly in the stars. Tommy didn't have a clue where he disappeared to half the time. But the kid's eyes worried him. Tommy'd seen eyes like that before. He'd never forget them. Karl Lundquist's eyes.

And now the new kid had vanished again.

Tommy pulled Ed aside. "Where's that other greenhorn?"

Ed pulled at a meaty cheek and looked over the gathered miners. "Dunno. Did you tell him to help the powder monkeys?"

"No, sir, I didn't. He worries me, Ed, I don't mind sayin'."

Ed paused, weighing his next words. Tommy saw it on his face. Ed thought the same thing. "Yep, I reckon he bothers me some as well."

"The yellow-eyed fever" is what Ed and other long-time miners had taken to calling it. Tommy's crew'd been lucky. Since Karl, they hadn't had any more "yellow-eyed fever" experiences. But miners talk. There were stories of incidents in other mines, horrifically similar to the Gold Pot Mine Massacre. Some of the men said Mr. Gannaway covered them up as mining accidents.

"Ed, don't start talkin' yellow-eyed fever again. You'll get the fellas all riled up." Tommy didn't believe in the yellow-eyed fever. At least, not with the supernatural stigma the others attached to it. It was clear as crystal to him the victims suffered from dementia, brought on by their poor working conditions.

Ed shrugged. "I seen his eyes, Tommy. They're yella. Like Karl's. And he's talkin' all sorts of nonsense."

Ed carried his own ghosts; it was as obvious as the straining overall straps on his back. Tommy remembered how Big Ed had ignored Karl's peculiar behavior. Until he'd started killing miners. Tommy guessed Big Ed didn't intend for that to happen again, not on his watch. Tommy didn't, either. "I'm watching him."

"Well, hell, then, where is he?"

A cough echoed down the drift. Not an uncommon sound down in the mines. Smoke rolled back, exposing a thin figure walking their way. He had one hand on the wall, guiding his unsteady gait.

Then he laughed.

Tommy approached him, a pit of dread building in his belly. "George, you feeling okay?"

George's uncommonly close-set eyes wandered. *Yellow eyes.* He opened his mouth to speak. Nothing came out but a hiccup.

"George, I'm sending you home. Go see Doc Wilkins and get his blessing. Then we'll put you back in the mines. Okay?"

George said nothing. A weak smile earthquaked across his lips. Tommy rattled his employee's shoulder, struggling to grab his attention. "Okay, George?"

Tommy looked back at his crew. Furrowed brows and nervous glances suggested they were worried—and for good reason—about what had happened to the greenhorn. Before questions—and worse, fears—could arise, Tommy draped his arm around George and walked him toward the bucket. The men spread. Tommy glanced over at Ed and jerked his head. Ed sprang forward and helped hoist George into the bucket.

Tommy yanked the cable and hollered up the shaft, "Man coming up!" Jim Reaper poked his head over the collar and nodded.

As Tommy watched George lift, a chill spread down his back. A familiar and very unwelcome chill.

George's roving gaze finally landed on Tommy. "They're coming, you know. Ain't no escapin' 'em, neither."

Ed whispered into Tommy's ear, "You done made the proper decision, kid."

"Maybe Doc Wilkins can figure this out. Before..."

Ed shook his head and belched. Sometimes Ed's belches spoke more than words.

Yes, sir, luck seemed to be on Tommy Donnelly's side. But what kind of luck?

Claire Donnelly hefted the potato-filled burlap bag onto her shoulder and left the boarding house. One of the benefits of cooking at the boarding house was the uneaten food she brought home to her family. Today's haul had been more bountiful than usual.

The warm temperature and greening of the trees suggested springtime. At least, spring as she remembered it as a child. But instead of birds chirping and welcoming the thawing climate, the air filled with the chugging of steam and gas engines hauling ore cans out of the ground. She saw school children on the playground next to the mines, but the constantly shrieking mine whistles drowned out their laughter. She drew in a deep breath, smelling the putrid stink of industrial waste. Something she had grown used to.

Still, she took pleasure in the beautiful day, and even after a nine-hour shift in the kitchen, there was lightness in her step. Tommy Junior and Margaret would be waiting for her at the door, full of questions about the food she brought home. Today she wouldn't disappoint. It's not every day they had potatoes. Claire bet she could make a week's worth of meals out of it.

Even Mother Donnelly proved to be a Godsend. Sure, she could test the devil, and she wasn't always a joy to live with. Particularly with her salty language and penchant for constant smoking in the house. But Claire wouldn't be able to bring in extra money and food without her watching the little ones.

As Claire passed the line of tents, she gave thanks again she and her family had a roof over their head. Each of the four rooms was smaller than a rich man's closet, but at least they could afford to rent a house. Many of the poor mining families had to make do with tents. Some of them resorted to squatting in discarded blasting powder boxes and piano crates. But Claire felt certain the Great Depression would end soon. President Roosevelt said as much when he talked on the radio.

She walked across the wooden planks covering the rain-flooded road and stopped in front of the mines. She hooked her fingers into the fence and watched. And wondered how Tommy fared below ground.

There weren't any alert whistles today. Every day she dreaded, practically anticipated, that sound. It announced a mining casualty. And every day she'd send Tommy off to work, his metal lunch box as full as she could pack it (sometimes not much, granted), with the same goodbye.

"You'd better come back to me, Tommy Donnelly."

"I will, Claire Donnelly. Nothing will keep me from you," he'd say in return.

And always, sealed with a kiss.

They fit the mold of a penny romance pamphlet. High school sweethearts. He'd been the star quarterback of the Gannaway Lions; she, the head cheerleader, both on and off the field. The promises they made to one another throughout school stuck. A year into a blissful marriage, she was pregnant. Tommy, Jr. jumped into the world, and like a fresh flower, Margaret popped up shortly after. Not once did they worry about having enough money to raise a family. Sure, times were tough, but they had it better than most folks.

Tommy also had a plan, one that germinated in high school. And like all of Tommy's plans, Claire knew he would follow through. He'd make enough mining money to go to college. He had his heart set on that university in Lawrence, Kansas, engineering his chosen field. He figured he already knew enough about machinery and geography to give him a leg up.

Claire cocked up a corner of her mouth, warmth spreading through her chest. Just a means to an end, that's all mining was. Tommy wouldn't die down in the mines like his father did. Soon, they'd all, including Mother Donnelly, she supposed, be migrating to Lawrence, Kansas, where they would live a better life.

Claire dipped the bucket into the barrel, filling it with water. She shaded her eyes and peered down the dirt road. Still no sign of her husband.

Her neighbor called out, "The men-folk will be home soon, honey. No need to fret."

"I know, Annie."

Inquiries as to neighbors' welfare were never made. They didn't need to be. They lived in a small town, their homes mere inches apart. Everyone knew everyone else's business at any given moment, sometimes before it even happened.

She stirred the potato soup as the children played at her feet.

"T.J., why don't you go on and take your little sister outside to play. Go on, git!"

The fresh air (as fresh as it gets in Gannaway) would do them good, but the children also served as her personal siren when Tommy made it home safely.

Sure enough, moments later, high-pitched greetings filled her heart with reassurance. She heard the sound of Tommy's boots clomping across the front porch and heaved a sigh of relief.

"You're home." Claire wiped her hands on her apron before wrapping them around her husband's back.

"I'll always come home. Always."

Again, they sealed their verbal contract with a kiss. But this kiss tasted much sweeter than the morning one.

They lay in bed, arms around one another.

"Mother Donnelly was smoking in the house again to-day." Claire kept her voice hushed as the walls were thinner than wet crackers.

Tommy laughed. "I'll talk to Momma."

"It ain't funny, Tommy Donnelly." She swatted his naked chest. "The house smells like it's on fire."

"I'll talk to her."

The quiet nights came as a welcome respite from the sounds of mining that overtook the days in Gannaway. "What happened in the mines today?"

Claire felt Tommy tense. "Same," he said.

"I know when you're keeping something from me. What happened?"

"All right, then. There's a greenhorn. Young fella straight outta high school named George Kendricks. You know him?"

"I know his family."

"Well...something ain't right with him. I had to send him on home."

"How's he not right?"

Tommy sighed. Claire knew the sigh, the sound of sur-render. Tommy's honesty always outweighed his desire to protect his loved ones from potentially upsetting news. "Now, I'm not saying it's connected or anything of that nature—"

"You'd best be telling me right now."

"Shh! Anyhow, back in '29...Karl Lundquist..."

Claire sat up in bed. She'd never forget that day. The mine whistles had jolted her out of a pleasant daydream in English class. Her singular thoughts had been with her fiancée on his first day underground. The panic she'd felt had nearly sent her into a screaming fit. "Oh, my—"

"There's no need to get in an uproar. Nothing hap-pened." Tommy tried to pull her back down alongside him. She shoved his hand away and glared at him. "The boy looked...confused. It reminded me of how Karl looked that day."

"Oh, my sweet Lord. Did he hurt anyone?"

"No, ma'am. I sent him on home to his Momma and Doc Wilkins."

"You said he looked confused. He's only been there for a short time. Maybe—"

"It was more than that, Claire. I could just feel it in my bones."

Claire trusted Tommy's "bones." They said a miner's best instrument was his ears, knowing when to detect tell-tale signs of falling rocks. When something didn't sound right. Tommy's instincts had led him out of many near scrapes.

"And he was talking away at nonsense. Not making any sense. Almost as if he were talking to ghosts."

"But you don't believe any of the miner's superstitious hoo-ha."

"I don't. That ain't changed. But I can't put the men at risk if I see something off."

"Well, you let me know what Doc Wilkins says about it. And don't you put him back in that hole 'til he gets checked out and done over again. You hear me?"

"Yes'm."

"I mean it, Tommy Donnelly. I find out differently, and I'll come over there and yank you outta that hole myself if need be. And I'll bring Mother Donnelly along to keep you in line." Dead serious as she was, the image made Claire smile.

Tommy reached around her waist and pulled her on top of him. "Claire, you can't come into the mines."

"You just watch me."

"If it's all the same to you, I'd rather watch you here, right now."

Claire giggled, clamping a hand over her mouth. "You behave! Our little ones are right on the other side of that wall." Claire often bandied about this warning. An unheeded warning. They both knew what always happened next.

They made sweet, but very quiet, love.

Chapter Four

1969...

Curiosity drove him. It practically drove the van, too. Dennis set out with good intentions that morning to put in a full day of work. But he blew past Gannaway, barely affording it a glance, and traveled seven miles down the highway. He wanted to see what the Native American did with the trashed eight-track cartridge. And maybe he wanted to restore his faith in humanity, too, after the ugly visit from Sheriff Stokes last night.

The gravel crunched under his tires as he pulled into the drive. He hopped down, chunked the door shut, and saw the Indian sitting in a lawn chair on his front porch, still wearing his fedora and sporting a weathered jean jacket. The man flashed Dennis another peace sign salute. Dennis grinned. He'd experienced peace and hate in the last twenty-four hours within a fourteen-mile radius of Gannaway, Kansas.

"Mornin'." Dennis beat the man to the punch and offered him a soul handshake.

"Mornin'."

"Name's Dennis Lipstein."

The man tilted his fedora. "Ahanu Littlefish. But you can call me Bob."

"Well, nice to meet you, Bob. How do you get 'Bob' out of Ahanu Littlefish?"

Bob's smile produced a tidal wave of creases and dents across his face. It was impossible to gauge if they were the result of age or too much sun. His eyes twinkled with youthful vigor, suggesting he might be younger than Dennis had earlier guessed.

"Long story, that. Maybe some time I'll tell you about it." He stood up and dug his hands into his jacket's pockets. "Lipstein. You Jewish?"

Maybe Dennis miscalculated the friendly Kansas natives. "Why does everyone ask me that?"

Bob laughed, more of a wheeze. "Welcome to Kansas, Dennis. And welcome to my nightmare. Get used to it if you plan on bein' around a while."

"Yes, I'm Jewish. No, I don't practice the faith any longer. Yes, I'm—"

"Whoa, slow down, brother. I'm not casting judgment. Native American, in case you didn't notice." He tossed his thumbs at his belly. "You don't think I get judged being who I am? Just color me curious. Don't get to meet many Jewish folks this neck of the woods."

"Okay, okay. It's just...sorry I snapped. Last night I was called a 'Jew-boy' by a sheriff and—"

"Stokes?" The smile slid from Bob's face.

"That'd be him."

"Yep. He's a real peach, ain't he?"

Dennis laughed. "Guess that's one way of describing him. Anyway, you can color me curious as well. I wanted to see what you did with the eight-track cartridge."

"Come on then, brother Dennis." He ambled by Dennis and around the corner of the house.

Dennis caught up to him standing in front of a large piece of plywood. The painted background captured a beautiful tapestry of wildlife and vegetation, an orange sun setting over mountains at the top. An array of trash—beer cans, cigarette butts, fast food wrappers, shoes, and Dennis's tape cartridge—hung off the board, nailed into place.

"You like it?"

"Actually...I do."

"Huh. You sound surprised, brother." Bob stepped back, studying his own work. "I call it 'The Raping of the Land'."

"Cute."

"I think so." Bob brushed by him again, turned and said, "Come on. Let's get acquainted."

Bob gestured toward the empty lawn chair next to his. Dennis took a seat. The strapping underneath him sank, ripping a bit, weathered from outdoor habitation. Bob reached down next to him and pulled a can of beer out of a cooler. "Want one?" He popped the top and put the lid in his pocket.

"Um, no thanks. It's, uh, 8:30 in the morning."

"What? You afraid this red-skinned man can't hold his firewater? Maybe I'll go wild on the white man?" Even though Bob's expression smacked of amusement, Dennis felt his bitter underlying tone. But something much worse bothered Dennis.

"No. I...don't drink. Not anymore." Dennis leaned back, pursed his lips, and waited for the inevitable follow-through questions.

"Oh. Sorry, brother. Alcoholic?"

Dennis nodded and said nothing.

"How long you been off the firewater?"

"Five months, twenty-three days." Dennis consulted his watch. "And three-and-a-half hours."

"Nice, brother. Congratulations." Bob held the can up, jiggled it. Beer sloshed over the side. "You want me to toss it away?"

After hesitating, Dennis said, "No, it's okay. I've been around it since. I need to get used to having it around me."

"Okay, fine, brother. Why?"

"Excuse me?"

"Why'd you become an alcoholic? Everyone has a story."

Harder than hell to pull off, but Dennis managed a

weak smile. "Well, as someone recently said to me, 'long story, that. Maybe I'll tell you about it sometime'."

Bob laughed long and hard. "Fair enough." He took a gulp and followed it with an "ah." "For me, a morning beer gives me artistic motivation."

"So, you're an artist?"

"What, you can't tell by looking around you?" Bob waved his hand across his aviary of oddball artifacts. "You're sitting in my world."

"Nice work. Can't say as I understand all of it...but nice work."

"Art ain't necessarily supposed to be understood all the time. It just...is. Everything you see here? I've found it along the roadside. Or scavenged it out of the wreckage of Gannaway. My purpose is to turn trash into art."

"It's a mighty fine purpose."

"That it is." He took another swig. "Don't pay worth shit, but, hey, artists ain't in it for the money. What's your purpose, Dennis?"

"I'm an environmental scientist."

Bob brought the beer can down, staring down into the opening. "You don't say."

"I do. The US Army Corps of Engineers assigned me the task of looking at Gannaway with my test tubes, chemicals, and microscopes."

Bob's extended silence reinforced the quiet surrounding them. No singing birds, no sound of wildlife. Nothing traipsing through the surrounding woods, no snapping limbs. Even the wind seemed to have packed up its bags to head for a more suitable environment.

"Huh." When Bob set his can down, Dennis knew he struck a chord. "Seems like you've got a mighty big task ahead of you. What do you hope to achieve?"

"Not really sure. It depends on what my findings show on the water and air samples. I hope to find out if Gannaway's habitable for its current few residents. Maybe we can obtain government funding to rebuild Gannaway. Maybe Gannaway's a lost cause and the land should be flooded. Or maybe—"

Bob turned in his seat. He held his neck stiff and straight. "That's a lot of 'maybes.' But here's a maybe for you that's a definite certainty. Maybe you should be very careful."

Dennis shook his head. "What do you mean? Stokes?"

"He's the least of your worries. There're some things a-bout Gannaway...things you should know. But you're a man of science. I want you to get your feet wet first. Then we'll talk."

"Um...okay."

"You plannin' on talking to ol' man Gannaway?"

"Yes. He's on my list. I've been told I have to. Since he apparently owns what's left of Gannaway and Kwashau County."

"You do that. He's another peach, you'll find out." Bob flickered a quick smile, then dropped it. "Just remember what I told you. Be careful. Be careful who you talk to, what you say...and be careful what you see."

"I...don't even know what that means."

"You'll find out. But like I said, anything I'm gonna tell you won't make much sense until you pop your Ganna-way cherry, so to speak. Excuse my French, brother."

"Okay, fine, but—"

Bob jumped to his feet and clapped his hands togeth-er. "Time for both of us to get to work. The day's a-wastin' and the sun waits for no man." He dropped another soul shake onto Dennis, hastening the end of the visit. "Just heed my word. And come back. I'll fill in the missing gaps for you. Peace, brother." With that, Bob skedaddled around the corner and out-of-sight like a man with something to hide.

Gullet Creek snaked through Gannaway, looping around

the outskirts of town. At one time the creek had been the primary source for water, feeding into the town wells. But when they shut down the mines and turned off the water pumps, the mines flooded. The water ate away at the chemicals within the rock, producing acid water that undoubtedly seeped into the creek and wells. A hint of orange tinted the water, a sure sign of acidic tainting.

The sparse vegetation surrounding the creek, comprised mostly of sickly looking mushrooms, seemed off and discolored. The land resembled a moonscape, fairly barren with spotty patches of grass.

Dennis snapped the rubber glove at his wrist. He knelt and dipped the vial into the creek, then capped it. In the dead woods across the creek, he spotted movement.

A man wearing dark blue overalls and a hardhat stood next to a tree, hands relaxed at his side, unmoving, his skin color startlingly white.

Dennis fished out his glasses. By the time he'd put them on, the man had vanished. Just dark, skeletal tree trunks, none of them large enough to hide behind. Maybe he hadn't seen anyone at all. Maybe Bob's ominous words struck a chord and conspired with his brain to play tricks on him. Either way, it jarred him. He hadn't hallucinated since he drank.

No. He wouldn't allow himself to go back down that dark path. He saw a man. Just knew it.

But why would there be a miner when the mines had been shut down?

Back at the van, Dennis ran some preliminary tests. He didn't have much of a set-up. A small table, a pump sink with saline solution, a few other various odds and ends. Not really efficient to accurately gauge the characterization of surface water and sediment samples. The variability, quality verification, and pH testing would have to wait until he mailed his samples back to Los Angeles. But he should be able to determine if there were contaminants in Gullet Creek.

A loud crack sounded outside the van. Dennis twisted, dropping his test tube.

"Goddammit, get on outta here!"

Dennis duck-walked to the front of the van and peeked out. A man dressed in flannel aimed a shotgun through the windshield. Dennis dove to the van floor.

"You get your city ass outta here! Leave us be!"

Another shot blasted by the van, rattling the windows.

Dennis threw his hands over his head and called out, "I'm a government scientist!" He felt ludicrous screaming into the van's floor, and his defense sounded admittedly weak. He had no idea if the man could even hear him. But in insane situations, insanity isn't a bad defense.

The van's door handle rattled. A hand thumped the window. "Get out here! Come on!" The gun barrel clicked at the window. *Tap, tap, tap.* "Get out here now 'fore I blast your van to Kingdom Come!"

Bang!

Dennis's heart jumped at the sound of the blast.

"Okay! I'm coming out! Don't shoot!" Dennis clamped his eyes shut. He tossed out a quick prayer to a God he'd thought he'd abandoned six months ago. But it was time to hedge his bets. He pulled himself up against the back of the bench seat and tossed back the sliding door.

The gun barrel wavered in Dennis's face like a black, upright snake.

"What're you doing here in Gannaway? You a metal scavenger?" He lowered his gun while coughing violently into a cupped fist.

"No! No, I'm an environmental scientist with the government. My credentials are in the van—"

"Don't care about no damn credentials!" His eyes widened, wild and unsteady. The few teeth he had looked yellow as corn.

"Let me explain—"

From behind them, a shrill laugh rang out. On the high-way shoulder, Sheriff Stokes leaned up against his car with folded arms and a big grin on his face, just enjoying the show. "That's enough, Harlan. Put the damn gun away." He took his hat off and wiped his brow. Then he sauntered slowly toward them, taking his sweet time.

"You know this boy, Eddie?" The gun-wielding man looked confused, swaying the gun back and forth.

"This here's Mr. Lipstein. Big City hotshot." Stokes pushed down on the gun barrel. "Let's not cause him to wet his Big City britches."

"What's he doin' here?"

"Oh, you know how the government is, Harlan. Always pokin' their nose into others' business. Just let him play with his science toys. He'll be outta here in no time. Mr. Gannaway knows about him."

Harlan cocked his head to one side and spat. "Mr. Gannaway vouches for him?"

"Never said that. But he's given his blessing for Lipstein's…scien-teefic research."

Caught between terror and disbelief, Dennis lowered his hands. "I was trying to tell you that." He may as well have been talking to himself. A minute ago the man wanted to blow Dennis's head off. Now he wouldn't even acknowledge Dennis's existence.

"Go on home, Harlan. Go on. Git." Stokes waved his hat.

"All right then. But I best not be catchin' this fella steal-ing metal outta Gannaway."

"Go on. He ain't gonna steal no metal."

Harlan stalked off, his bony shoulders pitching up with every step. He looked back and said, "Best not." He disap-peared down the road, stroking the gun barrel as he walked.

"How long were you watching that, Sheriff?"

"Long enough, I reckon."

"Were you going to wait until he shot me to do some-thing about it?" If this was the quality of law in Gannaway and Kwashau, it shocked Dennis the town hadn't been overridden by outlaws.

"No one got shot. I had it under control." Stokes edged closer, bouncing his vast belly off of Dennis's. "You weren't in any danger."

Dennis saw it differently. His world consisted of desks and test tubes, not shotgun-carrying crazies. "Could've fooled me. Isn't it illegal to fire a gun at someone?"

"Nobody shot at you. He just shot up in the sky." Stokes peered up and squinted into the sunlight. "Hunting."

"Nothing up there to hunt. Unless he wanted a hawk dinner. Or maybe he wanted a scientist on his mantle. What was that about anyway?"

"Harlan? He's harmless. Just a chat rat."

"'Chat rat'?"

Stokes replaced his hat, tilted it back. The better to glower at Dennis. "Chat rats are the leftovers in Gannaway. Folks who refuse to leave. They grew up here, their mommas and poppas, too. They been through a lot, Mr. Lipstein. Last thing they wanna see are more scavengers, looters, and folks wantin' to make their life miserable."

Stokes' not so subtle message again. "I'm not trying to make their lives miserable. I'm trying to improve their lives—"

"Well, now, folks don't see it that way. Hope you learned your damn-fool lesson. You can't go traipsin' all over God's green earth here by yourself."

Dennis looked around at the anything-but-green Gannaway land. "I suppose you want to babysit me while I collect my research."

Stokes lifted an eyebrow. "Be in your best interests. Unless, like you said, you want to end up on someone's mantle."

"I'll take my chances." Dennis might have to put a call into Meyers. Surely Meyers could put the fear of the government into Mr. Gannaway and his cronies. "I think it's time I met Mr. Gannaway."

The sheriff straightened and put on a show of pulling

up his pants. "Well, why didn't you say so? Mr. Gannaway's been waitin'."

Chapter Five

1935...

Tommy's day had just begun. It didn't take long for fortune to change the course of what at first seemed like a promising day.

In front of the Gannaway Lead & Smelting Company office, Mr. Gannaway's new 1935 Bentley sparkled beneath the sunlight. Rumor had it he paid a small fortune to be one of the first Bentley owners in the country. In the passenger side sat his pretty Indian wife, Naira. Tommy had never met her, but that didn't surprise him. Mr. Gannaway kept her on a tight leash, never let her out of his sight. Many conflicting stories circulated around Gannaway surrounding their strange marriage. Tommy didn't give heed to those, though. Just more rumors. Still, he had to admit to a certain sense of curiosity.

He tossed a wave her way. She offered the most imperceptible of smiles. It was a beautiful smile, though, one capable of starting wars. Then she lowered her gaze to her folded hands.

The corrugated door ground open, and Tommy entered the office. Calling it an "office" seemed somewhat misleading. A tin box would be more accurate. The shed's inhabitants were already cooking from the morning heat.

Mr. Gannaway sat behind Joe Darling's desk. Joe Darling was a timid bean-counter of a bookkeeper, but a fair man. Mr. Gannaway looked right at home, even with the sweat trickling down his face, no doubt induced by his neck-strangling suit. Darling and Doc Wilkins shuffled nervously by the wall, standing ready for orders from the owner of Gannaway Ore And Smelting Company. Or to offer him a handkerchief should he sneeze.

Tommy already had an idea why they were meeting. "Mornin', Mr. Darling. Doc." He tipped his hardhat to both men. "How are you, Mr. Gannaway?"

"Doing good, Tommy." He stood and shook Tommy's hand. When he fell back into his seat (or rather, Mr. Darling's seat), he gestured toward the wooden chair across from him. "How's your family?" He flashed his practiced smile, the kind only money can buy.

"They're fine. And your wife?" Tommy made it his business to know everything he could about people he worked with, from Mr. Gannaway on down to the newest greenhorn. He knew Gannaway had no children. More rumors abounded as to why.

"Just fine." He drew a finger around his tight collar, a sure sign the time for pleasantries had ended. "Doc Wilkins tells me you sent George Kendricks home yesterday."

"Yes, sir."

"Why?" Gannaway never beat around the bush, and Tommy appreciated that about him.

"'Cause he looked ill. And he was actin' funny."

"Funny? In what way?"

Tommy suspected Gannaway knew, but he played along. "He was talking to himself. Laughing. Vanishing into the mines. He was a danger to himself and the other miners."

Mr. Gannaway looked at the men hovering behind him. "Do you agree with this assessment, Mr. Darling?"

"Um, yes, sir, I do. Tommy's word is—"

Gannaway's hand shot up, cutting him off. "You took his *word* for it, Mr. Darling? Without assessing the situation yourself?" Although speaking to Tommy's boss, Gannaway's gaze remained planted on Tommy.

"That's not quite accurate—"

Another hand ax. "Regardless. Doc? What did you make of the boy?"

Doc toyed with his mustache's waxed tip, twisting it like a pretzel. "As far as I can tell, there wasn't nothin' physically wrong with the boy."

"Nothing wrong." Gannaway rolled his fingertips over the desktop.

"Now I—"

"Nothing wrong. That's your final evaluation, Doc?"

"Well, I didn't—"

"As you said, there was nothing wrong with the boy." He shot Wilkins a look. "Tommy, Tommy. I run one of the largest mining companies in the country." His smile returned, but Tommy saw no joy behind it. "This is a business committed to helping out our country in times of need. Wouldn't you agree?"

"Yes, sir." He'd heard it all before, but he'd found it best to let Gannaway deliver his speeches. Made life easier for everyone.

"And to run a business properly, I need every man pulling his weight. What makes this country great. I can't afford to have a boy off work 'cause he misses his momma. The boy's officially back in the mines this morning."

Tommy blinked and then looked at Doc Wilkins. "Doc... he had *yellow* eyes." He didn't want to bring up "yellow-eyed fever," but he couldn't allow George back into the mine, either. Not yet.

"Tommy, when I looked him over, he didn't have no yellow eyes."

A lock of Gannaway's greased-back hair curled over his forehead like a question mark when he slapped his knee. "Tommy, I don't want to hear any of this 'yellow-eyed fever' horse shit! It's just a story concocted by our boys...somethin' to kill time with. And I don't want you talkin' about it down in the mine."

"Doc, did he seem all right to you? You said he checked out physically. But what about what's goin' on in his head? What's your honest opinion?" Tommy jumped at the risk, perilously close to defying Mr. Gannaway. But it felt like the right thing to do. The *only* thing to do.

"Son, he...the boy...was a little weak. Nothin' more, nothin' troublin'. Mining work's hard, we all know that. He just ain't accustomed to it yet." As Doc Wilkins stuck a hand-rolled tobacco stick between his lips, his fingers trembled. "I fixed him up good with a shot. Fixed what ailed him." One of Doc's infamous mystery shots. No one knew, never asked, what went into the shots, but Wilkins passed them out indiscriminately, no matter the sickness. Not exactly the most comforting of treatments.

"Well, now, that's good enough for me." Gannaway stood, abruptly ending the meeting. "The boy goes back to work. Thank you, Tommy. And keep up the good work. You're a hard-working man."

Tommy stared at his extended hand, finally took it. "Sir, if you don't mind my sayin', this is a mistake."

Gannaway's cold, gray eyes narrowed. His hand gripped Tommy's harder. When Tommy tried to release their handshake, Gannaway tugged him back in. "I said, 'That's good enough for me.'" He clenched his teeth so tight, Tommy feared they might splinter. The other two men stood still as death.

"I understand, Mr. Gannaway, and I mean you no disrespect. It's just—"

"Darling. Doc. Leave." Gannaway flourished his hand toward the two men. As they scuttled away, Tommy swore he heard Darling sigh with relief.

"Tommy, you say you don't mean me any disrespect. But your actions speak differently. You questioned my authority in front of two of my employees." Strictly speaking, Doc Wilkins couldn't be designated an employee of the Gannaway Mining Company, but he certainly came running every time Gannaway snapped his fingers. "Whose name is on the company, Tommy? Hm? Hell, son, what's the name of our town?"

"Yours, sir. I know that, but—"

Gannaway's jaw tightened. Lines knifed across his forehead as he glowered. Unblinking. End of discussion.

"I just hope something doesn't happen, sir."

Gannaway finally released his hand. "It won't. It better not." He rapped his knuckles against Tommy's chest. *"Pray it won't."*

While Gannaway scraped the door shut behind him, Tommy had already taken Gannaway's advice into consideration. Praying for his men's safety.

Although Claire's back troubled her, it felt like a *good* pain. The kind of pain her mother used to say hard work earned. Brought on by helping others.

Today, the dining area housed a full group, more crowded than usual. The boarding room had opened up their food service to everyone. For a small fee, miners could eat a warm meal—usually potato- and bean-based—and have a roof over their heads while doing so. The men welcomed that roof in this unusually soggy spring.

As Claire collected the licked-clean plates, she noticed the men seemed particularly solemn today, their temperament no doubt influenced by the rainy weather. Chatter stayed at a minimum. Constant coughing filled the room, something she accepted as fact in Gannaway. And she'd also learned to accept the collective body odor. Not everyone could afford the luxury of daily baths. "The smell of hard work," her mother would've said.

Back in the kitchen, Claire scrubbed the plates over the basin. Kaya stood next to her, drying.

"How's that boy of yours doing, Kaya?" asked Claire.

Kaya smiled. Despite their ethnic differences, they had bonded over tales of motherhood. "Ahanu's got his head in the clouds. Always will, that one. Seventeen years old and he's talking nonsense about being an artist."

"But he's still working at the school. Maybe he can become a teacher there."

"I don't think so. He's a strong boy with a mind of his own. I don't reckon his dream will ever pan out, but I can see in his eyes, he's going to try. Or give it hell trying."

Claire burned red over Kaya's salty language, but a giggle slipped from her lips anyway. She had a lot of empathy for Kaya and her Kwashau tribal people. Twenty years ago, when Claire was just a wee lass, the town of Gannaway had been predominantly an Indian reservation, Claire's family had been amongst the first white settlers. Her late poppa had big dreams of striking it rich in the mines, just as Tommy's father had. As fate would have it, premature death struck them down instead of riches. It hadn't been easy for the Indians either. As rich, white settlers sublet the land out from underneath them for a penny, the Kwashau found themselves pushed off the reservation and moved to even more remote locations. Mr. Gannaway, of course, presided over all as the biggest landowner in the area. And for some odd reason Claire couldn't fathom, Indians weren't allowed to work the mines. As an Indian mother of three, Kaya lucked into her job at the boarding house. The future didn't shine so bright for her three sons, though. Finding work other than mining in Gannaway seemed near impossible. The entire town was built around the mining industry. It constituted ninety-eight percent of the town's jobs.

"Maybe Ahanu will surprise you, Kaya. I've seen him with the children at the school. He's very good with them. Has a natural way about him." Claire and Tommy, with the Kwashau tribe's blessings, had enrolled their children in the local Indian school. A lot of the townfolk disapproved of their decision, no matter it was none of their business, but Claire thought the Kwashau School had stronger educational merits than the public school.

"We'll see. What about you, Claire? I can tell something's bothering you."

Claire never could hide her feelings. Tommy always said he could read her like a book. A very beautiful book, he'd add, but a book that's easy to read. "I suppose there is. Tommy told me there's a boy in the mines. A sick boy—"

Kaya dropped a plate to the floor. White shards bounced at the women's feet. "Yellow-eyed fever?" Kaya's voice dropped to a whisper, her eyes wide with fear.

"It's what it sounds like. But Tommy says the yellow-eyed fever is nothing but a bunch of bananas."

Kaya gripped Claire's wrist and forcibly turned her. "No, child. The yellow-eyed fever is real. Your husband's a good man, but he needs to believe in forces outside of his control."

"You're frightening me, Kaya!"

Kaya tightened her lips, the color draining out of them. "I know what I've been told. I've said too much already—"

"Tell me what you know! My husband's down there!"

She hesitated. "You must keep what I tell you to yourself. You can't tell other white folk."

It stung Claire that her friend felt the need to differentiate their skin color. Given everything the Kwashau have been through, though, Claire understood the bad blood between the races. But she valued her husband's safety first. When challenged, Claire could transform into a lion, more ferocious than the mighty Gannaway high school football team. Especially with her family's welfare at stake. If she needed to keep information quiet, so be it. But she couldn't sit by, doing nothing. "I won't tell anyone. I promise."

"There's a man in our tribe. A very old man. A medicine man name of John Blackbird. If I've met him, I don't even recall. He stays to himself. But my people talk. They talk of the yellow-eyed fever. Story goes John Blackbird was horrified at what the white man had done to the land. Land they bequeathed upon us in the first place. Land they stole from us and destroyed with their mining. John Blackbird put a curse on the mines. What the miners call yellow-eyed fever."

Claire had no idea how to respond. What Kaya told her challenged everything she grew up believing. It went beyond her Christian capacity to comprehend. But the urgency in Kaya's eyes said she believed it with all her heart. "But... what does the curse do?"

Kaya shrugged. "Depends on who you listen to. Drives a man out of his skull. Makes him hear and see things that aren't from the mortal realm. *Dead* things."

"Oh, my sweet Lord. Most of those men, Kaya...all of them...they're innocent. They're just trying to make enough money to provide—"

"I understand. And I feel pity in my heart for those men. But what's done is done." She grabbed Claire's shoulders and gave her a squeeze, not comforting in the least.

"Anything that's *done* can be undone. Could you talk to your tribal chief?"

"I'm sorry, but they won't listen to a woman. And I believe a lot of the tribe sees the curse as a good thing. There's been lots of ill feelings built up over the years. You won't find much sympathy on the reservation, my friend."

Claire said nothing and fell into a chair. A rolling boulder filled her stomach with queasiness. What she'd heard sounded unbelievable. But she couldn't discard it.

Her inner lion roared. And lions weren't afraid of anything in the jungle. If she had to, she'd go talk to John Blackbird herself.

"I done heard you went toe to toe with Gannaway." Big Ed's wealth of knowledge never ceased to amaze Tommy. Tommy had no idea how he knew the things he did, what with spending so much time underground.

"I reckon you heard right. Where's the kid?"

Ed jerked his chin down the corridor. "Soon as he came

down, he headed straight into the drift."

"Maybe that's the best place for him now. Keep him away from the other fellas."

"I think you'd be right. Goddamn Gannaway." Ed didn't share many of the men's admiration for Kyle Gannaway. He placed the blame for everything wrong in the mines squarely at Gannaway's feet. Tommy thought he might be right.

"I tried to get him to see reason, but he wouldn't listen."

"Course not. He ain't down here. You'da been better off spittin' in the wind."

"I need to go find the greenhorn."

Ed patted his stomach and sighed. "I know better than to talk you outta that." He looked around and bent over a collection of tools. "Here. Take this. Just in case." He handed Tommy a small hand-pick.

"I'm not gonna use that, Ed."

"The hell you ain't. You use it if you need to. Your daddy would—"

"All right." Tommy grabbed it, shoved it in his back pocket. Whenever Ed brought up Tommy's father, he played unfair, using him as leverage. Tommy never won those battles.

As Tommy entered the stope, he tossed out waves to his crew.

"College boy underground!"

"You still readin' them fancy books, college boy?"

He didn't mind being called "college boy." Sort of fancied it, in fact. Ironically, the men didn't even know his plans to attend college. The nickname came about because of his reading habits and how informed he stayed about doings in Washington.

"Seen the greenhorn?"

The powder monkey pointed toward a freshly dug drift and said, "Last I saw him, he was wanderin' off down yonder."

Tommy entered the drift. Torches hadn't been mounted on the walls yet, so he lit his helmet. He stopped and listened. *Singing.* Goosebumps prickled his skin when he heard the gospel lyrics. A horrifically familiar hymn, a nightmare of sound.

He found George sitting on a fallen clump of rock, his hands held behind his back. He swayed back and forth, keeping beat with his song.

"George?"

George's gaze flit back and forth before settling on Tommy. "Mr. Donnelly?"

"I'm just Tommy down here."

"Just Tommy." George giggled as if privy to a private joke.

"How're you feeling?"

"You know something? Not so—" Convulsing, he doubled over, dry-heaving as if trying to bring up yesterday's soup.

"You sick?"

He looked up at Tommy, his eyes brimming with tears. "I...don't know what's wrong with me."

"Tell me what's ailing you."

"It's the...can't you see them? Can't you *see* them?"

"We're alone in here."

"No! No, we're *not!*" When he shot to his feet, Tommy stumbled back. "There's one!" He pointed into the darkness. "There's another! And they're tellin' me to do things! Horrible things!"

"George, there's no one down here! Just us—"

"It's gotta *stop!*"

George brought his arms up, a railroad spike gripped in each hand.

"George! *No!*" Tommy grasped George's wrists, shaking them. He closed the gap between them, ensuring George had no room to move. They twisted and turned, dancing around the boulders. "Drop 'em, George!"

A spike's tip grazed Tommy's hand. He swung George face-first into the cavern wall. The spikes dropped into the water with a splash. Still holding George's wrists, Tommy pinned him to the wall, covering him like a straitjacket.

George went slack, breathing heavily, but the fight had left him.

Tommy made a managerial decision. If Mr. Gannaway wouldn't take George out of the mines, Tommy'd make damn sure he wouldn't be able to work.

"I sure am sorry about this, George. I surely am." Tommy slipped his hand around George's fingers. He yanked back. Hard. When he heard the bones crack, he grimaced, practically feeling the pain himself.

George's scream brought the men running.

"What in the *hell?*" Big Ed's jaw dropped when he saw the two men.

Tommy had George's good arm draped around his shoulders, barely managing his dead weight. "Mining accident. Let's get him to the bucket."

Chapter Six

1969...

Dennis rang the doorbell. Stokes stood propped up against his car in the winding driveway, watching Dennis with a bemused expression.

Kyle Gannaway lived in a massive house, a southern-style mansion seemingly plucked from an era long past and dropped onto the outskirts of Gannaway. It was the only sign of wealth Dennis had seen in the area. It was definitely one of the few intact buildings still standing.

Dennis spotted a blur of movement behind the stained glass doors. When the doors opened, a tall, egg-shaped man with a tuft of blond hair stood before him.

"May I help you?" Dennis detected a slight European accent, one untouched by the Midwest.

"I hope so. I'm Dr. Dennis Lipstein with the—"

"Ah!" The man slapped his hands together with child-like glee. His grin brought a rosy color to his full cheeks. "Of course! Dr. Lipstein with the United States Army Corps of Engineers! We've been expecting you!"

Dennis shook his hand. The man's iron-like grip surprised him. Based on the man's size, he'd misjudged him as being all flab, no muscle. "I'm Gustav Eberstark, Mr. Gannaway's personal assistant. Call me Gus." He knocked back his head and let fly a chuckle to the arched ceiling.

"Hi, Gus. Pleasure to meet you."

"Likewise, Dr. Lipstein." More laughter, more like a nervous tic. "May I get you something to drink? A glass of wine, perhaps? Mr. Gannaway has an excellent selection from all over the world."

Dennis swallowed, his throat dry and parched. For the briefest of moments, he almost tasted the tang of a dry red wine and smelled the bouquet-like aroma. "No, thanks. I'm fine."

Gus pressed his thin lips together, appearing perplexed someone could possibly reject his hospitality. But it didn't take long for him to bounce back into full-on Santa Claus mode with a hearty laugh. "Please let me know if you change your mind."

"I'll do that."

Something whirred and clicked at the top of the center stairwell. A motorized chair lift hummed down, slow and steady. A thin man, hunched over, as crooked as the gold cane he carried, rode it down. Dressed in a red velvet bathrobe, he clutched the cane like treasure between his knobby knees. When the cart landed at the foot of the stairwell, he said nothing. Just stared. Even though he appeared ancient, his full head of wavy, white hair would've made men half his age jealous.

Gus hustled over to meet him. With surprising ease, Gus cradled him up into his arms. The old man dropped his arm around Gus's shoulders like a bride being carried over the threshold. Not once did the old man avert his eyes from Dennis, fully ignoring his manservant.

Gus deposited the man into a wheelchair sitting behind the stairwell. After fidgeting with the controls, he placed the cane in his lap and zipped up to Dennis, nearly running over his toes. "I'm Kyle Gannaway." His voice was deep and resonant, shocking coming from such a frail-looking frame.

"Hello, Mr. Gannaway. I'm Dr. Dennis Lipstein." They shook hands.

"Call me Kyle."

"I hope I'm not intruding, Kyle, but I was hoping to talk to you about your mines and Gannaway."

"Of course, of course. My town, after all. Been waiting for you to come around these here parts." Even though his accent and words carried a Midwestern bent, Dennis suspected he played it up for show. Probably something he'd adopted to deal with the locals. But underneath that "aw, shucks" exterior, Dennis recognized a man used to getting what he wanted. His icy eyes said it all. "Let's retire to my study." He flourished a hand in Gus's direction. "You're dismissed, Gus."

"Yes, Mr. Gannaway." As he trotted up the stairs, Gus dropped another string of chuckles.

"Follow me." Gannaway backed up, spun the chair a-round, and sped by Dennis. He pulled to an abrupt stop in front of two oak doors and nudged one open with the tip of his cane. The room had been designed with a comfort-able darkness, warm wood paneling and rich burgundy-colored carpet. In contrast, framed photographs of gaunt, dirty-faced miners graced the walls.

Gannaway moved behind a desk and flipped on a small table lamp. He flicked the lampshade back, the arc of light dazzling Dennis's eyes. Gannaway's prodigious, hawk-like nose jutted out from the shadows.

"So, tell me, Dennis. What can I do for you and the gov-ernment?"

"I suppose, for starters, I'd like to have your blessing. From what I understand, everyone in Gannaway and Kwa-shau pretty much listens to you."

Dennis couldn't see much of the man but felt fairly certain his statement brought a grin to his face.

"Well, now, seems to me like you learn fast. I did build these two towns, you know. Before Gannaway became the shit-hole it is now."

"That's my understanding, sir."

"Now cut that 'sir' business out. Ain't no 'sirs' in here. Just you and me. Kyle and Dennis."

"Didn't mean to offend, Kyle. Just my upbringing, I guess."

"Well, Mama Lipstein would be proud. So, Sheriff Stokes tells me you had a run-in with one of the locals today."

"A 'run-in' is putting it mildly. He pulled a gun on me."

Gannaway laughed hoarsely. "I'll have a talk with Harlan and the others. I actually don't get out much anymore, but I'll have Gus talk to 'em. You don't need to worry about them bothering you. My town is your town."

"I really appreciate that."

"But it's a two-way street, Dennis. I scratch your back, you scratch mine."

"I'm sorry?"

"All I ask is that you keep me apprised of your work. Where you're goin', what you're doin', that sorta' thing."

If it meant safety from the "chat rats," Dennis could live with the compromise. "Sounds fair."

"I'm more than fair, son. That's how I made my fortune. You ask anyone."

"I believe you."

"Now. Where do we start?"

"How about telling Sheriff Stokes to give me some breathing room?"

Gannaway swiped his hand through the air and snorted. "Who? Eddie? Don't let him get your knickers all up in a bunch, son. He gets a little carried away sometimes with the power of the badge, but I can knock some sense into him. Does seem to me, though, that he saved you from gettin' shotgunned today."

"He could've intervened earlier."

"Eddie's there for your protection. Might be wise if you understand that." Judging from Gannaway's tone, it sounded more like intimidation than a suggestion.

"I'd just rather not have him following me around while I work."

"Just what *is* the nature of your work?"

"The government wants to find out what to do with Gannaway. I need to test the water, soil, and air for contaminants. Make sure Gannaway's habitable. See what we can do to help."

"If you really want to help, you'd mind your own damn business!" His sudden ferocity startled Dennis. The yokel accent vanished along with his kindly, humble act. *"My* damn town! Nobody's asking me what I think!"

"I *am* here consulting with you. I want your input. I—"

"Goddamn government!" Gannaway's breath expelled in ragged patches, filling the otherwise silent study. "Always think they know what's best. I *know* what's best. It's my damn town."

"Believe it or not, we're trying to help—"

Thwack! Gannaway's cane came down onto the desk. *"Enough.* Just let me know what you're doing."

"I will." Dennis waited a beat, giving Gannaway time to settle down. "Would it be possible for me to get into one of the mines in the next couple of days?"

Gannaway leaned forward, his features coming into the light. "You know the mines are all closed down."

"That's my understanding, yes, but it'd be helpful—"

"Government made me close down the last of the mines a year ago. Said the land was depleted. A hazard. I thought it was poppy-cock, but I'm an American. I listen to my government."

"I'm sorry to hear your mines were closed. But if—"

"Fine, fine!" He spat the words out like a chastised child. "We can get you into a mine. But you'll need to be escorted. Ain't gonna have no government casualty on my hands!"

"Thank you." A sudden thought snagged Dennis as surely as a hooked fish. "If the mines are closed down...why are there still miners around?"

Gannaway tapped his cane on the desk. In a low voice, nearly a whisper, he said, "What are you talking about?"

"Down by Gullet Creek, I saw a miner. He wore overalls, a hard helmet—"

"Impossible! There ain't no mining going on. What you saw was *nothin'* but a chat rat."

Dennis knew when to cut his losses. Time to cut the meeting short before Gannaway changed his mind. "Could be. Doesn't matter."

"Damn right it doesn't matter. Now, we understand one another?"

"I believe so. I'll let you know what I'm doing, and you'll spread the word that I have access to all of Gannaway."

"Supervised access."

"Okay. Supervised access." Dennis had no intention of being constantly watched. But what Gannaway didn't know wouldn't hurt him.

"Fine, then. As I said before, my town is your town, Dennis. Just ask me for anything. I'm an open book."

But what kind of book? Dennis wondered.

Dennis turned his back to the nosy hotel clerk.

"I can barely hear you, Dennis. You're going to have to speak up." Dennis heard the frustration in Meyers' voice, but he didn't want to broadcast his business to everyone in town. Although it seemed everyone already knew anyway.

"Sorry, Martin. The hotel doesn't have phones in the rooms. I'm using the pay phone in the lobby. I'm not exactly living in the lap of luxury." The clerk leaned over the counter, uttering a surly growl. Dennis flashed him an apologetic smile.

"Hey, you wanted the job. How go your findings?"

"Not sure yet. I'm being hampered by the local law, and some nut went after me with a shotgun."

"Science can be dangerous."

"Funny. Listen, I should have something to send you in a couple of days. Kwashau doesn't have a post office, so I may have to travel south, somewhere civilized. In the meantime, can you put the screws to a Mr. Kyle Gannaway in an official government capacity? Put the fear of Uncle Sam into him?"

"Gannaway. Kyle. Got it. Why?"

"He's the town patriarch, owner of the mining operation. Everyone does what he says. But he's on an anti-government kick, and I don't know how much access he's going to give me to the mines."

"I'll see what I can do."

The bell above the door tinkled. A sharply dressed American Indian woman walked in, her skirt tight, impeding her stride. With a nod to the clerk, she stood behind Dennis. She folded her arms, tapping a tremendously heeled shoe.

"Um, Dennis?"

"Yeah?"

"How're you doing?"

"Fine."

"I mean...how are you *really* doing?" Meyers' walking-on-eggshells routine tore at Dennis. His boss meant well, but Dennis hated it when people treated him with kid gloves. It made him feel pathetic. And vulnerable.

"I'm fine, Martin. Really." Dennis felt the presence of the woman behind him and turned to meet her gaze. "I'm not...well...you know. And I'm not having a break-down or anything." The woman's expression remained stolid.

"Okay, Dennis. Just...take care of yourself."

"Yeah, look, Martin, I've gotta go. Be in touch soon." Before Meyers could say goodbye, Dennis hung up the phone.

The woman reached around him, plunging a finger into the coin return pocket. She smiled, shrugged, and said, "You never know."

"You never do. Hi. Can I help you with something?"

Her eyes reminded him of saucers full of chocolate, deep and rich. He could easily sink into them. While alluring, her smile remained business-like. "I think maybe I can help you, Dr. Lipstein."

No real surprise she knew him. Everyone in town probably did by now. "Okay." He glanced at the clerk who made no attempt at hiding his eavesdropping. Tommy swayed his hand to the door. "Step into my office."

When they walked outside, the woman pulled her snug-fitting jacket even tighter. "I'm Therese Greentree with the Bureau of Indian Affairs. Great Plains division."

"Ah! It's nice to see another government face around here. I was beginning to think this one-horse town didn't believe in government."

"Careful. I grew up in this one-horse town."

"Sorry. Let me yank my foot out of my mouth time."

She laughed. "I'm used to it. So, local trouble?"

"Yeah."

"Figured as much. Our mutual friend, Bob, said you might need babysitting."

"Everyone here wants to babysit me." Dennis ticked off his fingers. "Sheriff Stokes, Kyle Gannaway—"

The smile slid off Therese's face. "Careful who you trust, Dr. Lipstein."

"It's Dennis. I've also been getting a lot of warnings. What is it with this place, anyway?"

"Gannaway's been through a lot of upheaval and turmoil. It's just natural that the remaining townsfolk are upset. And wary of strangers."

"Yes, but...it's almost like the wild west out here."

"You're getting dangerously close to stereotyping again."

"That would be my other foot in my mouth. Getting full in there. So, you grew up here and now work for the good ol' USA? Why in the world would you come back?"

"I don't live here now. But it's an area I volunteered to represent. My people need the Bureau now more than ever. At least what's left of my people. I check in on them from time to time, mostly to make sure they're doing well, health-wise."

"Are there still people out on the Reservation?"

"A few. Not too many. The damn mining boom and all of the surrounding hoopla almost did them in. But there're a few remaining stragglers. Like Bob."

"Well, I appreciate Bob's concern, but I can take care of myself."

"No offense to you, Dennis, but don't be so sure of that. Other than the obvious chat rat problem, there are...well, let's just say Gannaway has other things going on."

"Especially people dropping ominous warnings."

She grinned again. "Bob knows the history better than anyone. Talk to him." She snatched a business card out of her pocket, flicked it toward him. "Don't hesitate to call me. I'm in town this week. Lucky for you. In the meantime, I would suggest you don't call on Stokes or Gannaway unless you absolutely need to."

"I was given the not-so-subtle hint that I have to call on them."

She looked down into the gravel and kicked a pebble away. "Your call. You'll figure out who you can trust."

"You said to call. Can I call you for a..." He almost said "drink." Old habits die hard. But frankly his blatant flirting surprised him. The notion of dating hadn't crossed his mind in some time. Not since Laura left. "How about a cup of coffee?"

She shook her head, yet her smile hinted at promise. "I never mix business with pleasure." She walked toward her car, then turned back. "But I'll consider an exception."

"Sounds like a date."

"Dennis, I said I'd consider it. I've only just begun considering."

She punched the gas pedal hard. Gravel spit from beneath her tires in Dennis's direction. She slowed, rolled down her window and said, "Whoops." She drove off, wiggling her fingers out the window in a very "un-whoops" like fashion.

Crunch.

Dennis bolted up in bed, unsure if he had heard something. Or dreamt it.

Crunch. Crunch.

Someone was outside. Walking on the gravel.

He held his breath and listened carefully. The footsteps stopped. Something clicked in the room. Probably nothing more than the wooden floor settling.

Scrank. The unmistakable grind of metal scraping against metal. Dennis flew out of bed, jumped into his jeans and opened the door.

His eyes settled into the darkness, the moonlight his guide. No-one in the parking lot. Just his van, the only current resident at The Kwashau Motel.

The gravel bit at his bare feet as he hobbled toward the van. Beneath the blue lamp of the moon, he saw a long scrape alongside the driver's door. Metal showed beneath the flaked paint. He ran his fingers over it. A deep groove, but narrow, delivered by a strong tool of some sort. A wrench or screwdriver, maybe. His mind leaped to another possibility. *A pickaxe?*

He focused his gaze on the woods set off from the parking lot. A figure darted. Maybe two? Fleeting and ducking. Or shadows weaving in and out between the trees. Tricks from the moonlight playing across the skeletal branches. Dennis blinked, rubbed his eyes, looked again. *Nothing.*

Dennis scuttled back to the room, his feet stinging from the pebbles. He locked the door and leaned against it, catching his breath. When he closed his eyes, an image took form, like a slowly developing photograph.

Had he glimpsed something yellow in the woods? *A hardhat?*

He gave up on the idea of sleep. And wished he had a bottle of vodka instead.

Chapter Seven

1935...

By the time Claire left the boarding house, she'd worked herself into a tizzy. What Kaya had told her didn't sit well. The more she dwelled on it, the more ridiculous an Indian curse sounded, but she believed it. It made sense in a way things shouldn't but, against all odds, sometimes do.

When the casualty whistle shrilled across the street, she felt it reverberate all the way into her teeth. She bunched her skirt up in one hand and broke into a run. *Tommy. My God, Tommy!*

On the other side of the fence, miners gathered. Raised voices, pregnant with panic. Men racing to and fro with no discernible destination. A group of them stopped in the center of the grounds, peering down into a hole. Around Tommy's mine.

Claire bypassed the man at the gate, running past him before he had a chance to raise any objections.

Two men propped up a young man between them. Slack-bodied, his head bounced with each hurried step the men took. Immediately, Claire thought it had to be George Kendricks. His eyes remained closed, as if he were sleeping. Or dead. A circle of miners formed, shuffling along-side Kendricks and the two men. Claire overheard snippets of questions, tidbits of conversation. Just enough to whip her into a tornado of fear.

"The boy's *dead*."

"He *ain't* dead!"

"Was it a cave-in?"

Claire ran past them, yelling, "What *happened?* Tell me what happened!" She didn't slow to hear their answer. Even if she had, she wouldn't have heard anything over the hellish pitch of the casualty whistle. Her heart galloped in her chest as she hurtled toward the shaft.

Jim Reaper sat in his perch, showing about as much emotion as Claire had ever seen from him. For once, he looked uncertain, nervous, his eyes brighter than his usual reserved demeanor. Gripping the bucket's rim, she climbed onto the platform.

"Um, Mrs. Donnelly? You can't get in the bucket."

"Jim Reaper, you just watch me! Where's Tommy? Is he all right?"

Jim scratched the back of his neck. Claire didn't like the way his lips twisted. "I 'spect he's fine, ma'am. Reckon he's still down below."

Claire struggled to hike her legs into the bucket. Her long skirt impeded her movement. She failed at tearing it, so she hitched it up. She rolled into the bucket and fell on-to her hands before climbing to her feet. "Well? What're you waiting for? *Lower it!*"

"Can't do it, ma'am. Against regulations."

"I don't give a hang about your regulations! I *need* to see how Tommy is. You lower me right now before I go up there and smack some sense into your thick head!"

Jim's hand wavered over the lever. Finally, he said, "But...you're a..."

"A *what?*"

"You're a red-head, ma'am."

"Oh, for heaven's *sake!* Don't give me that superstitious baloney! Lower me. *Now!*"

Jim took off his hardhat, studied it like he didn't realize it had been on his head. "Yes, ma'am. But at least wear this." He tossed it to her. Catching it, Claire flipped it on.

"Let's *go.*"

"Yes, ma'am."

The bucket lowered, Claire's stomach rising. Every time the bucket clanged against the wall, her heart jumped faster. *Please, God, let Tommy be fine. Let him come home to me again.*

Claire had one leg hanging over the rim before the bucket landed. Clutching the cable, she hoisted herself out.

Several miners stopped what they were doing. A chorus of groans went up.

"Woman down below!"

"Redheaded woman!"

"We don't need no more bad luck!"

"You boys *best* be showing this redheaded woman some proper respect. Now hush and tell me where Tommy is!"

A miner she didn't recognize knew when to shut up and pointed down the drift.

"Is he fine?" she called back.

"Yes, ma'am."

More cries of outrage flared as Claire entered the stope. One miner high-tailed by her, averting his eyes as if afraid he'd turn to stone if he met the intruding redhead's gaze. When Big Ed saw Claire, he nudged Tommy. Tommy's eyes widened. He tilted back his hat and came at her, arms open.

"Claire, *what* are you doing down here?"

"Tommy Donnelly, you darn near gave me a heart attack! That whistle goin' off and the Kendricks boy dying and...and..." Sweet relief drained her adrenaline rush. Her eyes filled with tears as she fell into her husband's embrace. "I thought..."

"It's okay, Claire. I'm okay. And George isn't dead. Just... an accident. I don't know why they set the whistle off." She looked into his eyes. Saw hesitation, an edgy shift. Withholding the truth. But they'd talk tonight. He wouldn't get off that easy.

"Told you I'd come down here, didn't I?" Claire wiped her eyes with the back of her hand.

"Yep, you surely did," he said with a chuckle. "Come on, let's get you outta here."

Tommy wrapped his arm around her shoulders. She heaved a sigh and looked about her. Miners still grumbled, but soon took up their posts again.

"That's right, you big ol' tough miners! Look out for the scary redheaded woman coming through!"

She could tell she'd embarrassed Tommy, but it didn't stop him from grinning. Even if he did turn ten shades of red, deeper than her hair color.

"Tommy Donnelly, don't you slurp your soup! You're settin' a bad example."

Tommy smiled at his giggling children. When he saw Claire's stern glare, he put on his obedient face. Here in their dining room, she ruled as the ground boss. "Your mother's right, kids. I'm puttin' on poor manners."

"The boy's just makin' out his meal." Mother Donnelly raised an eyebrow in Claire's direction. As if in defiance, she lifted her spoon out of the bowl and took a loud swig, much to the children's delight.

Tommy thought it best to change course before Claire truly took offense. "What'd you think of your momma goin' down into the mine today, kids?"

"Momma, are you a miner now?" T.J. sat on the edge of the chair, his eyes dancing with the possibilities.

"No, I'm not a miner." In spite of herself, Claire laughed into her napkin.

"I wanna be a miner just like Daddy."

The color drained from Claire's face. Tommy felt her disappointment, but he saw something else there, too. *Fear.* He knew she wanted better for their children. "Well, right now, young man, you're gonna get ready for bed. You need a good night's sleep so you're ready for school tomorrow. A good education just might land you a better workin' position than a miner."

"But... Daddy's a miner. So was Grandpa."

Mother Donnelly sputtered, then dropped her spoon into the bowl. "And thanks to those damn mines, he ain't around no longer! God rest his soul."

Tommy beat Claire to the inevitable reprimand. "Mother! Language!" He inclined his head to T.J. and Margaret.

"What? What'd I say?" Mother Donnelly switched her head back and forth, obviously befuddled as to any wrongdoing.

"What will I be when I get older?" asked Margaret. "A miner's wife?" She wrinkled her nose. "Yick. I don't like any them boys in school."

"'Any *of those* boys in school'," corrected Tommy.

T.J. prodded a finger into Margaret's shoulder. "You're gonna be a miner's wife, you're gonna be a miner's wife."

"Am not!"

"That's enough! Leave your sister alone, T.J., or so help me, I'll give you somethin' to whine about!" Claire stood, arms akimbo, her "don't cross me" stance.

"Okay. You kids go get washed up and ready for sleep," said Tommy.

The children scampered off, T.J. still haranguing his sister.

"I swan," said Claire as she fell back into her chair.

"Oh, they're just children being children, Claire. Land's sakes!" Mother Donnelly dumped a pouch of tobacco into a paper and rolled it into a tube. She popped it into her mouth, licking it with relish.

Claire cleared her throat. "Ahem!"

"Um, Momma?" said Tommy. "Would you mind taking that outside?"

Mother Donnelly raised her eyes from her busy work and stared at her son like he'd asked her if she could fly. She scraped back her chair, muttered, and slammed the screen door behind her.

"Thank you." Claire shook her head. "She's doing it all the time now. The house smells bad, Tommy. I smell tobacco all day long at the boarding house. I don't like smelling it in my own home."

"I know." Tommy empathized, but couldn't smell the smoke. Hadn't been able to smell much of anything for some time. "I'll talk to her."

"You always say you'll talk to her. Doesn't ever do any good."

Tommy reached across the table, placing his hand on top of hers. "I'll talk to her. You know I will."

"All right, fine, then. But right now, I need you to talk to me."

Actually, he'd anticipated this moment, dreaded it, in fact. Since they had a clear room, though, he couldn't avoid the talk any longer. "Fine, Claire. I imagine you're curious about George Kendricks. Just a clumsy, greenhorn accident."

Claire snatched her hand away. "What really happened down there today? Tell me the truth, Tommy. And swear it on your children's heads."

He scratched at his stubbled chin. *Where to start?* The events seemed jumbled in his mind now. He didn't understand it, not completely. "Like I told you before, George was acting all sortsa queer. He didn't look good. Talkin' to himself and what-not. I followed him into the mines. Found him out-of-sorts. He, ah...he came at me with a coupla railroad spikes."

"Oh my—"

"Don't fret. I handled the situation."

"And just how did you handle it?"

"Well... I'm not real proud of this, I don't mind sayin'... but, I, um, broke a coupla his fingers."

"Thomas Kevin Donnelly!" Whenever Claire resorted to using all three of his Christian names, an annoying habit she picked up from his mother, he knew the tide had turned. For the worse. "How on *earth* does breaking some poor boy's fingers fix anything? Are you tetched?" She leaned in, carefully scrutinizing Tommy's eyes. No doubt checking for the so-called "yellow-eyed fever."

"No, honey, I'm not tetched. Mr. Gannaway made me put the boy back to work. But I could see he was sick. He was endangering himself and my men. I had no other choice. As much as I hated doing it—" Tommy's stomach lurched as he recalled the snapping sound of the fingers. "I didn't want to do it, Claire. But it was the only way to keep him outta the mines."

A surge of sympathy washed over Claire's face. It made him feel like his actions weren't so heinous after all. "Sweet Lord, Tommy. Do the men know what you did?"

Tommy shook his head, glanced briefly at his soup bowl, and then pushed it aside. "No. I lied. Said it was a mining accident. Some rocks tumbled down on him—"

"But won't he tell the truth to Mr. Gannaway?"

"Don't think so. He was clean out of his mind. I doubt he'll remember any of it."

"Yellow-eyed fever." She said it nearly under her breath. Of course, Tommy heard her. It was damn clear to Tommy she'd meant him to.

"Claire, there is no 'yellow-eyed fever.' It's just another silly miner superstition."

"Don't be so quick to toss that notion away."

He drummed his fingers on the table and leaned back. Experience taught him not to argue with folks about superstition. Religion, too, for that matter. And his Daddy taught him to never go to bed with harsh words hanging between a man and his wife. But it struck him as odd, Claire giving the yellow-eyed fever true consideration. She'd always been as level as their hardwood floor.

"Claire, I'm fairly sure what happened to George Kendricks was due to the working conditions in the mine. He's a greenhorn. He's not used to the dust and the dark and the—"

"How do you explain the eyes, Tommy? You even said they were yellow!"

Tommy shrugged. "Maybe the mines affect folks differently. I've read in the newspaper how other mines across the country are improvin' their conditions. Better dust prevention. Showers. Electric torches. Safety goggles. Health—"

"You believe everything you read in that newspaper, but you don't believe what you see with your own eyes."

"Well...yes. I believe what the newspaper says. It's journalism. They report facts. Not superstition. And I betcha' George's yellow eyes was caused by something in the mines. Maybe he has a sickness to the dust—"

"And *maybe* you should believe in more things, Tommy!"

Her sudden anger puzzled him. He stood and moved around the table. His hands on her shoulders, she shook at his touch. He nuzzled his lips to her ear and whispered, "I believe in us, Claire."

She patted his hand, then squeezed it. "I know. I do, too. I just want you to be careful. Look out for yourself."

"Always. If it'll make you feel better, I'll talk to Mr. Gannaway. See if we can't do something about the work conditions down below. I'm sure Mr. Gannaway'll be open to—"

"No, he won't!" Claire didn't like Mr. Gannaway much. Never had. But Tommy always thought of him as a fair, though sometimes pig-headed, man. "He doesn't care about the miners, Tommy. Just his big, fat wallet!"

"I'll talk to him. I'll make things better."

"What if you can't make this better? Today I found out—"

The door banged open. T.J. and Margaret raced around the table, T.J. holding Margaret's jump-rope just out of reach.

"T.J.! Give your sister her jump-rope!" bellowed Tommy. By the time he turned his attention back to Claire, she'd corralled the children, guiding them into their bedroom. But not before giving him one more worried look over her shoulder.

On the reservation, Kyle Gannaway stretched back behind his desk, mulling over his employee's recent actions. Even though Steffen Eberstark preferred his God-given name, Gannaway took a certain amount of perverse pleasure in calling him "Steffen Fetchit," based on the colored actor in Hollywood. After all, he *did* do everything Gannaway ordered him to do. Even some things folks might frown upon.

"How's that new baby boy of yours doin', Fetchit?"

"Fine, Mr. Gannaway. Gus favors me."

I hope not in every way, thought Gannaway. He always tried to focus on Steffen's good eye. Not the bad one. A quarter-moon scar ran from his blond eyebrow to below his eyeball. The iris itself glowed like a full moon, white and cold. Gannaway never asked him what happened. Didn't want to know.

"Good to hear. So, it's my understandin' there was another accident today down in the Gold Pot mine."

"That's right." Steffen's tone was as frosty as his eye. It always was.

"What do you hear?" Gannaway valued Steffen's talents. Like a shadow, he drifted in and out of crowds and listened. If anyone knew more about the town's hidden secrets, Gannaway would gladly eat his hat.

"I'm hearing it might not have been an accident."

Gannaway glared at the unblinking man, waiting for elaboration. After a moment of silence, Gannaway spread his hands in an impatient gesture.

"I'm hearing Tommy Donnelly broke the Kendricks boy's fingers."

"Gawd *damn!*" He clumped his fists down onto the desktop. "That Donnelly kid again! I swear...he already gave me a cupful of grief the other day about the Kendricks boy. Tried to tell me how to run my mine. Thought I didn't know better and told me—*told me*—I was making a mistake by putting the boy back down there!"

"Yes, sir."

"Can't *believe* him. I imagine he done broke the boy's fingers to keep him outta the mines." With a chuckle, he leaned his head back on the chair. "Didn't think he had it in him. While I must admit to a certain...admiration for his work ethic, something like this just can't go unpunished."

"No, sir."

He jabbed his finger toward Steffen, but, really, he aimed his frustration toward Donnelly. "Gettin' too big for his britches, that's what Tommy Donnelly is."

Steffen nodded. "Would you like me to...fix the matter, Mr. Gannaway?" A sadistic sliver of a smile curled onto Steffen's lips.

Gannaway contemplated the offer. "Naw, let's just see what happens next. The men seem to respect Donnelly. And since he's already covered the story up with an accident, it wouldn't be good to let anything else out. Wouldn't be the first time we used the ol' 'mining accident' excuse, would it?" And, of course, by *we*, Gannaway meant Gannaway *himself*.

"No, sir."

"But keep an eye on him." Gannaway knocked his knees together, performing a sitting down Charleston almost, a habit he fell into while planning. "He's married to that pretty young gal, Claire Donnelly, ain't that right?"

"Yes, sir." A flicker of life entered Steffen's dead eyes. At least the *good* one.

"She might be the answer to keeping Donnelly in line."

"Shall I pay her a visit?"

"Not yet. Patience is a virtue. So the good Lord says. Haven't I *told* you that?"

"Yes, sir."

"Can't go runnin' off before a plan's had time to properly hatch. Keep an eye on her, too, though."

"Sir?" Steffen hesitated, the first sign of nerves Gannaway had ever noticed in the German.

"Yes?"

"The men are also talking about...the yellow-eyed fever."

"Horse shit!" He tossed a thick stack of papers at his employee. Steffen accepted the paper shower without flinching. "I don't wanna hear no talk about that *shit!* You *hear* me?"

"I hear you, Mr. Gannaway."

"Now, go on and git, Steffen Fetchit!" He dismissed him with a wave. "Go do your work."

"Yes, sir." Steffen stood, tidied his ill-fitting suit jacket, and strode out the door. It unnerved Gannaway how he always kept his hands glued to his side while he walked. Almost as if they were incapable of movement.

In the hallway, Gannaway saw a shadow dance across the doorway. *Naira. Eavesdropping again.*

Looks like he had more than Tommy Donnelly to put into their rightful, respectful place.

Moonlight bled through the cotton feed sack curtain. Claire couldn't sleep. She stared at her dozing husband, the moon's rays alighting on his face. Bone-white skin. No, not even white. *Blue.* Blue, like poor Dora's baby boy who'd died in his sleep last year.

She stroked his hair. He snorted, sighed, and rolled over. Her man. Her wonderful, honest, and *frustrating* man. For someone as smart as Tommy, he could be dumb as a bucket of ore at times. He thought he could fix the problems down in the mines by talking to that no-good scoundrel, Kyle Gannaway. But even if he could wrangle Gannaway's attention, it wouldn't fix the problem. Not by a Kansas mile. Some things you just couldn't fix by talking about them.

There had to be a reason Kaya had told her about the yellow-eyed fever. Maybe God was sending her a sign. A sign she needed to take action.

Tommy wouldn't believe her. Let him read his newspaper and gather his facts. Probably he'd even forbid her to go onto the reservation. But it fell upon her to try and fix this. Before someone else gets hurt. Especially her Tommy.

Chapter Eight

1969...

When Dennis pulled up, he spotted Bob studying three tires in his yard.

"Peace, brother," said Bob. They performed their soul shake ritual.

"Peace."

"So, whaddya think?" Bob stepped back, inviting Dennis to investigate the tires.

"I see three tires."

"That's the problem with you scientific types. You're so hung up with the reality of the here and now, you can't see the forest for the trees. Look again."

Dennis cupped his hand over his eyes and gave his best studious look. "Still three tires."

"I see art, brother. I'm thinking of building an automobile outta trash. I'll call it..." He scrawled his hand through the air. "...'The Industrialization of America.'"

"Needs a little work, I think. How about 'The Auto Industry Boom'?"

Bob tapped his fingers over his chin. "Who's the artist here? Come on over. Let's get caught up." Before Dennis sat down, Bob popped open a beer.

"Artistic inspiration," said Dennis.

"Yep. Artistic inspiration."

They watched a hawk swoop down into the field across the road. It lifted, trailing a curling snake in its beak.

"Nature," said Bob. "So, how're you finding Gannaway?"

"Some good, some bad. Last night someone scratched up the van door." Bob squinted to look at the van, even though the driver's door faced the road. "I guess another local gave me their own special brand of welcome."

"I guess." Dennis heard a note of disbelief in Bob's voice. "Might've been something else, though."

"Meaning?"

"Meaning you ain't quite ready for that lesson yet, brother."

Dennis liked Bob quite a bit, but he realized Bob intended on dolloping out information in small servings. Still, the leisurely pace at Bob's domain provided a nice respite from the tension he felt elsewhere. "I suppose you'll let me know when you deem me fit for that lesson?"

"I suppose so."

"Hey, thanks for sending Therese Greentree my way. Appreciate the gesture. But I really don't think I'll need her help."

"So says the stranger in a strange land. Don't underestimate Therese just 'cause she's a woman."

"That's not really what—"

"*Mm-hmm.* If only I was a few years younger." Bob snatched off his fedora and fanned himself. "Therese's a mighty fine-looking woman."

"That she is."

Bob broke out a devilish grin. "Now, hold on, brother. Don't tell me you're sweet on young Miss Greentree."

"I never said that." Even though Dennis felt his cheeks, possibly his loins, warm at the thought of her. "But, yeah, she's very striking."

Bob laughed, sputtered out a little beer. He finished with a deep, chesty cough. "Can't say as I saw that happening. Your aura spoke of a mighty deep hurtin', one I didn't think would allow for any romantic thoughts."

Of course, Bob spoke the truth. What *had* he been thinking? His romantic impulses fluttered away with a cleansing sigh. "Anyway, again, thanks. But I work better alone."

"Stubborn. I like that. But it could get you into trouble. You remind me of someone else I knew. A long time ago."

"Oh? Who's that?"

"Different history lesson, brother."

"I'm not ready for it yet, right?"

"You lookin' to stay after class?"

Dennis laughed. "No, Professor Bob. I'll behave. What's today's history lesson?"

"'Professor Bob.' Suits me, don't ya' think? We start at the beginning. To understand Gannaway today, you have to know its origins."

"I'm all ears, Professor."

Tilting back the beer can, Bob finished his drink in seconds. While Dennis watched Bob's Adam's apple moving up and down, he felt a touch of alcohol tickling his own throat. A phantom taste. And the burn was so *warm*.

Bob belched, and said, "Sorry, brother. I needed that. It's gonna be a long morning." He wriggled in his chair, getting comfortable, and kicked his legs out onto the porch. "You're a college-educated sort. Don't suppose I need to start at the very beginning with the pilgrims." Dennis shook his head. "All right. My people—the Kwashau tribe—were first recorded as living in Arkansas. I'm sure they existed before that, but stories differ depending on who you talk to. In the early 1800s, settlers and traders started moving into Arkansas, tossing around their big stick, so to speak. They made life rough on the Kwashau. You really need the whole song and dance? I mean, you're Jewish, you know the drill."

"Sure do. Head 'em up, move 'em out."

"You got it, brother. Moved my ancestors to a hellish, uninhabited land nobody else wanted by the name of Kansas. Wasn't called that then. Handed my people a few farming tools and seeds. 'God be with you,' the white man said. But the white man's God, of course, not theirs. Adapt or die."

"Yep. Your people and my people, been there. Lotta similarity."

"Don't I know it? Things were fairly okay for a while, until the oil and mining boom of the 1880s started. As luck would have it—more like bad luck, I reckon—the hellish land they'd given my ancestors was right in the middle of it."

"Of course. And the white man wanted it back."

"In the worst way. Tried to buy it back. In one of the few moments of business savvy my tribe ever had, they finagled a deal. They'd sublet it back, but they wouldn't sell it. Only problem was, the price for the subletting looked so damn good at the time—it really wasn't, mind you, but when you're damn near destitute, pretty much anything looks good—but anyway, that's where they lost their business savvy. Didn't read the fine print. The fine print that said they didn't retain the mineral rights to the land. Mineral rights belonged to the white man."

"Shit."

"Double-shit, brother. Still, they did all right or as all right as they could. Learned some farming. They still owned their land—what little that wasn't dug up—and were welcome to try and farm using white man's equipment and tools. For a price, of course. Formal schools and education were set up, strictly from a white man's perspective. Sure, there were still a few Indian schools. Hell, I worked at one when I was a teen. Our education was superior, but don't tell the white man that."

"Bob, that's...awful. Really awful. I'm sorry—"

"Dennis, it's history. It's done. And I don't believe your tribe had a bed of roses, either. Want me to apologize for Auschwitz?"

"Um, glad you feel that way. Still, history can be a fickle bitch sometimes."

Bob waved a hand, then folded his arms. "Couldn't agree more, brother. But you know something?"

"What?"

"Kyle Gannaway came to town. And everything got worse. In a red-hot hurry."

"Ah." Dennis scooted to the edge of his seat. "This I can't wait to hear."

"So you've met the illustrious Mr. Gannaway?"

"Yeah, I had the pleasure yesterday. He's...easily irritable."

Bob tossed the empty beer can next to him. "That's puttin' it mildly."

"So...then what happened?"

Shielding his hand over his eyes, Bob stared up into the sky. "Sorry, brother. Part two of Bob's history lesson will have to wait. It's goin' on 1:00. Time to get to work."

Dennis had no idea so much time had passed. He had to get to work as well. But he couldn't help but feel disappointed. "Okay. Busy tomorrow?"

"Tomorrow suits me just fine." Hands on his back, Bob twisted. An audible crack sounded.

Taking this as his dismissal, Dennis stood. "Bob, are there 'chat rats' who dress up as miners?"

"Why you ask, brother?"

"No reason, really. But I might've seen a miner. A couple of times." As soon as he blurted out the words, Dennis wanted to retract them. Because the alternative to mysterious miners worried him even more. It meant the hallucinations had started up again. "Ah, maybe not. My eyes aren't what they used to be. I didn't have my glasses on. Probably nothing. Just letting my imagination run away from me. You know, like you say scientists don't do?"

"Sometimes it's best to believe in your imagination, brother. Trust your instincts, your senses over your intellect."

"Huh."

"Anyway." Bob walked off into the yard, end of discussion.

Halfway to the van, Dennis turned around. "Bob, you mind my asking you something?"

"Shoot, brother."

"If Gannaway's such an awful place to live...why do it? I mean, your art's good enough to be in a gallery on one of the coasts. Why not move?"

Bob cocked a loopy half-sided grin. He splayed his hand about the yard like a Vegas showgirl. "What? And give up show business?"

Down the highway, another meeting of a different sort took place. A meeting reminiscent of one that occurred thirty-five years ago. But, this time, instead of talking to Steffen Eberstark, Kyle Gannaway barked orders to Steffen's son, Gustav.

"Just tell me what you want me to do, Mr. Gannaway." Gus finished with his traditional nervous chuckle. It set Gannaway's nerves on edge. Gus didn't have much of his daddy in him. No steely resolve, no fiery determination. Just endless, annoying laughs and inappropriate affability. Gannaway knew he scared Gus. He'd seen the same sort of apprehensive behavior from plenty of his employees over the years. It *did* give Gannaway a kick, though. The ability to instill fear packs a powerful thrill. And he had to hand the boy a smidgeon of credit. Gus had proven his loyalty over the years. The *only* thing he had in common with his late daddy.

"You tell Stokes to spread the word. I want to know what Lipstein's up to. Every moment of every day and night. If he so much as farts, I wanna smell it."

With a deep intake of air, Gus threw back his shoulders, preparing to belt out a laugh to the ceiling. Gannaway chopped his hand down, silencing him. Not in the mood. "For God's sake, Gus, is everything a joke to you?"

Gus caught himself, switched his chuckle into a cover-up cough. "No, Mr. Gannaway. I'll talk to Stokes. And anyone else who I should run into if you'd like."

Damn toadie. Too eager to please. "Just do what I tell you, Gus." They locked eyes until Gus looked away, a pathetic boy in the principal's office.

"Yes, sir."

"And I don't care what it takes. Keep Lipstein out of the mines. We can't have him poking around there. For obvious reasons. And should he get too nosy, we'll find another way to deal with him."

"Yes, sir." Squirming, Gus picked at his slacks like a kid in church. Gannaway wanted to slap some adult behavior into him.

"Needless to say, our financial concerns may very well ride on this." Again, when Gannaway said "our," he meant "my." But no sense telling Gus that.

"I understand, sir." He bowed his head and slowly rolled his hand over, ending with it palm up. Yet *another* annoying trait.

"I mean it, Gus. No pussyfootin' around. The sooner we get Lipstein out of town, the better off we'll be. Watch him like a hawk."

"I'm on it, sir." When Gus crossed his legs, the chair's leather squeaked. His foot dangled over one knee, wiggling in an out-of-control fashion. Gannaway considered thwacking it with his cane.

"What the hell you waitin' on, then? You've been given your orders."

"Yes, sir!" Gus scrambled out of the chair, dropping a chuckle on his way out.

"Go get 'gussied up!'" It didn't have the same ring as his nickname for Gus's father: "Steffen Fetchit." But it would have to do. Everyone needed to enjoy their work.

The water tower stood tall, but not as tall as many of the chat piles. The tower's shadow crawled over the remains of the dilapidated public park. The bronze statue in the middle of the dead park, surprisingly polished, depicted a proud man holding his lapels and jutting out his chin. Maybe the statue's stellar condition shouldn't be such a stretch to believe after all. The plaque read *Kyle Gannaway, Founder of Our Proud Town—1930.* Not a very good likeness, but the hair remained the same as the man he had recently met. Except for the bronze color, of course.

A stone bench crumbled at the statue's feet. A skeletal swing-set rose from the dirt, chains dangling from the rusted bars. It seemed odd that some enterprising looter hadn't tried to cut them away, salvaging the metal. Maybe the statue of the lion, representing Gannaway's high school mascot, had frightened them off. The lion still maintained its noble appearance—just this side of menacing—even after all the indignities the town of Gannaway had suffered. The blank eyes stared off into nothingness, lost in the past. Its jaw hung open in a silent, frozen roar. One paw remained forever uplifted, prepared to pounce. *Gannaway—Home of The Lions Since 1930.* Dennis lowered his head for a moment. It seemed appropriate. *Rest in peace, Lions.*

He regarded the fence surrounding the mines. Felt drawn toward it for reasons he didn't understand. As he circled the long-ranging fence, he drew his hand across it, rattling it like a passing school kid. At the gates, he gave the padlocks a good tug. Rusted and locked tight. Deciding to backtrack, he spotted a clump of dried weeds on the west side next to the park. On a whim, he pulled them back. Apparently, someone had had the same idea. Several links had been cut away, leaving a hidden opening large enough for a man to slither under.

The fence wrenched back with a rusty cry. After crawling under, he jumped to his feet and clapped his hands free of dirt. And whatever other contaminants might be melded with the dirt.

Cracks zig-zagged through the dry ground, black lightning bolts. Huge crevasses appeared ready to split wide and devour Dennis into the earth. An old car had been flipped over, sealing off an abandoned shaft. It was impossible to decipher the make and model due to the damage and rust. Railroad ties covered other shafts, sort of a lazy man's cap. He hoped kids never played here. If Gannaway had any kids left, that is.

Not too far from one of the shafts, he found what he wanted. A froth flotation pond. Practically everything else in Gannaway had died. He fully expected all of the froth ponds to have dried up by now. But, unbelievably, the pond seemed alive. At least as much as a pond could be considered alive.

An orange-colored substance swirled within the pond, the water reaching to the brim. Back in the day, miners dumped chemicals along with excavated ore into froth ponds to separate tiny particles of minerals from the rock. The ore would float to the top, making for easy pickings. Dennis realized collecting a water sample from a froth pond could easily taint his findings, but he wanted to leave no stone—mineral, water, whatever—unturned. No matter where it took him.

With the sun falling, Dennis moved quickly. Too many daylight hours spent at Bob's had taken a big bite out of his work day. And not a chance in hell did he desire to get stuck out there in the dark. Not with the chat rats about. Strapping on rubber gloves, he dipped the vial into the orange water. It filled, a bubble plopping to the top. Capping it, he labeled it and placed it in his bag.

The sun loomed behind the chat pile in front of him, producing a halo effect. *Beckoning him.* He always wondered about chat piles, their consistency and solidity. Since mountain-climbing probably would never leave his day-dream realm, a chat pile seemed like the next best thing.

The closer he walked to the pile, a hundred feet tall at least, the more insignificant he felt. Hard to believe so much earth could be dug out from below. He kicked at the bottom. A cloud of dust whirled around his foot, but the pile appeared solid as granite. Walking around the perimeter, he discovered what looked like a path. Stairs almost. Apparently, others had shared his desire to scale a chat pile.

He stepped onto it, stopped, thought it best to put on his gloves again. Just in case. Hell, maybe he'd better wear his goggles and respiration mask as well.

With every footfall, the steps crumbled, a minor avalanche of dirt tumbling down the hill. About half-way up, he second-guessed his spur-of-the-moment decision. But Bob's words came back to him. Not his exact words. Something to the effect he should use his imagination, not let facts and science derail him from seeing the bigger picture. He felt oddly liberated. Not constantly looking over his shoulder for his demons to swoop him away.

And he didn't see Devin's face for the first time in months.

Once his legs grew heavy, he stopped. Not quite at the top, but close enough. He looked around. A blip of the falling sun peeked over the horizon. Literally, hundreds of ugly, black-headed piles blemished the face of the land for miles around. All in the name of the mighty dollar.

Broken-down machinery sprawled across the landscape. Rusted dinosaurs caught in the ice age of industrialization. But something a half-mile away or so looked different, drawing his eye. The last sunbeam of the day gleamed on something. Struggling with his gloves, he plucked out his glasses.

A drill. In better condition than its fallen brethren. *And are those two men next to it?*

Instinctively, he dropped to his knees. His feet slipped backward. Scrambling for a hand-hold, he failed to grip the slick, sun-hardened surface. Chat gave way beneath him. Dust kicked up as he slid down the hill. *Chunk.* His feet landed in a deep pocket. He took a deep breath, as much as the mask allowed, and dug finger holds into the hill. Slowly, he crawled back down.

When he reached the bottom, he rested. Standing, he scanned the area. No sign of life, but the sun had given up for the day so he couldn't trust what he saw. Or didn't see.

Stupid. A flashlight had never even entered his short list of tools he might need. He blinked, trying to adjust his eyes to the dropping darkness.

Clouds rolled in overhead, blotting out the rising moon. *Fast.* Thunder rumbled. Rain hadn't been in the forecast. Chalk it up to unpredictable Midwest weather.

Shuffling his feet across the dirt, he moved one foot slowly in front of the other. He held his arms out in front of him, a blind man stumbling for points of reference. A vague sense of direction drove him. When his hands smacked the fence, he clasped it, thankful for something solid. Dropping on all fours, he crawled through the dirt, tugging at the fence. After what seemed like hours, he still hadn't found the opening. Resigning himself to waiting until the light of early morning, he sat back against the fence. The fence gave way, his back sinking into the hole. He released an involuntary whoop of victory.

After he rolled out, he heard the sound. Tapping. No, more like shuffling.

Click slitch, click slitch.

Someone stepping through water? Impossible. The rain hadn't started yet, and the streets were desert dry.

Click slitch, click slitch.

No. A foot dragging. Coming toward him.

Lightning flashed, vanished, then lit up the sky again. The light flickered on Gannaway's statue above him. Now he had bearings. He looked up to where the statue stood draped in shadows. Another bolt of lightning sparked.

The statue *smiled.* Turned its head toward him. Damn sure of it.

But, *of course,* it had always been smiling. It *had* to have been. Statues don't change. Just shadows and lightning conspiring to kick his imagination into overdrive.

Click slitch, click slitch.

The footsteps jolted him again. *Growing closer.*

Thunder growled. Something else growled, too.

Lightning shuddered through the sky, nervous and tentative. Violent hiccups of thunder rumbled above, reverberating into his chest.

Near hysterics, Dennis's mind raced, halting at the memory of the lion statue. He swiveled toward the statue. The lion looked back at him. *Hungry.* No. Just more tricks provided by nature's sky flashes.

Click slitch, click slitch.

But the footfalls weren't tricks.

Dennis ran through the park. When another jag of lightning flared through the sky, he dared a look back. The lights went out again, but not before he saw it. *Him.* A man walking through the park. Not dragging a foot, either. A *pickaxe.*

Dennis hitched his knees high, increasing his stride until his thighs ached. Another strike of lightning showed he had miscalculated his location. Abandoned houses surrounded him. Some wore giant orange "X's" on their front, signifying their condemned status. Wind whistled through broken windows, a fast-approaching train.

Tip pat, tip pat, tip pat.

Someone running toward him. Or *something. Closing in on him.*

Dennis turned and froze.

Lightning illuminated his visitor. Dennis yelped. The dog appeared equally frightened, shoulders up and tail down. Glowing eyes stared back at Dennis, the way dog's eyes sometimes do. It scampered off, somewhat in a sideways fashion as if it had been hit by a car. *Peace go with you, brother,* Dennis thought, channeling his "inner Bob."

A thunder blast rattled him out of his momentary reprieve, propelling him on. His foot left soft earth, landed hard on the tarmac with a smack. Dashing across the highway, he spotted faraway pinpricks of light, no doubt a few chat rats keeping the home-fires burning. But enough light to spot his van parked a quarter mile down the highway in an empty lot.

Click slitch, click slitch.

"Jesus Christ!"

The man following him sounded like he had gained speed, coming on strong. Dennis surged, using muscles that had lapsed for years. His arms pumped like pistons as he fled down the shoulder.

Scritchhhhhh.

Good God, what was that?

His keys jangled in his hand before he reached the van. He banged into its side and fumbled through the keychain.

Where's the key, give me the right key...

The keys slipped out of his sweaty hand and dropped to the ground.

Click slitch, click slitch.

Not gonna look behind me, not gonna look behind me...

When he snatched up the keys, the correct key miraculously flipped upward. He hopped in, fired up the ignition. Locking all doors, he checked and double-checked them.

He shifted into reverse. Something scratched at the back of the van, the creaking sound like those tree limbs make when they ask for entry on chilly fall nights.

Dennis didn't care. Nothing mattered but getting the hell out of there. If he took out a chat rat, the intruder had it coming. He jammed the gas pedal down. The van hurtled back. When he braked, he lurched to a stop. But the expectant thump didn't follow. Spinning the van around, he wrenched out onto the highway.

For the first ten minutes, he couldn't bring himself to look into the rearview mirror. When he felt enough distance had passed, he ventured a glance. But he saw nothing.

Lightning zapped the sky again. Next to him, blue-white magnetic charges snapped and sparked at the top of several chat piles.

And he swore—*God damn swore*—he saw a figure standing on the tallest chat pile, the one he'd climbed. Wearing a helmet with a lit torch burning brightly.

He didn't look again.

Chapter Nine

1935...

"Mr. Darling, could you see fit to giving me an hour or two off?" Tommy held his helmet in front of him, probably unnecessary, but a nice show of respect nonetheless.

"I don't reckon that'd be a problem, Tommy, but you know I gotta ask why."

"Well, sir, I don't feel I did a powerful enough job yesterday explainin' to Mr. Gannaway how things are down in the mine. I'd like to give it another go."

"Son, your funeral. But if it'll keep Mr. Gannaway outta my office, you can even take my car." Tommy snagged the tossed keys into his helmet, then high-tailed it. He knew better than to look a gift horse in the mouth.

The closer Tommy got to the Gannaway mansion, all the while thinking about his men's working conditions, the hotter his fire burned. Not that he looked forward to his conversation with Mr. Gannaway. No sir, not one bit. But he needed to keep his word to Claire. And to himself.

He chunked the gear down and bounced over the rough, muddy road. Several times he thought he'd get stuck, but the tires whizzed, caught hold, and shot him forward.

Most of the houses on the reservation had seen better days, in much worse shape than his own. Gannaway's house—a constant work in progress with more rooms added on daily, it seemed—by comparison, resembled a palace. Sure enough, when Tommy pulled up, workmen stood, arms reaching, tacking up the framework on the house's exterior.

He killed the ignition. The car sputtered to a stop.

Gannaway's manservant, Eberstark, answered the door. He remained silent, his face betraying nothing. Lean, rigid and upright like a knife-blade. Tommy'd never heard the man speak, had no reason to converse with him. But he'd seen him at Gannaway's side. And he *chilled* him.

"Mornin'. I'm here to see Mr. Gannaway."

"Is Mr. Gannaway expecting you?"

"No, but I'm sure if you tell him Tommy Donnelly—"

"Then you can't see him." When he started to shut the door, Tommy wedged his foot inside.

"This is important."

"Mr. Gannaway's not expecting you."

Tommy braced a hand against the door and yelled over the manservant's shoulder, "Mr. Gannaway! It's Tommy Donnelly, sir!"

To Tommy's shock, Eberstark kicked his foot out of the door with a pointed, hard-toed shoe. As fast as a snake, his hand lashed out, landing on Tommy's chest. "I *said* you're not going to see Mr. Gannaway."

Tommy smelled something like mint rolling off his breath. The man twisted his head, targeting Tommy with his good eye. Undeterred, Tommy raised his voice louder. "Mr. Gannaway! Sir, I need to talk to you!"

Tommy'd been in enough schoolyard brawls to know what to expect next. His fists coiled at his sides for protection, self-defense, but he wouldn't be the one to throw the first punch.

"I suggest you leave now."

"Mr. Gannaway! It's important, sir—"

"What in the *hell's* all this ruckus?" Gannaway appeared

in the doorway, hair standing up, cinching a robe about his waist.

"I'm sorry for comin' by unexpected, sir, but it's important I talk to you."

Gannaway snorted, then said, "Steffen, leave the boy be."

Tommy couldn't help but smile. When he tried to step around Eberstark, he countered, shadowing his moves.

"Leave him be, Steffen."

"Yes, sir." Eberstark moved aside, but not before bumping Tommy with his shoulder. As he trotted up the stairs to the porch, Tommy swore he heard the manservant growling.

Ruffling a hand through his hair, Gannaway retreated down a hallway. "Why in hell are you here at this ungodly time of morning, Tommy? You should be in the mines."

Tommy followed him. "I know, sir. But Mr. Darling gave me a little time off to talk to you."

"Better be good, then, boy. I'm busy and I ain't even had my mornin' cuppa joe."

"Yes, sir."

Gannaway tossed open a door and plopped down behind a desk. Tommy sat across from him.

"Well? Say what's on your mind." A miniature gold-plated derrick rested on the desk. Gannaway fondled it. Judging by the tarnished spots, Tommy suspected it was a habit.

"Sir, yesterday I—"

"This ain't about that Kendricks kid again, is it? We closed that topic."

"In a way, it is. I believe what happened to the boy is due to our working conditions. And it could just as easily happen to anyone else."

Gannaway cocked up an eyebrow, a sudden twinkle in his eyes. "I think what happened to the boy has *nothin'* to do with the mines. I might've heard a little somethin' about that."

Tommy shifted uncomfortably. "Dunno what you heard,

but facts is facts." He flipped out his index finger. "We don't have proper ventilation in the mines. The dust is a health hazard, harmful to the lungs and—"

"How's that account for broken fingers?"

"That was...an unfortunate minor cave-in. Rocks hit George. But...the boy shouldn't've been down there in the first place. If he'd been in his right mind, he might've avoided the falling rock." Tommy hated lying. Almost as much as what he did to George. Not much good at it, either. But helping his men came first.

"Or maybe...just maybe..." Gannaway leaned in, a smile spreading wide. "...someone broke that poor boy's fingers."

A lump formed in Tommy's throat, one he couldn't force down. "Don't think that's what happened." He waved his hand, hoping to abandon the uncomfortable topic. "What I was sayin' is, if things could change, I'm bettin' productivity in the mines would increase." He knew the fastest way to Gannaway's heart. His wallet. "There'd also be fewer accidents."

When Gannaway looked heavenward, considering more money with a lustful grin, Tommy knew he'd hooked him like a fish. "I'm listening."

"We could start with better ventilation, some sorta' dust prevention. Miner's consumption is terrible, as you well know, and—"

"Tommy, I need to stop you right now. How in the world can we reduce the dust? It's one of God's byproducts, for heaven's sake. It'd be like trying to get rid of dirt. It's not up to us to rid ourselves of God's blessed work." He let out a throaty laugh.

"I've some ideas, sir. I've read some things—"

"You *read?*" Disbelief, perhaps anger, fueled Gannaway's simple question.

"Yes, sir, I surely do. The newspaper, books—"

"Fine, fine. We can't drop in air holes or prevent dust, Tommy. You and I both know that."

"That's not necessarily—"

"What else?"

Obviously, Gannaway had closed his mind's vent on dust prevention. But Tommy had other issues to press. He'd gladly take a minor victory. Open the doors down the road for future improvements. "Most of the other mines in the country are using hardhats with electric torches. And using electric torches to light up the stopes. Seems to me that might be safer than the ol'-fashioned ones we're using."

"Mm-hm. Go on."

Tommy had every intention of continuing his fishing. But the disinterested glaze in Gannaway's eyes told him the big fish just swam away from the hook. "There'd be a matter of putting in showers for the men—"

Gannaway snorted. "Showers down in the mines? That's ridiculous!"

"It's a matter of health, sir. At least please consider putting them on the grounds."

"We'll see. We'll see." The way Gannaway stroked his statuette—harder and faster now—unnerved Tommy.

"And safety goggles. That'd be a real boon underground."

"Let me ask you something. What makes you think this isn't just idle talk from the men? Making up...fantasies of what they'd like to see happen? I betcha' there ain't no mines in the country that allows for this...*nonsense.*" His hand continued to fondle the neck of the mini-derrick, almost in an obscene fashion.

"As I said, sir, I read." Of course, Tommy left out one of the most important elements of his findings. *Unions.* But he'd learned Gannaway regarded "unions" as a curse word, never to be mentioned, definitely never practiced. "It's a fact that—"

Bang! Gannaway brought the statue up and slammed it down onto his desk. His eyes filled with rage. His cheeks and forehead turned red, nearly purple. A vein pumped in his neck like a thick nightcrawler. "I don't wanna hear any more of this talk! And don't you say a word to the miners about it!" He held the statuette back over his shoulder, looking like a Gannaway Lion quarterback ready to lob a football. Tommy hoped he wouldn't follow through.

"Sir, other mines across the Tri-State area are leading the way to safety. I just want—"

Gannaway ratcheted his chair back and jumped to his feet. "And I want *you* to shut your goddamned pie hole! You hear me? No more *horse shit!*" He looked about his office, almost as if newly aware of his locale. Gingerly setting the statue back onto his desk, he ran his thumbs behind his robe's lapels and took a deep breath. "You hear me, son? *Never* again." His voice had quieted to the point where Tommy had to strain to hear him. "If you know what's good for you."

Obviously, the meeting had ended. For all the good it did. Not only had the big fish escaped his hook, Tommy now felt like the lowest on the food chain. He stood and held his hand out. "Thanks for your time, sir. I hope you'll at least give some thought to what I said."

Gannaway glowered at Tommy, ignoring his hand. As he folded into his chair, he said, "Get back to work, Tommy. You and I both got a lotta work to do."

Tommy hurried down the hall. As he brushed by Eberstark, he didn't afford him a look. Plain and simple hadn't earned one. But out of the corner of his eye, he saw Steffen grin. Shark's teeth, a carnivore in the Gannaway ocean.

Once behind the wheel of the car, he took a last look at the expanding house money and privilege bought. Gannaway cared more about his expanding house than his men's safety. Or lives.

An upstairs curtain drew back. Tommy stuck his head out the window to get a better look. *Naira, Gannaway's wife.* When she saw him watching her, she pulled the curtain closed. It billowed like a flag disturbed by a soft breeze.

As Tommy started the car, he realized Mr. Gannaway'd just helped him make an important decision. Tommy'd never even *thought* about unionizing before. Now it was his priority. His new mission in life.

Beyond the mines, Claire entered the Indian reservation where the small schoolhouse nestled. Ahanu Littlefish stood in the pasture in front of the Kwashau School, the children gathering around him in a circle. With his eyes closed, he turned round and round. The children linked hands, giggling. He snapped open his eyes and hollered, "Go!" They raced off scattershot with Ahanu in exaggerated pursuit. When T.J. and Margaret spotted their mother, playtime ended for them. They ran toward Claire, nearly knocking her over with their full-bodied embrace. An embrace Claire never tired of.

Tugging at her skirt, Margaret rambled on about the things she'd learned today. T.J., on the other hand—growing up much too fast in Claire's eyes—broke quickly away as if embarrassed by his childish display of affection.

"How're my babies?"

T.J. pointed at his sister and stuck his tongue out. "She's the baby. I ain't."

"Tommy Junior! Don't you be mean to your sister. And it's 'I'm *not* a baby.'"

"Yes, ma'am."

As Claire watched Ahanu chase the children around the field, an idea struck her. "You children go on and play for a bit. I've adult business to tend to."

Given a reprieve, the children didn't bother to ask questions and scampered off.

She approached the Indian teen. "Ahanu?"

Ahanu turned and grinned. Tall and handsome like his father, but most definitely Kaya's boy. The eyes were unmistakably hers; inquisitive, brown, and bigger than half-dollars. "Afternoon, Mrs. Donnelly." He swept his long dark hair back with a confident crack of the neck.

"Afternoon. Your momma tells me you're fixin' to be an artist. That so?"

"That's so."

"Well, you just keep trying. I'm sure you can do it."

He eyed her warily. Claire suspected his family didn't support his dreams. For a white woman to offer encouragement probably sounded suspicious at best. "What can I do for you, ma'am?"

Claire drew closer and lowered her voice. "I know I can trust you to keep a secret, can't I?"

"Yes, ma'am, I reckon so."

"Do you know John Blackbird?"

His grin disappeared, aging him instantly. "I hear you right, ma'am?"

"Sure as I'm standing here."

He gestured toward the woods and walked away. Claire followed.

"Pardon my presumption, ma'am, but why are you asking about John Blackbird?" His eyes narrowed into hard slits, full of suspicion.

"Ahanu, I've known you and your mother for many years."

"Reckon so."

"You know I'm not one to beat about the bush."

"Yes, ma'am."

"And I don't want you gettin' into any trouble with your momma, either. So—"

"Ma'am, why are you asking about John Blackbird?" He asked it politely enough, but Claire knew Ahanu had never been a bush-beater either.

"The yellow-eyed fever. The curse. I know John Blackbird put the curse on the miners."

Ahanu fell back against a tree trunk, drawing a hand down his jaw. He sighed. "That's what I hear. We all don't cotton to it, though. Blackbird's hatred for the miners, I mean. Your husband's a good man. Lots of the miners are."

"That's why I need to talk to John Blackbird." She reached for his hand. Claire felt guilty, just a smidge. But she knew from experience a few bats of the eyelashes and a little bit of contact went a long way in putting women at an advantage over men. "Can you take me to him?"

He shrank back and tugged his hand away. "No, ma'am. I think that's a bad idea. A very bad idea."

Claire gripped his hand again. "Why is it a bad idea? I need your help. *Please*, Ahanu. Please? For me?"

Again, Ahanu took back his hand. "Ma'am, I respect your family. Likewise, I respect my people, too. But with John Blackbird...most of our people fear him. We stay away. Stories have it he hasn't left his home in ten years. If he scares his own people...I just wonder what he might do to someone...like you."

"A white woman. Is that what you meant to say?"

He looked down, apparently ashamed. "Yes, ma'am."

"This isn't a matter of color. I'm trying to save my husband's *life*. And maybe all of those other men down there!"

Claire took his extended silence as a sign her feminine magic had ensnared him. She watched different emotions pass over his face like a moving picture show. Finally, he said, "You ain't gonna give up on this, are you?"

Claire withheld her inner smile. "No, I'm not."

"Fine, then. I'll keep your secret. And I'd much appreciate if you don't tell anyone about my doing this."

"Sound's fair."

"I don't know about that," he said under his breath.

"Won't say a word."

"I'll only take you as far as the outer edge of his land. I'm not settin' foot on it."

"All right."

"And I really wish you wouldn't either, ma'am. For your safety. I can't guarantee what might become of you."

"It's a chance I'm willing to take. For my husband's life. I know you'd do the same for your momma." Claire knew she wasn't playing fair, but she pushed anyway.

"Reckon I would. Fine, then. You go tend to your children. I'll be ready in the shake of a 'coon's tail."

Uncertain of how long such a "shake" might take, Claire scurried after her neighbor, Annie, to arrange an escort home for her children.

Tommy made one last stop before returning to the mines.

"Mrs. Kendricks? Ma'am?" Tommy whipped his hat off, holding it politely to his chest.

"Oh! Mr. Donnelly." Tired, raccoon-like eyes peered out from behind the screen door.

"It's just Tommy, ma'am."

"I wanted to thank you for what you did for George. I understand you pulled him out of a small cave-in."

A big bout of guilt kicked Tommy square in the arse. "I...didn't do anything, ma'am. How's your boy?"

She stepped aside and held open the door. "He's quieted down. Doc Wilkins gave him some shots. He got some rest he really needed. But...he just ain't right, Tommy. Doc don't know what's hurtin' him so bad. Had him tied down for a while, but Doc finally took the straps off. Still ain't eatin', though."

"I'd like to see him, ma'am. If that's okay with you. But if he's sleeping, I'll come back later."

"No, no, he's awake. And he ain't carryin' on like he's been doin'. I'm sure he'd like to see you."

Tommy doubted that. But he had to see George's condition, hoping for the best outcome. If nothing else, to appease his guilt. "I'd be much obliged, ma'am."

Mrs. Kendricks's smile barely turned up, a strong effort for Tommy's benefit. A sudden urge to toss his arms around the fragile woman and hug her tighter than snug boots swept through Tommy. But he stuck to his original undertaking. If Mrs. Kendricks could be strong right now, he owed it to her and the men to be strong, too.

The house had the same floor plan as Tommy's. Most of the houses in Gannaway did. He wagged a finger between the two bedrooms. Mrs. Kendricks pointed. "Room on the right."

Tommy pushed the door open. George lay in bed, his head turned toward the window. "George?" Not a muscle moved, not a sound.

Tommy sat on the chair next to the bed, nervously kneading the edges of his hat. "George? You doing okay?"

With a snap, George twisted his head around, the rest of his body inert. Eyes still sickly yellow, but not near as bad as they'd been in the mines.

"George, I wanted to see how you're farin'."

Tommy's hopes rose when he saw a flicker of recognition pass through George's eyes. "Mr. Donnelly?" Contrary to what George's momma thought, not much had changed since yesterday. George still seemed lost, incapable of comprehending the world around him.

"Yep, that's right. It's Tommy. How're you?"

"I dunno. I dunno what's wrong with me. Don't feel so well. And..."

When he paused, he looked at Tommy as if hoping for encouragement. But Tommy thought it best to not to interrupt the boy. Give him time to collect his thoughts. Besides, Tommy had no idea what to say.

"They're still talkin' to me. They're...still here."

"Who, George?"

"They won't leave me alone. Thought it was just in the mines. But they're here...*now.*" His sharp, sudden laugh startled Tommy. "They keep at it. They keep wantin' me to do things. Things I don't wanna do. Why are they doin' it, Mr. Donnelly? Why? Why won't they leave me be?" The tears flooding down George's cheeks stirred Tommy's innards. But George's contrary saintly smile truly set him on edge. "Can you make 'em go away? And leave me alone?"

"Who? George, there's no one here but us."

George gawped at Tommy like he didn't understand a word he said. "Miners. *Dead* miners. They ain't happy 'bout havin' died. They want all us others to join 'em."

Clearly, consumption had taken hold of the boy, regardless of what Mr. Gannaway said. Not just his body, but his mind as well. Tommy knew the mines caused George's odd nature; the mines aren't for every man. The lingering aftereffects of Doc's "miracle" shots surely didn't help either.

Tommy thought it best to tread lightly. No sense in feeding the boy's wild flights of fancy. Anything might set him off again. "George, I'm sure sorry you're not feelin' up to snuff. But there aren't any dead miners talkin' to you. I think maybe the mine dust is clouding your thinkin'—"

"Your daddy talks to me, too."

Tommy's jaw clenched tighter than a fist. A chill crawled down his back, the kind you got when you heard rock cracking underground. Tommy's daddy died when George was just a runt on the playground. How could he even know about his father? "You're talkin' nonsense, much as it pains me to say it. My daddy died a good ten years ago."

"No!" George's hand shot out from under the blanket, latching onto Tommy's wrist. Soiled bandages covered the two fingers Tommy broke. Splinted, they pointed skyward. George pulled himself up, his face inches from Tommy's. Putrid breath blew out, the smell of decay. "You *gotta* believe me! I ain't makin' this up!" His yellow eyes flickered, then dimmed. "*Help* me. Please, oh, dear Lord, *help* me..." Once George's voice broke into deep sobs, Tommy placed a soothing hand on his shoulder.

"George, I'll do anything I can to help you. You know I will. I'll talk to Doc again. See if maybe we can get you to the hospital in Lawrence. And—"

Shudders overtook George. Violent ones, the type brought on by influenza. His shoulders fluttered like hummingbird wings, rapidly folding into his neck and falling. Tommy's left arm trembled along with the boy until George dropped it. As abruptly as the shakes started, they stopped. George fell back in bed, seeking solace out the window again. He breathed in, the calm after the storm, then let it out in a shuddering sigh. For the first time in days, at least as far as Tommy could see, he seemed at peace. Until he spoke. "Ain't no doctor or hospital can fix this, Mr. Donnelly. Nothin' can help me. They won't leave me be. I just wish...it would stop."

"George, there's gotta be somethin' a big hospital can do. I just know it."

He rolled over to face Tommy, his smile scrawnier than his mother's. "Tell my momma I'm ready to eat now."

"I'll do that." Eating, always a hopeful sign after a sickness. "Get some rest. We'll get you fixed up in no time."

George said nothing in reply. Just that hollow, hopeless chuckle.

Mrs. Kendricks lit up brighter than a blazing sun when Tommy told her George was hungry.

Doc Wilkins, uneasy on his feet as if he'd been enjoying a whiskey breakfast, stumbled up the sidewalk as Tommy came out.

"Mornin', Doc."

"Tommy." He tipped his black bowler. "How's the boy doin'?"

"You tell me. That's one mighty sickly young man in there." Tommy hitched his thumb behind him.

Doc's shoulders sagged. "I'll tell you something, Tommy. It's the damnedest thing I've ever seen. I've checked all my books, and I've found nothin'. All my years, I ain't never come across this illness. I hope it ain't a new sickness..." Looking around, the doctor hushed his voice. One of his eyes twitched, a response Tommy recognized whenever Doc felt beyond himself.

"You'll agree, then, the boy doesn't belong in the mines?"

"Tommy, that ain't for me to say—"

"Oh, horse shit, Doc! If it ain't for you to say, then who else?" Generally, Tommy prided himself on using proper grammar. Nor did he curse as a rule. But times like these were meant to break rules.

"You know it's more complicated than that, Tommy. Mr. Gannaway—"

A scream erupted from the house. Tommy raced inside, Doc struggling to keep up.

They found Mrs. Kendricks down on her knees in George's room. Potatoes surrounded her, several rolling away across the warped floorboards. The apron pulled over her face did nothing to muffle those screams. George lay on the bed. A steak knife's handle jutted from one of his eye sockets. His other eye dangled by red tendrils, resting on his cheek. Tears of blood streamed from the excavated holes. With what little life he had left, George Kendricks pulled the knife out of his eye and plunged it into his throat. He twisted the handle, yanked up. Then he did it again.

Chapter Ten

1969...

Dink-dinkety-dink-dink...

The coffee cup clattered over the saucer. Several farmers glanced toward the source of the racket. Painfully familiar, Dennis's shakes reminded him of the DTs. Back in his drunken life, his method of avoiding the DTs had been simple. Stay drunk and avoid the fallout. But when he'd kicked booze cold turkey, shaky days and sweaty nights were the new order of the day.

Try as he might, he couldn't still his hands now.

He set the cup back down. Bending over, he sipped. The coffee burned strong and sour, caffeine straight from the bottom of the pot. It scorched his throat and rested poorly in his stomach. Food would be a wise supplement, but he just couldn't bring himself to eat.

Without saying a word, the waitress at the small Kwashau diner refilled his cup. Before sashaying off, she shot him a derisive look, the kind that said *I've got your number, buster.*

He mentally replayed last night's events while he stared down into the dark liquid, searching for a logical explanation. Chat rats trying to chase him out of town, more than likely. So why did logic not comfort him the way it always did?

Someone scooted into the booth across from him. Therese Greentree looked at him, her eyes deep and brown as the murky coffee he struggled over. But unlike the coffee, she made deep and brown attractive, a lovely distraction.

"Aren't you a sight for sore eyes?" Dennis said.

"And you're a sore sight for my eyes," she countered. "You not sleeping?"

Dennis pressed his hands against the table, hoping to steady them. No sense in giving her the wrong idea about him. "No, not too much."

A tantalizing smile perked her lips up. "Okay. Why not?"

"I think the chat rats are trying to spook me out of Gannaway. Last night, one chased me back to my van. Scratched the back of it. Oh, and he was dressed up as a miner, complete with the obligatory pickaxe."

Worry lines rippled across her forehead, Dennis's first clue she might be in her thirties. "Dennis, I'm not so sure that's the chat rat way."

"They have a 'way'?"

"As much a 'way' as anyone, I suppose. But they're pretty blunt. If they don't want you in Gannaway, I can't see any of 'em playing hide-and-seek games with you. And I really don't see any of 'em dressing up to put a scare into you."

Dennis spread his hands, saw they were still shaking, and quickly dropped them to his lap. "I know what I saw. There was definitely somebody out there. Dressed up in overalls and wearing a hardhat."

"You do know overalls aren't a fashion choice exclusive to miners, don't you?"

"Yeah, I've seen that style worn by a few of the locals." He inclined his head toward an overall-wearing farmer in the corner. "Don't see a lot of hardhats and pickaxes, though."

Her long fingernails rapped out four counts on the tabletop. "Reckon not. I'm curious... What else did you see on your nocturnal adventure? And why, for the love of God, would you venture into Gannaway at night, anyway?"

"I didn't mean to. Time just got away from me."

"Yep. Time flies when you're having fun."

He managed a smile. In the eye-opening reason of day, his fears seemed silly. Sitting across from a pretty, intelligent woman helped in no small part. "Nothing but fun in Gannaway, Kansas. But I did see something else last night. At least I *think* I did. Hard to tell with the clouds moving in and the sun going down. And I didn't have my glasses—"

"Yeah, okay, I get it. You're making excuses." She caught the waitress's attention and pointed at Dennis's cup. "But what do you think you saw?"

Her accurate assessment brought him up short. Guilty as charged of excuse-making. "Fair enough. I think I saw two men working in the mines."

"Interesting. And how, might I ask, did you happen to see this? No, wait. How did you *think* you saw this? The mines are locked up tighter than government budgets."

"Well, I guess I sorta found a hole in the fence and took a stroll up a chat pile."

Therese appeared on the verge of exploding. She brought her shoulders back with a deep breath, obviously preparing to lay into him. The waitress appeared just in time. After she unceremoniously dumped a cup of coffee and left, Therese said, "I thought you were a scientist. But no. You're a juvenile delinquent posing as one."

"You caught me. Wanna go cruising in my hot rod?"

"In your dreams. Why would you do something stupid like that? Seriously, you could've been hurt. In any number of ways. Besides the obvious hazards of a closed-down mining area, there're the chat rats, not to mention if any of Gannaway's men found you breaking into the mines—"

"Therese, I was sent here to investigate every part of Gannaway's...ecology. That's what I intend to do."

"Yeah, we've covered that already." He appreciated her no-bullshit policy. *Immensely.* The Gannaway regulars seemed to operate strictly on pure bullshit. "So, how sure are you about the miners?"

"Pretty damn sure. Well...maybe not so sure. I don't know."

Again she tapped out a staccato beat on the table. Her smile supplied the crescendo. "Talk about a confident man."

"That's me. Could it be chat rats doing a little work of their own with scavenged equipment?"

"Hard to say. Nothing's ever as it seems in Gannaway."

"Fancy that."

"I'm fancying. So...you still don't want my help?"

He had to admit, an ally might prove useful. Or maybe he just wanted to spend more time with Therese. "To quote my favorite Bureau of Indian Affairs agent...I'm considering."

"Don't consider too long. Offer's good for a limited time only." She took a swig from her coffee cup. Pulling the cup away, her mouth twisted into a grimace. "What's *in* this?"

"Piss and vinegar, I think. Sorry. I thought about warning you. Guess I forgot."

"Cute. Just for that, you're paying for my piss and vinegar."

"My treat. Speaking of 'considering,' are you still considering my offer of meeting me for a cup of coffee?"

"Wow, man. For a scientist, you really are dumb. What do you think we just did?"

"This is our date?"

"That was our date." She slid out and stood, smoothing out her skirt. "Hope you enjoyed it. Don't forget to tip."

And like that, she bolted, the Queen of the Hasty Exits.

Unlike Therese, Dennis's next surprise visitor he could've done without.

Stokes stood outside the diner running his hand alongside the van door. "Hoo-wee! Looks like you got yourself into some sorta fender-bender!" He straightened and tipped his hat back. His open-mouthed smile gave him the appearance of a baby suffering from gas.

"No fender-bender. One of your fine citizens took it upon himself to do some body work. What can I do for you, Sheriff?"

"Now, why would you go blamin' something like this on one of ours? Maybe you had a little too much..." He knocked a cupped hand back toward his mouth several times. "...and got yourself into a scrape. Somethin' you wanna tell me?"

Fiery-orange dots pricked Dennis's vision. *Rage*. He'd fought long and hard to conquer his alcoholism, and he despised Stokes' insinuation. But Stokes couldn't know about his drinking problem. Not possible. And judging by the size of Stokes's beer belly, his favorite past-time involved gallons of alcohol.

"I don't drink. And I wasn't in a wreck. Two nights ago I heard something outside my motel room. One of Gannaway's citizens indulging in some good old-fashioned vandalism."

"You don't say. You see anyone?"

Telling Stokes what he thought he saw would be pointless. The ensuing "investigation" would lead to spending more time with Gannaway's finest, something he wanted to avoid. "No. Just the aftermath."

"Then I reckon you shouldn't be blamin' the townies."

"I've got work to do." Dennis zipped by Stokes and jumped into the driver's seat.

Stokes shot out a beefy hand and grabbed the door before Dennis closed it. "Now, hold on, son, we ain't done here yet."

"What do you want?"

"You know somethin'? I don't care much for your attitude. You been nothin' but hostile since you came into our neck of the woods."

"And you and the rest of the town have been so very

welcoming."

Stokes "aw, shucks" smile faded. He pulled his hat over his eyes and squared his shoulders. His law-keeping look, no doubt. "What's your business with the Injun squaw?"

"If by 'Injun squaw,' you mean Therese, we had a cup of coffee. I'd highly recommend their coffee, by the way. Go have a cup."

"Uh huh." Stokes looked off across the horizon for a good, long moment. Dennis practically heard his rusty mind grinding away. Finally, he said, "Where were you last night, Mr. Lipstein?"

"Sleeping. At the motel."

"Before that."

"Gathering some soil and water samples in Gannaway."

"Now, you wouldn't happen to have been trespassin' in Mr. Gannaway's mines, would you?" With one eyebrow raised, Stokes wore the smug appearance of a lawman arresting a notorious criminal. Case closed.

"Even if I were, it's my right as an employee of the United States government to take my investigation wherever it takes me. But...no. I wasn't in the mines."

"I done heard you was."

"You 'done heard' wrong, Sheriff."

"Like you said, Lipstein, it's my right as the duly elected law official in these parts to take my investigation wherever it takes me. And it's taking me right to you."

Dennis fought the temptation to explain his government stick measured bigger than Stokes's. He let it pass. "I didn't trespass. But I think there're lots of other crimes going on around here."

For once, Stokes seemed at a loss for words. He licked his lips, bent over, and spit. "You leave that determination to me, son."

"More than glad to. Tell you what. Why don't you do your job and I'll do mine. Maybe you should look into chat rats vandalizing automobiles."

"Maybe you should shut your *mouth.*" The good humor man had vanished. Stokes's eyes burned as he prodded a finger into Dennis's face. "You stay out of them mines, y'hear?"

Not particularly fond of the idea of doing jail time, Dennis kept his indignation in check. "I hear you, Sheriff. I won't go in the mines. At least, not without Mr. Gannaway's approval."

The smile reappeared. "That's all I'm askin'. As you hippies say, give peace a chance."

Afraid he'd burst out laughing, Dennis nodded and started up the van. As he passed Stokes, Dennis flashed him a peace sign.

Sometimes he couldn't help himself.

When Dennis arrived, several crinkled cans of "artistic inspiration" lay at Bob's feet.

"Back for more, brother?"

"Back for more." Dennis dropped into the student lawn chair next to his teacher. "Hey, is there still mining going on at the Gannaway mines? Mining from some of the chat rats, maybe?"

A crack sounded in Bob's neck as he turned. "I've heard could be. Don't know if it's chat rats or not. But, sometimes, late at night, I hear things."

Must be a helluva pair of ears you're sporting, Dennis thought. "It's seven miles to the mines, Bob."

"Didn't say I actually hear the mines. I said, 'I hear *things*'."

Deciding it best not to antagonize Bob over his mystical beliefs, Dennis let it go. "Okay. So you hear things. But you do think there's still mining going on?"

"Why you askin'?"

"Come on, Professor. I asked my question first."

"Fine and dandy. Yes, I think there's mining still going on. I suspect it's that damn Gannaway, too. Bad enough he ruined the land for forty-some years. But when the government shut him down, his greed musta kept itchin' at him. He won't stop 'til there's nothin' left but a huge hole all the way to Hell."

"You know for a fact Gannaway's doing this?"

"No. But there're new subsidences—"

"Cave-ins, right?"

Bob tapped his temple. "Give the boy an 'A.' Yep. Just a couple months ago, a house fell into the ground. The house was abandoned, thank the spirits, but it plummeted right through to the center of the earth. Left a hole 500 feet wide by 400 feet long, too. Hell, right out here on US69." He closed an eye and pointed toward the highway as if taking aim with a gun. "They say in some spots the earth's dug out to twenty-five feet below it. Ain't gonna be long 'fore some big ol' truck comes soaring along and the highway opens up and eats it alive."

"That doesn't exactly incriminate Gannaway, as terrifying as that sounds." Dennis added highway traveling to his list of current fears.

"Reckon not. But I 'spect he's cutting through the remaining support columns carved out of stone to mine the rest of the ore. Once they're gone..." He spread his hands like a stage magician. "...then all of Gannaway's gone. But, nope, no proof. Just what I hear."

"What you hear."

"Something wrong with your hearing, brother? That's what I said. Now. Answer my question. Why do you think there's mining going on now?"

"Last night, I thought I saw some workers at the Gannaway mine site."

He chuckled, then stretched out his legs. "I'll be damned. You were in the mines?"

"Yep. Sure was."

"Heh. What else did you see?" Amusement, then anticipation, danced in his eyes. "Nah. Don't tell me. Not yet."

Even though Dennis had pretty much discarded the notion of anything unnatural happening last night, temptation brought him to the brink of laying it all on the line. Bob would believe him. But he didn't know if he wanted to be believed. It would lend more credence to things Dennis didn't want to think about. Things that made no sense in his fact-based scientific world.

"Before we chat about current matters, you need to know more about Gannaway's history. So, without further ado..." Bob lifted his eyes expectantly, nudging his hand toward Dennis.

It finally struck Dennis what he wanted. With a grin, Dennis vocalized a drum roll. *"Rrrrrrrrrr..."*

"Professor Bob's History Of Gannaway, Part Two." Bob raised his hands to an imaginary audience. Dennis finished with a cymbal sound, the best he could manage.

"Okay, where were we?" Bob set his beer can on the cooler and picked at his fingernails. "The mining boom was in full swing. The population of Gannaway, though it wasn't called Gannaway yet, grew from 5,000 to 30,000 practically overnight. What was once considered 'Indian territory' was now 97% white. Of course, there wasn't enough housing for everyone. People slept where they could. Fields were covered with tents and boxes with folks crowdin' into them. Loud machinery drove out birds and other wildlife. And the holes! The damn miners dug thirty huge holes each before finding a place to sink a shaft. Giant, mechanical prairie dogs diggin' up holes everywhere is what it looked like.

"Then Mr. Kyle Gannaway rolled into town, big as life, but not half as nice. He'd had some success in the Oklahoma mining business, built up a huge wad of cash, so he thought he'd try his luck in Kansas. He sublet a small area out on the reservation and dropped a drill. But Gannaway ran into a problem. The Kwashau deal they'd negotiated with the government limited the number of acres an outsider could sublet. It was a fine idea, I think, but wily ol' Gannaway found a stipulation. If you lived on the reservation, the sky was the limit.

"So you know what Gannaway did?" Dennis dutifully

shook his head. "He found the prettiest, youngest Kwashau woman around and started courting her. Naira Blackbird was hesitant at first, wary of the white man's ways. And her father was dead set against it in a bad way, but more about him later. Soon enough, though, she started to come a-round. Gannaway possessed a certain amount of charm and good looks, I suppose, but the way he tossed money at Naira and promised her the world? It'd make anyone's head swoon, regardless of race.

"The day after they were married, Gannaway started building a house on the reservation. Didn't take long, either. He must've had an army of fifty men putting up that man-sion. And it stuck out like a sore thumb, too. He flaunted his wealth. His new home towered over the humble shacks already out there. The Kwashau people didn't like it, but they were powerless. Indian law is Indian law. Even if the white man refuses to abide by it, we're beholden to it.

"But what nobody knew, Gannaway was quietly buying up all the surrounding land leases. He'd go door to door, using his salesman snake-oil, makin' offers too good to be true. And he swore them all to secrecy, told them not to let their neighbors know, 'cause they were one of a kind. He knew it'd get their dander up if the Kwashau found out he was monopolizing their land. And then, *bam!*" Dennis had nearly been lulled into a trance by Bob's lilting tone until Bob clapped his hands like thunder. "Gannaway now owned most, if not all, of the reservation. Over 8,000 acres. Hence the birth of Gannaway Lead and Smelting Company. And the death of my people."

If Dennis didn't like Kyle Gannaway before, he abso-lutely abhorred him now. "So Gannaway married Naira just to get his hands on the land?"

"Didn't see your hand raised, student. But I'll let this one go. Who knows? Different stories were told. My people saw him as the devil. Some white folks thought it was a romantic fairy tale, others saw it as an abomination what with a white man marrying outside his race."

"Yeah, some things don't change over time."

"Preach it, brother. But I know for a fact he didn't treat her very well. She rarely left their home, don't think he'd let her. The few sightings of her told the tale. She always looked downtrodden, never met anybody's eyes. I even saw a few welts, maybe a black eye, on her lovely features once myself."

"Son-of-a-bitch."

"Eloquent, brother, eloquent. We'll get back to her tale in Part Three." Dennis almost groaned. "In the meantime, Gannaway had over 160 separate mines and mills spread out over a five-mile radius. My people were lucky if they had shacks to live in. And Gannaway was their landlord, of course. The whole reservation—if you could call it that anymore—was a hazard. Kids fell into bored holes. Cave-ins started. And Gannaway made more money than the whole town put together. Ran the town and was more or less the law, too. Too many people, not enough folks to keep 'em in line. Gannaway made himself the authority on mining disputes. And people listened. What other choice did they have in a lawless land? Folks wanted some form of authority, as slanted as it was. Gave 'em a little comfort. Soon enough, he named the town after himself. Nobody objected."

"Surely he had some dissenters."

"Not really, brother. He controlled the white men's jobs. The Kwashau weren't even allowed in the mines, so they didn't matter. Who was there to speak up? One man—John Blackbird, Naira's father. Once Gannaway married Naira, Blackbird disowned his daughter. After that, not many folks ever saw him again. He became a recluse, holed up in his shack. People talked about him in hushed whispers. My people were terrified of him."

"Why?"

Bob leaned in and placed a hand on Dennis's shoulder, almost an anchor. "Because, my student, he was a man of magic. What your popular fiction might call a 'witch doctor' or a 'medicine man'."

Dennis waited for Bob's stony demeanor to break into

a wide "fooled ya'" grin. But he didn't. "Come on, Bob, really?"

"Yep. I was afraid you weren't ready for this part of the tale yet."

"Regardless if I'm 'ready' or not, I'd like to hear more."

"John Blackbird put a curse on the mines. The 'yellow-eyed fever,' the miners called it."

That's when the tale really started. Several times Dennis wanted to snort in disbelief, but when Bob grabbed a beer and downed it in three unpleasant gulps like he had a demon nipping at his tail, Dennis knew he'd better leave it alone

"That's some story, Bob."

"It is. I can see you have doubts, brother."

"Well...if you believe it, then I do."

Finally, Bob broke out a laugh. "What a crock of shit that is! In other words, you don't believe it."

Holding his hands palm upright, Dennis sheepishly wagged his head. No, he didn't believe it. But he knew better than to argue with one's personal, spiritual beliefs, as out of this world as they may be. "Bob, is this just old superstition passed on down through the ages, or..." He hoped Bob would pick up on his trail of thought so he wouldn't have to ask the obvious.

Bob did. "Yes, I believe it. Dennis, one thing you have to know, I saw some things. Now before you go gettin' the men in the white coats, let me tell you I was a skeptical young lad back in the day. Didn't put much faith in all that supernatural nonsense. Sorta made me unpopular with a lot of my people. They even said I had one foot in white man's land. Doesn't matter. But 'til I saw what I did, I was just like you."

"Care to elaborate?"

"I care not to. Not now, at least. Wouldn't matter what I said to you now, anyway. I can see it in your eyes."

"I didn't mean any offense, Bob. But I'm a man of science—"

Bob sliced the air with his hand. "Yeah, so you've told me time and again. I'm just waiting for you to see some things. Maybe expand your mind some like the kids are doing in San Francisco with their LSD."

"Don't know about that."

"Next up in Professor Bob's history lesson? It's time to meet the Donnellys."

"Can't wait. So. History lesson's over for today?"

"History lesson's over. Always leave 'em on a cliffhanger."

The story rattled Dennis more than he expected. Of course, he didn't believe in curses and ghosts, but when a man speaks with conviction, it's hard to disregard him out of hand. And something else scratched at Dennis's mind, a particularly persistent itch.

Maybe Dennis had seen things, too.

As Dennis and Bob discussed the town's history, fourteen miles down the road, Kyle Gannaway considered Dennis Lipstein's present status.

Gannaway watched Gus waddle across the bedroom. With an effeminate flourish, his manservant whipped back the drapes. The sunlight scratched at Gannaway's bloodshot eyes. He cursed and rolled over in bed.

Gus, jovial as ever, set the serving tray over Gannaway, careful not to pinch his arms as he'd done last time. *Nothing like his father*, thought Gannaway.

Gus pulled the lid away unveiling the breakfast, and Gannaway grimaced. Grapefruit and dry toast. "Gus, I don't give a good goddamn what the doctor says, I want bacon, eggs, and coffee!"

Ho, ho, haaaa. Always the same damn three-note laugh. "Doctor's orders, sir."

Gannaway grudgingly gave in. As he picked at the grapefruit, Gus lingered, hands folded in front of him. Afraid to speak his mind. "Don't just stand there like an idiot child, if you got somethin' to say to me, spit it out!"

"Ah...sir...there was trouble last night—"

"Oh, *goddammit!* How many times I tell you I don't want to wake up to bad news?"

"Yes, sir. But I thought you'd want to hear as soon as possible." Gus inclined his head, wagged it with a silly smile. Talking down to Gannaway as if he didn't still possess a sharp mind.

"For Christ's sake, then, get on with it!"

"It's about Dr. Lipstein, sir. He—"

Gannaway dug his bony elbows into the mattress and propped himself up. "What?"

"He, ah, he was spotted last night. In the mines."

It took a moment for the information to sink in. Once it did, Gannaway hurled the grapefruit at Gus. Gus twisted, tossing up sissy hands in front of his face. *Whap!* It thumped into his shoulder, then plopped to the floor. "Quit pussyfootin' around and tell me the whole damn story."

"Seems some of the men saw him—"

"What men?"

"Decatur and Jones. The ones in the mines."

"Did Lipstein see them?"

"Hard to say. It could be he didn't."

"All your run-around speech ain't helpin' matters! Where'd they see him? What was he doin'?"

"He, uh, climbed one of the chat piles. They saw him near the top. That's when they hid."

"Dammit." The toast didn't fly as far as the grapefruit had, and the results were much less satisfying. "What in *hell* was he doin' climbin' a pile?"

"I don't know, sir. I'm just reporting what I was told. Seems—"

"Seems like *horse shit.* We can't have him knowin' the operation's still goin' on."

"No, sir."

"And they're sure it was Lipstein? Not one of the locals?"

"Pretty sure. His van was spotted across the highway."

"Pretty sure don't cut it." He ran a hand through his hair, searching for inspiration. Lipstein could be a huge problem.

"There might be a silver lining, Mr. Gannaway..." Gus paused in hopes of an "atta' boy." Should know better by now.

"Tell me."

"I had our man do some checking on Dr. Lipstein." The first promising thing Gannaway had heard. "Our man"—a particularly sleazy, but resourceful, private detective Gannaway kept on retainer—rarely let him down. Gannaway gestured with a backhand motion for Gus to continue. "Seems Dr. Lipstein is an alcoholic. Had some major issues with it in the past."

As soon as Gannaway smiled, Gus deemed it an appropriate time to insert a chuckle. Without saying a word, Gannaway killed it with a glower.

But Gannaway could work with Lipstein's alcoholism. He never touched the stuff himself. Seen it kill too many good businessmen. But he kept it on hand at all times, a valuable weapon to even the playing field. Or to get men to talk. Thirty-five years ago, he even cleverly used alcohol to dispose of an opponent.

"Well, now, Gus, why didn't you start my mornin' off with this spot of news?" Given his sudden good mood, he even allowed Gus another *ho, ho, haaaa.* "Got a little job for you. Go get gussied up."

Yes, sir, it felt like olden times. Always nice to sharpen up the battle skills against a new opponent.

Chapter Eleven

1935...

They finagled Mrs. Kendricks into bed, and Tommy barely made it outside before his stomach exploded. His guts convulsed. A squeezing fist clamped down, bringing up breakfast and continuing with gut-wrenching dry heaves. *Oh, God, the boy poked out his own eyes and throat!* He'd seen some terrible mining accidents in his life, but never anything like that. *The blood everywhere. And the loose eye sliding down like a gray egg yolk.*

Just as he thought it was over, his stomach tightened again. He pitched straight into the dirt. Specks of dirt adhered to his face and turned to sweaty, dark streaks of mud.

He clambered to his feet. The world spun out from underneath him. Thrusting a hand out for the porch railing, he missed and plummeted into a box of scrap tin.

A neighbor came running at the commotion. She stared down at him with wide eyes. "You all right, Tommy?"

The woman seemed familiar; in fact, he knew her well. But by God, he couldn't recall her name right now. "George... he's dead." His voice came out raspy, much worse than the ravages of miner's consumption. "Get...Durwood."

The screen door banged shut, followed by the inevitable scream. Tommy pulled himself to his knees, gradually working his way to his feet. As he reentered the house, the neighbor woman blew past him, shrieking.

Doc sat on the bed next to Mrs. Kendricks. His hand rested limply on her forehead. Mercifully, she'd given in to sleep. More like she gave in to one of Doc's shots. Based on Doc's coloring, he looked like he could use a shot himself. Something a little stronger than his usual self-medicating whiskey shots.

"Good God in Heaven, Tommy..." Even though the heat seethed inside, a shiver shook through Doc's thin frame. His grinding teeth sounded like a mouse skittering across the floor. "Never...never..."

Tommy drew his arm across his face, wiping away the mud and sweat. "I know, Doc. I know."

"Why would he...do such a thing?" Doc's eyes, usually large behind his bifocals, looked small and unfocused.

"The boy was sick. No denying that now." Tommy knew better than to have it out right then and there, but he saw the chance at gaining an ally, someone Gannaway might listen to. "You need to tell Mr. Gannaway the boy shouldn't have gone back in the mines. Maybe this wouldn't've happened." *And I wouldn't have had to break George's fingers.* His next thought followed like a gut punch. *Maybe if I didn't break his fingers, he wouldn't be lying in there dead.*

A rap at the door saved Tommy from further self-inflicted punishment.

"Hello? Mrs. Kendricks?"

It hadn't taken long for Harry Durwood to get there. It never did. The way word spread among Gannaway inhabitants provided a more-effective communication system than the telephones they couldn't afford. And like a bad penny, Harry had a way of showing up shortly after a death. Almost like he *smelled* death. Some of the miners thought Harry had made a deal with the Devil. A rarity amongst Gannaway businesses, the Durwood Funeral Home absolutely thrived, courtesy of the mining accidents that comprised most of Harry's clientele.

Tommy opened the door. Harry entered, dressed in his usual natty black suit, the only clothes Tommy'd ever seen him wear. Town scuttlebutt had it he slept in the clothes.

"The boy?"

Unable to find words, Tommy jacked a thumb toward the bedroom. He lurked outside the room while Harry conducted his business. The boy's death would haunt him forever, no sense in revisiting it.

Harry hurried by Tommy, anxious, maybe even a tad bit excited. Seconds later, he came back carrying several potato sacks and reentered the bedroom.

Skirtch. Skirrrrrrrrtch. Harry tearing the potato sacks. Or cutting them, probably with the knife from George's throat.

"Tommy? Give me a hand?"

Tommy fought the impulse to run and run until he could run no longer and reluctantly entered. Torn potato sacks covered the boy's body. Blood seeped through the bag rendering the "Ottawan Potatoes" logo illegible. In place of George's eyes were two round brown spots on the burlap. Blood from the throat puncture spread across the bag, curling up at the corners like a grotesque smile.

Harry stood at the head of the bed, the underlying sheet's corners bunched up in his hands. "How 'bout grabbing the bottom?"

Tommy kept his gaze locked down on George's feet, unable to look elsewhere. They lifted him, carried him outside, and unceremoniously heaved him into the bed of the "Durwood Funeral Home" truck.

"I'll take care of things on my end," said Harry. "The boy did this to himself?" Tommy nodded. "Shame. How's his momma?"

"She's...out." Tommy caught himself from saying *dead to the world.* "Doc's shots." Nothing else needed to be said. His words had dried up anyway. Harry's truck hit a bump as it drove down the road, and George's hand popped up ever so briefly. Almost as if waving goodbye. Or *see you soon.*

Tommy shuttered his tears through sheer willpower and dried his eyes raw with his shirt sleeve. There'd be plenty of time for tears later. Right now his men needed a strong leader. It wouldn't do for them to see him crying.

As soon as he drove through the gate, he smelled trouble. Expected it, even. A throng of men surrounded the office. Anger was evident in their defiant stances, in the fists they shook in the air. Some of the miners looked adrift, wandering about, helmets gripped uncertainly to their chests. Mr. Darling stood in the middle of the mob, impotently patting the air. He deflated with relief when he saw Tommy.

"Tommy! What happened to the greenhorn?"

"Is he dead?"

"Did the yella-eyed fever take him?"

Tommy squared his shoulders, girded himself as if going to war, and approached the men. "Fellas, let's all calm down a bit." With folded arms, Big Ed leaned up against the shed's side, staying out of the ruckus. But even he stepped forward to hear what Tommy had to say. Tommy dug a boot tip into the dirt, stalling, searching for inspiration. Impatient as the wind, Ed plucked the tooth-pick from his mouth. "What happened, Tommy?"

"I'm...sorry to say George Kendricks passed away a little while ago." Out of respect for George and his momma, Tommy kept quiet about exactly how it had happened. Word would get out soon enough, anyway.

A collective murmur built, the men wearing their uneasiness like overcoats.

"How'd it happen, Tommy?"

"He...he..." Tommy saw George's eyeball drooping down,

heard his strangulated cry. He stuck his fingernails into his palm, forcing the memory away. "He was sick. He died from—"

"Yella-eyed fever." Harvey Quick, one of the old-timers, stepped forward, itching for a fight. Harvey had been a thorn in Tommy's side for years. A lot of the men didn't cotton to his constant whining, but he had his supporters.

"Now, fellas…it wasn't the yellow-eyed fever. That's nothing but superstition. Ain't no such thing."

"Say what you will. But I don't buy it. No sir, not for a plugged nickel." He spat, his load of tobacco streaking across the dirt. "I know the yellow-eyed fever's a for-sure thing. Look what happened to Karl all them years ago. And all the others."

"Damn it, Harvey, that's all superstitious nonsense. We can't let fairy tales run our lives." Tommy recalled his earlier meeting with Gannaway, his anger sweeping away his grief. "But I'll tell you something. I do believe, with all my heart, what happened to poor George Kendricks could've been prevented. What happened to George happened because of the working conditions below. George got sick because of the mines. The dust alone's enough to cause miner's consumption, you all know that. With the right kind of ventilation, maybe we could improve our chances and—"

"How you reckon to do that?" Standing in front of Tommy, Harvey hitched his thumbs behind his overall straps and tossed his shoulders back. Several men fell in behind him.

Tommy hadn't wanted to bring it up then, but he couldn't pass up this opportunity. "I've read about unions." He knew some of the men thought "unions" were a bad thing. Un-American, some had said. So he tested the waters, letting the word sink in slowly before continuing. "If we unionize, I guarantee you every man here will be less likely to get sick. Pay raises—"

"Shit, Tommy," said Harvey, "everyone knows them

damn unions are run by foreigners and darkies!" A smattering of cheers and whistles brought a grin to Harvey's face.

"That's not true." Tommy shot a desperate glance to Big Ed for support. Ed shrugged his shoulders, no help whatsoever. "Listen to me, fellas. I believe—"

Something roared, grumbling across the grounds. Gannaway's Bentley sped toward the miners, an angry mechanical beast kicking up a trail of dust in its wake.

When Gannaway heard the Kendricks boy had plucked his eyes out, he knew there'd be trouble in the mines. Absolutely knew it. And from the looks of things, the miners were enjoying an unscheduled holiday on his pay.

"Goddammit, Steffen, go faster!" Gannaway leaned forward, squinting into the crowd. Just as he suspected. Tommy Donnelly stood amidst the miners, stirring them up. The boy needed a lesson. A hard lesson.

"Yes, sir." Steffen stepped on the pedal, propelling them across the dirt. The Bentley bounced to an abrupt stop, jostling Gannaway in the back seat. Gannaway jumped out and ran toward the men before Eberstark cut the engine.

"Boys! Boys!" He waved his hat through the air, corralling their attention. "I know we've lost one of our own today. A terrible tragedy. And the Gannaway Mining Company will be more than happy to pay for his funeral even though he didn't suffer a death in the mines." The thought of paying for another funeral—particularly one not his responsibility—irked Gannaway. But he also realized the importance of maintaining goodwill with his employees. Even if it smelled like a load of horse shit. "But let's put it behind us and get back to the mines. Do young Kendricks proud by honoring his memory."

"Sir, the men just need a little time to mourn." The young upstart, Donnelly, again. Just never knew when to shut his mouth.

"That's all fine and dandy, Tommy. They can do it at the funeral. But I sure as shootin' ain't payin' 'em all to stand around gawkin'. You men get on back down there. Go on, git." With an underhanded flourish, he shooed them like a farmer would his livestock. That's all they were, anyway. His livestock. He owned them. Some of the men grumbled as they passed him, others knew to stay quiet. Like the most stubborn of pigs, Donnelly didn't follow them. "Somethin' else I can do for you, Tommy?"

"Mr. Gannaway, I saw what happened to George. I've... I've never seen anything like it before. Once word gets out, the men're going to be afraid to go into the mines. We really should do something to—"

"Since when do *we* make the decisions around here, Tommy?" He bared a tiny row of white teeth in a vicious grin. "I don't recall you bein' my business partner."

"No, sir. I'd just like to talk to the men. Maybe tell them some changes will be made. If George hadn't gotten sick in the mine, he'd still be alive."

"You listen to me, and you listen good." He lowered his voice to a quiet growl, one he'd perfected over the years. "First of all, it ain't my business to make promises. 'Specially promises that ain't gonna get delivered. Second, it sure in hell ain't your business. Do your job and be happy you got it." Gannaway poked his finger into Tommy's chest.

Steffen trotted up in his odd, stiff gait, smelling blood and eager to join the fray. "Everything fine, Mr. Gannaway?"

Gannaway dismissed him with a curt gesture. "Nothin' I can't handle. Go on back to the car."

"Yes, sir." Before he left, Steffen flashed Tommy a smile; a smile that threatened, *One of these days...*

"Don't make me have this conversation with you again, Tommy. This is the third one I've had with you. Not a one of 'em's made me very happy. Trust me, you wanna keep me happy."

"Yes, sir, I reckon I do." He spoke the words Gannaway wanted to hear, but the fire in Donnelly's eyes gave away his true feelings. Not much of a poker face on that boy.

"Get back to work and don't do it again." He didn't wait for Donnelly's response and stormed off to his car.

After he'd settled into the back seat, a rap sounded at the window. Harvey Quick stood outside, his filthy knuckles tapping at the window. Gannaway didn't much care for Harvey. Too overeager to please. Showed no sense of loyalty to the men he worked with. Still, those very qualities had proven beneficial in the past. Gannaway rolled down the window.

"What can I do for you, Harvey?"

Harvey bent down, hands on his knees, and studied the Bentley's interior with a lustful intensity. "Might be somethin' I can do for you, Mr. Gannaway. Can I step inside your automobile?"

The man had some audacious nerve. Plus he smelled worse than a dead skunk. Gannaway would probably never get the stench out of his car if he allowed the man access. "No. You need to be gettin' back to work. State your business. I'm a busy man."

Harvey licked his lips, and said, "You should know Tommy was talkin' unions just afore you pulled up. Got some of the men rightly stirred. But, not ol' Harvey. No, sir."

No surprise, really. Gannaway considered himself an astute people person who could size up a man's character in just one encounter. Donnelly held onto the dim-bulb notion he could make things better, but he was too short-sighted to see what was really best for the townsfolk of Gannaway. Which was the Gannaway Lead and Smelting Company. Without his company, folks would probably be shootin' guns still, living like savages. Time to make a business decision.

"Thanks for bringin' this to my attention, Harvey. Tell

you what. I surely would look at it as a favor to me if you'd keep an eye on Tommy. Report back to me if he talks more of this union nonsense."

Harvey's left eye twitched, then he brazenly held his hand out, rubbing his fingers together. "I'd be honored to do you this favor, Mr. Gannaway."

Damn vultures! Everyone wanted a piece of his pie. Gannaway sighed and said, "Steffen, give the man five bucks."

Holding the bill up to the sunlight, Harvey smiled. "Thank you, sir. Won't let you down."

As the Bentley pulled away, Gannaway saw Tommy Donnelly standing by the office, looking mighty worried.

Good. A nice dose of fear might bring Donnelly to his senses. Otherwise, Gannaway might just have to resort to more drastic measures.

Claire wished she'd worn clothing more appropriate for trekking miles through fields and woods. But the trip had been a spur-of-the-moment decision.

Besides, she didn't have a lot of clothing to choose from. Four dresses and the skirts all dragged the ground, hand-me-downs from her momma. She wished she had some shorter skirts, the daring kind they wore in Hollywood. She grinned at the thought of exposing her calves, how the townsfolk would talk.

The cardboard reinforcing her shoes rubbed against her toes, burning them.

Ahanu maintained a quick pace, nearly impossible to keep up with. She needed to rest. "Ahanu, I have to stop for a minute." Ahanu didn't seem winded at all. Nothing new to him, he walked this route twice a day. But he remained uncharacteristically tight-lipped throughout their journey.

"We don't have much farther to go." He pointed up a

hill that may as well have been a mountain to Claire. "Just over yonder."

Claire hitched up her skirt and trudged on. Her legs grew heavy as she ascended the hill. Chiggers hidden within the deep grass bit at her ankles. The sun beat down, roasting her fair complexion. Still, she welcomed the sun's rays after the week-long rains they'd suffered through.

In the distance, horses galloped across the terrain. Small farmhouses spread throughout the hills, like a child's wooden toys. A bird, possibly a hawk, cawed overhead.

Once they mounted the peak of the hill, Claire dropped onto her bottom, refueling her energy for her impending encounter.

Ahanu hopped back a step as if bounding into an invisible barrier. "We're here. It's as far as I'll go, Mrs. Donnelly."

At the bottom of the hill, a gray shack sat in a wooded area. Bowing trees formed a nearly perfect circle around it. The shack looked uninhabitable and certainly uninviting. The walls, warped with age, leaned, ready to slide away if someone so much as sneezed. Splintered porch planks poked up like fingers. One window peeked out, dark and curtain-free.

"Thank you, Ahanu, I—" Ahanu was already halfway back down the hill. Claire hadn't even realized he'd left.

"You're welcome," he called back. "I just hope..." His last words were lost to the wind.

Apprehension gripped her. She wanted to run after Ahanu. Put all this silliness behind her. But reality grounded her. She'd come all this way, no turning back now. Carefully, she made her way down the hill, but the slope pushed her faster. By the time she reached the hill's bottom, she'd broken into a running gait.

The door buckled at her knock. Claire jumped back, afraid it might fall. She listened. A floorboard ticked beneath her. The constant bird chatter around her quieted. Humidity claimed the air, still and smothering. Claire's pulse thumped in her ears. Time had stopped. Finally, a hook unlatched. The door pulled back, revealing an older Indian woman. Her face showcased the ravages of time, a hard life lived. Unmoving, she said nothing, didn't even blink.

"Uh—hello, I'm very sorry to stop by uninvited. I'm Claire Donnelly. I—"

"I know who you are." Her voice sounded raspy, almost a male's voice. "What do you want?"

"It's...very important I speak to your husband." Of course, Claire assumed her to be John Blackbird's wife.

"My husband's not well."

When she started to close the door, Claire said, "Wait! *Please*. My husband's life may depend on it."

The woman stepped outside. "Tell me what this is about."

"My husband...Tommy...he works in the mines." Claire didn't want to appear weak, but desperation drove her. "I'm afraid for him. I'm afraid of the yellow-eyed fever. I'm *afraid* for my children. I heard your husband—"

The old woman held up an authoritative hand, stopping Claire. "I'm not sure what you've heard, white woman. But my husband is sick. Ready for his spirit to move on. He hasn't wakened in days."

"No..." Dizziness overtook her. The gray floorboards grew, rising toward her. As Claire felt herself falling, her world blinked out.

She woke with her chin on her chest, propped into a hard chair. Darkness surrounded her, a harsh contrast to the sunlight she'd left behind. So dark, Claire at first thought she had lost her eyesight.

"Drink this." The woman thrust a cup into her hands.

Without hesitation, Claire drank. It tasted strong, smelled pungent, but the soothing wetness felt good to her parched throat.

The Indian woman sat down across from her. "I take pity upon you. I know what it's like to lose a child. And I will soon lose my husband. But I'm afraid I can't help you. And John is beyond helping you. Even if he could, I don't believe he would."

"You said...he hasn't woken up. Can he hear you? Can I at least talk to him?" Claire knew her chances of seeing John Blackbird were slim, but she wouldn't leave without attempting everything within her power.

"Of course he can hear me. If not in this realm, then within the next. But he won't—"

"Please? From one wife to another?"

Finally, the woman cracked a smile. Small, skeptical, but clearly empathetic. "Very well, child. You can try." She grabbed Claire's hand and tugged her out of the chair. Claire followed her to a room where a hanging rug served as a door.

The small room barely held the cot where John Blackbird lay, eyes closed, long gray hair splayed out on a threadbare pillow. He might have been peacefully slumbering instead of knocking at death's door.

Claire leaned down and spoke quietly. "Mr. Blackbird... I'm Claire Donnelly. My husband is...Tommy Donnelly, a miner in the Gannaway mines. Lately...there've been some incidents. Involving the yellow-eyed fever. It's my understanding you put the curse on those men. But those men— my husband—don't deserve to die for...for...what that son-of-a-bitch Gannaway did to your people...and the land."

Mrs. Blackbird chuckled at Claire's off-color language. Under other circumstances, Claire would have been embarrassed by her unladylike outburst. Not now, though.

"If you can hear me, Mr. Blackbird...please, *please* release the curse. Don't let it take any more men...don't let it take my Tommy...please...please, I *beg* you..."

Claire's sobs filled the sweltering room, sounding so very helpless, pathetic even, to her own ears.

Blackbird's eyes shot up like window shades. Claire screamed. His pale, glassy eyes fixed on Claire. Running to his side, Mrs. Blackbird grasped his hand. His tongue darted in and out between cracked lips as if searching for his voice. Struggling, he whispered something too hushed to hear. His wife dropped her head, placing her ear next to his mouth. When she pulled away, worry lines creased her forehead. Her husband's eyes closed just as suddenly as they had opened. Mrs. Blackbird snatched Claire's hand again and dragged her outside.

"What did he say? *What* did he *say?*"

Mrs. Blackbird looked less than hopeful. Her frown brought her jowls down. "I'm sorry, child. So very sorry..."

"Oh, my..." Claire steadied herself against a post, then slowly slid down to the porch. Mrs. Blackbird's ankles cracked as she sat down next to her.

"I'm sorry, Mrs. Donnelly. But John said...the only way to release the curse is for Gannaway to close down the mines. It's the only way."

"Gannaway's not going to do that." A bird fluttered overhead and squawked, almost mocking Claire.

"That's what John said. It's out of his hands."

"'Out of his hands,'" Claire said. She felt numb, foolish for having thought she could fix the situation. But lionesses don't give up. "Why didn't your husband put the curse on Gannaway if he hates him so much? Why harm all the other men?"

Mrs. Blackbird's grimace looked physically painful. "I'm not supposed to talk about the yellow-eyed fever, child. Sworn not to. But...as I said before, you're in pain. This I understand and sometimes, family is more important than a sworn oath."

Claire thought, *Welcome to the lion pack.* "Please help me understand. Maybe if I understand, there's something I—"

She shot up a finger and held it to her lips. "There's nothing to be done about the curse. But I can answer your question. Earlier I told you I'd lost a child. We lost Naira to Kyle Gannaway."

Claire knew, of course, Kyle Gannaway had taken an Indian woman as his bride. But she had no idea he'd married John Blackbird's daughter. She'd never even heard John Blackbird's name until yesterday. Now she wished she'd never heard any of their names. "But...your daughter is still living. That's something to be thankful for."

"She's dead to John. Has been since she took up with that...white man. So John decided to take away what was most important to Kyle Gannaway. His money. That's why he placed the curse on the mines. He wanted to make him feel the loss we have. Hoped that the mines would be shut down. For good."

Claire wanted to tell Mrs. Blackbird how unfair, how insane it all sounded. Her husband and the other miners were caught in the middle of a silly family grudge, their lives at stake. "What if...what if Naira made peace with your husband?"

Mrs. Blackbird shook her head. "Doesn't matter none, child. What's done is done. Can't be undone. I'm sorry."

When Claire pulled herself up by the post, a sharp splinter slid into her palm. It didn't matter. Her physical pain paled in comparison to what she felt inside. "Thank you for seeing me, Mrs. Blackbird."

As Claire began her hike back, she heard Mrs. Blackbird muttering apologies. A tiny, inconsequential voice, unable to help.

The weather had turned. Clouds blanketed the sky. Thunder rumbled, God's upset belly. It matched her defeated mood.

What in the world had she been thinking? That she could just go ask John Blackbird to lift the curse? *Stupid, so very stupid!*

But even if she had lost the battle, she might still stand a chance of winning the war. She had an idea. An idea that posed a bigger challenge, but a sound idea nonetheless. And where there are ideas, there's hope.

A bird cawed above. *Laughing* at her. Cupping a hand over her eyes, she looked up. The bird circled over her repeatedly, flying dangerously closer with each pass. It swooped low, zipping past her shoulder. A *blackbird*. Other calls and squeals sounded far away, growing louder. A flock of blackbirds looped above her, dipping down. *Watching* her. One fluttered in the air next to her head and dropped a scornful scream into her ear.

She threw her arms over her head and ran, the long skirt tripping her with every step. The birds fell behind, but she didn't stop running until she left the reservation.

For the first time, Tommy found it a chore making it through supper. Even the town's children knew about George, and T.J. and Margaret bristled with questions. But Tommy strapped on a smile, made small talk, asked about school, and tucked his children into bed with kisses. For several minutes, he looked at them, loving them, feeling a small bit of guilty jealousy. The innocence of youth, so untainted by adult worries.

Even though he'd managed to avoid talking about George at the dinner table, Claire absolutely knew. He caught her stolen glances, the sadness inherent in her eyes. He could read her like a book.

But now, in their bed, with her arms around him, he could finally release. The tears came slowly at first. Then they burst forth, a natural flood that wouldn't stop. Tommy bit into the pillow, howling at the unfairness of the world.

Claire stroked his head, cradling him close. "I know, Tommy, I know. Let it out, my love. I know..." Before too long, Claire cried right along with him.

Chapter Twelve

1969...

"A working vacation" is how Dennis justified his constant visits to Bob. Like Bob said, he had to learn about the past to understand the present. Of course, a lot of the hocus pocus in Bob's history lessons sounded preposterous, but Dennis looked forward to those lessons, including the tall tales. He suspected Bob enjoyed them as much as Dennis himself did, maybe even more. They perfected their routine to an art form. As soon as Dennis pulled into the drive, he headed straight for "his" chair. Bob always waited for him, beer can already half-drained.

"So. Claire Donnelly visited John Blackbird and tried to get him to lift the 'yellow-eyed curse'."

"Yes, sir, that's about the size of it."

"But the curse continued."

"You not been payin' attention to my schoolin', brother? It's what I said. And don't ask if it's gonna be on the test."

Dennis still didn't buy into the mumbo-jumbo folklore, but Bob's storytelling abilities couldn't be denied. "Sorry, Professor Bob. Consider my wrists whacked with a ruler."

"They still do that in school?"

"I don't know. Been a while since I've been in school. But did they ever find the real reason this...George kid poked his eyes out and killed himself? I mean, a medical reason?"

Dennis never saw the beer can coming. When the empty can *thwacked* his temple, he let out a startled yelp.

"Sorry, brother." Bob shrugged, a half-grin on his face. "But you need a wake-up call. What I'm telling you just might help save your life in the future. It's more important than ever you start acceptin' science can't explain everything. If you don't believe what I've told you, there's no use in my goin' on any further. Things get even... hairier."

Finding that hard to believe, Dennis sighed. "All I can say is...I'll try to keep an open mind. How's that? And no more projectiles." He picked up the beer can and lobbed it back at Bob. Bob caught it without blinking an eye. "Show-off."

"Hey, if you got it, flaunt it. Anyway, I suppose you keepin' an open mind is better than where you started. And to answer your question, no, they never found a medical explanation for the yellow-eyed fever. That's 'cause there ain't one."

"Okay, fine. But back then, they didn't have the medical knowledge, equipment, or experience that's available now. It could've been an undiagnosed disease sweeping through the miners. Or, maybe Tommy Donnelly was right and—" Based on the serious look Bob gave the empty can in his hands, he let it drop.

"Tommy Donnelly was right about many things, brother. But this wasn't one of them."

"How can you be so sure?"

Bob cleared his throat several times and gently set the can beside him. He crossed an ankle over a knee with a painful-sounding crack and settled back. Story time. But not before he popped open another beer. *Spulit.*

"I've never told anyone this before, Dennis. And you can take it or leave it. Wouldn't be surprised if you think I'm a crazed lunatic and never come back again, but—"

"That's not gonna happen, Bob."

"Quiet, brother. Let me finish before I lose my nerve..."

Ahanu didn't let any grass grow under his feet after he left Claire Donnelly. Of course, he didn't put a lot of stock in the old tribal tales, but there was no sense in taking a chance. "Borrowing trouble" his momma called it.

Clouds rolled in faster than a fish swimming downstream. Spring had been an endless grind of rain and thunderstorms. From the looks of things, the April showers planned on sticking around for a while.

He was still a couple of miles from his parents' farm and hastened his pace, attempting to outrun nature and beat the storm. The woods lay in front of him, a shortcut that could easily shave off a half-mile. He didn't know the woods well, generally steered clear of them for that reason. And even though folks said he had "one foot in white man's land," he'd inherited an unerring sense of direction from his family.

The mill engine's constant chugging carried across the land. The burning stench of industrialization filled his nose. When he entered the woods, the machinery's thrumming vanished. The smell disappeared as if God had dropped a blanket over the woods. All odors. This time of year the woods should have been vibrant with the fragrance of newly bloomed foliage, but all he smelled was his own musky perspiration.

Above him, tree limbs entwined, greeting one another like long lost relatives. Fallen leaves, not yet reintegrated with the earth, crunched underfoot. He welcomed the noise, his intrusion into the woods the only sound around. *Strange.*

Something fluttered to his right. Two feet away stood a blackbird, larger than any he'd ever seen and darker than night. Unfazed by Ahanu's presence, it balanced on one foot, craning its head. As Ahanu passed, the bird kept watch, nearly human with curiosity.

Caw, caw, caw.

The shrill cry lit a fire in Ahanu's stride. He ran through the woods, and in his speed, he lost track of the man-made path. The bird's shrieks followed him. He couldn't see it, but he heard it as if it rested on his shoulder. Lost, he turned in a circle, hoping to gain his bearings. He felt like a small boy again, his trumped-up teenage courage dried up and blown away.

Just a bird, he thought. *Nothing but a bird. But the way it watched me...*

Cold sweat chilled him. *What if the bird's following me?* A silly thought, for sure, but he looked over his shoulder anyway.

He strained to catch a breeze and gauge its direction, an indicator of the way out of the woods. The acrid smells of the Gannaway mines suddenly overwhelmed him, stronger than before, so powerful he felt like he'd stumbled into one of the mines.

"Ahanu..."

A whisper. Someone whispered his name. Maybe a trick of the wind, but *dear God, there is no wind.*

"Ahanu..."

This time it was clearer, his name drawn out, almost like a song verse. He spun around, expecting to see one of his peers laughing at his fright. But it didn't *feel* like a game.

A shadow detached itself from the other shadows. A figure, a man, swaying by the trees.

"...'cause the old man is deaddd..."

A song, hollow and sharp, a nail scraping against tin.

"You would see a brand new mannn..."

"Hello? Who's there?"

When the man stepped forward, the torch on his mining helmet lit. Orange light, the color of Hell, washed over him. Ahanu froze. He recognized the Kendricks boy. Same goofy grin and unruly red hair. But in place of his eyes were two dark, wet cavities. A red line rippled across his throat. Blood split the skin and trickled down onto his overalls.

"Come join us, Ahanu..."

Ahanu stumbled back against a tree. "Get...*away* from me!"

As terrifying as Kendricks looked, his laughter nearly stopped Ahanu's heart. Ahanu clamped his hands over his ears, trying to block the gasping croak, the sound of a man gargling his own blood.

Ahanu scooted around the tree, putting the barrier between them. But he had to look again. Just *had* to.

Kendricks' throat opened wider, invisible fingers ripping at the skin. A dark red torrent spewed forth and kept spewing. The miner's head bounced in a lazy half-circle like a sprung jack-in-the-box.

A primal hand of terror gripped Ahanu's guts and squeezed. *"Stop* it. Please, stop—"

With a moist snap, Kendricks' head detached and fell back. His helmet tumbled to the ground and rolled to Ahanu's feet. The torch extinguished with a *"tch."*

Ahanu's eyes adjusted to the darkness within seconds, but it felt like an eternity. He could barely make out Kendrick's silhouette, blacker than the surrounding shadows. Just enough to see the headless man's body standing.

Oh my God, he's still standing!

Grasping for the helmet at his feet, Ahanu latched onto it. Cradling it under one arm, he struck a match and lit the torch. He held it out at arm's length like a rifle.

Kendricks had his back to Ahanu. Dangling by ropey tendons, his head swayed against his back. His mouth gaped open, twisting into an upside-down smile.

"Come join usssss..."

Ahanu screamed. At least he thought he did. Maybe it had been Kendricks. He ran, fists pumping, feet stamping over the ground cover. He didn't know his location, couldn't be sure of his direction. Didn't *care.* All that mattered was putting as much distance as possible between him and the dead man. Branches lashed at his face and arms like a demon's fingernails. A low-lying limb bit into his forehead, knocking him to the ground. Ignoring the pain, he bolted to his feet and continued. He galloped like a runaway stallion, his heart thumping to keep up.

It must've been an hour before he reached the clearing. And during that time, every last minute, he heard the singing. Always one step behind him. Singing from a man who couldn't *possibly* be alive.

Dennis struggled to suppress a laugh. Bob's grim demeanor made it pretty clear a laugh wouldn't be appreciated.

"Bob, you can't expect me to believe this story."

Bob stared past Dennis, his eyes unfocused. "Thought you'd have that reaction, brother. Probably way too early for you to hear that tale."

"So...you saw a ghost? Of the Kendricks boy?"

"I did."

"Okay. But...ghosts aren't real. Maybe you heard about Kendricks's suicide and your imagination—"

"Imagine *this!*" Dennis flinched, half-expecting Bob to lob another beer can his way. "I had no idea what happened to George Kendricks at that time. It happened that morning, and I was at school all day. *On the reservation.* How else do you explain I knew he had no eyes...and a cut throat?"

"I don't know, Bob. I really don't."

"Yeah, well, I can see you're still a non-believer. But I know what I saw. When I got home, I heard Kendricks killed himself. And all the gory details of how. Because of the yella-eyed fever."

"The yellow-eyed fever again. So you're telling me this Indian curse caused miners to see ghosts, kill people... then turn into ghosts themselves?"

"That's about right, yeah." Bob hitched up his shoulders and sighed. "No one ever much talked about it, just knew it was bad."

"If you didn't have the yellow-eyed fever, how did you see Kendricks's ghost?"

Bob stood, placed his hands in the small of his back, and stretched. "Some folks are just more attuned to the spiritual world, brother. Reckon I'm one of 'em."

"Huh." Dennis drew his hand over his mouth to hide his grin.

Picking up a blowtorch, Bob made his way into the front yard. "So you seen anything you wanna talk about yet, brother?"

Dennis considered, and said, "No. Nothing that can't be explained away by chat rats. Or Stokes, maybe."

Bob's look of disappointment struck Dennis, damn near heartbreaking in its intensity. "End of today's lesson, then. Come back when you believe."

"How's your research goin', Dr. Lipstein?" Gannaway sat across from Dennis, acting like a fidgety child with a secret to tell. His inexplicable smile—a leer, almost—unnerved Dennis.

"It's coming along. That's why I'm here."

"Ah!" Gannaway uncapped a bottle on his desk and poured a two-fingered drink into a shot glass. Dennis hadn't seen the bottle on his previous visit. He'd definitely remember it, being acutely aware of such things. "Have a drink, Dr. Lipstein. These warm Kansas days makes a man thirsty."

A single bubble in the golden liquid floated to the top and popped. The phantom sensation of alcohol tickled his throat and warmed his chest, haunting him. The only "ghost" he believed in. Six months ago, alcohol had been his only friend, helping him through the worst part of his life. Sometimes he missed their acquaintance, longed for a re-union. Just one more time to reminisce about the good old days. *No, Goddamnit.* He'd said goodbye to his so-called friend, slammed the door, and never looked back.

"No thanks. I don't drink." The lack of conviction in his own voice troubled him. Not a good sign. He stole a few more glances at the tempting glass like a kid sneaking up on a firecracker with a questionable fuse.

"I see." Gannaway recapped the bottle, keeping his gaze locked on Dennis. Dennis shifted in his chair, feeling like a specimen under Gannaway's microscope. "Please tell me what I can do to help."

It bothered Dennis that Gannaway hadn't touched the brandy either. Almost as if he knew about Dennis's past, playing a twisted mind game. "We'd discussed the possibility of my going into one of your mines for some samples. I'm ready now. Just letting you know."

Gannaway's lips twisted into a grimace. "Well, Dr. Lipstein, you know the mines are flooded. When the government closed 'em down, we shut off the pumps. No sense in going down...'less you got scuba gear."

"I know shutting the mines down is a long process. I've been told you still have equipment down there you're try-ing to bring back up. And I know for a fact there's at least one mine still open."

Gannaway dropped a hand on a miniature statue of a gold derrick sitting on his desk. He stroked it gently with a lover's touch. "Where you get your information, boy?"

Judging by the way his status changed from "Doctor" to "boy," Dennis knew he'd struck a nerve. "My bosses. They've filled me in."

"Hm. I see. The government. Well, I reckon there ain't no keepin' anything from Uncle Sam, now, is there?"

"I reckon not." Dennis meant no insult by mimicking Gannaway's diction, it just slipped out. Being around the locals, he found it easy to fall into Kansas slang. "Anything you can do to help would be greatly appreciated."

"We can probably get you down in one of the mines tomorrow. Say, noonish? I'll have a few of my men meet you at the main gate then."

"I really don't think it's necessary for your men—"

"Oh, the hell it *ain't* necessary, boy. I can't have you traipsin' all over my property and fallin' down a hole! I don't need any more damn *government* problems." His hand stroked the derrick faster and harder. Dennis half-expected it to ejaculate oil. "You meet my men there or you *ain't* goin' down. You hear me?"

"Loud and clear. And thank you. I'll see your men at noon."

Since Gannaway insisted on giving Dennis an escort, maybe he should enlist an aide of his own. For reasons he couldn't quite pinpoint, a bodyguard made him feel safer. Or maybe he just wanted to see Therese again. But dangerous or not, he knew he didn't trust Gannaway.

The diner was almost identical to the one on the outskirts of Gannaway. Same long-faced, John Deere cap-wearing patrons. Stained menus promising greasy food and bitter coffee. Dennis thought it best to meet somewhere away from Gannaway, where eavesdropping ears and curious eyes were at a minimum. He needn't have bothered. With his long hair, scraggly beard, and faded jeans, he couldn't help but be the center attraction. *Step right up and see the West Coast hippie.*

When Therese entered, she mercifully drew the locals' attention away from him. She glided through the aisle with perfect poise and determined confidence, a striking woman impossible to miss. She slid into the booth and hit him with her dazzling smile. "Surprised to hear from you. Thought you didn't need my help."

"It's a man's prerogative to change his mind."

"Think you got that backward."

"It should go both ways. You ever hear of 'men's lib'?"

Therese buried her grin into the menu. Hard to tell with her dark complexion, but Dennis thought he spotted a blush rising in her cheeks.

"So I traveled twenty miles to come to this fabulous place?"

"It's Kansas, Dennis. What do you expect? Another thirty miles down the road, there's a Howard Johnson's. If that meets up to your lofty Big City expectations."

"No, no, this'll do fine. It's the company that's important." Sudden temptation to grab her hand flitted through his mind. Instead, he gripped the menu tighter.

"Tried the coffee yet?"

"Nope. Haven't been that daring. Maybe I'll stick with water. Can't go wrong there." Then again, that might not be true. Maybe Gannaway's contaminants had traveled into the Drexell, Kansas water supply.

"So...what help do you need? And what changed your mind?"

"I'm going into the mines tomorrow. Gannaway was adamant his men were coming with me." Leaning in, Dennis lowered his voice. "I don't know what it is, Therese, but I got a bad feeling about Kyle Gannaway."

"Good instincts will take you far. What're you worried about exactly?"

"Not sure. Maybe nothing. But someone's been playing games with me, trying to spook me. Someone scratched up my van and chased me by the mines a couple nights ago."

"You think Gannaway's worried you might find something out?"

"Either that, or the chat rats are being territorial. But I think Gannaway's still operating his mines."

"You mentioned this before. You sure this time? It's a serious accusation. There've been rumors that Gannaway's still mining, but nothing's been proven. Or no one's had the balls to push the issue."

The waitress approached, looking like she drew the short

straw on serving them. After taking their orders, she served an eye roll with a snap of her pad on the side.

"Tough crowd, these Kansans." Dennis bit the bullet and told Theresa what he'd seen in the mines several nights ago.

"If this is true, Dennis, Gannaway needs to be reported. He's bleeding my people dry...literally."

"I agree. But we need more proof. I'd like you to come with me tomorrow. Maybe keep an eye out for any current mining operations. You know more about it than I do." Feeling compelled to add "and I'd like you to be my bodyguard," he bit his tongue.

"Not sure if I'd know a drill from a refrigerator, but I suppose I can try. Especially if it means Gannaway's still depleting the land. I'd love to put the bastard away."

"Okay. Now, I have to warn you, I—"

The waitress dropped the plates in front of them and scurried away. Dennis stopped the wobbling plate with a finger.

"Warnings are never good." Therese bit into her burger. Setting it back down, she wiped her mouth with a napkin, visibly trying to banish the aftertaste. "Burgers aren't safe."

Even though Dennis's stomach grumbled from hunger, he heeded Therese's words. He had to trust someone. And he implicitly trusted Therese. "Damn. What I wouldn't do for a good meal here in the boonies."

"Enough of the Kansas put-downs. You were gonna warn me about something?"

"I didn't tell Gannaway you'd be coming along. I imagine it'll be quite a surprise to his men."

"Huh. I like surprises. Except in my food."

"Can't say as I agree with you there. I'd rather know what's coming, when it's coming, and why it's coming. Scientific to the core, that's me, I reckon."

"'I reckon?' You're putting too much time in with the locals! We need to get you some culture before you turn into one of them. Maybe the Howard Johnson's next time?"

"You mean you're asking me out on another date? To Howard Johnson's?"

"You just don't quit. I didn't say anything about—"

"You said 'next time.' At the Howard Johnson's. I'd love for you to guide me to culture at the HoJo's."

"Play your cards right, mister, and we'll see. Now quit derailing our business. What time tomorrow?"

"Noon. At the front gates. But do me a favor? Show up thirty minutes early? I don't want to go in without you." Fear crawled down his back. Crept up on him like a silent killer. Therese's assured presence, though, gave him some small peace of mind. Surely if Gannaway put his men up to something, they wouldn't pull it with her there.

"Okay. It's a date."

"Wow. Another date? Heavy."

She shook her head while scooting out of the booth. Still, her contrary smile seemed genuine. "Give it up, Lipstein."

Before she left, she shot Dennis a look over her shoulder. An invitation? The waitress snatched up the ten dollar bill as soon as he tossed it down. Dennis brushed by her, hurrying for the door. "Therese, wait!"

Dennis ran toward the car before she could back out. Obviously startled, she cranked down the window. "Our date's ended, Dennis."

"I just want to thank you—"

"Oh, shut up." Snaking out a hand, she grabbed his neck and pulled him toward her. Her lips played over his, exploring, her tongue teasingly darting into his mouth. A breathtaking floral scent, so strong he could taste it, flooded his senses. She tasted fresh as pure spring water. As his fingers dove into her hair, she broke the embrace, holding up a hand like a traffic cop. "That's enough. For now."

Dennis fell back, helpless as a smitten schoolboy. "Wow... man." Realizing how foolish he sounded, he attempted to save face. "Wasn't expecting that."

"What? Haven't you heard of women's lib?"

"Sure. Just never been attacked by it before. I mean...

in a good way."

"So, you've been attacked by a lot of women's libbers? You a chauvinist?"

"No, of course not." Not the wittiest of comebacks, Dennis knew, but Therese confounded him. No science on earth could explain her. But exploring those uncharted territories seemed like a very worthy expedition. "You, um, made—"

"I'll see you tomorrow, Dennis. Move before I run your foot over."

As soon as Dennis dutifully hopped back, she sped out of the parking lot. She kicked up gravel and dust and tossed out one last wave with her delectable fingers.

For the first time in a long time, he felt optimistic, wondering where the possibilities might lead. Excitement bulldozed over and through him. Yet a sensation of terror dampened his enthusiasm. He didn't feel quite ready to date. And he couldn't ask Therese to get involved with an unstable wreck of a human being. With a laugh, he realized how ridiculous he sounded. Jumping the gun. Maybe she's only looking for sex. Either way, emotional and physical intimacy felt *much* more frightening than tales of ghosts and yellow-eyed fever.

Chapter Thirteen

1935...

On Sunday afternoon, the small graveyard overflowed with miners and their families. The new electric tower loomed behind them, the red light blinking at the top like God's mournful eye. Thunder rumbled, the clouds considering when to unleash their tears.

Most of the men hadn't worked with George long enough to know him, but it filled Tommy's heart with pride so many had shown up on their day off.

Mrs. Kendricks, George's only surviving relative, sat in front of the freshly dug grave. His daddy had passed away from miner's lung. She looked tired and cried out. Tommy supposed, even after such a tragedy, one had only so many tears to shed.

Tommy and five other volunteers lowered the coffin into the ground with ropes guiding the course. Big Ed, huffing like a steam engine, gave Tommy a look, one he couldn't decipher. A chill ran down Tommy's back when he remembered George's hand, flapping up in the back of Durwood's truck. He kept his gaze locked on the coffin, unblinking, until his eyes burned, an anchor to the present.

Thump.

Tommy heard it clear as day. But the others kept about their business, dragging the ropes up, snakes slithering out of the earth.

Thump.

Tommy's heart hammered in tandem with the sound. He straightened, stiff as a board. Cold sweat prickled the back of his neck. Something had bumped inside the coffin.

Thump. Thump.

He couldn't be certain, wouldn't swear to it, but the coffin lid jumped, hopped like a toad. Wood cracked. Nails inched up with a wrenching grind. Tommy took a step back, bumped into Big Ed's gut. Ed grabbed his shoulders, steadied him. Tommy kept his chin planted on his chest, afraid to look Ed in the eye. Afraid of what Ed might see there. *Madness.*

Thump. Rrrrnchhh.

Tommy couldn't help himself. He had to see, had to know. Had to assure himself he hadn't gone around the bend. One step forward and he looked into the hole.

Oh my God...

The coffin lid slid off. A bloated hand rose, propped the lid up against the dirt wall. George sat up, white as a bleached sheet. *Smiling.* His head tilted back. Black holes had replaced his eyes, and Tommy saw something deep inside, something horrible. Red flames licked out, melting George's face. His hand raised toward Tommy, a final salute. Just like he'd done in the back of Durwood's truck.

Tommy sucked in his breath, held it. Fought the urge to scream. His eyes clamped down tight, so tight his skull hurt. Ed still had his hands on Tommy's shoulders, gave him a shake. Slowly, he opened his eyes. The coffin lid was back in place, keeping George locked down where he was meant to be.

But really, Tommy knew it'd never happened.

All the supernatural nonsense the men had been chatting about the last couple of days must have crawled its way into his mind.

He rejoined Claire and squeezed her hand firmly, more for his support than hers. She'd been his rock throughout the weekend, remaining strong even when he broke down. Not since his own daddy's funeral had he been in such bad shape. Guilt gnawed at him like a hidden gut worm. Had he not broken George's fingers, maybe they wouldn't be burying the boy.

Claire kept glancing at Mr. Gannaway. Head bent humbly, Gannaway fixed his gaze onto the ground, his manservant standing directly behind him. As usual, his wife hadn't attended the funeral.

After Reverend Charles delivered some words (short on comfort, long on the sins of suicide), he introduced Mr. Gannaway, another tradition at a miner's funeral.

"Friends...saddened relatives..."

Mrs. Kendricks let out an anguished howl and buried her face in her hands.

Undeterred, Gannaway continued. "...my employees... today, we've lost another comrade, someone we'll all miss dearly. A tragedy. Simply, a tragedy..." He raised his head, sticking out his sharp chin. Tommy knew the gesture too well. Time for Gannaway's rallying speech. And it bit at Tommy's craw. Had Gannaway listened to him earlier, they might not be here. Or maybe he needed a scapegoat to lighten his own guilt. "It's always tragic when we have to bury our own, but life in Gannaway goes on. The Gannaway Lead and Smelting Company carries on. The work we're doing makes our country stronger, providing safety for our families and loved ones. We honor this dear, departed boy today. But we also honor him by going back to work. Showing him how we do things in Gannaway. Tomorrow, when you're working the mines, give it a little extra effort. Do it for...ah..." Gannaway stuttered and stopped, looking toward his manservant as if for enlightenment. A smile lit up his face when he saw Mrs. Kendricks staring woefully at him. Obviously, he'd forgotten George's name. "Do it for George Kendricks. We all know that's the way he would've wanted it."

Gannaway trotted over to Mrs. Kendricks and enveloped her hands within his own. "Mrs. Kendricks, I'm so very sorry. Let me know if there's anything *else* I can do." Gannaway emphasized "else" as he always did when consoling family members. Tommy supposed it was just his little reminder how generous he'd already been.

Gannaway turned to the mourners and waved like a politician. "Carry on, folks. Be careful, and I'll see y'all in the mines tomorrow."

Always the same speech, rarely modified. Tommy glanced down at Claire. Her attention remained focused on Gannaway. Her mouth wavered as if she wanted to say something but couldn't find the right words. When she took a tentative step forward, Tommy squeezed her hand again. Looking like she awoke from a dream, she offered Tommy a small smile.

They filed out of the graveyard gate one by one. A man stood against a nearby tree, one foot hiked up behind him. Tommy didn't recognize him, but he had "out-of-town city slicker" written all over him. No locals wore their hair combed back with enough grease to start a brush fire. He straightened his fancy suit jacket, too warm by a mile for the humid weather, and approached Tommy.

"Excuse me, Mr. Donnelly?" His accent confirmed Tommy's suspicions. East coast, he guessed. The man extended his hand well before he reached Tommy.

Tommy took his hand. "Yes, sir. But it's 'Tommy.' Who might you be?"

"I'm Kenneth Dickinson with the International Union of Mine, Mill, and Smelter Workers. I'd like to discuss certain...opportunities with you."

Claire dug her fingernails into Tommy's palm. Tommy ignored her, furious at the man's poorly timed intrusion. "Claire, why don't you go on and see if there's anything we can do for Mrs. Kendricks." When she hesitated, he released her hand. "Go on, honey, I'll be with you in a minute. Promise." She left, scuttling sideways, watching Tommy and the union man.

Tommy wheeled, ready to cut the union man down at the knees. He had to be either new at his job or the stupidest union man alive. Not only did he show inexcusable disrespect by bringing up business at a funeral, Gannaway stood within earshot. Tommy would have to make this look good. He raised his voice to a loud growl. "You listen here, Mr. Dickinson. I don't know *how* you got wind of my name or what you've heard. We just buried one of our men, if you can't tell. And for you to come into everyone's time of grief, wantin' to discuss Big City unions, well, sir, that don't sit right with me, not one bit! Gannaway miners ain't interested in unionizing!"

Dickinson's color faded, his air of confidence dissipating faster than a nail-struck tire. "I'm mighty sorry to be making your acquaintance on this...terrible occasion, Tommy, but—"

"Maybe you'd best get your ears checked, mister. I said we *ain't* interested." Tommy grabbed Dickinson's jacket lapels and yanked him close. He whispered in his ear, "Tuesday night at the pub down the street a ways. Nine o'clock."

The man seemed startled by Tommy's sudden change of mind, but kept his voice low. "What's the name of the pub?"

"Pub."

"I'll be there," he said, with a small smirk.

Tommy gave Dickinson a hard shove for show and rejoined the crowd. Still fuming at the union man's brazen appearance, Tommy desperately wanted to physically escort him from the grounds. But the union man dangled a carrot, one Tommy'd been thinking about nibbling on for the last couple days. It could be the turn-around his men needed.

He glanced over at Gannaway. Even though his hand rested on Mrs. Kendricks arm, he held his gaze firmly on Tommy. Gannaway gave a half-mast grin, like a man unsure of what he'd just witnessed. Tommy thought he'd been pretty convincing, though, and he didn't think Gannaway had heard the whispered conversation.

Tommy didn't realize Harvey Quick had been within

earshot until it was too late.

Kaya stared at Claire as though she'd sprouted wings, but agreed to cover for her at the boarding house Monday morning as long as the owners agreed.

The farther Claire ventured through the reservation, the deeper her hopes sank. Maybe she should have listened to Kaya. What she'd planned seemed impossible, like parting the sea. Then again, miracles happened.

She spotted Gannaway's mansion a mile away. His car gleamed under the sun like a black jewel. *He's home.*

Tommy would *not* approve of her visiting his boss, but she'd do anything to save her husband's life. Surely that would buy some good will with Tommy when he eventually found out. And this being Gannaway, it was guaranteed he would.

But now an entirely new set of problems filled her with worry—that union man who'd confronted Tommy yesterday. She'd heard stories about union violence breaking out across the country. Still, if the men went on strike, the yellow-eyed curse might be lifted.

She knocked at the front door. Gannaway's tall, thin sliver of a manservant, Steffen, answered the knock. The man chilled her to the bone. Whenever she saw him in town, Claire looked away. His lifeless, marble-like eye made her uncomfortable. She wasn't in town, though. Now she needed to enter his territory. She forced herself to lock eyes with his. At least, his good one.

"Yes?"

"Hello. I'm Mrs. Tommy Donnelly. Claire. Is Mr. Gannaway at home?"

Steffen grinned, his pointed teeth lining up like crooked gravestones. "Let me inquire." He closed the door and left her standing on the porch, mulling over her conflicting thoughts.

On the other side of the house, workers hammered and hollered. She tried to imagine what it'd be like to live in a house this size, where her children wouldn't have to share a bedroom with Mother Donnelly. A house with indoor plumbing and a servant to answer your door seemed outlandish, really, yet appealing in a way she'd probably never experience. The daydream brought a smile to her lips. Someday maybe, after Tommy graduated from college. She kept her fantasy in check, though. Four bedrooms would do just fine.

The door swung open. "Follow me," said the manservant.

"Thank you." She followed Steffen down the hallway and gasped at the fine furniture and decorations filling the rooms. The room with the long dining table looked bigger than their entire house.

Steffen rapped on a door.

"Come in."

Claire forced a smile as Steffen retreated, his arms motionless at his sides.

Mr. Gannaway startled her when she opened the door. She hadn't expected him to be so close, close enough for Claire to smell his cologne. "Oh. Sorry. You gave me a fright. Hello, Mr. Gannaway, we've never been introduced. I'm Claire—"

"Of course, of course, my dear! I know who you are. Tommy Donnelly's lovely wife, Claire. And I must add you are a pretty little thing." Claire couldn't help but blush. She felt her complexion burning as red as her locks. The way Gannaway's eyes roved up and down her body, as if she were a cow being sized up at auction, unsettled her. "Please, have a seat." He settled into a chair behind his desk, gestured toward a facing chair.

"Thank you for seeing me, Mr. Gan—"

"Please, Claire. To my friends, I'm Kyle."

"Okay, then, Kyle." Even though Momma always taught her to treat prominent men with respect, she let slip a small giggle. Such boldness made her feel brave and strong. It fed her lioness needs.

"Now...what can I do for you?"

"Mr. Ganna—" He raised his eyebrows, visually chastising her. "Kyle. You know there've been... incidents down in your mines. Certain deaths..." Claire's throat tightened. What she had to say—to ask—suddenly seemed impractical, nothing more than a hopeless request. She knew she couldn't ask Mr. Gannaway to stop operations, but she thought she could appeal to his humanity. Even though John Blackbird was in no physical state to reason with, maybe she could persuade Gannaway to make peace with the Kwashau tribe and the curse would be lifted. Now she felt like the world's largest fool, ashamed even. "I shouldn't be here—"

"Nonsense. Say what's on your mind, girl."

Claire folded her hands and clamped down on her fingers, fortifying herself. If she didn't follow through, she'd regret it forever. "The yellow-eyed fever," she blurted out.

Gannaway leaned back, falling into a disinterested pose. "Nothing but a superstitious pile of horse...*dung.*"

"But it's true, Mr. Gannaway. George Kendricks, Karl—"

Gannaway didn't just laugh. He roared, and Claire jumped. He moved out from behind his desk and scooted into a seat next to her. "Little lady, Doc Wilkins says it's nothin' but a matter of how men react to being underground, nothing we can do about it. Ain't no damn—excuse my ungentlemanly language—such thing as the yellow-eyed fever. It's just the men tryin' to get outta work. Trust me when—"

"It isn't superstition. And it's not the men shirkin' their responsibilities." Wavering on the verge of tears, she wouldn't allow herself to spill over. "It's an Indian curse put on the mines. I'm worried about Tommy."

Gannaway's hand landed on Claire's knee, jolting her again. Her momma's words echoed in her mind, *Sometimes you have to let men give you a li'l touch now and then. Makes them happy and we lady folk get what we want.*

Patting her knee now, Gannaway finished with a squeeze. Claire wondered how much of Momma's teaching she should disregard.

"Now, why don't you and I put this silliness behind us? We're friends, am I right? There ain't no Indian curse. And if you're worried about your husband...then maybe I could give him Mr. Darling's job in the office. How would that suit you, little lady?"

"It'd...be fine for Tommy, but what about the other—"

"Whoa, whoa, there, little lady!" He held his hands up. "One step at a time. I'm a businessman. For every good deed, I 'spect to be paid back." Another knee squeeze. Claire finally realized what he meant. She brushed his hand away and jumped to her feet.

"Mr. Gannaway, I *sincerely* hope I'm misreadin' your intentions here. If I am, I surely do apologize. But if you're suggesting that I...do unfaithful, sinful—"

With a hitch of his trousers, Gannaway stood. "Young lady, I'm not suggestin' anything. I'm telling you...you want something for your husband, you have to pay for it." He patted her bottom.

Smack.

She regretted slapping him the instant she did it. But not much. "I'd strongly suggest you *not* touch me again! If Tommy found out what you just—"

"Oh, hell, honey! Ain't nobody gonna find out! Think of the fun—"

She lashed out at his face again. Two red welts glowed on his cheek. The friendly, welcoming Gannaway vanished. His eyebrows arched down. His face contorted in seething fury. "I let you get away with one tap, little lady. But now you've made a mistake!" He walked toward her, backing her into a corner.

"I just came to talk to you about the yellow-eyed curse! John Blackbird put the spell on the mines 'cause you took away his land and his daughter! Everything he cared about and—" She stopped, fully expecting to feel the lash of Gannaway's hand.

Instead, he returned to his chair. "Get out of here. Now. And take your bullshit talk with you."

"But...Mr. Gannaway, if—"

"I said get out! Get out *now!* And *never* come back! You've made more than one mistake, little lady! And you tell your *goddamn* husband if he even mentions unionizing, that's just one mistake too *many* for me to tolerate!"

Claire raced through the door and down the hallway. Behind her, she heard a sudden clatter and an explosion of glass.

She reached the field and tripped. She thrust her hands out to try and break her fall, but her elbows buckled. Her face landed in the mud, numb pain surging through her jaw. She pulled up on all fours. Her hands slid away, pitching her back into the mud. She rolled over on her back and cried. The sun tightened the mud on her face and pulled her skin taut. *Enough.* She climbed to her feet. She felt dirty inside and out, no better than a filthy trollop. She picked at the scabs of dried mud and wiped away tears of shame, limping as she slowly made her way across the reservation. She knew she'd just made a mistake. A very bad mistake.

Gannaway's bleeding knuckles didn't bother him. Neither did the broken glass frame holding his photograph with Teddy Roosevelt. Just trash now, easy enough to replace. But the goddamn Donnelly family bothered him no end, trying to undermine him. *Goddamn woman.* The whole town owed him. As God created man in his own likeness, he'd fashioned the town of Gannaway. People prayed to God to show their appreciation. He didn't ask for that, but he was damn sure owed a show of proper respect. *Damn worthless ingrates.*

He yanked open the study door and caught the tail-end of Naira's robe whipping up the stairwell. *Another god-damn troublemaker.* Eavesdropping again. And all this horse shit about yellow-eyed fever was her fault. He'd deal with her in a minute.

"Steffen," he bellowed.

Ghost-like, Steffen stepped out of the shadows. "Sir?"

"You got our goddamn man ready to be at that bar?"

"Yes, sir."

"We need to put an end to this *horse shit.* I mean now!"

The rare occasions when Steffen broke into a smile gave Gannaway pause—a facial blanket hiding his true thoughts, whatever they may be. But he'd never owned a more capable man, and more importantly, Steffen remained loyal, unlike the rest of this shit-hole town. "Make sure he is. You be there in case he gets cold feet."

Another skull-like smile. Sometimes Gannaway thought Steffen enjoyed certain aspects of the job too much. "Yes, sir."

Gannaway bumped into his manservant in his hurry to mount the steps.

Locked again. He pounded on the bedroom door. "Naira! You open this goddamn door now! I'll knock it down if I have to!"

The door swung open. Naira stood trembling, quiet as death. But her eyes held another message. *Absolute contempt.*

"You was listenin' in again, weren't you? How many times I gotta tell you a man's business ain't yours?"

"You don't need to tell me again. I understand." She kept her voice controlled and complacent. The way he expected her to.

"How much did you hear?"

"I heard...the woman begging you for her husband's life." She backed away and lay down on her bed. At least he'd trained her to know how to properly respond.

"And this yellow-eyed fever horse shit! This woman says your daddy's spreadin' the word he placed a curse on me and my mines! What do you know 'bout *that?*"

"Maybe you should listen to her. I believe there's truth in what she says."

"You ain't gonna tell me what to *do!* 'Specially based on that *horse shit!*" He crossed the room, his shadow falling over her motionless body. A blinding headache—something that occurred more frequently these days—stabbed spikes into his brain. "So I think you need to spread word these yellow-eyed fever stories are just that! Stories!" His fist rose, even though he didn't remember raising it. It, too, had been trained properly.

"Yes." Some years ago, she'd stopped calling him by his Christian name. She didn't call him anything anymore, really. Didn't matter. Just as long as she knew her place. "I'll do as you say. But they're not just stories."

"Goddamn it!" Naira winced before the first blow landed.

A "kangaroo court" seemed like a good idea at the time. The men always enjoyed them. It would soften the blow of George's death, not to mention help raise a little money for Mrs. Kendricks. Besides, what Gannaway didn't know went on in the mines wouldn't hurt him.

Tommy donned the cardboard crown crafted by his children and sat astride Tulip, the men's favorite mule. Tommy suspected the men liked Tulip because she took after them in many ways. Ornery and foul-natured, Tulip lowered her head and kicked her back legs in protest, and Tommy struggled to stay astride her.

"And, now, please bring forth Earl. Earl?"

Earl strutted forward, wearing a sheepish grin. The men cheered and hooted.

"What say you, Big Ed?"

Ed unrolled an old newspaper and pretended to read from it. All for show, of course. Everyone knew Ed couldn't read. "Earl, you smelly bastard..." Laughter rose through the stope, something Tommy hadn't heard down there in a while. "...you're so stinky, the fellas say they can't stand to work next to you."

"Hm. This is a serious mining crime. I, Judge Tommy, fine you one dollar. And hereby order you to take more baths."

Earl plopped a bill into the bucket at Tulip's hooves. Usually, the men grumbled about letting go of that kind of money, but they knew the favor would be returned when their time came. *If they're that unlucky,* thought Tommy.

"Donald. Big Ed, please bring Donald front and center!" The men got a kick out of Tommy's posturing, and he played it to the hilt. It was the only time he felt comfortable ordering them around.

Ed hitched an arm around Donald and dragged him toward Tommy.

"Big Ed, please relay this miner's crimes."

Ed unfolded the newspaper again, enjoying his turn as the royal jester. "Donald, you dirty son-of-a-bitch. You're charged with soldering shut a greenhorn's lunchbox." This time the men's whistles and cheers resounded in approval over Donald's actions.

"But...we all do that."

"Then they'll be in front of my court soon." Tommy looked out over the crowd and added, "Verily." Laughter rang out even though Tommy suspected not many of them understood the word. "One dollar, Sir Donald, and an apology to the greenhorn!" Donald cashed in at the bucket although he shied away from a formal apology.

"Next up, please bring me Jimmy D., not to be confused with Jim R. up above!"

Jimmy shuffled forward, his head hung low, playing along with the charade. "Ed, what are Jimmy D.'s crimes against his fellow miners?"

"Whistling in the mine..."

A hush settled over the miners. It took a moment for Tommy to understand why. *Superstition.* Another mining superstition, whistling in a mine invited death. Warily, the men drifted away, picking up their tools as they left. They eyed one another, wondering who would be next. Tommy heard "yellow-eyed fever" frequently repeated, like a frightening children's verse.

Tommy dismounted Tulip. Court had been adjourned.

Holding out half his bread-and-butter sandwich as an offering, Tommy saddled up next to Big Ed on his favorite boulder. Fancy white bread being such a rarity, he knew Ed couldn't resist.

"That the good stuff?" he asked.

"The finest in the land," said Tommy.

Ed devoured it in three bites, followed by a thorough finger licking. "What's on your mind, Tommy?"

"Unions."

Ed groaned, but since he'd accepted the sandwich, Tommy knew he'd feel duty-bound to listen. "I don't think you should be pushin' for that."

"Why not? Ed, the men are dying down here. If we can make their lives better—maybe save some, even—how could unionizing be such a bad thing?"

"I just think it's a bad idea, I reckon. And Gannaway's gonna sure as shit fight you on it." He turned to face Tommy. "What would happen if the men striked? They ain't gonna be able to feed their families."

"For a little while, maybe. But the end goal is what counts. I think we can do it. I think we should do it."

Ed fell silent and picked at the mud on his boot heels. When he looked up, Tommy detected a glimmer of hope in his eyes. "You really think we can do it?"

"I do."

"And...how would we get started?"

"Already workin' on it. I'm meetin' a man down at the pub tomorrow night. Union man from the big city. Wants to talk opportunities. Ed, I need to know if I can count on you for support."

Ed looked out at his tired coworkers and finally nodded. "I've heard about them electric torches. Better masks."

"Health clinics especially for miners," Tommy added. "Better ventilation."

"Okay. But only 'cause of your daddy—"

"Oh, don't say all that again." Tommy rolled his eyes. "Do it for the men. For yourself."

"More and more like your daddy every day, you are. It goes against my gut...but what do you want me to do?"

"Spread the word to everyone you think will be friendly to the idea. But only the men you trust. I trust your gut. It's a good gut." He thumped Ed's belly with a flick of his finger. "Reckon I don't need to tell you to leave out Harvey Quick and his buddies."

"Reckon not." Ed took a look at Harvey in the distance and spit. "He's a goddamn rattlesnake."

"That he is. Tell the men to come on down to the pub at eight o'clock tomorrow night." Tommy stood, stretched, and rubbed his back. "I'm ready to get goin' on this."

"I can see that. Just be careful, Tommy."

"Ed, I work in a mine. Nothing up top's gonna get me."

What to do? What to say? All day long, Claire wrestled with what to tell her husband. She'd overstepped her boundaries, and she knew it. Women didn't seek out their husband's bosses for favors. She didn't regret it though, not one iota. Maybe it had been a poor decision—in fact, it had been an *awful* decision—but what if she hadn't tried it? At least, now she had no doubt she'd done everything she could to save Tommy and the other miners.

Still, she didn't want any secrets in their marriage. And she sure didn't want Gannaway presenting Tommy with a one-sided recounting of the events. If Tommy found out what Gannaway had suggested, he'd be fit to be tied. Tommy had that Irish temper smoldering inside him. He was usually a level-headed man. Something like this, though—oh, he'd fly into a rage for sure.

Tommy chased the children around their table, and Mother Donnelly nattered on about visiting Mrs. Kendricks that morning. Something about bringing her a warm potato dish. Claire couldn't hear her through the conflicting voices in her head.

Eventually, honesty won out, as awful and inevitable as the repercussions might be. Anxiety filled her. It couldn't wait for their nightly bedtime chat.

"Mother Donnelly, would you kindly look after the little ones, while their daddy and I take a walk?"

"Land's sake, it's stiflin' out, child. You gonna walk in this humidity?"

Lying on the floor with Margaret hoisted above him, Tommy looked puzzled but wisely stayed out of the women's debate.

Claire sighed and said, "You can smoke by the window while we're gone. If you open it."

Mother Donnelly grinned a near-toothless smile, one weaned on too many potatoes. She said to Tommy, "Don't be too long out there, now, you hear?" Without pause, she rolled a cigarette in anticipation.

They deposited kisses on both children's heads and strolled out into the clammy evening, hand in hand.

"Claire, what's this about?"

"You know me too well, Tommy Donnelly." They strolled on, Claire biding her time. Most folks were off their porches and inside their homes, fending off the humidity. But a nice breeze touched Claire's face and lifted her hair, giving her hope and a push. "I went to see Mr. Gannaway today."

Tommy stopped and turned. He raised her chin to look into her eyes. "Say that again."

"Oh, Tommy...I'm sorry. *Promise* me you won't get angry."

"Never with you, Claire. Never." His words calmed her even if they held uncertainty. As Claire hurried through her tale, Tommy never stopped for clarification or asked questions. She ended her story early, leaving out Gannaway's improper behavior. A decision she hadn't fully made until now. They had too much to lose—Tommy's job, their future. Their marriage? What if Tommy didn't believe her? *Blamed* her? She couldn't live with that. Withholding the truth from her husband carried a large burden, but one she could live with. Anything for her family.

She saw the disappointment in her husband's eyes. And it nearly brought her to her knees.

"I can't believe you did that, Claire." His voice remained calm, but it didn't disguise how he really felt. "I have to go apologize to Mr. Gannaway."

He turned back, and Claire grasped his arm. "No, Tommy, please don't!" He stopped, staring down at her hand. Her entire arm shook like a kite's tail in the wind. Caving his shoulders, he dipped his head like a man shamed into inaction and held her while she cried into his chest. "Please don't go see him, Tommy! I've already made a mess outta matters." She hiccupped out a few sighs and ended her crying jag. They remained silent, holding onto one another. Claire knew nothing—not Indian curses, Gannaway, not even a tornado—could ever tear them apart.

"Claire, you shouldn't make decisions like this without talking to me first. All this silliness about the yellow-eyed fever and whatnot. Mr. Gannaway probably thinks—"

"I know. I won't do it again. Just...leave it be. Please? There's no harm done, not really."

"Claire—"

"Leave it *be*, Tommy."

"I can't just—"

"I'm *afraid* for you!" She broke their embrace and rattled her fists at him. "I'm *afraid* of what he'll do to you! And what the yellow-eyed—"

"Claire!" He bunched her fists together and lowered them. "You need to stop with this superstitious nonsense.

Ain't no such thing. I can't believe you've been all over God's green earth, talkin' to witch doctors and Mr. Gannaway. You see what you're doin'? You're gettin' all worked up 'cause of what Kaya told you."

Optimism warmed her. She allowed a small smile to slip through. "Maybe you're right." Maybe she had worked herself into a frenzy over some old wives' tale meant to scare children. She saw death lurking in shadows even when it was sunny out.

"Course I am. There's no such thing as yellow-eyed fever. Just as there's no such thing as Santy Claus."

He lowered his voice and put a finger to his lips. "But don't tell T.J. and Margaret."

Claire giggled and hugged Tommy again. "You forgive me?"

"Always. And don't you worry about me. Mr. Gannaway ain't gonna do anything. He needs me. Besides I'm meetin' a union man tomorrow night. That'll fix the so-called yellow-eyed fever up but good."

While Tommy blustered with Irish bravado, Claire felt her new-found optimism float away like a barely recalled dream. *Unions.* Gannaway had sworn he'd never tolerate them.

She pulled Tommy in tighter as if her life depended on it. Or maybe her husband's. "You'd better come back to me, Tommy Donnelly."

"I will, Claire Donnelly. Nothing will keep me from you."

"You'd better see it doesn't."

Claire closed her eyes to shut out the unbidden vision of Harold Durwood, vulture-like in his black suit, knocking at her front door. In her vision, he jerked a thumb behind him toward his truck. In the cabin, a casket sat, dark and unpolished. "Where would you like Tommy, Mrs. Donnelly? I'm bringin' him back to you."

Chapter Fourteen

1969...

Dennis's nerves clanged like a firehouse bell. He stood on tiptoes every time a car drove by, straining to see the driver. Even though the thought of entering the mines with Gannaway's men left him feeling vulnerable, he attributed his jitters to seeing Therese again. He wondered if he should sweep her within his arms and kiss her. Last night's kiss could very well have been a glorious, spur-of-the-moment, one-time act of curiosity. He was out of practice regarding women. He hadn't felt so insecure since his first dates with Laura.

Therese pulled up and wiggled her fingers as she exited the car. Apparently, last night hadn't rattled her at all. He was beginning to think nothing did.

"Morning." Dennis stood straight and tossed his shoulders back, even sucked his gut in a bit.

"Mornin'."

They stood in silence until Therese's smile melted the ice. "Have fun last night?"

"Yep. Except for the burger. But dessert was mighty fine."

"We'll see if you're worthy of the main course." She winked a long lash.

Dennis stammered, words failing him.

Therese took pity on his obvious discomfort. "Relax, Dennis. Today's a business meeting." She gave his arm a squeeze, not a loving squeeze, but a familial touch of comfort. And she lingered longer than a relative might.

He had to get his head on straight. Get ready for a business meeting, not a date. An unpleasant one. Stokes' police car pulled up alongside them.

The car lifted visibly when Stokes hefted his weight out. A man Dennis didn't know stepped out of the passenger seat. He appeared in dire need of a shower, and his overalls could sure stand a washing. Gannaway's secretary, Gustav, climbed out of the back seat, looking uncomfortably out of place. He gave a comical double-take when he spotted Therese, then knocked back his head and laughed.

Stokes appeared less than delighted. He jutted a thumb toward Therese. "What in the hell is she doing here?"

"I asked her to come, Sheriff."

"That wasn't part of the deal you made with Mr. Gannaway."

Stokes ignored Therese, but Therese strutted forward, determined to make her presence known. "Relax, Stokes. I'm just here to observe. No harm in that. Besides, you have three on your team. I hardly think they're all needed."

"Listen here, missy. It ain't up to you to decide what's needed or not." Stokes's face burned more than his usual blustery, sunburned appearance. "I ain't keen on bringin' no *redskin* down into the mines."

Dennis saw Therese's fists clench at her sides. Things might get ugly before the tour even started. Dennis said, "Stokes, there's no need for name calling. We're all here for—"

"Name? What name callin'? I didn't say squat." Obviously, Stokes had no idea what he'd said. The way all bigots act.

"Never mind. Therese is here as an official government

employee and my guest. I really don't think Mr. Gannaway would appreciate a call from Uncle Sam ordering him to let her in."

Grumbling, Stokes hitched up his trousers and bobbled toward the gate, each footfall looking like agony on his knees.

Gus, ever the ambassador of peace, extended his hand toward Therese. "Hello again, Ms. Greentree. We've met before. I'm Gustav Eberstark. My friends call me—"

"I remember you, Eberstark." She swept by him, head held high. Gus watched Therese storm away, turned to Dennis and roared again. "She's quite a little spitfire, isn't she?" Gus leaned in, mouth agape, waiting for condescending corroboration.

Dennis tried to steer the potential shipwreck back on course. "I have to say I wasn't expecting you to be here, Gus."

He humbly spread his hands. "That's me, I guess you could say. Always unexpected." Another bout of jolly chuckles. "The other gentleman is Dick Swanson. He's one of the last of the miners. Until the mines were shut down, of course. No one knows the mines better than our Dickie." Straddled on Stokes's car hood smoking a cigarette, Dick looked like he had better places to be. In response to Dennis's wave, Dick flicked the butt to the ground. His form of greeting, Dennis guessed.

"Are we ready, Gus?"

"Ready as Eddie!"

Even though it relaxed Dennis to have Gus leading the pack—a civil man, to be sure—he wished he'd stop his incessant laughter. It began to penetrate Dennis's skull, each boisterous chuckle another hammer blow.

Stokes fiddled with his ring of keys while Therese waited impatiently behind him. Finally, Stokes found a fit and opened the gate. Leering at Therese, he said, "Ladies first."

"Oh, no, Sheriff, after you," she replied. Stokes grinned and led the group onto the grounds. Therese sidled up next to Dennis while the men flanked them like prison guards.

A tall, blue building with tin siding, not unlike a silo, hovered over them. Stokes banged a heavy foot onto the metal stairwell that crawled up outside the building. "Y'all comin'?"

As they climbed the stairs, Gus provided a running commentary, a helpful tour guide. "This is the elevator machine room building. We'll get on the elevator on the second landing." They bypassed Stokes as he leaned against the second-level railing. His asthmatically heavy breathing wheezed like a train's whistle.

Entering the building, a rush of hot air cloaked Dennis, roasting him like an industrial-sized pressure cooker. Sweat prickled his forehead and built under his arms. With all the loose wires dangling about, he was amazed the building hadn't burnt to the ground years ago.

Gus noticed his apprehension. With a chuckle, he said, "Don't worry. The elevator's been tested. Isn't that right, Dickie?"

"'S right." His toneless acknowledgment didn't relieve Dennis's tension.

"Oopsie daisy," said Gus. "Forgot the most important thing." From a barrel, Gus snatched out five yellow, aged hardhats. "Safety is everything."

They crowded into the open-faced elevator. Dennis's hand brushed up next to Therese's, a warmly human reassurance. She appeared calm, much more than him. He wanted to grab her hand, hold it.

Dickie punched a button on the control panel. Along with Dennis's heart, the elevator banged, jolted, and dropped a few inches.

Gus grinned. "No need to worry, Dr. Lipstein. Rusty equipment. Hasn't been used in a while, but still safe."

"Hope so."

The elevator plunged down into the earth. Layers of mud and clay drew up as they lowered. Dennis steadied himself against the elevator wall. He held on for another moment after they clanged down at the bottom, ensuring the elevator didn't have one more lurch left in it.

"Everybody out," said Dickie.

Dennis turned on his helmet lamp. It shot an arc of light down a long, hollowed-out passageway. The lack of fresh airflow was stifling, suffocating. Dennis inhaled deeper, hoping to catch a stray air stream. He imagined drowning evoked the same chest-tightening numbness.

Dickie nudged Dennis aside—a little too hard, Dennis thought—and stepped onto the wet path. He flicked on lamps set into the rock as he trudged by. The lights dimmed, then sparked. The walls animated shadows danced like living entities beneath the unsteady lamps. A spell of dizziness rushed through Dennis. He placed a hand on the cold rock for support.

"This is what you been waitin' for, Lipstein," said Stokes. "Go on, now."

Dennis looked down, saw Therese's hand in his. He didn't remember when that'd happened, but she hadn't protested. Encouraged, he gave her hand a squeeze.

Stokes noticed of course. "Ain't that sweet? We got us a romance down here." Gus chuckled. Nothing but good times down here.

Mud sloshed underfoot. Echoes bounced off the walls, creating an aural illusion of an army as opposed to their small entourage. "Why isn't this mine flooded, Gus?"

"Takes time to shut down the mines, Dr. Lipstein. We're working on it."

Dickie chortled, and Stokes shot him an angry glare. Dennis nodded, but he didn't believe Gus. It'd been more than a year since orders came down to cease operations.

"Gotta get some groundwater samples." Kneeling, Dennis filled a vial and capped it. As an afterthought, he pulled out a small knife and scraped at the wall, dropping the falling remnants into a container.

"You 'bout done playin' around down here, Lipstein?" Stokes stood over Dennis, his hands planted on his sides.

"That'll about do it." Actually, he would have preferred to gather more samples, but he wanted to leave the mine behind. Even more, he wanted to get away from Gannaway's men.

Therese grasped a handful of Dennis's shirt. Startled, Dennis shot up and turned. With wide eyes, she discreetly held a fingertip to her lips.

Taking her cue of silence, he mouthed, "Are you all right?"

She blinked several times into the darkness over Dennis's shoulder. "Later," she whispered.

Dennis breathed deeply when they hit the surface and open air. *Sweet relief.* He'd had no idea he suffered from claustrophobia; he'd never had a reason to find out. But how else to explain his unease below ground? Like he'd been buried alive.

"Stokes...was there anyone else down in the mine?" asked Therese.

He laughed. Derisively. "Little lady, ain't no one down there but us. And ain't nobody been down there in some time."

"Well, Dr. Lipstein, I certainly hope that satisfied your inquisitive nature," said Gus.

"For now."

"Just a huge ol' waste of time, you ask me," said Stokes.

Therese broke away from the group, swiftly walking deeper into the compound.

"Hey, where you goin', little lady?" Stokes huffed after her, shuffling across the cracked grounds.

"I'd like to see more." Stokes caught up to her and snagged her wrist. He yanked her to a stop.

She wrenched away and glowered. Dennis almost felt sorry for Stokes. "I wouldn't do that if I were you, Stokes."

Stokes ran his tongue over his lips, enjoying himself and his "big man" status. He grabbed her again. "You ain't goin' anywhere else. You saw your mine. Now we're done."

"I'm warning you, Stokes." She stared at the hand locked around her wrist.

"Said you weren't goin' nowhere else. Now come on." He pulled her arm up and twisted. Therese whirled, bringing her knee up into his crotch.

Stokes doubled over, cupping himself. "You damn *bitch!* You just assaulted an officer of the law!"

"I warned you, Stokes."

Dennis didn't applaud, but he couldn't help his grin.

Gus scurried toward them, hands frantically waving in the air. "Now, now, let's not let this little incident sour our scientific expedition. Sheriff, I don't think there's any need to bring her up on charges. Mr. Gannaway wouldn't want any trouble, after all."

Stokes turned his head and spat.

"If anything, Stokes, you assaulted me. I have witnesses," said Therese.

Dennis said, "It's true. I'll testify on her behalf."

"Ms. Greentree, let's all take a deep breath and calm down. Sheriff Stokes was just—"

"*Assaulting* me, Eberstark! I just wanted to see more of the mines."

"You seen one mine, you seen 'em all, girly," Dickie said.

"I'd like to see another mine, too, Gus." Dennis didn't want to, not really. But it was apparent the men didn't want them to see any more of the grounds. He wondered how far they'd go to keep that from happening. And why. "How about it?"

Gus sputtered, looked about the grounds, then clapped his hands together with finality. "I'm afraid that's impossible, Dr. Lipstein."

"Why's that?"

"The rest of the mines are closed and filled with water. They've been boarded over. There's nothing else to see."

Dickie snickered. Dennis suspected Dickie's loyalty to Kyle Gannaway didn't run deep.

"You sure about that, Gus?" said Dennis.

"Of course I am. Why do you ask?"

"Just wondering." Dennis no longer had any doubts he'd seen working miners the other night. But a confrontation would have to wait. The enemy outnumbered them, and they were definitely behind enemy lines.

"Splendid." Gus followed through with another clap.

"I do believe we're finished here."

Stokes straightened, his face crimson as a blood orange. Bumping his belly into Therese, he muttered, "Bitch."

Therese jerked her knee up as a warning. Stokes winced and turned quickly away from her.

After the men loaded into the police car and pulled off, Dennis said, "Okay, Therese, what happened to you down there?"

She shook her head slowly. "There *was* someone else in the mine."

"I didn't see anyone. And the mine's shut down—"

"I'm telling you I saw someone else. A *miner.* I couldn't see him clearly. But down in the stope, I saw a figure. Wearing a yellow hard helmet, just standing there, staring at us."

"Huh." He considered explaining it away as a shadow cast by the supports. Or maybe an effect of claustrophobia, but he didn't want to be on the receiving end of Therese's potent knee. "I believe you saw something, Therese, but—"

"Don't you give me that *shit*, Dennis. I'm not some scared little girl, frightened by my own shadow. I know what I saw, and dammit, there was a miner down there!"

"Okay, fine, you saw a miner. You think they're still mining?"

"I don't know. I just...there was a miner down there. And Gannaway's still raping the earth or..."

"Or what?"

"Nothing. Just forget it."

Therese jumped into her car. This time her fingers didn't wave, no repartee was shared. So much for Dennis's blossoming romance.

That wasn't what bothered him most, though. She had *almost* said something. Something too frightening to say.

They'd been in the mine a lot longer than Dennis had anticipated. He looked west at the horizon to gauge how much daylight he had. He kept an eye on the sunset's progress while he collected more ground samples next to the mine. No way was he getting caught in Gannaway after sundown, not with the chat rats literally gunning for him.

He capped off the last of his samples and placed them in an egg carton before securing it in his backpack. The sun had nearly vanished, the sky bleeding into a purple bruise. Six-thirty, much later than he realized.

He stole a nervous glance at the lion statue as he cut through the park. Its bronze hide faded under the falling dusk, no longer a fierce, vibrant beast. The blank eyes stared into oblivion. Of *course,* the statue hadn't roared at him the night he'd climbed the chat pile. The lion sat stationary as all statues do, just another dead monument like the rest of Gannaway.

He reached the van to find all four of its wheels resting on the gravel, the tires flatter than the highway. He dropped his backpack, ran his hand over the tread of the back tire. His fingers slipped into a long gash. A sure bet the other three tires had one, too. *Bastards.* Stokes? No, Stokes wanted him out of Gannaway. He didn't want Dennis's departure delayed. Clearly the chat rats.

Goddammit. Seven miles to the motel, seven long miles. Even if he jogged it, it'd be about a two-hour trip. Maybe more. And darkness was sweeping in fast. God *damn* it.

After reclaiming his backpack, he locked the van. As much good as that would do. Locks wouldn't keep the rats out. It'd be stripped and ravaged by morning. *Nope. Not gonna leave it for 'em.*

He gathered all the equipment he could reasonably carry. He swaddled the glassware in his jacket and stuffed it into his backpack.

He didn't notice the pile of rocks until he stepped back out of the van. Skull-shaped stones formed a five-foot pyramid. Indentations created shadows folding in like eye sockets. Smaller pebbles surrounded the pile like loose, gray teeth. The rocks hadn't been there when he parked. Something like that would be hard to miss. But where'd they come from? More importantly, *why?*

He shuddered as he walked by the man-made pile. Just a grouping of stones, nothing special about them. But their skull-like similarities chilled him. They grinned at him, *watched* him.

The moon was stirring as he set off down the highway shoulder. A thick blanket of humidity smothered the air. Sweat beaded on his forehead. He scratched at his damp beard, his skin irritated to the touch. Pressure built in his chest with every breath of stifling air, similar to his experience in the mine. An unseen hoot owl called out. *Who? Nobody but you and me, friend.* Other than the lone call of the owl, the night held a preternatural hush. Cicadas, usually so prominent in the Midwest this time of year, lay dormant. Possibly even locally extinct, driven away by Gannaway's toxic levels.

Something moved in the weeds to his left. Barely audible at first, but definitely there. He stopped and listened. *Silence.* An animal, frightened into stillness. Playing possum. Shaking it off, he continued.

So did the animal.

Weeds snapped. A sudden rustling tamped down the grass. The moon, full and pregnant with light, cast a white pallor over the fields. Tall grass waved to a standstill. Something—*someone?*—paced his every move, stopping when he stopped, moving when he moved.

Dennis gripped the straps of his backpack and picked up his pace, hoping to distance himself from his fellow traveler. At first, he jogged leisurely. Until a heavy thud landed in the brush next to him. Weeds swished, then broke, toppling like miniature trees. Heavy footfalls thumped down, four of them evenly measured out in giant leaps.

Oh, God, what's happening?

He didn't want to look, wouldn't allow himself time to slow down and look. Eyes locked down the highway. What he didn't see couldn't hurt him. Or so he told himself. He broke into a sprint, his fists jacking into the air.

Without breaking stride, Dennis cut right and crossed the highway. Pushing himself, he ran harder, faster than he thought possible. The road bounced in front of him with each plodding footfall.

Where the hell's all the traffic? There has to be someone out tonight.

A large *clump* sounded to his right, dull and heavy in the dirt, almost as if a body fell out of an airplane. He stopped, nearly tripping over his feet.

Don't look, don't look, don't you damn look!

His pulse thundered in his ears, his heartbeat a timpani. He strained to hear, not because he wanted to. Logic drove him to understand, seeking comfort in easily explained facts. He *had* to know.

The growl began short and low. Restrained. The next snarl rose in power, shatteringly loud and full of savagery. A *roar*. An animal's roar. A *lion*.

The weeds snapped like a string of firecrackers, dropping in the unseen animal's wake. A tremor pulsed through the ground. The vibrations traveled through Dennis's feet up into his legs. A scream built in his chest, bubbled into his throat, then lodged there. He couldn't release it. Afraid to release it. If he screamed, the sound would add concrete weight to the unbelievable.

Ahead he saw headlights. Two pale yellow eyeballs stopped in the middle of the highway stared at him.

Possible safe passage. Maybe he could pay the driver to turn around, take him to his motel. Money meant nothing as long as he was far from Gannaway. He thrashed his arms about and managed to eke out a yelp. The motor chugged, popped. A loud bang spat out of the tailpipe. Probably a chat rat. But facing a shotgun seemed better than being eaten by a lion. Or something far *worse*.

As Dennis approached the waiting automobile, he identified it as a pick-up truck. Old. *Very* old. Dark blue and dented, rust soldering it together, but still in workable condition. Smoke drifted out of the exhaust, floating up into the sky. The full moon presented a spotlight behind the group of men standing in the truck bed.

"Hey...could I...can I..." His mouth dried up as he drew closer.

Miners. All dressed in overalls and wearing hardhats. The one in front cradled a pickaxe in his arms like a baby. A large man stood next to him, his chest twice as wide as any of the others. They remained still as art and hushed as sickness.

Dennis dropped back. Gannaway's secret mining crew, they had to be. And that meant serious danger.

A flashlight beam snapped on, blinding Dennis. He shielded his eyes and called out. "Sorry to bother you... my van's broken down and—"

The miner turned the beam around, shining it back into his own face. Dennis screamed. Two black holes replaced the miner's eyes. A toothless grin formed a death's head smile. The things jumped out of the truck bed, light on their feet, and landed silently on the tarmac. One dragged his pickaxe along the highway, sparks flying underneath the scraping metal.

Dennis bolted back to the opposite shoulder. He tore past the dead crew, screaming between breaths, hoping— *praying*—someone would hear him. Someone *living.* The miners watched him, immobile except for their hideous smiles.

Please, God in heaven, what is going on? What's happening to me? It's not real, it can't be real, don't let it be real...

He braved a look back. The truck grumbled in the middle of the highway. The engine backfired again while the ghostly men hopped back into the truck bed. All but one. That one kept singing a song, low and resonant. A gospel song. The others swayed back and forth to the unholy rhythm, a choir from the church of Hell.

Dennis didn't look back again. His legs turned to heavy logs. Tears bled down his cheeks. His chest burned, on the cusp of exploding. Finally, he reached the hotel. With shaking hands, he latched onto his key, slipped it into the lock, and barreled inside. He slammed the door behind him, locked it, and checked a dozen times to be sure the lock had caught. He tweaked the blinds between two fingers. Nothing outside. No lions, no ghost miners. Nothing but his frazzled imagination.

But, dear God, it wasn't my imagination. It wasn't!

He flipped on the bedside lamp he intended to leave on all night, ready to collapse into bed. Except someone already occupied the bed.

The figure lay there, thin and unmoving.

Devin.

Devin opened his sad brown eyes, just barely. Dark bruises encircled them. His pale gray skin took on an even sicklier color beneath the yellow light. He had no hair, not even eyebrows. The same way he'd looked the last time Dennis had seen his son. *Alive.*

The bed shimmered, vibrated, blurred like a paint-shaking machine. A mechanical moan, possibly human—*who could tell anymore?*—buzzed around it. With a crack, the bed stopped moving. The bed that had transformed in-to a hospital bed. Devin's mouth gave birth to a plastic tube, a snake stretching, crawling on its own accord, to connect to a standing IV holder that hadn't been there sec-onds ago.

His son reached up one frail hand, gesturing toward Dennis. "Daddy?" A ravaged whisper. "Daddy...why aren't you here?"

This can't be happening, oh God, why are you doing this to me? This isn't real! I can't...I can't...

Dennis buckled to the floor. He curled up in a ball, and he pulled his knees against his chest. He wanted to contract into nothing, twist himself inside out, just as long as the pain stopped.

"Daddy? Daddy, where are you?"

No matter how hard Dennis clamped his hands over his ears, he couldn't block out his son's voice. His son's painful, *pleading* voice. He latched onto a chair leg, pulled it, and slammed it into the table repeatedly. Anything to make his pain—and his son—go away. *Anything.*

"You're not real! *None* of this is real! You're *dead!* Oh, *God,* why are you doing this to me? What—"

Something wobbled on the table above him. It fell with a clunk, then rolled in front of him. A full bottle of *scotch.*

Divine intervention from a God he gave up believing in long ago.

Chapter Fifteen

1935...

Claire knew Kaya was avoiding her. A body didn't have to be Doc Wilkins to figure out something ailed her.

Claire seized her opportunity while they washed dishes. "Kaya, is something wrong? You haven't been yourself today." *And I hope it's not 'cause you know Ahanu took me to see John Blackbird.* Ahanu wouldn't spread that news and neither would she, but small towns have unseen ears and big mouths.

Kaya smiled. Not like she meant it. "It's Ahanu. I'm worried. But I know you're worried, too, about your husband, so I don't want to bother you."

Claire looked around the kitchen, saw no sign of their boss, and dragged Kaya away to the pantry for privacy. "Kaya, that's nonsense. You tried to help me. I'd like to do what I can to help you."

Kaya pulled a fist up to her chest, almost as if in prayer, and closed her eyes. "Ahanu's been talkin'. He says he saw the ghost of the boy who took his own life. George Kendricks. Said he saw him in the woods...after he..."

Claire patted her hand, let it rest there. "I'm afraid...

that might've been my fault." She knew Ahanu didn't want his mother knowing about their outing, but Kaya needed support. Braving herself, Claire confessed. "I talked to Ahanu about the yellow-eyed fever. He agreed to take me to see John Blackbird. But he didn't do it willingly. I talked him into it."

To Claire's surprise, Kaya laughed. "Nobody talks that boy into doing anything he ain't got his mind set to. But... I'm surprised he took you. And that you went."

Claire told her about her visit to the Blackbird home. "Nothing came of it, I'm afraid. But please don't be mad at Ahanu. He didn't want to go."

"Hogwash. Boy's got a mind of his own. But I'm gonna have a talk with him about this."

"Kaya, please don't be too harsh on him. He—"

"You don't understand. That's not why I'm worried. He's been talking about...what he saw. Tellin' everyone in town. He's gonna get in trouble if he keeps it up. If Gannaway and his men hear his tale, they're not gonna look too kindly on him. Interferin' with white man's business and all."

Kaya's words hung in the air like a puff from Mother Donnelly's cigarette, pungent and harmful. She'd drawn the line between skin color with bold, harsh strokes. For the first time in their friendship, Claire wondered if Kaya saw her as an outsider, someone different from her. In the boarding house, they started on equal terms, ended as friends. But who knew where things stood outside of work? A deep, abiding shame ate at Claire. She'd never attempted to extend their friendship outside of the boarding house. When (*if?*) things settled down at the mines, she intended on righting her wrongs. "Kaya, the..." Claire caught herself before saying *white man.* "...Mr. Gannaway doesn't even believe in the yellow-eyed fever. He's not gonna give two hoots and a holler about some imaginative boy spinnin' tales."

Kaya's eyes smoldered. Another side of her friend Claire had never witnessed before. "You're not listening to what I'm sayin'. It don't matter none. The white man never listens to the Kwashau, 'cept when it's somethin' bad. Somethin' they see as bein' bad. And you mark my word, they're not gonna cotton to his tale. Not one bit." She held a finger up, wagging it in Claire's face. "I know what'll happen."

"Ahanu's a smart boy. He'll be fine." Although after having seen Gannaway's true nature, Claire doubted her own words. "Do you...believe he saw George Kendricks?"

Kaya shook her head solemnly. "Don't matter much what I think. And it won't matter one bit to...them."

"I can talk to some of the miners. Maybe—"

"You've done *enough*."

Kaya's verbal blow hurt more than a slap. "I'm sorry, Kaya. Please let me do what I can. I'll—"

Folding her hands in her lap, Kaya regained her composure. "I'm sorry for being angry. Ahanu's my only boy. He means more to me than anything. I just worry about him."

Claire knew she meant it as an apology, but for some reason, it still stung. "I'm sorry, too. Very sorry. If only... if only..." If only, what? Claire didn't regret what she had done. She'd go see Gannaway again if it meant saving her husband's life. But had she been so selfish as to not consider the consequences of her actions for those outside her family? "I'm sorry."

"It's not your fault. There's something you should know, though."

"What?"

"Several days ago, John Blackbird moved onto another life."

"He's...dead?"

"We don't see it that way. That's white man thinkin'. But, yes, call it that if you will."

Claire placed a hand on a shelf and rocked back against it. A bag of flour clumped to the ground and split open. White powder whiffed up, then drifted away. Just like the chances of stopping John Blackbird's curse floated away upon his death. "Several days ago?"

"Yes. Last Friday."

The day she visited Blackbird. Now she wondered if the

large bird she saw Friday had been John Blackbird's spirit moving onto the next realm. Delivering one final message. Telling her to abandon all hope.

It seemed remarkable—not in a good way—how much Claire's world had changed over the course of a few days. Before last week, she'd always sought comfort in her born-and-bred Christian life, knowing God would provide for her and her family. Quite possibly she'd even taken her beliefs for granted from time to time, although she'd be the last to admit to that small sin. But as bad as things looked at times, she knew God smiled upon her, and absolutely *knew* God's plans would work out for the Donnellys.

But ghosts and curses didn't sit right alongside Christian faith. The two sets of beliefs seemed uncomfortably at odds with one another, yet Claire couldn't deny both held validity. It made her less than secure in her religious ideology. Why would God allow the yellow-eyed curse to take good men?

Claire stumbled out of the boarding house, her mind elsewhere. She didn't see Eberstark until he stalked in front of her.

"Oh! You gave me a fright, Mr. Eberstark." His dead, gray eye, moist and glinting in the sunlight, reminded her of an olive overtaken by mold.

"I certainly didn't mean to do that, Mrs. Donnelly." He flashed a lifeless smile, his teeth pointed as church steeples. "How are you today?"

"Just fine. And you?" She sidestepped, hoping to end their conversation. He countered, blocking her path.

"I'd like to talk about your husband." His good eye blinked, the other at full attention.

"He's...doing just fine, thank you." Again she attempted to step around him. Like a magnet, he stayed attached to her.

"Let's hope he continues to do so."

His body language wasn't intimidating, but Claire felt the menace in his words. "What in the world is *that* supposed to mean?"

"Just as I said. I hope he continues to do well."

"Is this some sorta warning, Mr. Eberstark?"

Ignoring her question, Eberstark leaned closer. "Is it true Mr. Donnelly has been talking about unionizing?"

Finally, he'd made his point. Of course, it had to be about those damn unions. Even though Claire stood firmly deadset against Tommy's union talks, Eberstark wouldn't hear a word about it from her. "I don't understand what you're asking."

"Is Mr. Donnelly trying to form a union?"

"No. And even if he was, Mr. Eberstark, I hardly see how it's any of your concern."

He delivered a dry, mechanical *rat-tat-tat* of a laugh. At least Claire assumed it was supposed to be a laugh. "Oh, it's everyone in Gannaway's concern. Please keep in mind, if Mr. Donnelly chooses this...unfortunate path, he'll be putting the miners' jobs into jeopardy."

"Now you listen to me, and you listen good!" She thumped his chest with a finger. It sounded hollow, like a bad melon. No surprise, really. She already knew he had no heart. "There *haven't* been any union talks, and there's not gonna be. And if you think you can come 'round intimidatin' folks into...not unionizing, then you got another thought comin'!"

"Then he is unionizing."

"He most certainly is *not!* Now you best just get out of my way. What would Mr. Gannaway think if he knew you were bothering a poor housewife?"

"Why, Mrs. Donnelly...who do you think sent me?"

They performed another uncomfortable tango until Eberstark finally bowed out. "Good day, Mrs. Donnelly," he called out as she hurried across the street. "If I were you, I'd have a chat with your husband."

As soon as Claire rounded the general store's corner, she stopped, bracing herself against the brick wall. The potato sack slipped to the dirt, and she nearly followed it. Tommy had more than the yellow-eyed fever to worry about. Something had to be done.

"Again?" Mother Donnelly grunted, slapping her hands down on the table. "It's hotter than hell warmed over out yonder."

"Mother!" said Tommy.

Usually, Mother's language sent Claire into fits, but tonight she seemed preoccupied. Another new chapter in *The Book of Claire* Tommy would have to interpret.

"What? What'd I do?" Having perfected her innocent, puzzled look, Mother gawped at Tommy until the children tittered. Playing her usual games. But even she knew when to end the game. "Come on now, children. Looks like there's more grown-up time needed around here." Gathering up her tobacco pouch, she led T.J. and Margaret outside. Before she slammed the screen door, she muttered, "Damn hot."

Tommy grabbed Claire's hand. "What is it?"

"Tommy...about this union..."

"Just going to meet a man tonight, honey. Nothin' to worry about."

"But there is. From what I know about unions, it can lead to...fights and...and men losing their jobs. You don't want that to happen. And Tommy—meeting in the Pub! I mean, Mr. Gannaway's goin' to hear about it, sure as a gun's iron and he'll—"

"Claire, that's why we're meetin' at the Pub! Even Mr. Gannaway has to know when it's time to hang up the fight. Once he sees the majority of men supporting unionizing... well, he'd be foolish to oppose it. And I need to see who I can count on and who I can't. I suspect word'll get back to Mr. Gannaway, it's bound to eventually. Just wanna' know if I got any bad apples in my orchard. And, who knows? Maybe even the bad ones will come around once they hear what the Union's got to offer. Besides, the Pub's in the middle of town, not far from any of the miners' houses."

"I don't know, Tommy."

"And as far as the rest...the men'll only lose their jobs if we strike. I don't see that happening. I'm just talkin' to a man. Nothing more, nothing less." Clearly, Claire had something else to say, but she kept quiet. Tommy would find out about it soon enough. If he kept talking, his wife would find a way of keeping him home, sure as shooting. Best to let it go.

"*Promise* me you won't strike, Tommy. Please."

He wished he could, but uncertainty plagued him. And he hated breaking a promise to Claire more than anything. "I can't do that, Claire. I'm sorry."

"*Why?*"

"Because unions are a *good* thing. If—and it's a mighty big 'if'—we unionize, it'll help everyone. And us, honey. I'm doin' it for the men, but 'specially for *us*. I know you've been worried about my bein' in the mines lately. But this'll make things safer. I promise. You understand?"

"Yes. I understand." But she didn't, and Tommy knew it. She shrank into the chair, so small. Her shoulders heaved with each heartbreaking sob.

Tommy kneeled and enveloped her in his arms. "Look at me, Claire. *Look* at me."

She lifted her head.

"This is a good thing. A very good thing." He'd gladly do anything to protect her from heartbreak. But he couldn't understand her strong opposition to unionizing. Only good things would come from his meeting. This particular chapter of the complicated book of Claire Donnelly may as well have been written in a foreign language. "I can't make you the promise we won't unionize. But I can make you another promise..."

"What?" A momentary glint of hope lit up her eyes, her entire demeanor.

"I'll always come back to you. *Always.* Nothing will keep me from you." Usually, this put a smile on his wife's lovely face. But not tonight.

Harry O'Reilly's bushy eyebrows lifted when Tommy entered the bar. Everyone knew Tommy didn't drink. Not that he took the higher road or acted like he was better than anybody else. He just thought his money would be better spent elsewhere, and everybody knew that.

"What brings ya' here, Tommy?"

"Got a little meeting business to take care of, Harry."

Harry looked out over the bar. "Thought somethin' was up. More crowded than usual. Get you anything?"

"Just your charmin' company."

"Big spender." Sighing, Harry moved toward a paying customer. As one of the few men in town able to make a living outside of mining, Harry'd been a mainstay for as long as Tommy could remember. Truth be told, he'd taken advantage of the mines back in the days of prohibition. He'd set up a few stills in the depleted mines, building up a solid customer base. "Pub" started off strong, and Tommy suspected it would still be going strong long after the mines closed. If that day ever came.

Tommy spotted Ed across the room, hunkered over a table in the corner. A group of miners, including Earl and Don, sat next to him trading insults.

"Hi, boys."

"Boss."

Ed jabbed a stubby finger toward an empty chair. "Saved ya a spot." The group was larger than Tommy had hoped for. Possibly thirty men—all of them good men— filled the small bar, although a lot of them spent most of their nights there anyway. Mining made a man thirsty.

"What's the lowdown?" asked Earl. "We unionizing?"

"We'll see what happens. Right now, I'm just meetin' with a man. Maybe have him talk to y'all. See what ya think."

Kenneth Dickinson, the union man, strolled in with a city boy's wave, short and light handed. For a man whose job depended on connecting with working men, he'd sure made a bad choice, wearing a dapper suit. If the men considered Dickinson a rich city slicker, his credibility wouldn't be worth a scrap of wood.

"Hello, gentlemen." He offered his hand to no one in particular. No one accepted it, either. "Um, I'm Kenneth Dickinson with the International Union of Mine, Mill, and Smelter Workers. Our union was established in 1925—"

"Hold on, hold on," said Earl. "You sayin' you're 'international'? What's that mean for us Americans? You gonna take our jobs away and give 'em to foreigners and coloreds?"

Tommy shifted in his chair, almost taking pity on Dickinson. *Almost.* "Let's hear him out, fellas, before we go castin' judgment."

"Thank you, Mr. Donnelly. I can certainly see why you'd ask that question, sir. But, really, aren't we all foreigners in this great land of ours? From generation to generation, we all came from—"

A barrage of groans went up. "We ain't no goddamned foreigners. Born here and proud of it!"

Tommy shot to his feet, drawing attention away from Dickinson. "Hear him out, boys. I believe what Mr. Dickinson meant to say is we all have *past* relatives who struggled to come to America. My grandparents came from Ireland. But they helped to make America the country it is today, and we're all proud Americans now thanks to their efforts." Once the men calmed, Tommy reclaimed his chair. "Isn't that right, Mr. Dickinson?"

"Um, yes, it is." He drew a finger around his collar, his Adam's apple bobbing like a yo-yo. Tommy imagined he'd shed his tie before the end of the night. "And, no, we, ah, don't give jobs to...foreigners. We represent the American people, the hard workers who toil in this land for next to nothing."

The men liked what they heard. Grunts of approval circled the bar.

"And I guarantee you if you decide to ally with us, your working conditions will improve immeasurably—"

"A lot," Tommy translated.

"Ah, yes. Anyway, our record speaks for itself." Dickinson spread a handful of news clippings across the table. The men glanced at them indifferently. Half of them couldn't read. "As you can see, we've improved the conditions in mines across America. We've—"

"What about the yellow-eyed fever?" The voice hollered out from the opposite end of the bar. Harvey Quick stepped out of a dark corner, shadows peeling from his face. He strolled over, thumbs pinching up his overall straps. "How you gonna fix that, Mr. Big City Union Man?"

"Um, I'm sorry?" Dickinson looked to Tommy for clarification. But Tommy had a bigger issue now. What to do about Quick? He knew Gannaway kept him in his pocket, a no-good rat. Still, like he'd told Claire, it was a sure bet somebody in Gannaway's pocket was going to be there. Might as well have it all out in the open from the git-go. Let him know how it's going to be.

Big Ed tossed his hands up and shrugged. Not a lot of help.

"Harvey, if you're here to listen, you're more than welcome," said Tommy. "But I would also consider it a big favor if you'd keep the details of this meeting quiet. Just for the time bein'." *And if you don't, I'll know exactly who I have to watch out for.*

"Well, I reckon I jes' might be able to do that. Just maybe. It all depends." Tommy'd expected as much. Harvey was sure as shooting going to play both sides against the middle. But Tommy didn't intend to play with double-dealing scoundrels. He wasn't wired that way. He just wanted to know how potentially dangerous they were.

Big Ed rose to the rescue. "Let me buy you a drink, Harv." He strapped a large arm around Harvey's back, forcing him away to the bar.

"I'm sorry, Mr. Donnelly," continued Dickinson, "I don't know anything about this yellow-eyed fever. Is it some sort of—"

Before the men sidetracked the union issues into a spook-tale session, Tommy rallied. "Let's not discuss that now, Mr. Dickinson. Why don't you—"

"Why can't we hear about the fever, Tommy?" More men chimed in. "Let's see what Mr. Fancy Pants can do about that."

Dickinson swung in the wind, way out of his element. He gave Tommy a helpless look. Tommy's two-fingered whistle brought the chatter to a stop. "Fellas! Let's all settle down. The yellow-eyed fever is a sickness caused by mine dust. Some of the men are more susceptible to it than others. But we can fix it. Everything that's broke can be fixed again—"

"Can't fix no curse, Tommy!"

Tommy ignored the outburst, the best way to handle it. "What Mr. Dickinson's offering us would stop the fever and the miner's consumption. Other mines unionized and demanded better ventilation. And you know what? They got it! And how about health buildings 'specially for miners and their problems? Ol' Doc Wilkins and his shots sure can't cure us." The men's laughter diffused more tension. "These unionized mines? They have their own health clinics. How about electric lights? The Gannaway company still uses hand-lit lamps. That's why we have so many explosions. Any damn fool knows you don't mix fire with gas."

"You callin' Mr. Gannaway a damn fool, Tommy?"

With a grin, he said, "I ain't castin' no names about here. But...sorta seems plain as the nose on my face."

More laughter, followed by a smattering of applause.

"And goggles. How'd you men like—"

"What're goggles, Tommy?" asked Don.

"You idjit, they're to protect your eyes!" The men ribbed

Don with elbows and good humor. "You really think we could get some of these things, Tommy?"

"Yes, sir, I do. And a place to shower when we come outta the mines. Ain't y'all gettin' tired of your wives complainin' about how filthy you are after a hard day's work?"

"I can't stand my wife's smell most times, Tommy."

"Can't help you there, Earl." More laughter unified the men as a whole. Tommy saw the possibilities glowing in their eyes, a new sense of hope reborn. "These unions made this all happen. It's been documented..." Several blank stares met him. "...um, I've read stories about a lot fewer mining casualties 'cause of the new conditions."

"What about more pay, Tommy? I can barely put food on the table now."

"I think...no, I'm sure if we joined a union, we could barter for better pay, Kent."

Cheers spread out like a pond ripple, a contagious effect. Hands pummeled the tabletops. The men slapped backs and hoisted glasses. Amidst the chaos, Dickinson shriveled into the background. Tommy glanced around to check on Harvey. Ed had him engaged in some serious drinking.

Tommy tapped the air to quiet the crowd. "Now. That's the good news, boys. But I'm gonna be honest with y'all. It ain't gonna be easy. Right now, I just want you to go home and consider what you've heard. But if we're committed to unionizing, the best way to have our demands met would be to strike—" Just when Tommy thought he had them onboard, the tides turned, washing away high spirits. Shoulders sank. Weary sighs hissed out sparks of optimism. He needed to reel them back and do it damn quick. "I know, fellas. Strikes can be damn scary. Might just well put us hungry for a few days. But I can tell you, sure as my name's Tommy Donnelly, it's the best way to get what we want. What we *need*. And the Gannaway company needs us just as much as we need the work. I can't rightly see Mr. Gannaway puttin' on a helmet and chisellin' out ore!" Slowly, the men perked up again. "Like I said, boys, this is in the early stages of plannin'. But if you like what you heard today...spread the word to the right people. Tell the miners in the other holes what you heard. I guarantee we can build an army here. The more we have, the better our chances. And the better we'll be able to provide for our *families*. And stay alive and safe and see our grand-kids grow up!" This time the cheers rattled the front window and shook the floorboards beneath them. Behind the bar, Harry planted his hands against the wall as if trying to hold the timbers together.

"Tom-my! Tom-my! Tom-my..."

Dickinson popped out of his cave and latched onto Tommy's arm. "You just made my job easier." He had to shout to make himself heard over the cheers. He stuffed some wadded-up sheets of paper into Tommy's hand. "Call me when you get the men organized!"

Tommy shook his head and pantomimed holding a phone to his ear. "Don't have a telephone!"

"Then write me! We can do business!"

Tommy edged through the crowd, escorting Dickinson to the door. "I just might do that, Mr. Dickinson." When he reentered the bar, another round of cheers poured kerosene onto his internal fire.

Harvey Quick slid off his bar stool as soon as Tommy settled back at the table. He left Ed to settle the bill and shoved his way outside.

A man stepped out from a tree's shadows. "Well?"

"They're unionizing, all right. Sure are. You tell Mr. Gannaway I done good, now."

Steffen Eberstark grunted at Harvey's outstretched hand. He pinched two fingers into his pocket. He pulled out a five dollar bill and dropped it into the dirt. A light breeze brushed up and carried it away. Steffen grinned as he watched Harvey scramble after it on all fours. Most fun he'd had today. And his day had been full of mirth.

Chapter Sixteen

1969...

"Daddy! Help me! Why aren't you helping me? I don't want to die! Please, Daddy, help me! Where are—"

Dennis had closed his eyes a hundred times, willing Devin to be gone. Praying to forces he didn't believe in.

But his son remained in the motel room. *Pleading.* And *dying* all over again. His small bald head reminded Dennis of a gray egg, so fragile it could break open any moment. He tried to think of his son in the abstract. He knew Devin couldn't possibly be in the room. But terrifying doubt marred reality.

Devin struggled to push himself up on the pillows. His impossibly thin elbows folded, dropping him back into his nest of tubing and bunched-up sheets. His eyes filled with unbearable agony. Dennis *felt* his son's pain, the weight of it enough to crush his mind.

"I hurt, Daddy! Please, help—"

Had minutes or hours passed? Time's boundaries were broken, imprecise. For all Dennis knew, he'd died himself and was suffering in a hell much worse than any he could imagine.

"Daddy, where are you? It hurts so bad—"

Dennis sat at the table, his back turned on his son. He stroked the bottle of scotch, polishing the neck like a rifle barrel. And why not? A couple of shots from the bottle—oh, yes, that'd have a kick with a lot more power than a rifle's blast. If he had a gun, he'd have used it. No doubt in his mind. End his suffering. But was it possible to die if you were already in hell?

"Daddy—"

His mysterious benefactor had been considerate. The seal on the bottle had already been broken. A glass, just the right size, sat on the table. Waiting to be used and licked dry. When he held up the glass, he saw a miniature, distorted reflection of his ashen face. Trapped inside the glass as he had been six months ago...

Dennis couldn't pinpoint the exact time or even a reason why he crawled into the bottle, but a year ago he was definitely circling the rim. Once he'd heard his son's prognosis, he tipped completely into it.

But the real damage happened on a Tuesday night, the last night of his son's short life. Dennis sat by Devin's bedside, physically barricaded from holding his son in his arms. The night before, Devin had developed pneumonia, and now an oxygen tent covered him. A curtain of plastic wrap prevented Dennis from telling his son how much he loved him. That, and his own crippling faults and insecurities.

Leukemia. Such a harsh, fatal-sounding word. That's how the experts had diagnosed Devin's illness. At first, Dennis denied it. Just last month, Devin had been chasing butterflies with a giddiness reserved for healthy five-year-olds. Five-year-old boys just don't get leukemia. Except sometimes they do.

Now, cut off from the world and deprived of a normal

childhood, Devin waited at death's door. Laura sat on the opposite side of the oxygen tent, nothing but a blur through the plastic. A perfect metaphor for their marriage. They'd grown apart, oddly transformed into strangers. Instead of seeking comfort in one another, they'd sought out different companions. Laura, his once beautiful butterfly of a wife, now cocooned herself into a dark depression. Dennis devoted his time to studying leukemia, a constant flow of alcohol his research assistant. When Devin had been admitted to the hospital for his hellish treatments, Laura had fled their bed and taken up residence in Devin's empty room.

To no one's surprise, Devin had handled the news better than his parents. He possessed that wonderful coping ability children have—a curious nature superseding any thoughts of mortality. Filled with questions about his illness and overflowing with optimism, nothing could keep Devin down.

Then the treatments started.

Treatments. Torture would have been more accurate. The radical chemo- and radiation therapy tore Devin apart. Unable to hold down his meals, he lost a frightening amount of weight. His hair fell from his head in clumps. Tears replaced his optimism. Dennis's brave little soldier finally fell in the cancerous battlefield, joining his parents in the ranks.

That last night, Dennis had stopped for several drinks. Just enough to take the edge off. Alcohol was the only thing keeping him going, the gasoline fueling his motor. He'd been up for two nights straight, pouring over textbooks, searching for miracle cures to save his son from his inevitable fate. But he'd found nothing. His scientific background, his wealth of knowledge, his master's degree and accolades in the field of environmental science meant absolutely nothing. *Zilch.* He felt completely useless, mentally and physically exhausted.

Dennis arrived at the hospital just in time to witness Devin crying himself to sleep. Merciful sleep. Blessed sleep.

Peaceful, even, the first such peace he'd had in a while. The hospital lights shimmered off the plastic, producing a heavenly gossamer effect, like a halo for the small broken angel it shrouded.

Nurses made their rounds, frequently poked their heads into the room. Their tennis shoes squeaked across the linoleum as they glided across the floor. They checked Devin's chart and his vitals, but nothing changed, not even their bland expressions. Business as usual for the hospital staff while Dennis's son rotted away.

Machines blipped, a nice, steady, soothing beat. Laura sat out of sight across the room, her repetitive, low-pitched sobs segueing into an oddly melodic tone. *Hoo, hoo, hoo, sigh.* Over and over and...

So *tired.* So *very* tired. Maybe if he closed his eyes, just for a little bit, he could grab a quick nap.

But just for a little bit...

From such inconsequential thoughts, lives can change.

Screaming from somewhere far away. Voices raised in panic. Devin's voice, high-pitched.

"Daddy! Daddy, where am I?"

Something tearing. *Shhhrrrrrriipppppp.*

"Daddy! Where are you? Why aren't you here?"

Running footsteps.

Dennis clawed his way back to consciousness, the climb to the light of awareness a Herculean struggle.

His eyes opened. A loose flap of the oxygen tent waved in his face. Nurses gathered next to him, some kneeling. Laura screamed, her fingers raking at her hair. A machine screeched, battling for dominance over Laura's siren wail. At the center of the chaos, Devin lay on the floor. A crumpled, broken, baby bird.

Dennis jumped to his feet. A nurse pushed by him, a hand held over her mouth.

"What's going on? What happened? Devin—"

Laura continued screaming, oblivious to her husband's questions.

A tired-looking doctor hustled into the room. He went

down on one knee and studied Devin, took his pulse. With folded hands, he pumped hard on Devin's chest, counting out numbers and breathing life into his mouth.

Oh...God...

Dennis fell back, bringing his chair crashing down on top of him. He clambered to his hands and knees. He crawled toward his son with an outstretched hand. His fingers grazed Devin's leg. Unmoving, cold.

"Someone get him *out* of here," yelled the doctor as he pummeled Devin's chest.

But Dennis knew his son's time had ended. Five years old. Hardly a blip on a life-time's radar. His son would never know the joys of a first kiss, dating, sex, marriage, children. *Nothing.* His life had peaked at catching butterflies.

The doctor stood, mumbled something to one of the nurses. Dennis leaped onto his son's body, aching for one last embrace. He'd give his own life to have his son wake, whisper to him, "I love you, Daddy." *Just one more goddamn time!* He wrapped Devin's lifeless hands around his neck. They flopped back to the floor.

Sudden silence swept the commotion out of the room. A horrific moment frozen in time.

A foot kicked into Dennis's ribs. Laura hovered over him.

"Get up, you son of a bitch," she said in a controlled, icy tone.

Dennis climbed to his feet, brushing tears from his eyes.

"Your son was calling for you, you bastard. *Calling* for you! And where were you? Passed out *drunk!* He tried to reach you...he tried to..."

"No! Laura...I wasn't drunk. I was *tired.* I'd been researching..." Hungry for comfort and needing to feed the hunger, Dennis reached for her.

"Get *away* from me!" She lashed Dennis across his face. He wished he could feel the blow, that he could feel anything except the raw agony that deadened his heart. "I can smell alcohol on your breath! The last thing Devin saw... was *you*...passed out in front of him..."

"Laura...I'm so sorry. Please *believe* me. I wasn't—"

"You're...*inhuman.* How do you...think that made your son feel? Seeing you like..." She stopped. Simply gave up and ran from the room. The last time Dennis ever saw her.

Ten minutes. It took a mere ten minutes for Dennis to lose the two people who meant more to him than anything.

He dropped to his knees, pounding the floor next to his son's body. He didn't stop—*couldn't* stop—until his fists turned into bloodied ham hocks. A small offering of penance, but not nearly enough.

If he'd thought he'd crawled into the bottle before, now God corked him in and tossed the bottle aside.

Dennis stayed drunk for two months straight. Thanks to Meyers and other friends, he'd been sober ever since. *Alone.* But sober.

"Daddy, where are you? Please! I need you! Why are you doing this to me? Where—"

Dennis unscrewed the cap off the scotch bottle and poured a shot. The glass shook in his hands, worse than in his detoxing days. Golden liquid splashed over onto his fingers. Temptation taunted him to dive in, lick the precious fluid from his skin.

"Please help me, Daddy! Please, please, ple—"

The pungent caramel smell filled his nose. So strong. It would burn nicely in his chest. And he would forget. Forget everything. Just for one night, forget what he saw in Gannaway, forget Devin—

No.

He had passed out during his son's final moments. No way in hell would he forget Devin's memory. "God damn... Goddammit...*No!*"

He heaved the bottle across the room like a missile. It exploded against the wall, miniature projectiles bouncing onto the carpet. The scotch dribbled down, appearing blood red upon the orange wall.

"Daddy? Is that you?"

Devin sat up in bed. His eyes lit up, looking like the inquisitive boy Dennis remembered and loved.

His second chance to make things right.

Rushing to the bedside, Dennis dropped to his knees.

The tube in Devin's mouth shrank, receding into his mouth like a long spaghetti string. The IV bag and holder dissolved into a wisp of dust.

"Devin? Son? I'm *so* sorry. I'm so, so sorry I wasn't there for you. I love you, son. More than anything. More than *anything.* You need to *know* that. I've missed you—" Dennis leaned over, wrapping his arms around Devin's back, and pulled him into an embrace. His son's bare back felt cold. He tugged the hospital gown tighter, protecting his son from sickness.

Sobbing, Dennis repeated his words. The words he had wished to share with his son. The words he'd wanted so desperately to say but were stolen from him. "I love you, Devin. I'm sorry, I'm—"

The soft material of the hospital gown quivered as if alive. Beneath his fingertips, he felt the gown changing, growing coarser. *Denim.* His fingers searched, fell across a buckle. His son's already perilously thin body shrank, constricted, tightened. The skin melted away in his hands.

He shot up and stared at the thing that replaced his son. *A bag of bones wearing overalls.* Twin dark holes gaped up at him. Remnants of the inner matter encrusted the miner's eye sockets. His mouth opened, another dark cavern void of teeth. A gray tongue darted out.

"If you could see inside insteaddd, you'd see a brand new mannn..." The thing sat up in bed. Its right leg clumped to the floor.

"No...you're not real, *none* of this is real, not god damned *real!"*

"'Cause the old man is deaddd!" The ghost crawled out of bed. Its arms extended as if wanting to continue their

hug.

"You *bastards!* Why's this *happening* to me? You *sick* bastards! You don't get to sully my *son's memory! Fuck you!"*

Dennis turned and stumbled, landing on his face. He bellowed, wanting the nightmare to stop. *Anything, just make it stop!* The singing grew louder as the thing crept up behind Dennis. Its shadow swayed across the wall, keeping time to its death-knell song.

The door pounded as did Dennis's heart. A voice followed.

Not real. Nothing is anymore!

Dennis raised his voice, shrieking, trying to drown out the horrific croaking of the ghost.

The damn song isn't real, the miner doesn't exist, nothing is—

Then he heard her voice. *"Dennis! Open up! Dennis!"*

Like an anchor, Therese's voice dropped him back into reality.

The singing stopped, but Therese's pounding continued. Dennis twisted on the floor, daring a backward glance. The miner had vanished, the motel bed returned to normal. Nothing looked out of place, nothing was disturbed. Except for the broken Scotch bottle, lying on the floor like a drinking binge casualty. And all too real.

"Dennis, open the damn *door!* Now! *Dennis—"*

When he yanked open the door, Therese fell back in shock. "Dennis...what's wrong?"

"I'll explain everything. But, please, oh, God, Therese, get me *out* of here!"

He fell into her arms, ecstatic to be holding living flesh and bones.

"Dennis, it's not your fault your son died." They stood in front of Therese's open hotel room door. She clamped her hands over Dennis's cheeks, demanding his full attention.

"You don't understand...I wasn't there when he needed—"

"Enough." She pushed him into the room. Standing on tiptoes, she kissed him. Whether it was an act of pity or lust, he didn't care. Nothing mattered. He welcomed the warmth, the sensuousness of her full lips.

Plumes of breath billowed from her nose, tickling his cheek. His hands roamed her back, moving toward her hips. She pulled away, swiveled, and kicked her hotel room door shut. Her brown eyes flit back and forth between his. Grabbing his neck with force, she yanked his mouth toward hers again. Her tongue, so teasing and tantalizing the other night, voraciously probed his mouth.

Using his shoulders as a crutch, she hopped up, wrapping her legs around Dennis's back. The force propelled them across the room. Dennis fell back onto the bed, Therese collapsing on top of him. Her hands combed through his hair, kneading, massaging his scalp.

Thump. Without coming up for air, Therese managed to toss one of her shoes behind her. The other shoe flew across the room, landing on the table and setting the lamp to wobble. Light danced over their entwined bodies.

When Dennis reached for her breasts, she jumped off the bed. She smiled, her lips provocatively apart. Her gaze darted down toward the bulge in Dennis's jeans. With a shrug of her shoulders, she let her jacket slide to the floor. Unbuttoning her blouse, she said, "Well? This isn't just a show for you."

Dennis yanked his jeans down and kicked them away. Fumbling with the buttons on his shirt, he gave up, the anticipation too much, and tore his shirt away.

Therese swayed her hips back and forth, the skirt shimmying to the carpet. Holding one leg straight over the bed, her panties dangled from her toes, almost as an offering. Dennis reached for the trophy. At the last minute, she kicked them up over his head. He couldn't be sure where—

or if—they landed, but he didn't care either. As soon as she hopped onto the bed, he rolled on top of her.

She had a different idea. She clamped her legs around Dennis's back. Rocking side to side, she leveraged Dennis underneath her. *Even in the bedroom, she's a take-charge kinda gal,* thought Dennis.

Her way or the highway.

Dennis watched the first rays of daybreak sift in through the curtains. He'd been awake all night, but he hadn't moved, not an inch. Still sprawled on top of him, Therese slept soundly through the early hours of the morning.

No way he could have slept. After their night of love-making, the harsh reality of the previous night's horrors crept back into his mind. *Reality.* Strange term, not nearly as rigid as he'd once thought it. Ghosts had never existed before in his concept of reality. But now they did. He couldn't deny last night's events. He'd doubted his sanity, nearly went back to the bottle, even contemplated suicide. Therese had brought him back from the brink, made him realize something he'd tried desperately not to believe. Gannaway *was* haunted.

On the drive to Therese's motel last night, she'd surprised him again. He'd expected her to react with derision, ridicule, disbelief in his wild tale. To react like most people would react. Instead, she'd remained stoic for the most part, occasionally punctuating his story with appropriate gasps or one-word acknowledgments. An astounding woman who could definitely teach him a thing or two.

He gently brushed his lips across her forehead.

Stirring, she mumbled, "Time is it?"

"Shh. It's still early. Go back to sleep."

But the damage was done.

"I'm awake." She looked up at Dennis, yawned. Her

hand patted his face and moved back to his chest.

They needed to talk. He needed to know she fully believed the unreal story he'd spit out in incoherent sentences on the ride to her motel. There hadn't been much talking once they'd arrived.

"So...you're an alcoholic?" she asked. "I sure can pick 'em."

Dennis laughed, a pleasant surprise. "Everything I told you last night and that's the one thing you focus on?"

"Yeah. Guess so."

"Okay. Yes, I'm an alcoholic." He waited for his declaration to take hold in her mind. "But I've been sober for six months. And counting."

"Good."

"Well, it shouldn't have gotten so bad it needed to get good, but, yeah, it's good." Dennis hauled himself up in bed, prompting Therese to roll off. He leaned the pillow against the backboard and sat up. "Therese, you weren't shocked about any of my story."

Therese scooted over, nudging her nose against him. "Make room. It's my pillow you're bogarting. I'm Native American. Everything supernatural and spiritual's been ingrained in me since childhood. I've heard the stories of Gannaway all my life. Tales of ghosts, wandering spirits, curses—"

"Why didn't you ever say anything to me?"

"You weren't about to listen to me, Science-boy. Anyone could see that. Besides..." She shrugged, the sheet falling from her shoulders. "...I've never actually seen anything myself. I always thought it was nonsense, put it behind me really. But I never closed myself to the possibilities either. Too many people I respect believe in it. But yesterday..."

"When you saw a ghost in the mine."

She nodded. "When I saw the ghost in the mine. I know what I saw. It could've been one of Gannaway's miners down there, I suppose. Except for the little detail that Gannaway wouldn't have let us down there if someone was working. Then your story corroborated what I suspected."

"My story..." Apprehension washed over Dennis. He pulled the sheet up, flapped it out until it covered Therese as well. The warmth of her body against his took the chill off. "Okay. Gannaway's haunted by the yellow-eyed curse and miner's ghosts. Crazy, but...okay. Why would these bastards have brought my son...Devin into it?" Dennis choked on the words, tears stinging his eyes.

"Dennis...I don't know. You need to talk to Bob about that." When Dennis looked away, she brought him back with fingers guiding his chin. "Look at me. Dennis, *look* at me. I don't know why Devin appeared to you. But you need to understand something. From what you told me, you're in no way responsible for your son's death. He was sick... an illness no one could've cured."

"But I wasn't there for him...when he called me..."

"Yes, you were. Should you have been drinking before your visit? No. But you know that. You were tired, worn out; you fell asleep. You're only human. Quit eating yourself up alive over it. Devin knows you were a good father. He knows you loved him."

He wanted to ask her if she truly believed it, desperately wanted her to say "yes." Then he wanted to ask her another dozen times, hoping for the same outcome. The scientific research method. Instead, he said, "Thanks."

"You're welcome. Just remember what I said."

"I will." He planted a kiss on her cheek. "Therese?"

"Mmm?"

"Therese—that bottle of Scotch was *real*. And I didn't buy it. I swear to God—on Devin's memory—I didn't. It was just—*there*. The visions vanished when you knocked on the door. But the broken bottle glass was still there. Right on the floor where it fell when I threw it against the wall."

"The Scotch was real? Huh. That's—"

"Fucking Gannaway did it." It was the only thing that made sense. "Son of a *bitch!* He found out. Somehow he found out about my alcoholism. That's why he kept pushing the booze at me." Exploiting his alcoholism, hoping he would fall off the wagon, seemed much more heinous than ghostly visitations.

"Son of a bitch is right. Damn. What're you gonna do about it?"

"What *can* I do? I can't prove anything. But I'll tell you something. I'm going to get proof he's still mining. *That* I can do."

"I'll help you any way I can. I hate the bastard, too."

Shoulders touching, they lay in silence, taking in the sounds of the land awakening outside.

"Your motel room's much nicer than mine, Therese."

Therese inched away. She averted her eyes, suddenly uncomfortable. "Um, yeah, about that, Dennis..."

"Yeah?" He reached for her, landed a hand on her hip.

"This is *my* motel room. Last night was fun and all, but you're going to have to go back to your motel. I'm working. And I'm a girl who likes her independence."

"Oh. I...see." Although he didn't. Not really. Moving in with her had crossed his mind, at least until one of them completed their job. For more reasons than one. He couldn't hide his disappointment.

Therese took pity on him. "Oh, don't worry. You'll still see me. We have a common enemy. Besides, I can't have you keeping me up all night." She kissed him. Not the unbridled passion from last night, but a chaste, solid kiss, tongue firmly docked in her mouth. Maybe even a friend-ship kiss. Still, Dennis couldn't help his biological reaction.

Therese lifted the sheet and glimpsed underneath. "Speaking of 'staying up'..."

With a sigh, she straddled Dennis again before he could say anything.

Her way or the highway.

Reluctantly, he accepted it would be a short journey. But he'd gladly roll along her highway until they ran out of road.

Chapter Seventeen

1935...

In less than a week's time, most of the men had signed up. Naturally a few remained non-committal, just God's odds. Tommy imagined they'd come around once they realized the inevitability of it all. The savvier miners knew better than to resist progress. Except for maybe Harvey Quick and a few of his pals.

Quick posed a problem. True, Tommy had held that first meeting at the "Pub" for a reason, but he hadn't really expected Quick to be there. Quick never frequented the "Pub." Everyone in town knew his chintzy ways, so cheap he wouldn't penny up for a beer. Tommy wanted Gannaway to know the miners weren't just going to accept their lots and take his handouts for much longer, but he would have preferred Gannaway not realize that just yet. Not until they got a chance to get their union feet wet. Maybe the others who had agreed to unionize would persuade Quick to stew in silence.

Tommy had settled on the abandoned barn next to the Kwashau school for tonight's meeting. It offered plenty of privacy. Situated halfway between Gannaway's mansion and the town, not many of the men had even known the barn existed prior to tonight.

Hay bales scattered across the barn's floor provided makeshift seats. Lanterns hung on the walls to keep out the night's darkness. The other mines' foremen huddled together, oblivious of their day-long stench. Or, rather, simply used to it. If they worked in a perfume factory, they probably wouldn't smell that either.

"All right, fellas, hey!" Tommy banged on a rafter. "I reckon y'all know why I asked to meet you here—"

"Unions," said Dale. The oldest of the crew bosses, everyone looked up to Dale. If Tommy could convince Dale to sign, the other pit bosses would fall like dominoes. "Been hearin' about your union talks."

"That's right, Dale. Most of my men are with me. What do the rest of you say?"

The men fell silent. Dale scratched his beard, looked around at the others, gauging their reactions. Dale hobbled to an empty bale, the other men clearing a path. Hay puffed out when he dropped onto it. "Heard some things about unions. Good things, bad things. What's in it for my men?"

"Well, Dale, first and foremost, better working conditions for all of us. Working conditions to give us at least a little bit of protection from rockslides and such. Like the one that put the limp in your walk."

Tommy kept talking, listing his ideal changes, saving income increases for last. Talks of more money usually sealed the deal. The door wrenched open before he could reach his selling point. The union man, Ken Dickinson, stood outside. And he wore the same damn Big City suit. Definitely not a selling point.

A few men jumped to their feet, startled by the unfamiliar face. Dickinson looked like he hadn't slept in days, no doubt accustomed to better living conditions than the boarding house he had temporarily checked into.

"Um, boys, this here's Ken Dickinson, our union representative," said Tommy.

Several miners grumbled; none of them greeted him. The miner's way; distrust for anyone who didn't toil underground. Dickinson hadn't been of much assistance on the first go-round, but Tommy had thought his appearance might give tonight's talks more credibility. Right now, Tommy regretted his decision. He hurried through his speech before the miner's skepticism swept them away.

"...higher wages guaranteed, as sure as my name's Tommy Donnelly!" When Tommy finished, all heads turned to Dale, waiting to hear him weigh in.

Dale picked his teeth with a fingernail, squinting up at the roof. "What's Mr. Gannaway think of all this?"

"Well, now, I doubt he'll be tickled. But—"

"Why don't you tell everyone about strikes, Tommy?"

Tommy hesitated. But the men deserved the truth. "A strike could happen, boys. Worst thing to come of it might be we'd lose our jobs for a couple of days. But after that—"

"What if Gannaway replaces us with coloreds?" Dale again, the devil's advocate. "Plenty of them to go 'round. Or Injuns? Ain't no shortage of them."

Their voices rose in agreement, building to an angry mob. Like a drowning man, Tommy looked for a piece of flotsam to grab onto. For sure, he couldn't count on Dickinson, who'd backed his way toward the door.

"Boys, boys!" Tommy waved his hands, ending with a shrill whistle. "That ain't gonna happen. You can't train men to be miners in a couple days. Gannaway's not gonna want the mines shut down longer than they have to be."

"Tommy, the bigger problem's gonna be all the miners who lost their jobs over the past five years. By my count, there're at least 1,000, maybe more, still livin' here in Gannaway."

Definitely a potential problem, and in all fairness, Dickinson had warned Tommy of that possibility. "Ain't gonna lie to you, fellas. That could happen. And my heart goes out to all those men. The depression's been tough on all of us. But unionizing and a possible strike may be the only way to get what we need. Maybe then, some of those men can even get their jobs back. All it's gonna take from us is commitment and some union fees." Tommy fully expected the groans. "Sorry, fellas. But the fees are minimal. We should be able to make them back in no time with increased wages. We stick together, and Gannaway'll be forced to meet our demands. Hell, I wouldn't even call them demands. We're just asking for things to be better. So we can provide for our families. So we can live to see our children grow. Something we've earned while we've been making Gannaway mountains of money!"

Dale did something Tommy'd never seen before. He cracked a smile. "Fine, then. You talk a good talk, Tommy Donnelly. You can count on me and my men."

One after the other, the men strode forward, snatching paperwork from Dickinson. Tommy left no hand unshaken, thanking them for their support. "Fellas, I'd like to enlist all of you to be local union leaders. Y'all sign, your men will sign."

Before Dale left, he approached Tommy. "Just one thing."

"Speak your mind, Dale. You always do."

"Mr. Gannaway. I've worked for him longer than any of the fellas here. I know him better than most. He ain't gonna cotton to this idea. Things could get bad."

"Mr. Gannaway doesn't even know we're *thinkin'* about unionizing." Tommy spoke with confidence. "Best we keep it that way, too. Eventually, union rules state we'll need to bring him to the negotiating table. And I believe in giving every man a fair shake. But for now, let's keep things between us. If we hit him all together, if he sees how many miners he's dealin' with, he'll be less prepared to fight us on this. Ain't that right, Mr. Dickinson?"

"Um, yes, that's the best way to handle it, I believe," said Dickinson.

"You say so, reckon that's okay, then." Dale sounded less than convinced as he limped out of the barn.

"Count on it. Mr. Gannaway won't be a problem. He'll come around to seeing things our way! Things will work out just fine." Tommy believed that. Then.

Of course, Kyle Gannaway knew about the impending unionization plans. He already had a counterplan in motion. The strategy of war. That there would be blood spilled, he had no doubt. And he'd make damn sure it wouldn't be his.

The men gathered in Gannaway's living room were an unsavory bunch. Gannaway hated the necessity of them being in his house. Several of the hooligans kept their hats on, apparently having been raised in a barn. One man sprawled out on his sofa, scratching his privates as if digging for ore.

He'd dealt with some of these men before. He'd hired them to carry out some of his dirtier but necessary work when he'd created this town. They'd run rampant back then, some with guns, some with lead pipes, others with knives and whips, carving a town from a nameless shithole. Thugs, hoodlums, and gangsters, all of them. From these ranks, he'd acquired his manservant, Steffen, the only permanent holdover from the violent crew.

Once his town blossomed into civility, Gannaway put the screws to the toughs. Most were wanted men. He threatened to turn them over to the law if they didn't leave. He'd paid them off nicely, though. Gannaway was a fair man. Besides, he'd thought they might come in handy down the road.

As usual, he'd been right. He needed their special talents once more.

"Got anything to drink, Gannaway?" Gannaway couldn't remember the crotch scratcher's name for the life of him.

"No, I don't. Now, listen up, gentlemen. I've got a special job for you, one that's a little different—"

"What the hell you want from us?"

From a corner of the room, Steffen stiffened, ready to "Steppen Fetchit" if Gannaway gave the signal. Gannaway waved him back.

"I'm takin' matters into my own hands, protectin' my interests. Along with other mine operators in Kansas, Missouri, and Oklahoma, I've formed my own union, the Tri-State Union. I'm—"

"Still don't know what you want from us, Gannaway. Quit tip-toein' around and spit it out." Like a bird of prey, Steffen flew to the man's side and dropped a claw on his shoulder. His good eye locked onto Gannaway, waiting for the word. Strictly for his amusement—and because the man was shredding his very last nerve—Gannaway gave a small nod. Steffen dug his fingernails in, pinching until the man gasped.

"You're here 'cause I'll be paying you to shut your damn mouths and do what I tell you to do without asking questions. First thing, I need you fellas to talk to the miners around town who lost their jobs. Tell 'em they're guaranteed their jobs back should the current miners strike. And they're gonna strike, you mark my word." One man yawned, didn't even bother to cover it.

"When they do, the Tri-State Union's gonna fight back. Here's where your special, ah, skills are gonna be needed. You'll be deputized to carry guns."

That got their attention.

"Mr. Gannaway...if I'm...uh...understandin' you correctly, you want us to be your police?"

"More like my personal army."

"When's this gonna happen?"

"If I was a bettin' man, I'd say soon. Steffen here will take care of your temporary livin' arrangements. Then—"

"So we're just supposed to sit around waitin' for the strike to happen?" *Unacceptable.* Three strikes and you're out. Gannaway caught Steffen's eye and whirled his finger in the air.

Steffen grabbed the man by his lapels and yanked him off the chair. He jerked the man's arm back, corralling him toward the door.

"Wait, Mr. Gannaway! I'm sorry, I didn't mean nothin'—" His pleading receded down the hallway. Gannaway smiled in anticipation, savoring his new army's stunned reaction. If his soldiers didn't respect him, how could he possibly count on them to defend his property?

The front door slammed, and nervous fingers scratched the necks under shirt collars. Gannaway draped an arm over his chair and leaned back. He didn't say a word.

A shriek split the quiet. Loud and long and abruptly silenced like cats finished rutting in the night.

Throats clicked dryly, music to Gannaway's ears. Mission accomplished. "Now, where was I? Ah! Steffen will find someplace here in town for you. I'm willin' to put you fellas on a retainer if you—" A hand snaked up into the air slowly. At least this man appeared to have some grade schooling in his background. And he'd obviously taken note of the lesson just taught. "Yes?"

"What's a retainer?" Heads nodded.

"I'm givin' you some money upfront to keep you around and ready. The amount will be discussed later. Keep those guns loaded, boys. It could happen anytime. If anyone doesn't want to be a part of the Tri-State Union, well, then I reckon that's your choice. Just see my man, Steffen, on the way out." The men dropped their heads, gazing down at the carpet. Gannaway knew they feared Steffen. For good reason, too. The same reason he'd personally handpicked him. "No? Everybody fine? Then I'm fine. We'll be in touch." Steffen appeared in the living room doorway, a gaunt ghost. "Steffen, take special care of the men, please." Gannaway chuckled as he watched the men shuffle out the door, unsure of their fate. But a frightened army is a loyal army. More than he could say for his miners.

Gannaway didn't want a strike. Disruptions in work disrupted the flow of money into his bank account. But by God, if he didn't find himself looking forward to it now. Donnelly and his group of ingrates needed to be taught a lesson. Squished like the bugs they were.

Gannaway's parked black Bentley stood out like a marble in the dirt in front of the drug store. It was so clean and shiny Claire couldn't even look at it for too long underneath the harsh afternoon sunlight without her eyes hurting. She stole a glance inside, boldly prepared to confront her demons. The driver's seat sat empty, but someone occupied the passenger seat. Naira Gannaway.

Claire'd never met Mrs. Gannaway before. Only knew what her neighbors told her. But if the stories were true, she felt an instant bond with her. Kyle Gannaway held them both hostages.

She didn't know what compelled her to do it. But before she changed her mind, she knocked on the window.

Clearly startled, Naira's eyes widened, a hunted animal at the end of a rifle. She shook her head once and looked away.

"Please, Mrs. Gannaway! I'd just like a moment of your time." On tiptoes, Claire peered over the soda-pop sign into the drug store. Kyle Gannaway was berating Mr. Keppler, the druggist, prodding the man's chest with his finger. Apparently, it was the only way the foul man conducted his business.

Naira's hand darted toward the window handle, then drew back as if she'd been burned.

"Please. I just want to talk to you, Mrs. Gannaway."

The window rolled down. Naira shot an apprehensive look toward the drug store, then back to Claire.

"Please, go away. He'll see you," she whispered.

Claire didn't care. She'd set this ship into motion and wouldn't abandon it. "I'm Claire Donnelly. My husband's Tommy Donnelly, one of your husband's pit bosses. I'm—"

"You don't understand. If my husband sees you talking to me, it'll be bad for you and your husband. And me. *Please.* Go away."

Claire felt Naira's fear rolling off her in waves. Surely

Gannaway wouldn't hurt his own wife. "I know about the yellow-eyed fever. I visited your parents and—"

Naira sucked in a deep breath. "You...went to my parents? What did they tell you?"

Lowering her head, Claire said, "I know about the curse your daddy put on the mines. And why he did it. I'm terribly sorry for the pain caused your family. But I'm trying to keep my husband alive. Is there anything—*anything* at all you can do to help?"

"I'm sorry, too, Mrs. Donnelly, but there isn't." She paused, her lips quivering. "Now, please. You must leave now."

Behind Claire, the bell over the drugstore door tinkled, followed by a roar. "What in the *hell?* What're you doing bothering my wife?" Gannaway's neck and face burned red, sweat prickling his forehead. "You get *away.* You've already done bothered me at my home. Now you're pesterin' my *wife.* Go on! Git! Goddamn it, git!" He shooed at her as if waving away a stray dog. "I *mean* it, woman."

Remembering his earlier fit of rage, Claire backed away. In a quiet voice, she said, "I was just saying good morning to your wife—"

"I don't give two hoots and a *goddamn,* you leave her alone!" He stormed toward Claire, forcing her against the drug store window. As she slipped sideways, her hands screeched across the glass.

Gannaway dropped a paper bag into the dirt at her feet. He raised his foot and brought it down. The bag popped, glass tinkling within. "You're trying my *patience,* woman! You see how easily I crushed my medicine? What do you think I'm capable of doing to folks who *irk* me?"

Mr. Keppler looked out the window, then vanished. She considered running inside for protection but knew Keppler wouldn't do anything. Couldn't do anything, more like. Turning away, she fought back the tears. She wouldn't give Gannaway the satisfaction. As she scuttled down the street, she took one last glance.

Gannaway kicked the back fender of his car, then

punched the door, cursing like a sailor. The car wobbled, rocking back and forth. Inside, Naira held her head down, trying to stay afloat. Claire hoped she hadn't sent her drowning into the sea of misery.

It didn't take long for the men to sign, dot, and cross the paperwork. A few days after the Reservation meeting, everything fell into place. Dickinson practically salivated when he collected the forms from Tommy.

Down in the mine, the men showed a reinvigorated kick in their stride. For the first time since George's funeral, Tommy saw hope in his crew's eyes. Singing and joking were the new order of the day. Occasionally, a man would stop Tommy, drop his voice to a whisper and ask, "When we gonna strike?"

"Soon," he'd tell them.

Tommy knew it had to happen. The sooner, the better. It seemed inevitable. But like the most inexperienced greenhorn, he held out hope Mr. Gannaway would come to his senses so they could avoid any days without pay. Didn't seem likely, but he always believed in giving a man a fair shake.

"Earl, where's Big Ed?" Tommy hadn't spoken to Big Ed all morning. He'd only seen his bigger-than-life backside several times, his massive shoulders rounded and hunched. Almost as if avoiding him. Tommy suspected the union talks had set him on edge.

"Last time I saw him was down in the stope."

Grabbing his lunch bucket, Tommy sloshed down the drift. Claire had put a bread and sugar sandwich in his lunch today, the sure way to soothe Ed's union doubts.

Humming drifted toward him. Low and solemn. Mechanical and cold. Tommy froze. The melody sounded familiar, eerily so. He recognized the tune, plucked it out of his mind as if from a nearly forgotten dream. The gospel song Karl had sung years back. *Couldn't be.*

Ed sat in the dark, slumped forward on a boulder. He rocked back and forth, keeping stride with his song.

"Ed?" Tommy lit the torch on his helmet. The fire flashed, then settled, throwing an arc of light over Ed. Ed cradled his stomach as if holding a baby, singing it quietly to sleep. "What're you doing down here?"

Tommy dropped a hand on Ed's shoulder. Ed trembled at his touch, his entire body quivering. "Oh." One word. But that word spoke volumes.

"Ed? You okay?"

When Ed turned, he closed his eyes as if the light stung them. "Tommy? Not...feeling too good..."

"Are you sick? Tell me what's going on." Tommy had seen behavior like Ed's before. He gripped his lunch pail tight and hoped he wouldn't have to use it. "Look at me, Ed."

Ed's deep sigh sounded like the curmudgeon Tommy knew and loved. A great sense of relief surged through him. Until Ed opened his eyes. One eye appeared healthy-looking, squinting into the light. But the other eye, wide open and unyielding to the torch, had yellow speckles closing in around the iris.

"Oh, sweet Jesus, Ed. Are you—" *Are you what?* Tommy couldn't ask about the yellow-eyed fever, wouldn't allow it credence. But mostly, he didn't want to think of his friend—hell, his second father—suffering from the new miner's sickness. A bad sickness. "Ed, the dust botherin' you? Tell me what's wrong." Tommy's knuckles grew white over the lunch-box handle. *Please, God, don't make me use it.*

Something caught in Ed's throat. He forced a long, drawn-out swallow, wincing at the pain. "I'm...sick, Tommy. I think...I'm in a bad way..." He reached an arm out. Tommy grasped it, helped him to his feet. Ed fell back onto the boulder and nearly took Tommy with him. It hurt to see Ed in this condition. He'd always been one of the strongest—physically and mentally—men Tommy knew. Now he flailed about like an infant, uncertain of his footing. "Send me home, boss. Before something...bad happens."

The lunchbox dropped into the water. Tommy felt shame in even considering using it as a weapon. Not on Big Ed. Never. Tommy sat next to him and wrapped an arm over his shaking shoulders. "I'll get you out of here. You just get better. Promise me you will. I need you."

Ed laughed, a rattling, phlegm-filled sound. "You need me like a hole in the head. You just keep doin' what you're doin', Tommy."

It sounded like goodbye, but Tommy wasn't gonna have it. Wouldn't accept it. Big Ed was the only person he could truly count on besides his family. Hell, Ed *was* part of his family. Tommy took his time, making damn sure he had his emotions under control before he spoke. "I *do* need you. You ain't goin' nowhere. We'll get you through this, you'll see. With the new clinics we're going to get—"

"Ain't no time. Just see it don't happen again. I'm seeing things, Tommy. *Hearing* things. Terrible things—"

"Let's go." Maybe if he didn't hear about the terrible things, they wouldn't exist. Tommy shot to his feet and called down the drift. Men came running.

"Fellas, Big Ed's sick. The dust and damp done got to him. We need to send him home for the day."

It took Tommy and two others to get Ed to his feet. Dragging him down the drift proved harder work than a full day in the mines. Tommy almost put him on one of the carts to have a donkey haul him, but knew the men would crack jokes about it. A mining legend deserved better.

It took four men to hoist him into the bucket. With his gaze steadfastly earthbound, Ed clawed at the air like a blind man. "Tommy?"

"I'm here."

He found Tommy's shoulders and squeezed. "Do something for me. Promise me you'll do it."

"I will. Just name it."

"Promise me you'll strike. Before...before..." He shook his head, words failing him.

They watched Big Ed rise up into the sky, like an angel

delivered into his Heavenly afterlife.

"If you could see inside insteaddd, you'd see a brand new mannn..."

The song verse rang out clear as spring water. Tommy told himself he was still asleep, that in his dream he was underground listening to Big Ed hum the song. A vivid dream. No, not a dream, a nightmare.

Except Tommy lay fully awake in bed. And still, he heard the song.

" 'Cause the old man is deaddd."

Burying his head underneath the pillow didn't help. The song sliced through his protective sheath.

Claire rolled over, murmured, fell back to sleep. Probably the best sleep she'd had in a few nights. The yellow-eyed fever nonsense had been bothering her. Lately, she'd looked like she hadn't slept a wink in days. Not a chance Tommy would wake her, even if he did want to know if she heard the song.

"If you could see inside insteaddd, you'd see a brand new mannn..."

Tommy slipped into his overalls, grabbed his boots, and tiptoed out of the bedroom.

Once outside, it took a minute for his eyes to adjust to the darkness. Big Ed, in all his three hundred pound glory, sat on his front step. He swayed back and forth, hugging his knees to his chest, a particularly challenging position for a man carrying his girth. *Singing.*

"'Cause the old man is deaddd."

"Ed?" At first, relief rinsed away Tommy's earlier fears. Big Ed looked healthy enough, a far cry from his earlier bout with whatever it was he'd come down with. Didn't matter what time it was, either. Not if Ed was better.

"Ed, you all right now?"

"If you could see inside insteadd, you'd see a brand new mannn..."

That song. No, Ed wasn't all right. Tommy knew it, didn't want to believe it, struggled to keep knowledge from clawing its way out of his gut.

"Ed?"

Ed clambered to his feet, more spryly than usual, but with an odd stiffness dictating his every move. Like a puppet on strings, his arms wrenched up awkwardly, conducting an invisible chorus. He marched down the road, his boots kicking haphazardly at the dirt.

Tommy tied his boots quickly and followed. "Ed? Wait a minute!" Ed's bald spot glowed under the moonlight, pale and worm white. He tramped down the road, his arms moving back and forth in rhythm, as though marching.

For a big man, Ed moved fast. For a sick man, he moved incredibly fast. Tommy followed, calling out to him in a low voice. In the distance, a dog barked at the neighborhood interlopers. "Ed?"

"'Cause the old man is deaddd."

Ed walked into the grassy meadow skirting the reservation, surprisingly nimble, easily avoiding the holes in the earth. Tommy's toe caught the edge of a fissure and tossed him forward onto his knees. He watched as Big Ed beckoned him forward, teasing him like a child playing tag. His gestures rippled like water, smooth as silk.

If Tommy had stopped to think, he probably wouldn't have followed Ed. But another part of his brain had taken over, operating on a different plane, one step beyond dreaming. He had to follow, nothing could stop him. But his stomach churned with dread.

Ed blurred into a shadowy figure before he vanished into the woods. The same woods Tommy had played in as a child, the same woods he had memorized like his wife's beautiful face. But in the dark, it was *different.*

Twigs snapped underfoot as Tommy stepped onto the path. A creature flit in front of him, so close he felt a brush of wind as it took flight. Cicadas buzzed, stopped abruptly, and started again.

"Ed? Where are you?"

"If you could see inside insteaddd, you'd see a brand new mannn..."

Ed's voice lowered, croaking like a frog. Coming from a place far away. Tommy listened, following the sound, a skill he'd honed down in the mines.

"'Cause the old man is deaddd."

Louder now. From the clearing ahead. A clearing he knew well. Trees opened up above, inviting the moon's white spotlight. The singing halted mid-verse just as the cicadas stopped their deafening song. A branch creaked. Silence. Another creak. Steady, equally measured out, like the ticking of a Grandfather clock.

Whoosh. Creak. Whoosh. Creak.

A large, shadowy pendulum slowly swung back and forth.

Big Ed dangled at the end of a rope, his toes pointed toward the ground.

"Oh, my God, Ed, no!" Tommy raced toward him. He thrust his arms around Ed's legs and struggled to lift him. *"Ed! No, dear God, no!"* Ed's eyes were closed, his neck crooked at the noose. The branch groaned under the weight, threatening to snap.

Too late.

Tommy held on, prayed to be wrong, prayed for the nightmare to end.

Maybe if I'd checked on him earlier, this wouldn't've happened!

Ed had been sick, no doubt about that. And Tommy had been wrapped up in finalizing union business instead of taking care of him. "Ed, I'm sorry, *please,* oh, God. *Why?"*

Ed's eyes snapped open. His yellow eye, now completely doused in a sick shade of gold, glistened with moisture.

"Join us, Tommy...come join us..."

"No. *No!"* Tommy dropped into the leaves, scuttling backward like a crab until he butted up against a tree. His world collapsed around him.

This wasn't—couldn't—possibly be real.

Maybe just a reaction. Muscle spasms. He'd read sometimes that corpses displayed involuntary physical reactions.

Not this time, though. Ed stared at him. Whispered to him. Said things. Ed's words changed to gibberish, a language Tommy couldn't understand. Didn't want to understand, either.

Ed's eyes shuttered, and the branch broke. *Riiiiiiippppp.* Ed plummeted to the ground, wisps of dust rising from beneath him.

Crickets restarted their chorus. The buzz-sawing sound slithered into whispers. Human whispers from everywhere. Above. Around. *Below.*

"Come join us, Tommy…join us…join us…"

Tommy howled like a wolf, mad at the moon.

Chapter Eighteen

1969...

"I'm going to start charging you for gas, you know. A career as a chauffer's never been one of my loftier ambitions." Therese glanced over at Dennis, a smile taking the sting out of her words.

"Hey, it's not my fault it'll take a couple of days for the tires to come in. Never been in a town where a mechanic had to actually order tires. But I shoulda expected it around here. I'm just glad you knew a mechanic. Thank God for small favors, huh?"

"Yeah. 'Cause under these circumstances, we need all the favors we can get."

Therese turned smoothly into Bob's driveway. He greeted them with an ear-to-ear grin, the happiest Dennis had seen him since their chats had begun. "Well, now, looks like we have some things to catch up on."

"That obvious?"

"Brother, you look like you've seen a ghost. Therese, how are you?"

"I'm fine." She glanced at her wrist, checking the time. "Listen, boys, I'm gonna leave you to it. I've got work to do.

But I'll be checking in. You okay, Dennis?"

"Yeah. Thanks again. For everything." He studied her eyes. Nope, not the time for a goodbye kiss. She barely even returned his hug.

As Therese's car roared down the highway, the men settled into their lawn chairs.

Click. Sssss. Bob fortified himself amply with a can of artistic inspiration. "Well?"

Last night's events seemed ludicrous in the morning light. Old habits died hard, though, and Dennis searched for logical explanations. Maybe everything that happened last night hadn't happened. But he was just fooling himself; he had to accept it. No way around it. *Just tell it like it is.* He finished the story and waited as Bob knocked back the rest of his beer. Finally, he cracked open another can and spoke.

"Welcome to my world, brother."

"You're welcome to it. Not a world I want to visit again."

"Seems to me like you don't have much of a choice."

"What do you mean?"

Bob shifted, one knee cracking. "I mean the ghosts are appearing to you for a reason, brother."

"Kinda what I thought. What reason?"

"Now, that we don't know. Not yet." Dennis's spirits lifted when Bob said *we.* He wasn't alone. He had an ally. "But we can find out. Seems to me the ghosts want something from you."

"What?" Dennis's laughter edged toward hysteria. "What in the hell do I have to give these...ghosts?" *Ghosts.* Such a hard word to say. He hadn't had much reason to toss it around in the world of scientific study.

"Let's look at the facts, amigo. The ghosts of Gannaway are still around for a reason. I suspect they're lookin' to get laid to rest. Like it or not, brother, they must believe you're key to that."

"For God's sake, why? I'm just an environmental—"

"Yeah, yeah. We know what you are. Maybe this is about what they think you can be."

"I don't follow—"

"For such a smart fella, you're pretty dense sometimes." Bob tapped his temple. "The ghosts don't appear to everyone. Usually just sensitives. I don't see you that way. So they want somethin'. They're restless and tired at the same time. They want to move on. You're their conduit."

"Conduit?"

"That's right. Find out why they're still lurkin' about, put 'em to rest. Now if you've been payin' attention, I've been layin' out Gannaway's history for you. You already know the reason Gannaway's haunted."

"Yellow-eyed fever." Dennis said it without a hint of sarcasm. Just another component of his new world paradigm.

"That's right. But there's more to the story. Once we piece together what we know, maybe we can find out what we don't know."

"Bob, why would they use my son? He wasn't a miner. He didn't have yellow-eyed—"

"Damn it, Dennis! How in the hell do you think they'd get your attention otherwise? If your son hadn't visited you last night, would you believe in the miners' ghosts? Or would you have chalked it up to chat rats?"

"I suppose you're right."

"'Course I'm right." *Slurp.* A victory drink for Bob. "Always am. Just haven't been able to convince the white man about it. No offense."

"None taken." Dennis didn't want to ask, but he had to know. As painful as the answer might be. "Do you think that was really Devin I saw last night?"

Bob grimaced, the lines on his forehead deepening and riding high. He popped open his third beer. "Want me to hold your hand, coddle you like a babe? Or you want the truth?"

"The truth."

"I believe it was your boy. Maybe he was, oh, I don't know, trying to help in his own way."

"Oh...God..." Dennis slunk into his chair. His son was

a restless spirit? *Please, no.* He felt old, much more feeble than in his worst drinking days. "Does this mean Devin can't rest either? Is there something I need to do to give him peace?"

"Hard to say, brother. Sorry. It's the best I got. But you know something? If I were a betting man—and I ain't, so don't go gettin' into that Indian stereotype—from what you've told me, sounds more like you're hauntin' yourself over your son's death than Devin is. Wasn't your fault what happened. I'm sure he doesn't blame you. Maybe it's time for you to lay that ghost to rest."

"If only I could—"

"Dammit, brother, just do it. You know, sometimes the cosmic ways of the universe align. You think it's just a job, you being here. I think otherwise. You were sent here to put a stop to the haunting. Finally. But to do that, you gotta fix yourself first. So quit wallowin' in self-despair and get your *shit* together."

"You really think so?"

"I do. And stop doubting. Could be your downfall."

"Fine. But...what next?"

"I'll help you. Best I can."

"You'll be my Tonto?"

Crunch. The can bounced off Dennis's temple. "Damn it!"

"You don't get to make those jokes. Too many negative Indian jokes as it is. I'll be the Lone Ranger. You're Tonto."

"As you say, Kemo Sabe."

"That's better." Bob sat back with a satisfied grin. "Know your place."

Right now, Dennis's place remained in the lawn chair at Bob's side, the safest place within twenty miles. Knowing he had help made his impossible task feel less daunting. "So, you didn't say anything about the bottle in my room."

"What's there to say?" He shrugged. "You think it's Gannaway. Sounds like a good bet to me. Evil bastard."

"You've sorta hinted at that before. Why do you think he's evil?"

Bob stared off at the tips of the chat piles in the distance and rubbed his knee as if he'd been climbing them. "I'll tell you soon. But first, we have work to do. Best get on it before sundown. For obvious reasons."

"Where do we start?"

"Where do you think? You're the damned conduit."

Dennis was tempted to make a joke about being "Conduit-Sabe," but let it slide. None of this was a joking matter. "You say we need to explore deeper. What about that run-down mining museum down the road? Worth looking into?"

"I've been around long enough to know—trust intuition. If that's what your innards are telling you, then that's where you start."

"My guts have spoken then. But how do we get in? I really don't want to ask Gannaway for access."

Bob reached into a pocket and pulled out a ring of keys. He jangled them like sleigh bells. "The keys to the kingdom, brother."

Bob barreled down the highway in the 1962 Thunderbird, driving with a teenager's glee and deadly belief of invulnerability. Patches of cancerous rust ate at the car's body. Hot air rushed up through a hole in the floorboard and poured in through the open windows. If the T-bird had ever had air conditioning, it was long gone now. Bob's long hair flapped about his face, obscuring his vision. Dennis gripped the dashboard and hoped to survive the trip.

The car chugged into Gannaway and snorted out a blast through the exhaust pipe. Bob pulled a U-turn and stopped the death mobile in front of the stretch of abandoned stores. He banged on the dented glove box until it popped open. A wad of speeding tickets snowed to the floor. Bob grabbed a large flashlight, almost too large for any hand to easily handle.

"Best we park over here, brother. Fewer eyes upon us and all that."

Dennis jumped out of the car, happy to be on firm ground but not encouraged by Bob's warning. Bob trotted off down the highway, and Dennis scurried to catch up.

"If you have the keys to the museum, why do we care if anyone sees us go in?"

"You know the answer to that. Years ago, when the museum proprietor closed down and moved away, he left the keys. Said to keep an eye on the place. Not that anyone would ever go there again. Think he did it just for nostalgia's sake. Gannaway and Stokes don't know I have the keys. Doubt they'd care one way or another. But it's best to be cautious when dealing with them."

The wooden porch warped, and the lip of the roof slanted, tipping them a welcome. Or a warning. *Good luck, all ye who enter here.* One of the white pillars had crumbled, the other one was ready to follow. Most of the windows sat in pieces. Broken glass lay on the porch. A chill ran down Dennis's back. He wondered if people had been trying to break in. Or *escape.*

Bob flipped through the collection of keys, trying several before settling on the winning entry. "Now, be forewarned, brother, ain't much left in the museum. Most everything's been scavenged. All the old mining equipment's gone, probably sold off for scrap metal. But there're still photos and newspaper clippings. Guess those don't have much market value."

Hefting the doorknob up, Bob leaned into it with a shoulder shove.

The rectangle of sunlight stretched across the mostly barren floor. Bob closed the door.

"Can't we leave it open?"

"Best not to." Bob closed an eyelid and tapped it. "Watchful eyes and all."

The door shut with a wooden *thump.* The sound of a coffin closing.

Click. Bob swung the flashlight's beam across the room.

Curtains of cobwebs draped from the ceiling's corners. Water droplets stretched from the ceiling, then plopped to the rotting floorboards. "Careful where you step."

Something squeaked, followed by a pitter-patter of tiny feet. Red paint on the wall displayed a message. *Goodby Gannaway.* Streaks of thick paint ran from the misspelled graffiti, congealing into crimson teardrops. Glass-fronted display cases sat shattered, jagged shards of teeth surrounding the empty mouths.

Scrapbooks rested on a drooping bookshelf. Bob played the light over them. "Might find those of interest."

Dennis opened one of the books. A rancid, moldy odor filled his nose. Pages pried apart with a tug and a *squick*, but the articles, mostly yellowed news clippings, appeared legible. Dennis gathered the three books and set them by the door. Taking the books might be considered stealing, but reading them in the museum was out of the question.

"Come here, brother." Bob's light landed on a wall-hanging.

A decade of dirt covered the glass frame. Bob wiped it as clean as possible with his shirt sleeve, then coughed away the swirling dust. The strip below the black-and-white photo read *The Gannaway Lead & Smelting Company, 1934.*

"This was the year before everything went to shit." Three rows of men anchored the photo, the first line kneeling, one knee up like a posed football team. Grimy, serious, thin faces glowered out at them, the men's overalls ill-fitting. They had the gaunt appearance associated with serious health issues. Bob ran his index finger across the front row, stopping on a sandy-haired, handsome man, younger than the rest and one of the very few miners sporting a grin. "Tommy Donnelly. Told you about him. Got more to tell you about him, too. He was the youngest foreman in the mines. And the one who organized the strike of 1935."

Dennis nodded. "Looks a bit happier than the rest of them."

"He was. Good man. Knew him, knew his wife better. I've told you about Claire. If anyone could've organized the men, it was him. As much good as it did him."

Bob moved over to the next hanging photo, brushed the dust away. "1935. The year it all happened." As Dennis studied the photo, the image appeared to blur. For a moment, he thought Bob had fumbled the flashlight. But Bob's hand held steady, the butt of the flashlight planted solidly against his belly like a shotgun.

The image quivered. Dennis squinted, straining for a better focal point. The photograph vibrated again. This time Dennis didn't question his eyesight.

"Um, Bob, you see that?"

"I did."

The frame rattled against the wall, knocking like an anxious visitor at the door.

"No earthquakes in Kansas, brother."

Maybe not, but Dennis remembered Bob's stories of subsidences. The museum could be sinking into the ground, dropping into the mines below, delivering them into a lonely grave.

Bob said, "Uh-oh."

The contents of the photo stirred, distorted, transforming the tableau. The miners' heads moved, craning. Their puzzled looks suggested they had no idea where they were. Or how they came to be trapped in a photograph. Tommy Donnelly, or rather his photographic likeness, lifted off his knee and stood. He leaned forward, eyes searching. He gave a curt nod, as though he'd seen Dennis and Bob and offered a greeting. He walked forward. His image grew larger until he dropped out of the frame.

"Oh. My. *God*. Bob, *tell* me I'm not going crazy."

"You're not, brother. We're not that lucky." Bob's hand shook, the flashlight's beam dancing like a firefly trapped in a jar.

A hand flew up within the picture frame, sending them both back a step. It waved, beckoning them to the left.

"Jesus Christ."

Bob's ring of light tracked to the left of the photo. A small shadow of a man, no larger than a hand puppet, waltzed across the wall. Almost playful, it stayed one step ahead of the flashlight's beam. Dennis looked behind him. Nothing in the museum could've created such a silhouette. Then he hurried to the next hanging photograph.

Just a drill and a bucket dangling atop a mineshaft's collar. No miners. Bob maintained a cautious distance but recognized the shaft nonetheless. "That's Tommy Donnelly's old mine. The Gold Pot Mine, number thirty-seven."

Dennis poked a finger at the picture, quickly withdrew it. He cleaned the frame with his elbow. A shadow stretched across the ground by the collar. Tommy Donnelly strolled into frame. He stopped. Turning toward them, he pointed toward the bucket, then the mine's gaping collar, and ended with a thumb to his chest. He repeated the cryptic message slowly, over and over again, until Dennis had to look away.

"Bob. I've seen enough."

"You and me both, brother."

The beam bounced wildly about the room as they ran for the door. Dennis stumbled over an upturned floorboard and pitched forward. Splinters stabbed into his hands. Bob pulled him to his feet, stronger than he looked.

The door wouldn't open, permanently warped from the dampness. Dennis yanked, fear bubbling within him. The door wrenched off a hinge, fell, and clattered down beside them. Dust rose like smoke.

Dennis stood within the welcome rectangle of sunlight. He grabbed the three scrapbooks.

Impossible shadows bobbed across the sunlight-dappled floor, playing a perverse game of peekaboo. A five-fingered shadow reached out, close to Dennis's silhouetted head.

They tore across the highway, neither man looking back. They didn't even look for oncoming cars.

"Why did Lipstein and the Injun go into the museum?"

Gus squirmed in his seat. The inner lining of his trouser pockets showed distastefully, his pants near bursting at the seams. If Kyle Gannaway didn't hold the memory of Gus's father in such high esteem, he would've cut Gus loose long ago. Gus was dead weight, a *lot* of dead weight. "Aheh. Sir, with all due respect, I don't believe there's a threat, let alone a problem—"

"How's that showing me 'due respect,' Gus? God *damn* it. Lipstein's becomin' more of a problem every day."

"Yes, sir. We're watching him." *Ho, ho, haaa.* Not Gus's full-on laugh, but enough to annoy the living tar out of Gannaway.

"Stop laughin'! Be more like your old man and grow some man parts. Your daddy never laughed once in his life."

At this, Gus blazed red as a fiery sunset. Gannaway excelled at going for a person's jugular, and he'd long ago figured out Gus harbored "daddy issues." Knowledge, especially knowledge of weakness, was a formidable weapon, the best way to keep employees in line. "Yes, sir. Sorry, sir."

"What's he up to now?"

"As far as we can tell, he went back to Litttlefish's house."

"And if he goes pokin' his nose further? What then? What're you gonna do if he goes steppin' through the mines again? You gonna consider him a threat then?"

With his hands clenched between his knees, Gus took in a deep breath, then expelled it through plump lips. "Then, yes, he'll be a threat."

"And you're fully prepared to take care of the threat?"

"Yes, sir."

"How?"

"Sir?"

"How you gonna deal with the threat?" Gannaway held up a hand. A dare, almost. "Careful how you answer that."

"Gonna get gussied up," Gus said quietly.

Gannaway cupped a hand over his ear. "How's that?"

"Gonna get *gussied up*, sir!"

"Damn well better. One last chance we give the Jew.

One more. Then it's outta my hands. He brought it on him-self."

The chairs in Bob's front yard weren't nearly as appealing just before sunset as they were during the day. Bob parked his rattletrap in back of the house and fairly trotted inside. He hadn't slowed down since they raced out of the museum. Dennis followed him, making certain to lock the door behind him. He doubted a lock could keep out ghosts, but he felt safer nonetheless.

Dennis heaved a sigh and plunged into the soft, worn sofa. Bob vanished into another room. Dennis called out, "Bob? I know it's a huge imposition, but you suppose I could bunk on your sofa tonight?"

Bob reentered, struggling to look over a mountain of blankets in his arms. "Way ahead of you, brother. Hell, after today, I'd welcome the company." He heaved the covers at Dennis, a much softer bullet than a beer can.

"Thanks."

Comforting bric-a-brac cluttered every nook in the house, and paintings decorated the walls. A wild kaleido-scope of bursting colors and psychedelic patterns dazzled the eye. The chaos of the artwork looked like the effects of a bad LSD trip, but at least nothing moved.

Bob nestled into a recliner, a six-pack in hand.

"Are we going to...ah, talk about what we saw, Bob?"

Behind the beer can, he nodded. Dennis waited for him to finish the beer. Didn't take long. "You see what I saw? Tommy Donnelly moving in the photo?"

"Sure did. Couldn't believe it. What's it mean?"

"Might mean a lotta things, brother. Could be a warn-ing. Might be he's trying to tell us something. You ask me, I think he wants you to go to his old mine."

"Yeah, I kinda suspected as much. But I'm not looking

forward to it."

"Look at it as the night before Christmas. The longest, most never-ending night of the year for kids. But once you wake? Big rewards." Dennis suspected Bob had knocked back something stronger while he tinkered about in the other room. His words sounded slurred, his demeanor more relaxed.

"Not very helpful." But Bob's analogy supplied the laugh Dennis needed.

"You'll need me as lookout. It's too dangerous to go into the mines yourself." A thoughtful silence followed Bob's long drink. "Unfortunately, you'll have to go at night."

"Shit."

"Exactly. But there ain't no way you can sneak in by daylight. Also, you might have to go calling Tommy Donnelly out. See if he'll tell you what he wants. Be friendly to the ghosts this time."

"This just gets better and better. I have to visit a ghost in a mine at night. And make friends with him."

"Ain't the ghosts you need to worry about, brother."

They sat quietly. Dennis had no plans on sleeping tonight, too many nightmares lurked, waiting for him. He had his homework next to him, the stack of moldy scrapbooks, but he hoped Bob would keep him company until dawn. "Bob, you said there's more story to tell. Let's hear it."

"All right, brother. Got my storytelling supplies here." He patted the six-pack in his lap like a pet poodle. "May as well start with what Gannaway did to me. I suppose my story's part of Gannaway's history, too. Just the hidden underbelly of it."

Walking from lamp to lamp, Bob switched every light on. Then he talked through the night.

Chapter Nineteen

1935...

Ahanu stood in the tree shadows on the other side of the cemetery and watched as the men lowered another miner into the ground. The newest yellow-eyed fever victim. He didn't know the man, had just seen him around, but he felt connected in an odd way. The yellow-eyed fever had impacted his life as well, dropping a ghost in his path. He knew there was a reason behind that spectral visit, but he couldn't put his finger on it. Not yet. Maybe the spirits wanted him to spread the word. Maybe he could find a way to stop the curse.

He'd told everyone who would listen about his visitation. The white men would have no part of it, of course, even though the miners would've benefitted the most. They glared at him as he told his tale, contempt in their eyes. Some laughed. Most ignored him.

His mother thought it an unwise road to travel. But he'd be a fool not to listen to the spirits when they spoke.

Sticking to the shadows, he watched the funeral and hoped for a sign to steer him on his path.

That sign stalked toward him in the guise of the frightening German man with one eye. On the reservation, they called him "Evil Moon Eye." No one dared look him in the eye for fear of having their souls stolen. The real stories Ahanu had heard about this man, though? More frightening than any superstitious beliefs.

Ahanu didn't recognize the two men following closely on the man's heels. Surely they couldn't have spotted him hiding in the trees. But the one-eyed man walked directly toward him, seeking him out as if by smell. Ahanu withdrew into the trees, a frightened animal.

Eberstark said, "Boy, I know you're in there. Come out. Or we'll come in after you." He delivered his request in a calm, icy manner. His words froze Ahanu as badly as a winter storm on the reservation. He retreated deeper into the woods. The thought of stumbling upon another ghost seemed like a safer alternative.

He heard their plodding footsteps behind him, crashing through the brush. "You'd better *stop*, redskin! Best thing for you!"

Ahanu found the well-trod path and raced along it. Stealth made no difference now. Only escape. A man lunged from behind a tree and grappled Ahanu's legs. His chin cracked onto the ground when he fell, teeth snipping at the tip of his tongue. Ahanu rolled over, lashing his feet out at his attacker.

"God damn it, you prairie dog. Hold *still!*"

Ahanu planted his foot solidly on the man's face. By the time he scrambled to his knees, the other two men had caught up.

"Boy. We just want to talk. You running? Not very friendly." The one-eyed man reached down, his grin lean and hungry. He snapped Ahanu's head up by a handful of hair. "I've heard things. Things you've been saying about the yellow-eyed fever. This does not please my employer. Do you understand?"

One-Eye tightened his grip, and Ahanu nodded. "I didn't hear anything, redskin. Say you understand."

"Yes...yes, sir."

He knelt, cupping Ahanu's chin gently as if preparing for a kiss. "I'd like to believe you. I may believe you. But I'm supposed to make an example of you. This is not going to be pleasant. For you. For me? It will be very pleasant." A coal-black shoe kicked out, forcing Ahanu onto his back.

The wooden-handled knife materialized from nowhere. One moment his hand had been empty, the next...*not.* Maybe One-Eye did possess magical powers.

Ahanu caught a reflection of the man's eye in the extended blade as he brandished it before him. Silver on silver.

"I'm sorry...sorry. I won't say anything again. I swear—"

"No, you won't." One-Eye waved the blade over Ahanu's chest, twirling it one way, then the other. Ahanu clamped his eyes shut. With a swift downward stroke, the knife tore through Ahanu's shirt. The tip of the blade broke his skin, trailing a small stream of blood behind it. With a yank, the man stripped away part of Ahanu's shirt. He fastened the rag tight over Ahanu's mouth. "No, you will not say anything about this to anyone. You had an accident. Do you understand me, redskin?"

Ahanu mumbled, "Yes." Through the gag, it sounded like, "Eff."

The man stood, one foot in the air. He wiggled his dress shoe above Ahanu, teasing the pain to come. The shoe smashed down onto Ahanu's ankle. Bone cracked. A pain, sharper than any knife blade, sliced through Ahanu's body, exploding into every limb. His chest arched. The rag locked his screams within his head.

The man dropped to the ground again. Stroking Ahanu's cheek tenderly, he whispered, "Remember this lesson, redskin. It's a white man's world. You'd do best to heed that. You want to live amongst us? Adapt. Learn our ways. Respect those better than you. You're inferior. You don't get to talk about us, especially spreading your beliefs. Keep your mouth shut. The sooner you learn this valuable lesson, the better off you'll be. The better place our country will be."

Standing, he brushed off his jacket. "I know it's a hard lesson to learn, but it's essential. This might make you remember it better...redskin." With speed like a rabbit, he dove and clenched Ahanu's wounded ankle with an iron grip. He twisted until Ahanu's leg popped in a place it shouldn't have.

Serrated flames of burning agony melted his vision, his mind, his body. The last thing Ahanu saw before he passed out was the face of the one-eyed monster smiling down at him. But upside down, it didn't resemble a smile at all.

Tommy felt dead inside. An integral part of his soul, his history, had dried up like drought-ravaged crops. Might as well bury that part of his soul alongside Big Ed's body. It would never come back.

It took the combined strength of eight men to lower Ed into the ground. The sight reminded Tommy of happier times when the miners once tried to hoist Ed up in the air on a bet. When they all tumbled down, defeated beneath his weight, no one ever laughed harder than Ed.

God rest you, Ed. I'll miss you.

This time Tommy didn't bother hiding his tears. Those he couldn't bury. In fact, more miners shed tears at Ed's gravesite than any he'd ever witnessed, absolutely pouring down grief.

Claire clung to him as if afraid to let go. She knew how much Ed meant to him.

Of course, he hadn't told Claire what had happened that night, what he'd thought he'd seen. He told himself the vision had been caused by the shock of seeing his best friend kill himself. It had seemed so real at the time. *Too real.* But nothing good would come out of fanning Claire's imaginary flames. She'd be better off not hearing his wild flight of fantasy. And best for everyone.

Miraculously (if you could even mention "miracle" in the same breath of such heartbreak), Tommy managed to keep Ed's suicide a secret. The news would have devastated Ed's wife, Myrtle, a God-fearing woman if Tommy had ever met one. If she thought Ed hadn't been delivered unto Heaven, she'd have dropped into an early grave right alongside her husband.

Gannaway's manservant left half-way through the funeral, followed by two strangers. Tommy resented the fact they'd even shown up for the proceedings, let alone demonstrated such disrespect by leaving early. Gannaway spewed forth his same, soulless speech, good for nothing but boosting his own ego. Tommy shut him out.

At George Kendricks's funeral, despair and sadness had bound the miners together. But now anger hovered over the men like a thundercloud ready to burst. Anger at Gannaway, anger at their work situation, anger that Big Ed had been yanked prematurely from their lives.

Tommy gave one short nod to each man. They returned it. An unspoken agreement had been reached.

Time to strike.

"Kaya, I heard what happened to Ahanu. How is he?"

Kaya's eyes were red, her hair visibly grayer than it had been just a few days before. *She's in mourning.* Something Claire had grown accustomed to these last, hard days. That wasn't all, though. Something else was different. Tension. Tension so tight Claire was afraid to touch her lest her skin crack.

"His leg's bad. Broken in two places. Doc Wilkins did what he could, but he'll be in bed for some time."

"That's *awful.* I'm terribly sorry. How did it happen?"

"Ahanu says it was an accident. Fell out of a tree. But it wasn't any accident." Kaya stiffened when Claire reached for her hand. She wrenched it back to her chest and swaddled it within her shirtsleeve.

"Kaya...surely, nobody would *do* this to him."

"I know the truth."

"Why would someone hurt Ahanu? He's a good boy. He—"

"His chest was cut, Claire!" The spite behind her words bit deeply. "Knife wounds don't *happen* from falling out of a tree."

"Oh, my..." Claire collapsed into a chair, leaning a shoulder against the washing basin for support. "That's just..."

Kaya picked up a dish, wiped it clean. She glowered at Claire and held the dish at chin level, then dropped it to the floor. The explosion startled Claire. "And now he's different, Claire."

"Different? How?"

"He's turned his back on our ways. Wants to be called 'Bob.' Says it's a white man's world. That he needs to adapt."

Claire jumped to her feet. She wanted to hug her friend, give comfort. Kaya crossed her arms and warded off contact.

"Kaya, if there's anything I can—"

"You can't. In fact, it's best we don't talk again. White folk and Indian folk shouldn't mix."

"No, we—"

"If it wasn't for...I've said what I wanted to say. Respect my wishes. Don't talk to me again." Kaya left the kitchen, dropping her apron to the floor with finality.

Claire thought she'd grown accustomed to mourning. But the death of her valued friendship dug a new crevasse in her heart.

Dickinson looked whiter and wetter than a fresh coat of

whitewash. Sweat formed dark circles beneath his armpits and percolated across his forehead.

It didn't seem Dickinson was going to invite him in, so Tommy took the initiative and stepped inside the hotel room. No sense talking union business in the hallway for everyone to hear.

"Nice place." Tommy had never been in one of the hotel's rooms before. Never had a need to. After several restless nights at the Gannaway Boarding House, Dickinson had decided to upgrade to the hotel. The men's union fees at work, no doubt. "The way you look, I'm guessing your visit to Mr. Gannaway didn't go very well."

Dickinson sat down on the bed. Holes riddled his suit trouser's knees. Grass stained his once-pristine jacket. "You take it right. He...his manservant...my God..."

It took all the restraint Tommy had not to laugh. The Big City man had probably never met a violent man before in his life. "Did he—" Tommy paused deliberately. "—*escort* you from the house?"

"If you call being tossed out physically escorted, yes. My God..."

"What happened?"

"Things started out cordial, friendly. Once I said I was union...well, Gannaway went belly-up, stark-raving bananas! He said, hell no, he wasn't gonna negotiate. He won't even consider talking to us."

Tommy wasn't overly surprised, though he'd held onto a slight hope of fairness on Gannaway's behalf. He needed to quit thinking that way. "I figured it would be a waste of time. I gotta tell you, Dickinson, the men are ready to strike. Too many deaths lately. Deaths that could've been avoided. You just tell us what we need to do."

Bit by bit, color trickled back into Dickinson's face. "Well, in our successful strikes in the past, we've closed the mines."

"And just how in the hell do you propose we do that? It ain't like they're our mines to shut down."

"Just leave that to me. But get your men organized and

have 'em prepared. They'll have to picket the mines. Let me know when."

"Sooner rather than later. Dickinson, this whole thing is a mess. I've been keeping up with what's going on in Washington in the newspapers. The politicians argue all the time about whether unions are legal or not, but they never decide anything. I gotta tell you, I'm worried."

"Tommy, I've got everything under control. I'll be bringing in some international union men to help." Dickinson averted his eyes like he had something to hide.

"Dickinson?"

"Yeah?"

"How many successful strikes have you been involved with?"

"Um...this is my first. But, don't worry. Just leave it all to me."

Claire tried to keep a steady stream of chatter going with T.J. and Margaret on their way home, but she found it next to impossible. At one point, T.J. asked if anything was wrong. Just like his daddy, intuitive to a fault. But she couldn't stop playing the scene with Kaya over and over in her mind like a motion picture. Her guilt weighed heavier than a bag of ill-gained gold.

Hand in hand, they turned onto their road. Claire spotted a figure across from her house. A woman, heavily shrouded in an intricately designed shawl. The visitor tentatively stepped forward when she saw Claire, then ducked back into the cover of the trees. Claire recognized those rich, milk chocolate eyes even from a distance.

"T.J., take your sister into the house and stay with Grandma."

Claire watched them disappear inside before walking to the trees.

"Mrs. Gannaway?"

Naira Gannaway swiveled as if to leave, then stopped. She turned back and pressed a finger to her covered lips.

As Claire approached her, Naira pulled the shawl from her mouth. Her eyes flit back and forth. "Please," she whispered, "it's important we remain quiet. My husband mustn't know I'm here. And call me Naira."

"Naira." Claire tried to match her whisper. "What are you doing here?"

Her eyes blinked, full of empathy. She reached for Claire's hands and pressed something inside. Hard and round. A beaded pendant. A six-point star sat at the center, painstakingly crafted from bright orange, dazzling yellow, and candy-apple red beads.

"Take this, Mrs. Donnelly."

"Claire."

"Claire, I can't do anything about the curse. But I want to help you. Make sure your husband wears this. At all times. It will protect him."

"But...what is it?" Claire studied the beautiful pendant, stroking the smooth texture.

"It's the Fallen Star. Protector and Bringer of Light. It will protect your husband from harm."

Clasping the necklace to her chest, Claire hoped to feel the power of the Fallen Star. She felt something better. *Hope.* "Thank you. Truly. But...why do this? I thought—"

"I can't help all the miners. But if I can help one... maybe that will erase some of the damage I've done."

"Naira, you did nothing wrong."

When Naira's eyes closed, her eyelids fluttered as if batting away pain. "That's not what I'm told," she said. Claire knew immediately who'd told her such things. Her beastly husband, obviously berating his wife at every turn. Another woman treated as a secondary citizen, subservient to her dominant husband. An unfair role in a sometimes unfair world.

"It's not your fault. Don't let your husband—"

Naira's eyes grew wide at the mention of her husband.

She took a step back and raised her hands. Claire imagined she'd lots of practice doing that. "Stop. And please don't say anything to anyone about my being here." She wheeled and sprinted through the field, leaping over tall brush like a gazelle.

Claire nearly called out her name, but she stopped herself. She wanted to tell Naira she didn't have to accept such vile behavior from her husband. And so many other things. But the time had passed. "Thank you," she said, even though Naira had long vanished.

Kyle Gannaway moved the chair to the foyer. He nudged it once, inched it back a little bit. Dissatisfied, he picked it up and slammed it down with a crack. He sat down and grinned. *Perfect.* He'd be the first thing his wife saw when she returned.

Whenever that might be.

His mind traveled, concocting various scenarios. The longer he dwelled, the further his patience unraveled. Could she be sleeping with another man? Worse yet, a redskin? And bringing her diseased woman parts into his bed? *Unacceptable.*

Or maybe she'd taken to ranting like a lunatic about the yellow-eyed fever. Spreading foul lies, stirring up the miners. *His* men. The *nerve* of that lowly woman. Without him, she'd have nothing. Not a plugged nickel.

Didn't he see to her every need? She didn't lack for anything. A good husband, he ensured she had everything the rest of the town couldn't afford. But her *gall.* She *knew* she wasn't allowed outside the house without him. Her unwarranted actions screamed betrayal, plain and simple.

The very fact she'd asked him what he intended on doing today should've set his suspicions on alert. She never delved into his business. She knew better. At least he'd *thought* she did, but apparently not. He'd expected to find her in the bedroom after the Tri-State meeting. She rarely left it, the lazy sow. But he'd found it empty, the bed unmade.

How hard can it be to make a goddamn bed?

Tick-tock.

The grandfather clock next to him chunked out seconds, stretching into agonizingly long minutes.

Tick-tock.

The pendulum echoed every throbbing pain penetrating his head, stronger with each swing.

Tick-tock.

A vein in his head bulged, the cords in his neck pulled taut like ropes.

Tick-tock. Come home. Tick-tock. Come home...

Willing her appearance only agitated his headache.

The doorknob turned. Her dark hand slid inside, fumbling for the light switch. She entered quieter than midnight. She unwrapped her shawl before she finally noticed him. She stopped dead in her tracks, looking guilty as sin. *Filthy whore.*

"Naira."

"Oh...you frightened me." She rolled the shawl into a ball, toying with it, something to focus her guilt-ridden eyes on.

"Where have you *been?*"

"I...took a walk."

Liar. He knew it as sure as if he could peek inside her mind. "Horse *shit!* Now you gonna tell me where you *been?*"

"A walk." As she brushed by him, he latched onto her arm. The chair clattered to the floor when he jumped up.

One lie he could forgive after a good punishment. The same lie twice, however? Absolutely unforgivable.

His knuckles bashed into her cheek, sending her reeling backward. Her whorish tongue darted out, licking at the trickle of blood.

"Stop! No more!"

He reached for her, ready to show her who was boss.

"I'll stop when you tell me the *goddamned* truth!"

"No!" She'd never raised her voice before.

Gonna be the last time, too.

She leaped up the first couple of steps and turned. "I went for a walk. I can take a walk if I'd like to." She hurtled up the stairs, avoiding her deserved punishment. Gannaway stormed after her, his heavy feet pounding the steps, a thunderous precursor for what he had in mind for her. She stopped at the top. As he stalked toward her, fire blistered in his veins.

Tick-tock. Liar. Tick-tock. Ingrate.

He wrenched her wrists together. Gave them a few extra twists for good measure. Indian rope burn, some folks called it.

"Where *were* you?"

"All right! I went to see Mrs. Donnelly!"

Gannaway fell back as if a fist had hit him. "For *God's* sake, why? Ain't I had a bad enough day, what with the union man and all that *horse shit?* You know how hard it is to run this *goddamned* town, let alone tryin' to keep my wife in tow?"

He slapped her, open-handed, the kind that didn't leave marks. She staggered, twisting around on the stairwell rail. Her hateful glare stunned him. He certainly didn't deserve it.

Tick-tock. Show her. Tick-tock. Teach her.

"Bastard!" She ran at him growling, fingers clawing the air. Finally showing her true stock, nothing but a savage beast. Her hands rammed into his chest. It didn't matter.

"Why, you little *bitch!"*

Gannaway grabbed her arms, swung her around several times, a violent country hoe-down. His head swelled with dizziness, and he released her. When she spat at him, his head exploded. That's what it felt like, at least. His right hand hammered into her jaw. The resulting crack came from either her chin or his knuckles. Felt *good.* Sounded even better. She faced him, steadying herself against the railing.

Tick-tock. Kill her.

He shoved. Her bottom perched on the railing. Her legs flipped up, toes pointing at the ceiling. The way he usually liked them. Unbalanced and unsteady, she wavered, her arms flapping at her side. Better help the little bird fly away. With a smile, he pushed again. Not hard at all. Her arms went up, a backward dive. The expensive shoes he'd bought her kicked up toward the chandelier. Then she slipped away.

Her body landed with a soft thud, like a bag of potatoes dropped off the back of a truck into the dirt. Disappointing, really. Not the cathartic snapping of bones he had hoped for.

Leaning over the railing, he looked down.

Blood oozed from her mouth as she gasped for air. Her eyes clouded over. But the smile she managed before she died left him unsatisfied. That smile—it was almost as if she'd *won.* As if he'd done what she'd wanted. Like she'd been released.

Tick-tock. She's dead. Tick-tock...

"Steffen!"

Goddammit, where is he?

Gannaway prodded his wife's body with the toe of his boot. Dead all right, but he knew that. Still, he wanted the last word. He'd damn well earned it. He nudged her again. Her head wobbled to the side, and her dead eyes stared up at him. *One last act of defiance.* He pressed his fingers over her eyelids and drew them shut.

"Steffen! Get your ass in here!"

"I'm here, sir." Steffen stepped out from beneath the stairwell. For a minute, Gannaway worried that Steffen had witnessed the entire ordeal. But just for a minute. *So what if he had?* Steffen wouldn't talk. He knew which side of his bread carried butter.

His manservant stared down at Naira's body, his expression unchanged. A corner of his mouth flinched, then dropped, a smile almost completed.

"Well? Steffen Fetchit!"

"Sir?"

"I need you to make sure my wife's never found. You understand me?"

"I do."

Gannaway's head burned. The fires inside ignited his nerve ends. By the time he stopped the clock's swinging pendulum, Steffen returned with a large bedspread. In seconds, he wrapped her up, relishing the task like wrapping a Christmas gift for a loved one. He hefted her onto his sharp shoulders with ease. Naira's hair fell out and brushed the floor. Steffen stopped at the door.

"What do we tell everyone?"

"You let me worry about that. Just do as you're told!"

Gannaway heard his manservant humming as he made his little problem disappear.

Claire rested her head on Tommy's chest, her usual position after lovemaking. Her husband's heart thrummed in her ear, his life's essence. *Her* life's essence.

"So, Kaya gave you the pendant?"

"Mm-hm." Claire had thought about telling him it was a family heirloom, but with it being obviously Indian, Tommy wouldn't have believed her. Tired of lies—or at least withheld truths—she invented a story with just the smallest alteration.

"And you want me to wear it?" He chuckled.

"Mm-hm. It's supposed to protect you from harm." She sat up and slapped his chest. "Stop it. It's not funny." Unable to control herself, she joined him, his laughter as contagious as influenza. "Okay, maybe it is slightly funny..."

"Yep. A medallion that'll protect me from harm. Claire, I thought you were over all this spook story stuff."

"I am. Just do me this favor. Please? Do it 'cause you love me. It's silly, I know. But it'll give me a little bit of comfort. If you're worried about what the other miners will think, wear it hidden underneath your shirt."

"Okay, honey. For you, I'll do anything. You know that."

"I do."

"Even if it is silly."

"Hush."

Tonight felt almost normal, their carefree ways settling back into their lives. Tommy seemed less tense. And she could flip over the moon about the pendant's possibilities. Momma always said the only way to fight fire was with fire. Claire never understood that until now.

Outside, a dog barked from far away, lonely and forlorn. Going on two in the morning, Claire didn't care about sleep. Not one whit. In their bedroom, nothing mattered more than their love.

"Tommy?"

"Hm?"

"You still striking tomorrow?"

"That's the plan. Dickinson says he has men coming in." Claire felt Tommy tighten beneath her. "I hate not knowing the entire plan. Ain't my way."

"I know. The Donnelly way. Sorta like Mother Donnelly not knowing when she can smoke next."

"Little different than that."

Claire knew Tommy would never forego the strike. Stubborn as a mule, he wanted to do best by every miner who put their lives on the line. An admirable trait, usually. For once, though, she wished he'd put his own needs—his *family's* needs—first. But then, he wouldn't be the man she fell in love with in high school, the man she knew she would marry from the first moment he asked her out like a bashful wallflower.

"Just be careful. Promise me."

"Promise."

"You'd better come back to me, Tommy Donnelly."

"I will, Claire Donnelly. Nothing will keep me from you."

And for the final time, they sealed their promise with a kiss.

Chapter Twenty

1969...

Bob ran out of gas at four in the morning. Besides, he'd almost exhausted his beer supply. He cradled his final beer lovingly and savored the last warm gulps. He'd sunk progressively deeper and deeper into his chair throughout the saga, his voice settling lower with each descent. By the time he'd finished, the top of his head was level with the back of the chair.

Dennis still didn't want to go to sleep. And he had questions.

"So, man. Steffen Eberstark beat you?"

"Yup. Badly." He extended his left leg, and the knee popped like a knuckle. "Still have pain in the leg to this day. Couldn't walk on it for months after it happened."

"And you never told anyone who did it to you?"

"No. The silver-eyed bastard got away with it. Well... Guess I can't rightly say that. In a way. But that's a tale for the morning, not the dark hours. A morning full of sunshine and warmth."

"Huh. And that's why you changed your name to Bob?"

He grimaced and rubbed the back of his neck. "That'd be it. While I was laid up, I had a lotta time to think. And wonder if the son-of-a-bitch was right. About living by white man's rules if you wanted to survive in their world. I—"

"You know that's not really true—"

"Dammit, Dennis, you're interrupting Professor Bob again. Stop it, or I'll make you go stand in the corner. Sure, it's easy for you to say it's not true. You didn't live through it. And now in the enlightened 'Age of Aquarius,' everyone who's rich and privileged wants to champion the underdog's plight. Fine. But back then? And with everything I saw? You know how my people were treated from the beginning. Things hadn't changed by 1935. Maybe even became worse. And I didn't want to live a life in fear of the white man. Didn't want them beatin' on me when they felt like it. I wanted a chance to make a life for myself as something other than their lackey. How better to do that? Learn their ways and live by their rules."

Bob's verbal arrow struck a painful bullseye. Obviously, Bob considered Dennis born with a silver spoon in his mouth. Dennis wanted to dispute it but couldn't. Just as Bob spoke a sad truth about living in the white man's world, perhaps Bob's assessment of him held true as well. "Okay. You're right. I don't understand. But I sympathize. Really."

"Thanks, amigo. But what's in the past stays in the past." With a bitter smile, he added, "Except for what goes on in Gannaway, of course."

"Of course." Which brought all the ghosts rattling their chains to the forefront again. "So Mrs. Gannaway just disappeared? Right after she gave Claire Donnelly the charmed pendant?"

"Ayup. Kyle Gannaway's story was she ran off with another man. Some salesman. No one ever saw nor heard from her again."

"Okay. You say Kyle Gannaway's 'story.' I'm assuming there's an alternate version?"

"Depends on who's writing the history, brother. But most folks suspected Gannaway killed his wife and did away with her body."

Dennis blinked, trying to wrap his mind around the fact he'd met a murderer. But Bob knew all, saw all. The best "truth barometer" around. "Why? What made people suspect that?"

"Think about it. Use your scientific noggin. You've met the wonderful, illustrious Mr. Kyle Gannaway, right?"

"Right."

"Do you honestly think he'd be running around town, spoutin' off a story about how his wife ran off with another hombre?"

"No, you're right."

"Course I'm right. Haven't steered you wrong yet. Gannaway's such a prideful man, ain't no way he'd let folks know he was a cuckold. Unless he was coverin' up something worse. It was no secret he beat her for fun. Stood to reason, one day, the fun was gonna go too far."

"Okay, we'll go with that. What happened to Mrs. Blackbird, Naira's mother?"

"She died shortly after her daughter 'left.' White folks say from a broken heart. Which you and I both know is a common health ailment, right?" Winking, Bob crushed the empty beer can. "Indian folk say her family was reunited in the spirit world."

"What do you think?"

"Beats me, brother. Maybe the truth is somewhere in the middle."

"You're really putting your beliefs out there."

"Safest place to be. Just in case." He weighed his hands like the scales of justice.

"So...the next part of the story is the strike?"

"Next, last and final part of Gannaway's history. At least the pertinent part."

"You up for it?"

Bob squinted into the beer can, spelunking for missed liquid artifacts. "No."

"No?"

"No. It's beyond late. We need sleep if you're going into the mines tonight. Besides, my knowledge of what really went on during the strike is a little...undernourished. I was laid up, remember? You need to talk to someone else to get the full story."

"Who?"

"Claire Donnelly."

"She's still *alive?*"

"That she is, brother. That she is."

Tin kettle drums. No, not drums. Someone hammering at a door. Dennis clawed his way out from a mercifully dreamless sleep. He smacked his lips, mouth drier than a desert. Water. He needed water.

He put on his glasses and checked his watch. A little after 1:00 p.m. He'd slept for nearly seven hours. Not a single ghost had haunted his sleep, a nice change.

The pounding on the door continued.

Therese stood on the doorstep, looking sharp and professional in another tailored suit. Her face softened considerably when she saw Dennis.

"I've been worried about you. You weren't at your motel and—"

"Therese, calm down. I feel like I have a hangover."

"You were *drinking?*"

"No. No! Come in, okay?" He shaded his eyes against the sunlight and motioned her in. Therese headed straight for Bob's storytelling chair, obviously no stranger to the layout.

Dennis plummeted back on the sofa, wishing for another hour's sleep. Plus it'd buy him more time to not have to think about his inevitable task tonight.

"What happened? Did you boys have a slumber party?" She smiled, amused with herself.

"Yep. We talked about cute boys and did each other's hair."

"Chauvinist."

"You're the one who started in with the gender jokes. But, yeah, I slept over."

Therese remained stolid through his summary of their night at the museum. Nothing could shake this woman. If anything, she appeared envious she hadn't been invited to the Boys' Ghost Hunter's Club.

"Thought I heard you, Therese." Bob dragged in, trailing a six-pack by the polymer ring. Apparently, he'd broken into his emergency supplies. "Mornin'."

"Afternoon. Dennis just told me about your ghostly encounter."

Bob sat next to Dennis, popped a beer open, and hitched an eyebrow. "Yeah, it was one for the record books."

"I'll say. Ghosts walking from photo to photo."

A chill iced Dennis's spine. "Won't be visiting that museum anytime again."

"Amen, brother." Bob held the can up as a toast.

"What's next?" asked Therese.

Dennis opened his mouth, but Bob nudged his knee. He saw Bob's ever-so-slight headshake and clamped down. "Um, don't really know. Guess it's back to work for me."

"'Bout time. I checked this morning. Your van should be ready tomorrow. Need a ride anywhere?"

"No. Bob'll loan me his car if I need it. 'Til I get the van back."

"Only if you promise not to trash it. That car's got a lot of sentimental value to me."

"How 'bout if I promise not to wreck it? 'Cause no offense, Bob, but that car was trashed a *long* time ago."

"And there you go with the insults again."

"All right, boys. Glad that's settled. I've got work to do myself. You need anything, call. I mean it." She switched her gaze between the two couch-sitters. Dennis felt like a reprimanded child, the school principal holding court over him.

"Sure thing."

"Um, Dennis, can I see you outside for a moment? Talk to you later, Bob." Therese bolted for the front door without waiting for an answer. A new record for speedy exits, even for her.

Bob responded with a shrug and attended to his beer.

Outside, Therese scowled. It matched her folded arms and tapping foot. "What was that about?"

"I don't understand—"

"Oh, *bullshit!* What kind of fool do you take me for? I saw the look-and-shove routine you and Bob had going on! What're you not telling me?"

"Nothing. Honestly."

"You started to say something but stopped."

Desperate times called for desperate measures. He took a chapter out of Therese's playbook and kissed her. It always worked for her when she wanted to shut him up. Her shoulders dropped as she relaxed within his embrace. Until she shoved him away.

"Nice. But do something about the breath."

"Oh, sorry. Morning' breath."

"Afternoon breath, lazy."

"Fine. You win."

"Seriously, Dennis, if you're planning something stupid, let me know. I care about what happens to you. I can help. More than you know. I have connections. Plus I want Gannaway as much as you do."

"I know all that. I just...want to take another day off. Still shook up from the things I saw the last couple days, I guess." He feigned a shiver and didn't have to work too hard at it.

She tilted her head, narrowing one eye. Her other beautiful eye burrowed into him, the worst possible torture. "Why do I not believe you?"

"Scout's honor." He held up two fingers, splayed apart.

"That's the peace sign, idiot."

"Never was much of a scout."

"Just don't be stupid. Call me." With her hand out the window, she gestured for him to come over. Clutching his beard, she gifted him with a deeper, more soulful kiss. And broke it off just as abruptly.

"Wow."

"Can't pull my trick on me, Dr. Lipstein. I always get the last kiss."

Her way or the highway.

Dennis hoped it wouldn't be his last kiss.

Bob's beer flowed during the afternoon, but his word-well dried up. He remained quiet, more hushed than a serious churchgoer. Dennis followed him around like a curious student watching him work. He painted a child's wagon, adorning it with the earthy colors of camouflage. He stacked discarded shoes into a pile uncomfortably reminiscent of the pyramid of skull-like bones Dennis had seen earlier, finishing the project by lacquering a translucent liquid of some sort over it. Then he sat down at an empty canvas that remained stubbornly blank.

"Thoughts, brother?"

"Um, on what you should paint? Or tonight?"

"Either, I reckon."

Dennis sat down in the grass and pulled up his knees. "Why didn't you want me to tell Therese about tonight?"

"Don't want her involved. Wanna protect her. Her parents asked me to look after her some years ago. I have. I do. She's like a daughter. Anything else I need to protect her from? You having sex with her?" Bob kept his gaze glued to the blank canvas, brush poised in the air.

Dennis chose honesty as the best policy. It didn't feel right lying to his comrade-in-arms. No matter the fallout.

"Yes."

Bob stared at him, then coughed out a laugh. "You should see your face right now, brother! Talk about 'white man!' Relax, I like sex, too. Good for you and good for her. You make her feel nice?"

"Um..."

"Ah, never mind. She's happy, you're happy, I'm happy."

"Glad you see it that way."

With a dab at the palette and a swish of the brush, Bob delivered three broad, blue strokes onto the canvas. Three plumes of jet-plane smoke. "What do you think?"

"What're you painting?"

"Dunno yet. It'll come to me in time." He looked down at Dennis, eyebrows raised. "If we have time."

"Bob, besides Therese, do you have any children? I mean, of your own?"

"Nope. Never happened. Wasn't in the cards. Married once. Didn't take."

"Why didn't you have kids?"

A huge shrug, then a slump. "You know how I told you how everything aligns on the spiritual plane for a reason?" Dennis nodded. "Something's kept me tied to this place. I had a lot of chances to leave, start a family, become an artist somewhere else. But I always stayed. Felt compelled to. For whatever reason, I've become the unofficial caretaker of Gannaway. Maybe the spiritual caretaker. My lot in life. And I feel...I feel it's all gonna come to an end. Maybe tonight."

Watching Bob get into his groove took Dennis's mind off what lay ahead. He composed with his brush like a conductor leading an orchestra. Long swoops for defining lines, points and jabs for punctuation. He finished his painting before sunset. A beautiful pastoral skyline, untouched by industrialization, rested over grassy green meadows.

"It's great, Bob."

"You think? I call it 'Blue Skies over Gannaway'."

The painting captured Gannaway's ancient past beautifully. Or what might've been had Kyle Gannaway never destroyed the land. Dennis wondered if the town of Gannaway could ever rise to such heights again.

"You're brilliant, Professor Bob."

Bob dropped his tools of the trade to the grass and rubbed his eyes. "You know something, brother? Screw it. Call me Ahanu. It's beyond time I took back my heritage."

"Ahanu it is." Dennis clapped a hand on Ahanu's shoulder. He seemed different sitting in his chair, transformed. Small and frail. For the first time since Dennis had met him, he looked his actual age. His shoulder trembled beneath Dennis's touch. A few tears slipped down his cheek. He dabbed them away, patted Dennis's hand.

Night began to fall, and the men finally talked about what they'd successfully avoided talking about all day.

Ahanu's driving absolutely terrified Dennis, especially when he killed the headlights for the last half mile of the trek. A blind journey into pitch darkness, they may as well have been driving straight into Hell.

The Thunderbird wrenched to a halt, and Dennis's heart threatened to stop as well. Ahanu switched off the ignition. The car fought the loss of power and sputtered. Dennis swore he heard it sigh when it finally gave in to inertia.

"You think it's safe parking here?" They faced the highway, parked on the grounds that once contained the city park. Within spitting distance of the hidden mining compound entryway.

"No, brother, I don't. But if I parked where we did yesterday, you'll never hear the horn." He handed the flashlight to Dennis. "You think you can find the mine? Tommy Donnelly's old mine?"

Dennis waved the yellowed piece of paper in his hand. "Got the map, straight from the scrapbook."

"Good." Ahanu extended his hand and Dennis took it, squeezed it hard. "Luck to you, brother."

"Thanks. For everything."

Dennis exited the car and stayed low. Full in the sky, the moon draped white light across the devastated terrain. The grounds resembled an uninhabited planet, unfit for human or alien life.

Dennis stopped at the fence. As soon as he flicked the flashlight on, he smothered the beam against his stomach. He ran his fingers along the bottom of the fence and found the entrance. He pulled aside the bushes, lifted the loose fence, and rolled under.

Showtime. God's spotlight shined down, lighting his path. *Noise.* In the distance. A man, no, two men's voices. Hushed and barely audible. He turned off the flashlight, dropped, and listened.

Thunk. Grnnnnnnd.

Machinery. He'd never heard the sound of mining equipment before, a dinosaur's stomach rumbling with indigestion.

Dennis dodged between chat piles and defunct machinery, winding his way deeper into the compound. Ahead, electric lights cast the glow of progress over the dead lands. A lamp hung on a pole. Two helmet beams flickered each time a man turned his head. Behind the miners, lights brightened the lower half of the elevator building, the top darker than the sky surrounding it.

Squatting, Dennis inched closer. Sweat rolled down his face. His blood pumped into his ears so loud he thought the men might hear it.

Why the hell didn't I bring a camera?

In the distance, a car horn blared. His heart banged. He bolted to his feet too quickly and fell. The sunbaked ground punched the air out of him.

"Who's there?"
The back of his head exploded. His teeth bit into the earth. Before he lost consciousness, he watched the shadows coming for him.

The longer Ahanu sat in the car, the more useless he felt. Not only did his constant surveillance induce severe neck cramps, but he couldn't see a damn thing. His leg twitched, pitching a fit and screaming for exercise. He surrendered to his troublesome appendage and left the car.

His back ached from bending over to keep his hand hovering over the horn. Crouching didn't help either. The old body couldn't cut it with this cloak-and-dagger crap, and like a bratty kid, it intended to prove it to him.

The devil that was his inner voice spoke inside his head, heckling him. *What are you doing here, Ahanu? Leave now!*

He planted his feet. *I'm staying.* No more listening to voices other than his own, especially ones from his past.

Gravel crunched behind him. Just once. He turned, saw nothing. Gannaway's statue stared down at him, smiling. The smile he'd seen too often, awake and in nightmares.

More rocks shuffled. An animal? A *footstep.*

A low growl snagged into his craw. *A lion, a goddamn lion.* He squinted at the lion statue and wished he had a flashlight. A wind gust brushed tree limb shadows away. Ahanu saw the lion with bold clarity. Its front paws were both lifted into the air. *Not just one. Impossible. Then again, it's Gannaway, Kansas.*

Crnch, crnch, crnch.

Footsteps. Absolutely, positively.

"What the *hell* we got here?" Ahanu recognized the

helium-pitched voice before he saw the face.

Ahanu swung back to the car, slamming his hand onto the steering wheel. The horn didn't take. He punched harder, shot off one bleat before a strong arm enveloped his neck. A kick swept his feet from underneath him.

He tumbled to the ground, his knee on fire. A flashlight's beam blinded him. But he knew Stokes stood behind the light.

"God *damn,* Bob! Thought you'd know better than to get involved. You always was a nosy redskin. Now, why don't you save us all some trouble and tell us where the Jew-boy is?"

"Go to *hell.*"

Stokes's boot tip launched into his ribs.

"'Fraid you're gonna go there afore I do, boy. One more chance before I turn you over to my friend, here. Where's the Jew-boy?"

Ahanu coughed, then forced a hollow chuckle. "Probably with your mother, fat boy."

"Done playin' nice here. Time for fun's over."

Another man trudged forward. Stoke's flashlight splashed over the large oval figure. *Gustav Eberstark.* A nightmarish replay of the past. But this time, Ahanu knew the son intended on finishing what his father had started. A quote throttled Ahanu's mind. *The sins of the father shall be visited upon the son.*

Gustav reached into his jacket pocket, retrieved something. The carved wooden handle had seen better years, but Ahanu recognized it all the same. The knife Steffen Eberstark had cut him with back in 1935. The blade flipped out, shiny and sharp, nothing worn about the blade.

Gustav kneeled. Stokes aimed his beam on the men, shedding a new light over Gustav. The jovial, round face of Eberstark Junior melted away. Now Ahanu stared into the vile features of Gus's father. The cut, chiseled jawline. The long, aquiline nose. And the evil, sadistic glee in his eyes. But just one of them.

Unlike his father, though, Gus closed his eyes when he plunged the blade deep into Ahanu.

Ssssssss.

A snake. No, not a snake. Bacon frying in a pan. But it didn't smell right. Mold. Dirt. Gunpowder?

Dennis opened his eyes, half-awake and disoriented. Dreaming, maybe. Full-on dark surrounded him except for a small flicker of light. Alive and jumping like a birthday candle's flame. Sizzling. Traveling a winding path.

My God...dynamite!

His head pounded, his limbs were unsteady as he forced himself to his knees. He managed to dredge up saliva onto his fingers even though his mouth had dried. He pinched the fuse. The burning sensation jolted him awake. The fuse lived on, too strong, too hellbent on its destructive journey to be stopped with spit. He grabbed the stick and heaved it down the dark corridor. The spark turned over in the air, round and round like a Fourth of July pinwheel. It kept burning after it landed.

Matches! Patting his pockets down, he clawed out a box of matches.

Scritch. Tsss.

The fire grew in his cupped hand, then settled into a small spark of light. Instinctively, Dennis ran in the opposite direction from which he'd tossed the dynamite. His feet squelched into a puddle of standing water. One tennis shoe stuck, slipping off his heel, then freed with a *clop.*

Shit! He could've dunked the dynamite into it. *Go back for the stick? No. No time.* Best to take his chances. If he had any.

A fallen rock tripped him, but he stayed on his feet, propelling forward. Ahead he saw a large shadow, blacker than the rest. *A boulder.* It sat close against the cavern wall, with an opening behind the stone providing enough room to squeeze into. He sucked in his gut, held his breath, and wedged himself inside. The match singed the tips of his fingers. He shook it out, then tossed it. And waited. In the dark, his hand fell on something next to him. Hard and cold. Smoother than rock, but dirt-encrusted. Something that didn't quite belong.

He needed to conserve matches, but he had to know. The match light, so startling in the black, bounced over his neighbor. His hand jerked away from the skull. Open-mouthed, gawping at him in eternal agony. And he knew, just *knew,* he would soon join it in this forgotten grave.

The explosion drowned out his scream.

And the earth fell around him.

Chapter Twenty-One

1935...

Tommy stood with Dickinson, watching the international union men who'd rolled in earlier in a parade of trucks and swarmed off like a plague of locusts. Now they stood in front of the mine gates, brandishing rifles in their arms, looking glumly out at the horizon.

"I don't like this, Dickinson," said Tommy. "Don't like it one bit. You never said anything about guns." The men put Tommy on edge. They stood at full attention, well-trained soldiers, their itchy trigger fingers prepared to unleash death.

"Tommy, it's the only way to close down the mine. Otherwise, you can't strike. If you want your demands met, you have to take certain risks."

"Dammit, I don't want my men's *lives* at risk!"

First night of the strike, and the men's discouragement hung over the crowd like storm clouds. Three hundred or more, a good turnout. But they ambled about in front of the armed men like an insignificant afterthought. Tommy knew where their minds were. Wondering where their family's next meal would come from. Picket signs drooped at their sides, impotent weapons when compared to the rifles the union men carried. But against Tommy's orders, some of the men carried pickaxe handles. Worse, a box of handles sat off to the side. Things could turn ugly fast if he didn't straighten this out. Right now.

"Dickinson, this isn't necessary. I don't want this gettin' outta hand. I've been in contact with the editor of the Gannaway Lion. He's sympathetic to our cause. He's gonna—"

"You're not listening to me. Trust me. I know what I'm doing." Tommy wanted to belt the smirk from Dickinson's face, but no sense in drawing first blood. Particularly from his own team. "This is how unions work. Other—"

"And like you told me, this is your first hootenanny. You should've *told* me what you were planning." Tommy stormed off to talk to the miners. "Fellas! Fellas, can I have your attention?" They were anything but rowdy, but he needed them focused, their minds alert. "Now, I know this isn't the way you want to be spendin' your nights. Me neither. Just keep in mind what we're tryin' to accomplish here. And the way to do that is through peaceful, calm—"

"Tommy, don't look to me like the union boys are lookin' for peace. No, sir," called out Earl.

"I *know* that." Tommy tried to hide his distaste as he shot Dickinson a look. "That's not any of my doin'! But we're just gonna protest in a nice and easy manner. Keepin' the mines closed is our goal. 'Til Gannaway—"

"I know it as gospel that Gannaway's settin' up his own army now, Tommy." A few of the men clumped their ax handles into the dirt, a call for battle. "We can't just sit here and let 'em take shots at us!"

Tommy'd heard the rumors. And the men weren't blind. They'd seen the Kansas National Guardsmen trucks coming in. Gannaway knew a lot of folks. And he probably knew a lot *about* a lot of folks. Things that'd make those folks anxious to do him favors. None of the men had missed the new crowd of shady characters lurking around town, too. Sure as shootin', Gannaway had been busy putting together his own force. But things needed to be kept peaceful at all costs. Tommy didn't want lives sacrificed to save lives. "They ain't gonna shoot at us, Earl. Not 'less we give 'em reason to. So everybody, calm down, and I'd mighty prefer it if you'd drop your pick handles and lead pipes. Ain't gonna need 'em."

"I don't know." Earl scratched the back of his neck. "Might be I feel a li'l bit safer with some protection." He hefted the handle and whacked it into his palm. Men cheered, following his lead.

"Boys! We're not gonna get anywhere if we start fighting! The first man you harm is gonna be a strike against us! And if you end up in jail or worse, who's gonna feed your families?" One look at their faces and he knew his words meant nothing. He was trying to douse a raging fire with a bucket of water. And the winds of hostility just kept fanning the flames ever higher. But their collective silence gave Tommy hope. At least they were listening, considering reason. "Keep things nice, fellas. Calm heads prevail in situations like this."

From behind, one of the union men chortled.

Across from the mines and down on Main Street, the Gannaway Baptist Church overflowed to the rafters. The righteous reverend Charles Whilton looked pea green with envy at the attendance. Over five hundred men packed the church, most of them standing in the aisles, some waiting outside to hear the decision.

One hundred Kansas National Guardsmen stood in the front row, a human barrier. Kyle Gannaway's own personal human barrier. He ballooned with pride at the sight. The current Kansas governor had sent the guardsmen to him in his time of need. Damn well should've, too, after the money he'd coughed up for the governor's winning campaign.

Gannaway's own cadre of riff-raff sat strategically throughout the church, surrounded by the mass of unemployed miners. Just days ago these out-of-work men hated Gannaway for taking away their livelihood. Now they saw him as the Second Coming. He thought that sounded mighty appropriate.

Yes, sir. *Pride.* He beamed out over the adoring crowd, here to listen to him. *So this is what movie stars feel like.*

"Thank you for turning out this evening, gentlemen." Anticipation hushed the crowd. "Now, all of you know it's been a tough week for me and the company. The Gannaway Lead & Smelting Company. *Your* company." Of course he fed them malarkey. But the more the men felt like they had a stake in their own future, the better off he'd be. He sighed, properly and falsely humbled. "Tough times, tough times. My wife, she left me at this most trying of times. The current miners decided to unionize. My life...what I live for..." He snapped his fingers. "...all gone within a week."

A small chorus of boos. Gannaway loved the show of sympathy. He flashed his award-winning smile. "It's all right, fellas. It's okay. 'Cause you know why?" He cupped a hand over his ear and repeated, "You know why?"

"Why?"

"'Cause I ain't no quitter, that's *why!* And neither are *you!* That's why you're all here. Ain't that right?"

Feet stomped the floor. Voices and fists raised, weapons shaking over the men's heads like baby rattles. The large white cross behind Gannaway quivered as if Jesus himself had come down off the cross to join the righteous gathering. Outside, the men joined in the ruckus, sending cheers bouncing through the streets.

"That's what I reckoned! Now. With the help of Colonel Blacking..." He nodded to a walrus-mustached man in a pressed army suit. "...we're not gonna roll over and

be quitters. These men, these so-called 'unionizers'..."
More jeers. "...are taking what rightly belongs to *us*. Our
God-given *right*!" Holding a fist in the air, he squeezed
it tight. The blood drained, his fingernails digging deep
into his palm. He imagined crushing Tommy Donnelly's
traitorous heart within his grip. "Now, who's with me?"
Hands snapped up, heads nodded. A slow murmur bubbled, then overflowed into boisterous applause. "Let's go
take *back* what belongs to *us! Follow me!*" Gannaway
snapped his fingers. Steffen strode onto stage hefting a
box. After setting it down in front of Gannaway, he vanished. Gannaway reached into the box. He brandished
the pick handle proudly, lifting it like a king's scepter.
"Grab your *weapons,* boys! Let's go take back the *mines!*"

Men rushed the stage like ants to their queen. More
handle-filled boxes replaced the depleted ones.

They filed out, stampeding, roaring into the night. Lit
torches swirled in the darkness. From behind threadbare curtains, anxious wives peeked out from windows,
watching the procession of men march past.

Gannaway brought up the rear, grinning. The world's
most satisfied circus ringleader.

Claire dropped the cotton sack curtain back into
place. T.J. and Margaret stood behind her. They hadn't
left her side since the noise began. Margaret reached out,
clung to a leg.

"Momma', I'm *scared!*"

"Shh, it's all right, honey. Just mining business."

"But all the *yelling!*"

Mother Donnelly hovered in the children's bedroom
doorway, a cigarette dangling from her lips. "Land's sake,
I've never seen anything like it."

"Mother, you're not helping." Claire knelt to speak

with her children. "Now, I want you to go with Grandma and get in bed. Go to sleep. Things'll look better in the morning. You'll see."

"But, Momma—"

"You heard me now. Git." They stood frozen, terrified. Claire planted a kiss on both of their feverishly warm cheeks. "I promise everything'll be all right. Now go get ready for bed. Love you both."

"Is Daddy okay?"

Claire straightened, looked at Mother Donnelly for assistance. But she appeared nearly as frightened as the children, at a rare loss for sass. "Daddy'll be fine. Good night."

As soon as Mother Donnelly ushered the children into the bedroom, Claire took another look out the window. *Bloodlust.* She saw it, felt it, practically smelled it. Backs were slapped, and arms draped around one another in camaraderie. Their humorless laughter gave her a chill.

But what she saw on top of her bedroom dresser froze the blood in her veins. The beaded sun pendant blazed gloriously in the otherwise drab room.

Oh, my Lord, Tommy forgot the pendant.

Snatching it to her chest, she ran toward the window again. The procession had already stomped past her house, almost to the mines. A few latecomers lagged behind, staggering. Drunk on alcohol, smelling blood.

Naira had told her the pendant would protect Tommy from harm. Especially from the yellow-eyed fever. But when all's said and done, harm is harm. And tonight, Tommy stood right in the eye of the storm.

Claire took one last look at the closed door to her children's bedroom. What would happen to them if she became a casualty of crowd madness? But she had no choice. The Devil take her if she didn't at least try.

With a deep breath, she opened the door.

She stepped into the night, following the noise and staying close to the shadows.

Tommy heard the voices first, then the dropping hammers of footfalls.

"They're coming," he said. Dickinson dropped a shade paler than the white moon, his eyes nearly as big. "Now what, Dickinson? We ready for this?"

Dickinson said nothing. He turned and ran behind the line of armed men. *No surprise there.*

"Men, they're headed toward us. Remember! Keep things peaceful. We don't want anyone gettin' hurt!"

The marching men's footsteps fell into unison, thrumming throughout the streets, crawling up from under the dirt on which the miners stood. Rounding the corner of Main Street, the first torches appeared. They blazed in the night, angry fireflies darting toward their destination.

A line of armed guardsmen stopped just across the highway. The civilians behind them shouted, almost quivering in their lust to break through the barrier. The guardsmen nudged them back with shoulders and outthrust arms.

A man stepped forward, his body rigid as a rock. He lifted a megaphone to his mouth. "Attention, union strikers! This is Colonel Blacking with the United States Army. I have been given orders to bring a peaceful resolution to this strike! Lay down your weapons and leave the mines!"

Thumps sounded behind Tommy as a few men dropped their weapons. Most of the men lifted their ax handles higher. The international union men brought their guns up. *Click, clack, rack.* Gun hammers pulled back and locked.

A hush fell over Tommy's men. Across the highway, catcalls rang out. The opposing crowd strained to see over the guardsmen's cordon.

Dale strode toward Tommy. "What do you think?"

Tommy had no idea. But he couldn't let his men

know he was as terrified as they were. "Guess we try to talk with 'em. Can't give up now. You with me?"

Dale sighed, tucked his hands into his overall pockets, and nodded.

Tommy didn't know the first thing about military protocol, but he took his best guess. *"Colonel Blacking! Permission to approach you on the highway?"*

Blacking lowered his megaphone and prodded an authoritative finger toward the two men flanking him. They marched onto the highway.

Tommy whistled to put his own insurance plan into play. Cal Edginton, the editor of the Gannaway Lion, stepped out from behind a tree. He held up his shoebox of a camera and waved, ready to go.

Dale followed behind Tommy, favoring his bad leg.

Colonel Blacking ignored Tommy's extended hand. He locked his gaze on Tommy, his hands glued to his rifle.

"Colonel Blacking, I'm Tommy Donnelly, and this is Dale Hemmings. We're two of the local union leaders."

"Mr. Donnelly. Mr. Hemmings." Gannaway's crowd roared, fists pumping into the sky. "It'd be best if you surrender immediately."

"With all due respect, Colonel, I know we're within our constitutional right to assemble and speak our mind—"

"Not when it closes down a mining operation you don't own, sir."

"They're still debating that in Washington."

"This is your last warning, Mr. Donnelly. Are you going to surrender peacefully?"

Tommy shot Dale a look. Hard to say, but it looked like Dale gave the smallest shake of the head.

Then something brushed by Tommy, so close he felt a whiff of air. With a grunt, Dale buckled to the pavement. Dark liquid spread its wings beneath his head. A brick lay next to him.

"Dale?" Tommy dropped to his knees, cradling Dale's head. Dale groaned, weak and fading fast. Tommy pulled

his hands away. They were drenched in blood.

An overhead blast jolted Tommy to his feet. Blacking's smoking gun barrel pointed toward the stars.

Deathly silence blanketed the warring factions. Time teetered on the edge of a razor blade. Tommy raised his arms and screamed, *"Everyone! Stop! This man needs—"*

Shots ripped open the night. Lights flared across the street, followed by a series of small explosions. Behind Tommy, the union men returned fire.

Blacking and his soldiers retreated. But Gannaway's mob stormed the highway, coming at Tommy.

"God damn it! Stop!" Too late. With a roar, Tommy's men met the opposing mob, ramming into them, weapons crashing down. Flesh split, bone cracked. Cries resounded as the wounded fell. Men who had once worked alongside one another traded knuckles, fighting for their right to return to the mines.

More lights popped down the highway, Edginton's camera flashes commemorating the madness. Bullets flew toward the reporter, and he dove behind a tree.

Dale lay on the ground in the middle of the chaos. Tommy hooked his hands underneath Dale's armpits and dragged him across the highway. The trail of blood gleamed underneath the moonlight.

One of the armed guards lobbed a canister of tear gas into the middle of the fracas. It spun, hissed, and spat out toxic smoke.

"Damn it! Go, Steffen Fetch it! You have your orders!" Gannaway clenched Steffen's rock-solid arm, screaming into his ear. They'd stayed far from the bedlam in the drugstore's alleyway, but Gannaway still couldn't hear himself think.

"The electric tower? Sir, are you sure?"

God *damn!* The man had hidden his wife's body, even killed for him in the past, and *now* he was questioning an order? "Yes, I'm damn sure! Just do as you're *told!* Blow the damn thing up, bring it down, and make damn sure it looks like one of the strikers done it!"

The more bodies that fell in Gannaway, the sooner Uncle Sam would look in on his affairs. And if a toppled electric tower didn't make Blacking declare martial law, nothing would.

Gannaway urged Steffen on with a shove. "Go on! Steffen Fetch it!"

"Yes, sir."

Gannaway had one last piece of business to take care of. A thorn in his lion's paw. He hadn't come by the decision lightly either. But he'd seen how Donnelly rallied the men. And Harvey Quick had told him Donnelly had gotten an eighty-seven percent vote amongst the miners to strike. Time to cut off the head of the beast. Take away the head, and the animal would bleed out and die. The law of nature. *"Steffen!"*

"Sir?"

"Make sure you take care of the Tommy Donnelly problem."

A slippery grin stretched across his manservant's face. "With pleasure, sir. How do you want me to do it?"

"I don't care! And I don't wanna know! Just take care of it. Once and for all!"

Steffen's reluctance disappeared. A light jig hastened his step as he trotted off. Maybe the boy deserved a raise.

Claire hunkered between two trees. But she never let her husband out of her sight.

Damn fool. Always putting others before himself.

But she loved him for it, no way around it.

She watched in horror as Tommy dragged a man across the highway while the others beat each other senseless around him. She nearly cried out when a man kicked at him. He didn't even notice.

A waking nightmare ate away at her reality, the end of the world unfolding before her. Civil men morphed into primal beasts, battling over a damn stupid mine. Screams of pain vied with screams of victory. She couldn't tell who was on which side and didn't think the miners knew either. Bullets sprayed, random projectiles ending lives indiscriminately. She prayed.

Please, God, where are you?

God had abandoned Gannaway, Kansas. Tears welled up, but immediate rage turned off the tap. She knew what she had to do. She had to reach her husband. No matter what.

She stumbled over a fallen tree limb and snatched it up. She tugged at the bottom of her skirt and dug the branch's sharp end into the tautness. The skirt tore, and she pulled away a long strip of rag. She tied it around her face with a knot in the back and ran toward the mines.

Men dropped on all fours and retched. Bodies littered the pavement, rolling as if they were on fire. Moans formed a desperate chorus, mourning the loss of eyesight. Some men fled for the confines of the compound. Others took to the dark streets, winding their way home in the shadows.

Once onto the mine grounds, Tommy managed to haul Dale to his feet. He was barely conscious, his eyelids drooping.

Tommy shook him. "You okay, Dale?"

"Mmm."

The bleeding had stopped, matting his hair to his head. Tommy kicked open the office door and propped him into a chair. "Hang on. I'll go get Doc Wilkins to fix you up."

"Damn bastards..."

Tommy whipped off his shirt and bandaged it around Dale's head. "Put your hand on it. Hold it tight. Okay? Dale, you hear me?"

"Mm-hm."

Click. Cold metal pressed into his neck.

"Shouldn't've gone union, Tommy. Shouldn't have done it."

Harvey Quick. "Harvey, put the gun down. You don't know what you're doing." Tommy raised his hands above him.

"Never been more right in my head. Mr. Gannaway promised me your job when the mines reopen." The cold barrel pressed harder, nudging Tommy's head into Dale's face. Harvey was nervous, though. The gun wavered back and forth across his neck. That nervousness meant Tommy had a fighting chance.

Thunk. The gun clattered to the floor, followed by something heavier.

Tommy spun around. Claire held an ax handle above her head, ready to strike again if necessary. But it wasn't. Harvey lay on the floor, out cold.

"Claire! What in *God's* name are you doing here? You could be—"

"If it weren't for me, you would be *dead,* Tommy Donnelly!" His angel of mercy, his beloved wife, stood perched in the midland between anger and terror. She dropped the handle and clamped her hands over her mouth. "Oh, sweet Jesus, Tommy..."

"Claire..." He grabbed her and squeezed tight.

She pushed away and opened her clenched hand. The Indian pendant gleamed beneath the dangling light bulb as if it emanated its own light source. "You left this."

"You risked your life to bring me this?"

Her head bounced up and down. "I had to, Tommy. I *had* to!"

The pendant, the silly pendant. It seemed so out of place, a child's toy, in the midst of the upheaval outside. Tommy didn't believe in its power, but Claire did. He slipped it over his neck and managed a smile.

"Okay, Claire, I need to get you home."

"Come *with* me, Tommy!"

"I can't. The men need me. I—"

"I need you! The *children* need you!"

The fear in her eyes shone clear as day. He wanted to shake her fear loose and throw it away once and for all. "Claire, I know that. And I need you, too." He grabbed her hand and held it to his chest. "You're everything to me. That's why I need to get you to safety." He turned to Dale, still only half-lucid. "Dale, you okay?"

Dale grunted.

"I'll get Doc Wilkins. Just hang on."

Tommy grabbed the discarded rifle, checked the chamber, and tugged Claire behind him.

They retraced Claire's steps back out of the compound. Most of the men had either retreated or were down on the ground. Smoke drifted through the air, leaving a strong, lingering odor, rotting apples mixed with garlic. Across the highway, Blacking and his men tried to restore order. From the looks of things, they were failing miserably. Backed-up cars and trucks flanked the battle-field, bleating exultantly like trumpets.

"I'm going to take you to Cal Edgington. Need to check on him anyway," said Tommy. "He'll get you back to safety."

They found Edgington, head buried in the leaves, hands covering his head.

"Cal, you okay?"

Cal looked up, startled. "Jesus Christ, Tommy! I've never seen..." He managed to make it onto his knees before falling back. "Jesus..."

"Come on. You've got to get out of here. Is your camera okay?"

"I think so."

"Good. It may be our only hope now. Make sure those pictures get in the next edition. Can you make sure Claire gets home?"

Claire said, "I reckon I'd best make sure he gets home."

Tommy didn't argue. She was right. He handed her the rifle. "Be careful with this. What you need to do is—"

Claire cocked the hammer, swung the rifle over her shoulder. "Tommy Donnelly, I grew up with a damn rifle on the farm. Now, hush."

"You're the smartest, bravest Donnelly around." He kissed her, a quick peck. "Love you, Claire Donnelly."

"Love you, too, Tommy Donnelly. Be careful."

Once Tommy reached the mines, he realized, with regret, he hadn't told Claire he'd always come back to her. *Always.*

An explosion ripped through town, angrier and more resounding than thunder. The few men left scuffling stopped to look up. Weapons dropped, hands flew to ears.

Behind the cemetery, the red eye at the top of the electric tower snapped off with one last wink. The wire-connected poles toppled first, bowing down to their giant king. Sparks sizzled, the loose wires snaking between tombstones.

The top of the tower tipped, hesitated, then tumbled down. Gravestones shattered into pebbles, memorials of lost loved ones now nothing but dust. The bottom of the tower splintered and snapped like giant toothpicks. Beams hurled out across the highway. A top segment landed on a truck, flattening it easily.

Floomph.

The town of Gannaway dipped into darkness. Along the residential streets, house lamps shut off one after another. O'Reilly's Pub, empty for probably the first time in its history, went black. Floodlights over the mines disappeared. Frightened yelps replaced the sounds of violence. Hellhounds barked, howling the devil's symphony.

And Kyle Gannaway laughed. With unfettered, nearly hysterical, glee.

The armed guardsmen at the perimeter of the highway lit lamps, swinging them uncertainly. Car headlights focused a myriad of crisscrossing spotlights over the casualties lying on the highway.

Gannaway shoved his way through the mob toward Colonel Blacking, who shook his head and looked just as flummoxed as the rest of his Guardsmen.

"Colonel, you have to do something!"

"And what in hell might that be?"

"The strikers! They blew up the electric tower! If you don't claim martial law, there's gonna be rioting and looting, and God *knows* what!"

The Colonel's once squared shoulders rounded. "How do you know it was the strikers?"

"I *know* it was the strikers. Some of my boys saw them by the tower before it came down."

Blacking stuck his hand out to no one in particular. "Give me the goddamn megaphone."

The device squawked. Blacking cleared his throat a few times and spoke. "Citizens of Gannaway! Gannaway, Kansas is now under martial law. Stop what you're doing immediately! Surrender your weapons and go *home.* Your right to assemble is *revoked.* I repeat, the town is under martial law. I am fully authorized to *shoot* anyone who does *not* comply! Do so now, before we arrest every one of you!"

"What about the goddamn freedom of the press, Colonel?" asked Gannaway. Might as well take out that damn reporter and his photographs while he had the chance. He'd seen him skulking around, flashing that camera.

"Ain't that supposed to be revoked, too?"

"Don't press your luck, Gannaway. I'm doing what I can, how I can."

No matter, thought Gannaway. He'd already won. The miners weren't big enough fools to keep fighting, not against his government and military backing. The strike was over. God had surely smiled upon him. Like he always did.

The last of the remaining strikers gathered by the mining office. Matches hissed, producing small pockets of light in the darkness. Blood seeped from wounds. Those still standing propped up those unable to stand. Faces looked hungrier, leaner, more drawn than usual. Yesterday the men had been excited about their new, improved prospects. With the imposition of martial law, they'd become hollow shells, lost spirits.

The dream had ended, at least for now. "Fellas. God knows I'm sorry, but we can't fight this. Not like the way they want to."

They pitched their rag-tag collection of weapons to the dirt with clinks and clunks.

"But as sure as I'm Tommy Donnelly—"

"We done heard that before," said Donald. "Don't matter no more."

"You're wrong. This is a tragedy, no doubt about it. I'm not sure how many good men we lost, and I'm bettin' there're at least a couple still laying out there on the road. But this is a setback. Nothing more. I ain't restin' till I see us done *right*. But for right now, there just isn't any way to keep fighting. Not against martial law." His throat tightened. He had more to say. But what did it matter? Nothing could make up for all the death he'd witnessed lately. *Nothing.*

The door opened behind him with a teeth-grinding scrape. "Tommy, it's okay. We tried." Dale, aided by two miners, hobbled toward him. "We tried, did the best we could."

Tommy hung his head, kicked at the dirt in shame. The deaths shouldn't have been for nothing. George. Big Ed. All the others.

"We did try, didn't we?" It hurt to smile, but Tommy brought it up from a wellspring of great pride. "We tried. And I'm not done trying, either. Every day in Washington, we're one foot closer to having unions fully recognized. As long as you'll have me, I'll keep trying." The men left quietly. A few of them clapped Tommy's shoulder as they passed. "Go home, fellas. Go home to your families. Hold your hands in the air when you leave. Shout 'going home peacefully' if you need to. Walk slowly. Things will come our way. Eventually."

Everyone left the mines before Tommy. It just felt natural for him to close up shop. Standing by the gate, he watched all the men leave unharmed. Across the road, the opposing crowd had dispersed, bored with inaction. Tarps lay lined up on the ground next to the Guardsmen. Boots stuck out from underneath. Tommy counted at least nine pairs. Harold Durwood, never one to miss a chance to do business, hovered nearby as the military collected the last remaining bodies from the street. More bodies to haunt Tommy Donnelly's dreams.

But right now, nothing mattered except getting home to his family. First, though, he'd make one last check through the mining grounds for any wounded he might've missed.

When he turned around, the moon startled him. Not the moon above. That moon had long slipped away behind cloud curtains. He stared directly into a sliver of a moon covering a silver eye.

Claire sat up in bed and watched the hands of the clock tick off the hours. Two-thirty a.m. Waiting, she listened to the night, thankfully and finally quiet. The only sound she heard was the crickets, coming out from hiding. At three-thirty, emotionally and physically exhausted, she gave in to sleep.

She woke thirty minutes later, when Tommy cried out her name.

The cry came from far away, like a nightmare barely kept at bay. But it reverberated loud and sharp in her mind and threw in a kick to her gut for good measure. An awful, agonized cry.

Clairrrrre! I'll always come home. Alw—

Then nothing. Tears streamed down her cheeks, blood dripped from her nose.

She pulled her knees to her chest and hugged them as she rocked back and forth. Her hand soothed her husband's pillow, stroked the impression his head had worn.

Oh, Tommy, you lied to me. You lied. You're not coming home. Not this time.

Chapter Twenty-Two

1969...

The explosion rattled the cavern's walls. Dennis clung to the skeleton next to him. Even a long-dead person was comforting under the circumstances. He closed his eyes. Intense heat roiled above him. Rock chinked to the ground. Dust and smoke infiltrated his nose, his lungs. His eyes watered. He'd never been so thirsty.

But he'd been lucky, all things considered. He'd tossed the dynamite far enough away to avoid the walls and ceiling caving in directly on top of him. But he was still buried alive. *Alive, but entombed.*

The earth settled. A stray clink and plunk announced the end. Smoke cleared. He waited another moment and stood, his entire body trembling.

He struck a match and held it in front of him. The flame pulled down the drift. *Airflow.* A mining tip he'd picked up from Ahanu's tales.

He cupped the flame and moved the match carefully from side to side until he spotted a lamp on the wall.

Please, God, let it work, please dear God.

The last breath of the match burnt his fingertips.

But the visual imprint of the lamp's location stayed in his mind's eye. He fumbled in the dark, hands outstretched, until he latched onto the lamp. He flicked the switch and light flared briefly, then died. *Please, God!* The fifth click took. The illumination wasn't bright and grew weaker by the second, but it would have to do. He only had a few matches left and needed to conserve them to hunt down the airflow.

The skeleton called to him, almost as if he heard its long-dead voice asking for help. He guessed the skeleton to be female; the skull looked smaller than a man's. Filthy tatters of clothing draped the bones. The material disintegrated into dust when he picked it up. But he'd seen the pattern. Unmistakably Native American.

Naira Blackbird Gannaway. It had to be. Dumped here unceremoniously with no proper burial, the mine shaft her final resting place.

"Don't worry, Naira," he whispered, "I'll make sure he doesn't get away with this." He owed her that. Dennis's newfound respect for the spirit world compelled him to believe her ghost had drawn him to her and saved his life. At least for a while longer.

The oppressive air—or lack, thereof—thickened. His lungs weighed heavy. He wanted to gulp the precious remaining oxygen, lap it up like water, but forced himself not to. Short, measured, controlled breaths, like he'd learned to do in the birthing classes he'd attended before Devin's birth. *Devin...*

No. Stay focused.

Bastards. Son-of-a-bitching bastards! They killed me! No...tried to kill me. Gustav, Stokes, and Dickie. And Gannaway.

He had to sit. He was hyperventilating. He shut his eyes and contained his breathing.

Don't let anger overtake you.

He struck another match and walked down the drift. Water dripped. The long distances between each *plip* lasted an eternity. Every time a drop reached its destination, it echoed around him, a spike driven into his brain.

Rock and dirt blocked the drift. The match flame waved and bent toward a draft. At the bottom of the heap, two long slabs of rock formed a triangular opening, propping the debris up above it. A doorway to life. When he held the match beneath the rocks, the flame sucked in and whiffed out. *Air.*

He crawled underneath, the lantern lighting his way. A wall of dirt blocked him. Digging his hand in, the soil crumbled away easily enough. But what lay behind it? More rocks? Endless dirt? *Death?*

No, the draft originated somewhere. He scooped out a handful of dirt carefully and waited. The dirt might be the only thing holding up the rocks above. Nothing happened, just a sprinkling of dirt. Two more handfuls. Silence except for the endless water torture behind him.

Encouraged, he pulled the dirt away faster, shoveling it behind him. Sweat and grime streaked his face, seeping into his eyes. He had just enough elbow room to wipe his face on his sleeve.

The gap behind him was already full of discarded dirt. Worse, the wall ahead replenished its endless supply of earth as soon as he hauled out another batch.

One match left. *Scritchh.* The air flow pinched it right out.

Oh, God, please let me be making headway.

Second thoughts nattered at him. Would it be better to go back and wait for help? Ahanu had probably called for help by now. Then he remembered the car horn blaring before he lost consciousness.

He should've told Therese, shouldn't have listened to Ahanu. And what about Ahanu? Did the horn blast mean someone had caught him? Killed him?

He had no choice. He had to keep going. It was his only chance of getting out alive.

You can do it, Daddy.

He jumped, banging his head above him. Dirt showered down. He grasped the lamp like a life preserver. Had he imagined Devin's voice? Or had he actually heard his son urging him on? Anything was possible in Gannaway, Kansas.

Something shifted above. A loud thump sent his heart racing. First, a sprinkle of dirt dribbled down. Then, like an impatient storm, a torrential downfall of long-hidden earth followed. A cavern full of dirt tossed onto his coffin.

The lamp cracked under the weight, dropping darkness over him. Dirt poured into his mouth. He tried to spit, but falling debris sealed his lips. Holding his breath, he dove forward. He clawed his fingers into the dirt, but little gave away. He kicked his legs, now pinned beneath the earth's formidable weight. He couldn't move. He was swimming in cement. Immense pressure squeezed, pressing him down, his breath nearly gone. And still, the dirt fell.

Do it, Daddy.

As oxygen fled his brain, he strained to hold onto consciousness. He couldn't understand why, really. It all seemed hopeless. It would be so easy to just let go, to see Devin again.

Just one more minute, Daddy!

I'm sorry, son. Sorry I let you down...

He fell into a bottomless pit of nothingness.

Something grazed his fingertips. Strong. *Cold.* It latched onto his hand. Squeezed. And pulled.

Half lucid, Dennis swore he held a hand, fingers enfolding into his palm. Earth rushed past his face, cool and final. He kept his eyes nailed shut. His back strained under the weight, but his savior was stronger. One last tremendous surge nearly yanked his arm out of its socket. He felt his fingertips break through the wall of death, blessed air kissing them. Dirt tumbled from his face, sliding away with a whisper. Like a one-armed swimmer, he used his free arm to leverage himself away from his prison. Brightness teased his line of vision. The man yanked his hand one last time.

Dennis rolled onto solid, cold ground. He breathed

deeply, gasping, coughing out dirt. His eyes cleared.

Tommy Donnelly stood over him. Same sandy hair, same movie star good looks. His cocksure grin announced that even in death he could handle anything.

Dennis didn't question the ghost's timely appearance. He was far past the point where supernatural entities frightened him. Particularly one who'd saved his life.

By the time Dennis climbed to his feet, Tommy had already walked down the drift, gesturing for Dennis to follow. Once they reached the elevator, gears started clanking and rotating of their own accord. Machinery hummed above and the elevator dropped down. Tommy inclined his head toward the open gate. Dennis stepped inside. Tommy didn't.

"Um, you coming?"

With a half-smile, Tommy reached in, punched a button. The elevator jerked and raised Dennis back to the land of the living.

As soon as the elevator doors slid open, Tommy met him. Even benevolent ghosts were full of surprises. Terrifying ones. Silently, Tommy led him across the compound to a closed mine. An overturned, rusted car covered the shaft's opening. Above it, a sign hung by one chain. The wind blew through and around it, wheezing like an old man. *Gold Pot Mine*. Tommy Donnelly's mine.

The ground slithered beneath Dennis, coming alive. He hopped, replanting his feet the way he'd step onto a fast-moving escalator. The dry earth shifted, swirled, transformed into mud. Wooden planks grew and stretched across the grounds, *clack-clack-clacking* like bones. Machinery magically shed rust spots. The car vanished, replaced by a swinging bucket. The *Gold Pot Mine* sign reattached itself to a previously nonexistent second chain.

Three men appeared. They stood over something, kicking it. The tall, thin man had a scar over one eye. Steffen Eberstark.

Dizziness overtook Dennis. He might have fallen down, he was too disoriented to tell. The world blinked out, went gray, then roared back dazzling white.

When he opened his eyes, he lay on his back, staring into the faces of the three men.

And he shared the mind, memories, sight, the *essence* of Tommy Donnelly.

Liquid cooled Dennis's face, burned in his nose. No, not *his* nose. *Tommy's nose.* Alcohol. His eyes—Tommy's eyes—stung, blurred, adding three additional men to the ones pouring the whiskey down on him. When he tried to sit up, a boot crashed into his cheek. He fell back. Two men pinned his arms to the ground.

"Let me go, you *bastards!*"

The men hooted and hollered, a good time had by all. Except Tommy.

Eberstark stood astride him, then sat on his chest. He tapped Tommy's head. "Donnelly, I've been looking forward to this. Mr. Gannaway sends you his best."

Tommy rocked, attempting to toss his rider. He kicked his legs, his only unrestrained limbs.

Swack. Gannaway's manservant sliced a bone-solid palm across Tommy's face. "Now, you can either make this easy or hard for yourself."

"What the hell do you think you're *doing?* Everyone knows I don't drink!" A weak argument, Tommy knew, but maybe the other men would listen to the voice of reason. Eberstark sure as hell seemed beyond the bend.

"Everyone slips once in a while." Steffen grinned, a wisp of a grin. "Get him up, boys." Eberstark stood, wiping his hands together. The other men yanked Tommy to his feet. Eberstark turned away and then swiveled back with a gut-punch that doubled Tommy over. "That's an extra from me. Just so you remember me."

"Oh, I'll remember you all right, you *son-of-a-bitch!*"

"What do you intend on doing about it, Donnelly? Appears to me your luck's finally out." He twirled a finger in the air, something Tommy'd seen Gannaway do on numerous occasions. "Let's finish this."

The men dragged Tommy to the Gold Pot Mine's collar. Eberstark hopped up onto the wooden platform. He drew the hanging barrel back, holding onto the rim. "In you go. Unfortunate drinking accident. You were really distraught over how your strike turned out, don't you know? Anybody would be." His thin lips stretched and opened, tiny, jagged teeth showing yellow under the moonlight.

"You're not gonna get away with this!" Tommy had a gut feeling he would, though. But he wasn't going without a fight. He shook his shoulders. The men countered by wrenching his arms higher behind him. Pain shot through his body, lightning bolts zapping his brain. "Son-of-a—"

Another punch to the stomach. "Such foul language. What would your pretty young wife think of that?"

"She'll know the *truth!*"

"Doubtful. But I'll look in on her for you. Let her know the truth. Offer some comfort in her bereavement, even."

"Stay *away* from her!" *Oh, dear God, please don't let him touch Claire.*

Eberstark laughed, foul and mechanical, a *rat-tat-tat* stuck in his throat. "Oh, I'll give her special treatment. Get him up here."

The men prodded Tommy up the steps. They hopped off, leaving Tommy face to face with the demon in man-servant form.

No sense wasting time on praying now. Too late for a Godsend, Tommy knew. But he still had some fight left in him.

Tommy looked Eberstark in his good eye and said, "I'm bringin' you with me."

Eberstark thrust his arms out, his hands thumping

onto Tommy's chest. Tommy tottered over the hole, his arms flailing, trying to control gravity. With a last rush of strength, he heaved his weight forward. One hand missed his target entirely. The other didn't. It grabbed onto Eberstark's tie and yanked. The weight and momentum pulled them both back.

"Everyone slips once in a while," said Tommy as they plunged into the dark hole. Eberstark's good eye grew wide. His mouth formed a foul, shocked oval.

The last thing Tommy saw was the quarter moon over Eberstark's blind eye. The last moon he'd ever see.

His last thoughts belonged to Claire, though.

Clairrrrre!

I'll always come home. Alw—

Like a childhood nightmare where you're falling, Dennis woke up before he—or rather Tommy—hit the bottom of the shaft. He sat up, blinking his way into consciousness. The mine grounds were back to their modern, decaying state. The machinery was rusty again, their mechanical bones drooping from age and neglect.

Oh, my God. They killed Tommy Donnelly. And... and...

Nausea formed in his stomach, bile climbing into his throat. Rocking himself, he shivered in the humid night.

Ahanu! I have to get to Ahanu!

He pulled himself to his feet and staggered off of the grounds.

Another car sat running alongside Ahanu's death machine, the lights on. Survival instinct had him scrambling to hide, look for a weapon. Then he recognized the car.

"Therese!"

She jolted up from behind Ahanu's trunk, eyes wide with shock. *"Dennis!* My *God!* It's Bob! He's—"

Dennis raced around the car, heart pumping.

Ahanu lay on the ground, unmoving. Therese pressed a rag tightly over Ahanu's stomach. "Dennis, what in *God's* name happened here? I saw Bob's car when I drove by and found him here! He's been stabbed!"

"Is...is he—"

"He's still breathing. But we've *got* to get him to the hospital. Closest one is twenty miles away."

Dennis ran his hands through his hair. "Jesus...okay, I'll help you get him in—"

"What the *fuck* happened, Dennis?"

"I'll tell you later. Right now you've got to get him to the—"

"*Me?* Where are *you* going?"

"Therese! There's no time! Get him to the hospital! I've got to go finish—"

"Finish what?

"*Gannaway!* His men threw me into a mine and tried to bury me alive!"

"Jumping Jesus..." She switched her gaze between Dennis and Ahanu.

Dennis issued orders with the authority granted by surviving near-death. "Get Ahanu to the hospital. I'm going to Gannaway's house before they find out I'm alive and try and cut town. When you get Ahanu safe, call the Feds and send them out to the Gannaway mansion."

"You need to wait for them, Dennis! You can't just—"

"I can. I have to. The ghosts want me to."

"Say that again." Kyle Gannaway heard what Gustav said; he just couldn't wrap his mind around it. God *damn!* Everyone on his payroll was a damned idiot!

"Ah, sir, heh, heh—"

He hurled his gold-plated derrick at Gustav, who

pirouetted like a well-fed ballerina. Stokes started chuckling again, and Gannaway froze him silent with a pointed finger.

"You goddamned morons! Damn sloppy work! What if—"

"Mr. Gannaway, ain't no way they can tie this to us. We were careful. We thought—"

"I don't pay you to think, Stokes! And I sure as *hell* don't pay you to interrupt me. *Got that?*"

Stokes and Gustav stood, swaying humbly in front of his desk. Tweedledumb and Tweedledumber.

"Yes, sir."

Gannaway wheezed deep in his chest. "You buried Lipstein in one of the ol' mines?"

"Yes, sir," said Gus with a smile. Apparently, he thought he'd escaped the hook already. But Gannaway wasn't about to let this worm wriggle free so easily. Not until he felt confident everything had been handled properly.

"And how'd you do that again?"

"Ah, Dickie tossed a stick of dynamite into the drift. Lipstein was unconscious, sir. There was no possible way—"

"Jesus Christ! And you're sure he saw our mining operation?"

"Yes, sir."

Begrudgingly, he had to give it to the men for thinking fast on their feet. Wasn't about to tell them that, though. Give 'em an inch, they'd take a mile. "And there's *no* possible way anyone will ever find him?"

"Highly doubtful, sir." Gus's smile slipped away.

"Highly doubtful ain't *good* enough, Gus! And what about that ol' damned injun, Bob? You say you stabbed him dead. Fine. You fix that to look like a chat-rat incident?" He looked at Stokes for affirmation. Stokes nodded, his waddle jiggling beneath his chin. At least he remained silent, knew when to. "Why in hell didn't you toss the injun in with Lipstein?"

"There was no, ah, time, sir," said Gus. "As soon as I, ah...disposed of Bob, we heard yelling from the mines." He took a step forward as if anticipating a gold star for his bravery. Buncha school kids, always seeking positive reinforcement. "And it's a good thing we went to the mines when we did, sir. Otherwise, Lipstein might've escaped."

Dumbfounded, Gannaway stared at his men. They'd taken a bad situation and possibly made it worse. Still, the Lipstein problem had been resolved. He just needed a likely explanation for Lipstein's disappearance. It wouldn't take much. He was a known drinker; he'd fallen off the wagon and taken off to Mexico to drink away the rest of his days. That'd do nicely, yes, sir. God smiled down on him once again, always looking after the smart and the strong.

"All right, fine. But if any of this goes south, you two..." He pointed twin gnarled fingers at them. "...you're taking the fall for this. I had *nothin'* to do with it."

The men shuffled, eyeing one another warily. "Yes, sir."

"Now, go on. Git. Get the hell outta my study."

Stokes shuffled out faster than Gannaway had ever seen him move. Gus tried to follow him. "Not you, Gus, Goddamnit. Get me up to bed."

"Ah...yes, sir. Heh, ho, ho..."

Jesus Christ.

The Thunderbird rumbled down the highway, faster than Bob had ever pushed it, at least when Dennis had been a passenger. Dennis didn't quite have the pedal pushed to the floor—he didn't think the body would hold up—but it was damn close. He had no idea what to do once he'd reached his destination. Not a clue. But he had to do something.

All signs pointed to it. Naira Gannaway'd *called* him to her skeleton, damned if she hadn't. Tommy Donnelly had saved his life and shown him how he had died. There was a reason. A persistent voice in his head screamed. *This is it.*

The steering wheel came to life and shimmered in his hands. Unforgiving grinds roared with every gear change. Warm wind blasted through the floorboard, whipping his dirt-covered pant legs. His body was nothing but one sore muscle. He was filthy, grimy, and exhausted. He rolled down the window. The air beat on him, hot and humid, but it kept him awake. And determined.

A song played in his mind. He didn't know who sang it or where it came from, but it damn sure fit.

All roads lead here in the end...

The speedometer needle hovered at seventy-five miles per hour. Gannaway's mansion zoomed into sight over the hill. A car, headed in the opposite direction, zipped by so fast he didn't spot the cherries on top until it passed. Or the county sheriff star on the side.

Shit. Stokes. So much for stealth.

In his rearview mirror, Dennis watched the cop car fly onto the shoulder. Stokes whipped the patrol car around and sped back toward Dennis.

Dennis barely hit the brakes before yanking the Thunderbird into Gannaway's drive. The back left tire bounced into the yard and fishtailed before correcting itself. The black-grated fence loomed fifty yards in front of him. His headlights gleamed off the chain and lock.

He gripped the steering wheel until his knuckles turned white and floored it. Now or never. *Hold in there, Thunderbird.*

He felt the impact up into his teeth. The right gate flew off its hinges and blew back into the yard. The other half remained standing.

The T-Bird's front end smashed like an accordion. The back end whipped around and scraped against the fence, then lifted and dropped him back to the driveway.

His forehead cracked into the windshield. When he bit his tongue, the salt of blood tasted bitter in his mouth.

The T-Bird hissed into silence. Smoke billowed from beneath the crushed hood. Once the Thunderbird finally wobbled to a stop, Dennis fell out to the ground.

Behind him, red and blue lights swirled through the sky, a macabre merry-go-round.

"Stop right there, *goddammit!*"

Fat chance. Adrenalin surged and replaced exhaustion. He bolted forward in a nearly perfect sprinter's start and raced uphill toward the house.

Crack!

A bullet fired.

Almost to the front door.

Sudden light illuminated the front windows. An overhead floodlight swamped him with a jaundiced yellow brilliance.

Stokes thundered through the grass behind him, panting for breath.

"Stop...dammit..."

Dennis didn't look, he didn't need to. He felt them. The miners. The *dead* miners. On his left. On his right. Moving, swaying, dipping in and out of the shadows of the trees.

Zwing.

Stokes shot off another bullet. Either he was the world's worst shot or too winded to take aim.

The door wrenched open as soon as Dennis touched the knob. Gustav blocked him, his round face contorted with rage. His fist cracked underneath Dennis's chin. Dennis reeled back but kept his balance. Gus lowered his head and charged. Dennis sidestepped, latching onto Gus's arm and used the momentum to swing his attacker around.

Another gunshot cracked. Gustav slumped, arms outstretched like a needy lover, and carried them both to the ground. Dennis felt blood spreading across Gus's back. He grunted and pushed Gus's body off. Winded,

Stokes stood above them, his smoking gun at shaky aim on Dennis.

"God *damn* you, boy! Look what you did! Your time on this here world's come to an *end.*"

"You're crazy, Stokes! You just killed Eberstark!" Dennis pulled up on his elbows and scrambled back through the grass. Fearful uncertainty blazed in Stokes's eyes, making him all the more dangerous.

But Stokes hadn't noticed Dennis's cavalry of gathering ghosts.

Something moved in the bushes next to them. A dark figure shot up, then slipped away.

"Stokes, look around you."

"Boy, you just tryin' to buy time 'til you meet your maker, but you done met your destroyer." Ignoring his own bluster, Stokes turned to look. "What the *hell?* If'n there's anybody out there, this is police business! This here man's a wanted criminal. I'm the sheriff! If you don't want no trouble, go on home now!"

Disembodied laughter rose around them, stereo of the dead. Wet, gargling murmurs bounced off hidden barriers.

"Jesus, God, *almighty!* What the—"

"You value your worthless life, Stokes? Then you'd better get out of here." Stokes rotated in a circle, his gun jabbing ineffectually at the sky. Dennis climbed to his feet.

"What in *hell's* goin' on *here?*" He swung back on Dennis. The gun shook in his hands so violently Dennis thought he might miss even at this close range.

"The ghosts of Gannaway, Stokes. The miners. They're coming for you."

"Bull*shit.*"

Flickers of yellow flared from the surrounding foliage. Tree limbs waved in the wind-free air. Whispers replaced laughter. And singing. Quiet, deep, resonant singing.

"Jesus *Christ!*" Stokes raced down the hill, his pistol flapping at his side.

Dennis stepped over Gus's body and crossed the threshold into Gannaway's mansion. He left the door ajar. Company was on the way. Wouldn't want to shut them out. Not very neighborly.

"Gannaway!" The study was empty. Gannaway's beloved fetishistic derrick statue rested on the floor.

"Gannaway!" Dennis mounted the stairs. He didn't need to be quiet, not now. He had allies.

Boots tramped through the doorway behind him. Not loud, not very fast. They had all the time in the world. Or at least in *some* world. The ghostly feet fell into a militaristic marching pattern.

Tomp, timp, tomp, timp, tomp, timp.

Dennis knew not to look. It'd be better for his sanity, if not his safety.

A freezing sensation stroked Dennis's back. The small windowpanes next to the stairwell glazed over. Spidery tendrils of ice crept across them. Dennis saw his breath, small plumes shooting from his nose.

"Gannaway!" Dennis headed for the closed door at the end of the hallway. The largest door had to be Gannaway's bedroom.

The army of ghosts was already climbing the stairwell. He didn't have much time.

"Gannaway! It's *over!*" Dennis hugged the wall, waiting for the shotgun blast he knew was coming. The door exploded outward, and wooden shrapnel flew by him. Dennis waited a beat, then turned and kicked in the remainder of the door.

Gannaway sat upright in his bed, the smoking shotgun still in his hand. Dennis hurtled across the room and grabbed the warm barrel. He threw the gun out of reach. The old man didn't put up too much of a struggle. Gannaway's frail body went limp, his fight gone. The ragged whistling sound emitting from his throat sounded like an accordion radiator with holes punctured in it.

Damn. No satisfaction in beating the hell out of an old man.

"You're done, Gannaway. I know everything."

"I don't know *what* they teach you in your fancy-ass city, *boy,* but you've broken and entered!" His words struggled to form between gasps. "I'm gonna have you put in jail for—"

"I said it's over, you bastard."

Dennis didn't expect a confession. A little remorse, a smidge of guilt would've been nice, though. Gannaway's stubborn denial brought Dennis's rage burning back.

"You son-of-a-bitch! You had your men try to kill me!"

"I did no such thing! If they did somethin' like that, you can't blame me!" He peered around Dennis and bellowed. *"Gus!* God damn it! *Gus!"*

"Gus is dead. Stokes shot him."

"Gus—"

"And I know you killed Tommy Donnelly. You tossed him into a mine. Killed your wife, too. I found her body today. Down where my body's supposed to be." Gannaway's mouth fell open, round with decaying teeth. Threads of saliva stretched, snapped, dribbled out of a corner of his mouth. His eyes glossed over, hazy, unfocused. Nearly...*yellow?* "How...how could you possibly know that?"

"I had help." Dennis waved behind him. Footfalls shuffled down the hallway.

Even though they were on the same team—hell, the ghosts practically led him to this moment—Dennis still couldn't bring himself to look. He wanted Gannaway to get an eye full, though. "Here come the other men you killed, Gannaway. Killed just to earn a buck. The men who died because of the *shit* you orchestrated during the strike." He grabbed Gannaway's jaws between his thumb and fingers for emphasis. "And you know what, you dirty son-of-a-bitch? You're *still* killing off the people who live in this town. I know you're still mining. Still poisoning the water, the air, everything."

Whispers crawled into the room. The bedroom windows grew sheaths of ice, white frosting on a birthday cake. Something squeaked at one window. Dennis glanced and saw pasty worms of fingers drawing across the pane, pleading for an invite to the party.

"I didn't know what I was going to do when I got here, Gannaway. Now I know." The room grew cold as a walk-in freezer. "Nothing."

"You...you're gonna let me go?" *Hope. The son-of-a-bitch still thinks he's walking out of this.*

Dennis shrugged. "I'm not gonna do anything. Doesn't mean they're not, though." He hitched a thumb behind him.

Dennis didn't look up as he left the room. He kept his gaze glued to the floor as he walked down the hallway—some things weren't meant to be seen—but he still saw their worn boots and tattered, denim-covered, dirt-encrusted legs, held together by stitches of flesh. A foot peeked out of one torn boot. Or the remains of a foot. Mostly bone, but ambulatory.

One foot in front of the other. Just keep doing it, the only way out.

He didn't really know the ghosts meant him no harm; he *felt* it. Their ghostly foreman, Tommy Donnelly, would see to it. *At least he hoped so.*

He shuffled his shoes, slow and easy, not even lifting his feet. It seemed safer that way, with his feet tethered to the physical world by contact with the floor.

Slide, shuffle, and be mindful of the ghost's shoulder I just bumped.

Some of the men intentionally nudged him, several chuckled as he passed. *Just keep your head down. Show no fear. Or they'll smell it.*

Near the stairwell, he increased his pace and started down. He glanced up once, securing his hand on the stairwell railing. Once was enough. One of the last miners climbing the staircase carried his head tucked underneath his arm.

Out! Gotta get out! He raced through the front door and

breathed in deeply. From upstairs, Gannaway screamed.

God, I've always been a loyal servant to you. You've always rewarded me for my hard toiling on this great earth. Why are you forsaking me now? Why...

Gannaway prayed nonstop, silently and aloud.

"Jesus, God, Almighty, what in the *hell* is happening to me? Am I in Hell? Has time stopped?"

That had to be it. It was the only possible explanation for the horrors in his bedroom. Men, not quite alive, not quite dead, roamed the room.

"Let me wake up, *please*, God..."

He pulled the blankets up over his head, shrank into his bed the way he'd done as a child afraid of things unknown.

"Help me..."

The sheet couldn't hide their darting shadows. Faces hovered, uncomfortably close. Occasionally, a shadow poked him, trying to flush the rabbit out of his hole.

"This isn't *happening...*"

Tick-tock. Tick-tock...

The grandfather clock hadn't worked in years. But it did tonight. The chocking of the pendulum blasted through the room, keeping rhythm with his pounding heart.

Tick-tock. Tick-tock...

He clapped his palms over his ears, blocking the madness.

Tick-tock. You're dead. Tick-tock. You're dead...

Then it all stopped.

Silence.

No more footfalls. No grunting, no singing. No damned clock. Too impossibly good to be true. He waited an eternity to build up sufficient bravery to emerge from under covers.

First an inch. Then a little more. The cold air licked his forehead, froze his sweat into ice cubes.

Beautiful, sane silence.

He pulled the blanket down further, just enough to peek over the ruffled edge.

They're gone, all gone, never were here, thank you, Jesus, God, nothing but a nightmare, I knew you wouldn't...

"Hello, husband."

Kyle Gannaway's heart exploded before he could properly reacquaint himself with his wife.

Chapter Twenty-Three

1969...

An hour's drive away, Miami, Oklahoma might as well have been in another country. The locals waved at Dennis as he passed them, quite unlike the reception he'd received in Gannaway. A gas station attendant made sure Dennis knew how to pronounce the town's name properly—"Miam-uh"—with a patronizing smile and a knowing wink.

The house was small, but well-kept and cozy. A glorious garden, dazzling to the eye, celebrated springtime.

Fifties doo-wop music drifted out the screen door. Dennis rapped on the door.

"May I help you?" Her hair had lost the fiery red Ahanu had described, but it wasn't the gray Dennis had expected either. Like autumn leaves, it glowed gently, a mosaic of muted colors. Her eyes blazed with life, a cloudless, deep blue sky.

"Mrs. Donnelly? I'm Dennis Lipstein. I, uh...don't know how to say this, but...I need to talk to you about your husband. I know how he died."

Holding the door open, she swayed him in with a smile. Almost like she'd been expecting him. "It's Claire. Come on in, then. Lemonade or tea?"

Claire didn't interrupt him a single time. When he finished his tale, they sat in silence.

Claire dabbed tears from her cheek. "I knew it. I knew they killed Tommy. He didn't drink. They tried to tell me he fell down the hole after drinking..."

"I'm sorry."

"Oh, no, there's no need for you to be sorry. You've helped give me...closure. And I'm glad to know he took Eberstark with him. What a bastard that man was. They must've buried his body elsewhere. And Kyle Gannaway's dead?"

"Yes. They said it was a heart attack. But...who knows?"

Claire rocked in her chair thoughtfully. The last remnants of sunlight cast a sleepy orange radiance over her. Her rebound grin melted Dennis's heart. "You know something, Dennis? Tommy was right. He did come home again. One day in 1962..."

Dark clouds rumbled, turning over at a quick boil. The sky darkened, nearly purple and meaner than a three-day bruise, unusual for a springtime afternoon.

Claire whipped the last sheet off the clothesline and sniffed the air. The smell of rain. And her knees ached with the stubborn pain of a bad tooth. She'd lived in Kansas all her life and knew the signs well.

But she had time yet. She'd had nothing but time ever since the children moved away. She smiled just thinking about them as she finished folding the laundry.

When the siren blared, it chilled her to the bone.

First, the wind changed direction, tree limbs swaying one way then bending backward. Tiny pellets of dust shot across her arms, into her face. Her ears popped. Even though she lived far from any railroad tracks, the sound of a freight train chugged her way. Fast as a snap of the fingers, a funnel cloud materialized down the road. Large and angry and spinning her way at a ferocious clip. She watched Mrs. O'Connell's roof lift and fly like a Frisbee. The ground shook when it crashed down several hundred feet from her. She'd severely underestimated how much time she had. This tornado moved faster than any she'd ever seen.

The cloud seemed almost human in its fortitude, twisting down the road, devouring everything in its path. The wind whipped Claire's hair about, and her dress flapped like a kite.

The root cellar. Her only chance. She tugged at the door. *Stuck.* Fear boosted her strength, and she yanked at the door again. The force of wind threw her back. She fell down on the sidewalk, staring into the face of the funnel. Debris swirled around her, a miniature tornado offspring. A slice of wood, a lone survivor of Mrs. O'Connell's roof, slashed her cheek. The windows of the house she'd lived in for thirty-two years exploded.

This is how it ends. Alone, picked up by a tornado and abandoned God knows where.

A hand reached hers, pulled her to her feet. The winds and their cargo of debris inhibited her vision, but she knew—she *knew*—her husband stood before her. The touch of his hand wasn't just memory. Not this time. She remembered the touch of his hand. Calloused, but gentle as a baby's hug.

"Tommy?"

He smiled. The smile she remembered so well. He put an arm around her waist and opened the cellar door easily. Gently, he guided her down the steps, escorting her to safety. The hellish winds slid off and around him. He didn't look a day older than he had the last time she'd seen him.

Before he closed the door, she heard his gentle voice. Maybe his voice was in her head. Maybe it wasn't.

"I'll always come home, Claire. Always."

Claire shook her empty glass, rattling the ice cubes like a handful of dice. Sunset had passed as she told her story, cloaking the house in darkness. They'd talked for hours, swapping tales of Gannaway. She stood, walked toward Dennis and rested her hand on his shoulder.

"So you see—Tommy did come home again."

"Was that...the last time you saw him?"

"Yes."

Dennis didn't know how to respond. Not because he didn't believe her. He'd long since passed the point of disbelief in the supernatural. He just didn't know whether to offer sympathy or congratulations. Either choice seemed wrong.

"Claire, I'm truly sorry you lost your husband—"

"Me, too. But good came from it. The miners took good care of me after Tommy passed. And his work won out in the end. In 1937, the Supreme Court upheld the National Labor Relations Act. Gannaway's so-called Tri-State Union folded and the men unionized. So Tommy helped those men live longer and better lives. Everything happens for a reason, Dennis."

"Yeah. I've been kinda learning that lesson."

"Our son T.J.'s an engineer in Kansas City. Took after his father. Margaret's a school teacher in San Francisco with three children."

Claire took his hand and led him to the hearth, a history of life in photos preserved above it.

"T.J. looks like Tommy. And Margaret's as beautiful as you are."

She slapped his shoulder. "Oh, stop with the flattery. No need. You're welcome to visit anytime, Dennis."

"Thank you, Claire. And...well, I'm sorry. I've taken up your entire day. I really should get going."

"Dennis?"

"Hm?"

She fixed her solid blue gaze on him. "Everyone slips once in a while."

He didn't remember telling her Tommy's last words. But he knew what she meant even if he had no idea how. He hugged her. She buried her head into his chest as they swayed to the radio music.

He'd never slip again.

Ahanu inched up in the hospital bed, antsy, ready to make a break for it. Therese, scrunched down in the visitor's chair, had her feet kicked up onto the bed.

"Hey," said Dennis, "these are for you." Dennis handed him the bouquet of flowers.

"Flowers? You asking me out on a date, brother?"

"Look inside."

Ahanu peeked within the paper wrapping and grinned. It didn't take him long to pop the top of the beer can. "Thanks, brother."

Therese rolled her eyes. "And you really think that's a good idea? Ahanu just had surgery."

Dennis shrugged. "Artistic inspiration."

"You know it, amigo."

Dennis sat at the edge of the bed. "You doing okay, Ahanu?"

"Better now. Guess I was out of it for a day or so."

"Yeah. Thanks, by the way. For everything. Um, sorry about your car."

He waved his hand. "Ah, I can always get a new car. On its last legs anyway."

"And I'm sorry you're in the hospital. I—"

Within seconds, Ahanu drained the can and hurled it at Dennis's head. A new speed record. But Dennis's response time had improved, too. He ducked. "I don't wanna hear it, brother. We do what we can. And now…it's all over."

"Guess it is. I saw a lot of men in suits when I drove through Gannaway. *Scary* suits."

Therese nodded and moved her feet off the bed. "My FBI contact says they picked up Stokes on his way to Mexico. Blubbering like a baby. They also got Dickie, and they're looking into everyone else involved with Gannaway's illegal mining operation."

"Good. I guess my work's done here. I mean both professionally...and otherwise."

"I'm surprised you had time to wrap up your work," said Therese. "With everything else happening." Since the night Gannaway died, none of them had mentioned anything remotely supernatural. They skirted the topic. The ghosts had fled, and nobody wanted to stir them up again. Best to leave some things buried.

"Yeah, I finished. I'm going to recommend evacuating the remaining residents of Gannaway. See if Uncle Sam will help them out financially. The toxic levels of the water are near deadly. Surprised anyone's still living."

"You do what you need to do, brother."

"What's next for you, Ahanu? Still gonna live the bohemian life?"

Ahanu winced, whether from his wound or his thoughts Dennis couldn't tell. "Nope. Like you, my work is done here, too. Gannaway doesn't need a caretaker any longer. Think I'll head out to San Francisco. Become a famous artist and sleep with groupies."

Therese chortled. "Yeah, good luck with that."

He held his hand out, fingers up in the air. One last soul shake for the road. "Take care, brother."

"You, too, Ahanu."

Dennis turned to Therese and said, "Goodbye."

He heard the pitter-patter of feet behind him when he reached the van. He smiled. He'd known she'd follow him out.

"Dennis, wait a minute! That's it? A simple goodbye?"

"Had no doubt you'd come."

"Awfully cocky, aren't you?"

"How's this for cocky?" He pulled her toward him, slipped his hands behind her neck and kissed her.

"Pretty damn cocky. Show me more." This time she took the lead, damn near throwing him into the side of the van.

"Wow. Um, you know...I'm gonna miss this. I mean, you and me."

"Don't go soft on me now, Dennis." With a playful leer, she flashed her eyes toward the bulge in his jeans. "Though it doesn't look like that's gonna happen anytime soon."

"I am going to miss you. Really." He held her hands, wanting to anchor her to his boat. "Come with me."

"What?"

"Come with me. Come back to L.A. with me. We can move in together."

Her lips formed a grin, but her eyes clouded over with doubt. An unfamiliar look for her. "Dennis—"

"I'm serious. I want you to move in with me. I...hell, I just want you."

"Dennis, I can't. My work takes me all over the Midwest. Like it or not, I'm married to my job. I love my job."

Her way or the highway. Ah, well. It'd been a beautiful dream, even if it'd been a fleeting one. "I'm not gonna win this."

"You know me better than that. You ever win against me?"

"No." He laughed. "Never have, guess I never will. Will you at least call me? Come visit? I've got a few other tricks I'd like to show you."

"Now that sounds promising."

"Fantastic. My number's—"

She recited it to him before he could spit it out. "How'd you know my number?"

"I do homework on things that interest me. You interest me."

"You interest me, too."

T.J. and Margaret were worried. Claire heard it in their voices when she called them. She supposed she couldn't blame them. She had smart kids with lots of intuition. She'd hadn't come right out and said *goodbye*, but that's why she'd called. To tell them goodbye. And not to worry. It'd been a lot harder than she'd thought, telling them she loved them for the final time. She'd thought she'd been properly prepared for the task, but she hadn't been, not really. How do you say goodbye to your children?

Her time on earth had finished, this she knew. How she'd come by this revelation, she couldn't quite pinpoint. But she knew it as sure as she knew the sun would rise tomorrow morning. She just wouldn't be there to see it. She'd gotten a call right after Dennis had left. A psychic phone call from God. *Hello, Claire, we have an appointment...*

She lay down on her bed, dressed in her finest dress, and closed her eyes.

When she woke, she saw her body on the bed. Tommy stood in front of her. She ran into his arms. So solid, so real. How she'd missed him.

"I told you I'd come back to you, Claire Donnelly. Nothing will keep me from you."

"I know, Tommy Donnelly."

And as always they sealed their pact with a kiss.

ABOUT THE AUTHOR

Stuart R. West is a lifelong resident of Kansas, which he considers both a curse and a blessing. It's a curse because…well, it's Kansas. But it's great because… well, it's Kansas. Lots of cool, strange and creepy things happen in the Midwest, and Stuart takes advantage of them in his work. Call it "Kansas Noir." Stuart writes thrillers tinged with horror and horror tinged with thrillers, both for adult and young adult audiences. He writes at the crossroads of horror and sneaky humor. *Ghosts of Gannaway* is Stuart's second book with Grinning Skull Press, and Stuart feels funny talking about himself this way. Stuart spent twenty-five years in the corporate sector and now writes full time. He's married to a professor of pharmacy (who greatly appreciates the fact he cooks dinner for her every night) and has a twenty-two-year-old daughter who's still deciding what to do with her life. But that's okay. It took him twenty-five years to figure that out.

Stuart's blog can be found at http://stuartrwest.blogspot.com/

Drop in on him at Facebook at: https://www.facebook.com/stuartrwestwriter

Press
Presents

More Tales of Terror from Days Gone By

In the Spring of 1912, evil came to the small town of Kings Shore. A creature with a voracious appetite for blood took up residence within the town's shadows.

Network newsman Roland Millhouse arrived in town to interview Patricia Owens on the occasion of her 120th birthday. He envisioned a feeble old woman in a wheelchair. The woman he met was anything but. She possessed more energy than most people a half-century younger. And her life was far from boring.

Roland expected to leave Kings Shore with a fluff piece full of garden parties and church socials. What he got was a terrifying tale of death and monsters. A tale that would change his life forever.

Something lurks beneath the surface of Cooper Lake. Something hungry. Something intelligent. Something that preys on those who venture too close to its domain. The native Indians had a name for it. ONIARE In 1939, its victim was a young drifter. Dave Longo fought and killed it then, but it won't stay dead. It returned in 1956 to claim the lives of two young men. For Dave, its return was a reunion in Hell. It's now 2014 and the creature has returned again, but Dave Longo is not around to face it a third time. The task becomes the responsibility of Ryan Lowell, a child the oniare had terrorized back in '56, but can he overcome his childhood fears to vanquish the oniare once and for all.

Deep beneath the streets of Detroit, someone — or something — is picking off the miners of the Detroit Salt Combine. The company appears to be more concerned with the protection of their equipment than with the safety of their employees, so the miners take it upon themselves to approach the Attican Detective Agency to find out what's happening to their co-workers. Jasper O'Malley, an agent with a reputation for getting things done (at great cost), is assigned to the case.

Teamed with Sadie Dupree, a geological expert, and Amelia Rio, an ace driver for one of the Organized Crime families, Jasper ventures underground to investigate the fate of the miners. But there's another factor operating within the labyrinth of tunnels, a factor that would kill to keep its illegal operations undiscovered. And still another factor has infiltrated the hired detective's own group. Yes, there's a Judas working with Jasper, a traitor who knows the secret of the mine, and who will stop at nothing to keep the mine's secret. Can Jasper track down whom or what is responsible for the miners' disappearances, or will he and his one true ally suffer the same fate as the unfortunate workers?

The Caribbean Sea, 1708 AD. In Port Royal many have heard the legend of the Black Brig, a ship of the damned bringing a fate worse than death to the isolated colonies of the Caribbean Sea. But few know the true story behind the tavern tales. As the war between the Northern Alliance and the League of the Antilles looms on the horizon, an old captain is ready to embark on a venture to cease the blight of the Black Brig once for all and have his revenge. Set in an alternate historical setting, where a supernatural plague caused the fall of the European powers and where what was left of humanity struggles to survive in the New World, *Dead Men Tell No Tales* narrates the ghastly voyage pirate captain Daniel Drake Davies underwent in 1676, and the events that will force him to confront those same horrors thirty years later. For the dead do not rest peacefully in the Devil's Sea. Pirates, voodoo, and seagoing undead await you in this fantastic journey in a land that never was.

www.ingramcontent.com/pod-product-compliance
Lightning Source LLC
Chambersburg PA
CBHW070756190726
48292CB00002B/556